# Mission Murder

## Betty Kerr Orlemann

## A HATTIE FARWELL MYSTERY

First in the
Hattie Farwell mystery series

ShadowDance Press
*an imprint of Word Forge Books*
Ferndale, Pennsylvania
wordforgebooks.com

*Mission: Murder*
ISBN 978-0-9771329-1-1
Library of Congress Control Number: 2008931426


Published by ShadowDance Press, *an imprint of Word Forge Books*
PO Box 97
Ferndale, PA 18921
Phone 610-847-2456
Fax 610-847-8220
Admin@WordForgeBooks.com
WordForgeBooks.com


Written by Betty Kerr Orlemann
Author.BettyO@WordForgeBooks.com
BettyOrlemann.com




Edited and proofread by
Rebecca A. Valentine
Maxwell D. Valentine
The Write Stuff
Windsor, CO 80550
mzwrite@frii.com
TheWriteStuffOnline.com

Cover design and illustration by Laura Pritchard
Pritchard Design
Doylestown, PA 18901
Laura@PritchardDesign.com
PritchardDesign.com

Interior design and production by Caryn Newton

# Dedication

To the memory of my husband, Robert Duff Orlemann, December 29, 1926-December 27, 2001. For more than forty-eight years, Bob was my partner, my lover and my best friend. I'm sorry that he didn't live to see this book published.

5/24/18

To: Nancy Edden with my love and thanks for her contribution to happy memories of our Wyncote childhood!

Betty

Betty Kerr Orlemann

# Contents

# 1

Anna Turner ran up the marble front steps of her grandmother's Walnut Street townhouse in Philadelphia. She used her key to open the heavy front door to the hall. As usual, the day's mail was lying on the floor, where it had been pushed through the brass mail slot. Anna leaned over, scooped it up and laid it on a mahogany dropleaf table that stood against the wall to her right. She placed her briefcase next to the mail and shrugged off her coat, hanging it in a closet under the stairs. Hurrying to the foot of the stairs, she called, "Yoo-hoo! Are you home, Gram?"

An echoing *Yoo-hoo!* came from the second floor, and Anna grabbed up the mail and her briefcase and bounded up the stairs. She found her grandmother sitting on the loveseat in her upstairs sitting room. Sitting next to her was Hattie Farwell, her oldest and dearest friend. The two women had been drinking tea and poring over an old photograph album when Anna bounced into the room.

"Aunt Hattie!" squealed Anna. "What a lovely surprise!"

Hattie slid the album into Annie's lap and rose when Anna entered the room. She strode across the carpet to hug and kiss her.

"Do you realize how much she looks like you, Annie?" she asked her friend, admiring the petite, blue-eyed blonde. "You're a very pretty girl," she told the young woman.

"You think I resemble Gram?" asked Anna, with a big grin. "I'm flattered." She walked over to her grand-mother's chair and gave her a warm hug. "But time has flown by, Aunt Hattie, and I'm afraid I'm no longer a girl." She laughed. "I'll be thirty before you know it!" Anna turned back to her grandmother. "I've brought up the mail." She sorted through it and took out three bills addressed to herself, then placed the remaining pieces on a table next to Annie.

Ignoring the mail, Annie smiled warmly at her namesake. "Did you have a good day at school, dear?"

Hattie looked on with interest as Anna responded.

"Maybe it's this soggy weather, or the fact that Thanksgiving vacation is two weeks away, but those kids were a real handful today," she chuckled.

"Do you know, dear, that you're teaching at the same school where I taught when your father was just a little boy?" Hattie inquired.

Anna did know, had known for years, but she was too polite to remind her cherished "aunt" as the old woman continued.

"I, too, taught the fifth grade, and I loved those active youngsters," said Hattie, a faraway look in her eyes.

Hattie had been forced to give up her teaching job in Philadelphia when her brother was killed in Europe during World War II. Dutifully, she had gone home to Bucks County to care for her ailing parents and their farm.

"Very sad," her grandmother often said. "Very, very sad."

The two older women, the photo album once again open across their laps, launched into a series of "Do you remembers?" and promptly became lost in happy memories and laughter. They had grown up on neighboring farms in Plumstead Township, where their families had been close friends for at least three generations.

Anna smiled as she watched them. Her grandmother, still slim, her blond hair now gray but her blue eyes as lively as ever, leaned forward.

"Hattie, do you remember the time that mean-tempered old white gander chased us all the way up the hill from the pond?" She turned to Anna with the details. "He came at us with furious hissing and wildly flapping wings. We must have been about eight years old. It's a miracle we escaped!"

Grinning, Hattie answered, "Yes, how could I forget? And do you remember, we were wearing identical blue seersucker playsuits? How we used to love to dress alike."

"We wanted people to think we were twins," explained Annie, laughing. "Can you believe that anyone would think we resembled each other in any way? You, with your dark hair and gray eyes, and always at least an inch or two taller than I...in spite of the fact that you were only two months older!"

Anna poured herself another cup of tea and grinned as the old friends reminisced. Since they were paying no attention to her, she had the opportunity to study them. Her perky grandmother looked younger than her years, but Hattie looked every minute of eighty. Annie's hair was carefully permed and fashionable, while Hattie simply twisted her long, gray locks back into a bun at the nape of her neck. Maybe they had enjoyed dressing alike when they were youngsters, but no longer. Annie was wearing carefully pressed navy slacks and a dark pink sweater over a floral blouse. Low-heeled navy flats completed her outfit. Hattie, on the other hand, was wearing what she always wore. Anna could not remember ever once seeing her in any other attire.

"She wears what she finds comfortable," her grandmother had once explained, when Anna was a little girl and had asked why Aunt Hattie always wore the same outfit.

What Hattie found comfortable were long skirts—usually black— with lace-up boots and immaculate white blouses. She never wore make-up of any kind. If she were pressed to explain her choice of clothing, she would explain that her beloved grandmother—who had lived with her family in the old farmhouse from the time Hattie was born—had always worn such skirts, boots and blouses. It was her way of paying homage to a strong woman she respected and admired.

Despite what might appear strange to others in Hattie's choice of apparel, Anna loved her old family friend with her all her heart and thoroughly enjoyed her company. She believed that, besides her grandmother, Hattie was probably the kindest, warmest and most intelligent person she knew.

Hattie noticed that Annie was eyeing an envelope which Anna had left on the table.

"Go ahead and open it," she advised her friend with a smile. "I can see it's made you extremely curious."

Annie laughed. "You always could read my mind! Okay, if you won't think it's rude, I will."

She took the letter from the pile on the table, slit it open with her finger and removed the contents.

"Ah, the vicissitudes of age! Whoever sent me this note forgot to sign it, and look at the shaky handwriting!" She showed it to Hattie, who gazed at an envelope addressed to "Annie Turner" and agreed that the writing was indeed shaky.

"There is no return address on the envelope, either," observed Hattie.

"Hmm," said Annie, "let's see what she or he has to say." As she unfolded the note, two tickets fell into her lap. She picked them up and eyed them with interest.

"Orchestra seats for the Beethoven concert at the Kimmel Center on Saturday evening!" she exclaimed, waving the tickets in the air. She read the accompanying note aloud. "Annie dear, I know how much you enjoy Beethoven, so am enclosing two tickets for Saturday evening. Something has come up and we can't use them. Enjoy!"

"If you don't have a date or any other plans," Annie asked, "would you like to go with me, Anna?"

"How nice!" her granddaughter replied. "I'll be glad to go with you. If I had made other plans—which I haven't—I'd break them!" She smiled affectionately at her grandmother.

Hattie looked at her wristwatch and suddenly declared, "Oh, I had no idea it was so late! I'll have to get a taxi at once, or I'll never catch my train back to Doylestown."

While Anna phoned for a cab, Hattie and Annie went downstairs to get her cape. They were standing at the door when Anna joined them.

"The cab's on the way," she told them.

Hattie stepped onto the stoop to wait. The sky was already dark at four-thirty in the afternoon, and the chilly air held the promise of more rain.

"You two stay inside," she ordered, as they started to follow her. "It's damp and dismal out here." She looked back at them lovingly, as they stood arm-in-arm in the lighted doorway. "Anna, you look so young, you could pass for eighteen," she observed. "In fact, you both look young. You're like two peas in a pod."

"Yes, indeed," quipped Annie. "Before and after!"

They were laughing when the Yellow Taxi Cab pulled up. Hattie quickly hugged and kissed them both, before turning and hurrying down the steps. An afterthought suddenly occurred to her, and she called back, "By the way, Anna, how is your mother?"

Anna smiled understandingly, knowing her mother wasn't one of Hattie's favorite people.

"Thanks for asking, Aunt Hattie. She's just fine. As a matter of fact, she and Cameron should be getting home from the Bahamas this weekend."

Hattie had never met Anna's stepfather, Dr. Cameron MacArthur, but she knew that he had founded The MacArthur Facial Reconstruction Clinic for Children in Philadelphia. She was also aware that Doug Turner, Annie's son and Anna's father, had practiced with him all of her life. She recalled that Cameron had been a widower when he'd married the widowed Alexandra Turner ten years earlier. She'd never said one word against Alexandra, but it was always obvious to both Annie and Anna that neither she nor Hattie were fans of each other.

As she climbed into the cab's back seat, Hattie called out to her friends, "See you on Thanksgiving!" She couldn't know that she would not see Annie on Thanksgiving, or ever again...at least, not alive.

# 2

"Well, Anna, let's have a look at the rest of that mail," said Annie, as they returned to the sitting room.

While Annie was sorting through the mail, Anna stood for a moment, looking at two silver-framed wedding pictures on the wide front windowsill. One was a black-and-white photograph of her grandmother and grandfather. She smiled at her grandfather's youthful likeness.

It was with his blessing that she had come to live in this house when she began teaching in Philadelphia. Her plans to eventually rent her own apartment were irrevocably changed when he had died five years earlier with a sudden unexpected heart attack. It was then, amidst tears, that she and Gram had overseen the removal of her grandfather's dental office from the first floor, and turned the space into Anna's own suite.

The other photo was a color portrait of Anna's parents. Looking at it objectively, she had to admit they were two of the best-looking people she had ever seen. Both blue-eyed blonds, tall and regal, they could have been royalty.

Her father, too, had died from a heart attack. He was only forty-seven. Anna had been seventeen then. He had literally burned himself out, first with a busy dental practice on Philadelphia's Main Line, then by giving it all up to go to medical school to study plastic surgery.

"It's not facelifts that interest me," he had told her and her shocked mother when he'd made his decision. "I want to help children with facial deformities." His work had always involved him in children's facial problems, peripherally. As the years went by and he saw what a huge difference his work could make in the quality of their whole lives, he decided that was the way he wanted to go. His wife, less charitably inclined, mourned the loss of the big bucks she imagined a "nip-and-tuck" practice might have brought in, but he was adamant about his decision.

His long hours in school and studying, to say nothing of a lengthy residency followed by a hectic practice, kept him away from his family for most of Anna's life. She felt she'd never really known him very well. Her little sister, Brooke, who'd been just five years old when he died, claimed she scarcely remembered him at all.

Her mother hadn't taken his long hours well. She enjoyed being doted on when he was around, and suffered when he wasn't. At first, she'd pouted and complained. When that didn't have any effect on her distracted husband, she'd fashioned her own life. Attempting to take a cue from his service-mindedness, she threw herself into volunteer service—as long as the company in the organization was up to her social standards, and her presence was visible among those she considered important.

Anna remembered long stays with her grandparents while her parents had traveled to Europe and other foreign places for her father's professional conferences and seminars. When her father was away for longer periods on a speaking tour, she remembered her mother, bored and miserable, taking a sudden interest in politics and other civic activities. Before long, though, that exuberance, too, had died. Alexandra had clearly been flailing about to find her place in the world, but her attention span always proved too short for anything to really catch on.

Whatever Alexandra had been involved in at any given time, Anna could not recall her mother spending much time with her at all. What she did remember was being frightened that her parents would divorce, because it was obvious her mother was miserable without constant attention from her father. But then, when Anna was almost thirteen, Brooke had been born and her father had finally finished his residency and settled into his new practice. After that, he was home most evenings, and Anna's parents had seemed happier.

"Brooke," she said softly, smiling as she picked up a silver-framed photograph of her young sister. "She's beautiful, isn't she Gram?"

"Yes, she is," Annie answered, wistfully. "I wish her school wasn't so far away. I feel as though I hardly know the child any more, and I miss seeing her on a regular basis." She exhaled audibly. "Well, enough of that. Let's get dinner and then decide what to wear to the orchestra."

❧

Saturday evening was clear and crisp. Annie and Anna, who preferred walking to driving whenever they could, left their house early enough to enjoy the brief stroll to the Kimmel Center on Broad Street. Annie hooked her arm through Anna's, and they chatted happily as they walked.

They waited at Fifteenth and Locust Street until the traffic light turned green. They had barely stepped into Locust Street when a burgundy Chrysler with tinted windows pulled out of Fifteenth Street and sped directly toward them.

Both women turned at the sound of squealing tires to see the marauding vehicle bearing quickly down on them. Annie grabbed at Anna's arm and tried to pull her back to the curb, but Anna was frozen with fear and wouldn't budge. Her eyes fastened in terror on the oncoming car.

At the last instant, Annie jumped in front of Anna and pushed, throwing all her weight against her granddaughter's slight frame.

The impact sent Anna sprawling back onto the sidewalk out of the car's path, but it was too late for Annie to save herself. The speeding Chrysler struck her full force in her abdomen and propelled her into the air.

Her broken body landed with a sickening thud on the street. It was the last sound Anna heard before passing out.

# 3

Hattie had insisted on driving her own car to Annie's funeral. As she stood in the dismal dreariness of the church cemetery, she was thankful she had made that decision. She simply didn't want to talk to anyone just yet.

She felt a knot in her throat as she watched a spadeful of dirt being cast upon the casket. She listened to the deep voice of the minister reciting, "Unto Almighty God we commend the soul of our sister departed, and we commit her body to the ground; earth to earth, ashes to ashes, dust to dust; in sure and certain hope of the Resurrection unto eternal life through our Lord, Jesus Christ..."

She joined a line of nearly two hundred mourners as they circled the grave, dropping long-stemmed white roses on Annie's polished mahogany casket. As the casket was being lowered to its final resting place, its brass hardware glistened briefly in the dim light of the drizzly morning.

*What a waste of money*, Hattie thought, feeling immediately guilty for letting such a thought enter her head. *Annie would have said the same*, though, she rationalized.

"Annie...oh, Annie," she whispered. Tears welled in her eyes and crept down her cheeks as she continued to stare at the casket. Annie had been her best friend since either of them could remember, and now she was gone.

Hattie took comfort in the fact that Anna had requested that Annie be buried back home, in the cemetery of the church where she had been baptized, spent her growing-up years, sung in the choir, and where she and Hank had been married. Now Annie was next to Hank and her parents forever.

"Oh, Annie, how I'll miss you!" Hattie choked out. People began to leave the cemetery. The slamming of car doors and the soft crunch of tires on the driveway made no impression on Hattie, so deep in remembrance was she. Lost in the past, her eyes were still riveted on the casket, but she didn't see it.

She saw Annie as a child, sitting bolt upright on the other side of her big double bed, eyes wide, as Hattie told her ghost stories. Hattie smiled. They had spent countless nights sleeping over at one another's homes, often trying to scare each other with spooky stories and just as often succeeding.

She looked up at the church steeple where, less than an hour before, its large bass bell had tolled a sonorous farewell to Annie. Hattie's heart ached. Eighty years, she thought, and it seems like a country stroll.

A discreet cough from the other side of the grave reminded her that the minister was watching two men, shovels in hand, waiting to fill the opening with dirt.

Hattie lingered one moment longer, then turned and walked a few yards to her family plot. She stopped by the graves of her parents and brother, Fred, to ascertain that they were well kept. A fitful breeze blew a handful of leaves across Fred's grave and teased the small veteran's American flag in its bronze holder at the base of his headstone.

"How different my life would have been if you had lived," she whispered. She jumped at a light touch on her arm. Turning quickly, she saw Anna standing next to her. Anna's blue eyes, so much like Annie's, were swimming in tears.

"We've both lost our best friend," Anna said with a little sob.

Hattie nodded and placed her arms around Anna. They stood holding each other silently for a moment. Hattie was the first to speak.

"I'm so very grateful I had that lovely day with her last Thursday. It is a memory I will always cherish."

"That's how I picture her now," whispered Anna, "happy and laughing. Only now she's in Heaven, with Grandpa and Daddy."

"Yes," Hattie agreed, "and with her parents and everyone else she loved, who went on before. I do believe that, dear."

Anna looked thoughtful.

"Perhaps I shouldn't say this, Aunt Hattie, but I loved Gram more than anybody. She was more of a mother to me than my own mother. Much more, and I don't feel a bit guilty admitting that. I'm going to miss her so very much." She wiped her eyes with a soggy tissue, then continued. "I have a very special favor to ask of you, Aunt Hattie. Will you please come back to Mother's condo with me? I know she invited you."

"Yes," Hattie admitted, "she said she was having people back for a light lunch. But frankly, dear, I really don't have the heart for it."

"Oh, please, Aunt Hattie. Please come. I need you there," Anna pleaded.

Hattie couldn't help looking down uncomfortably at her long black skirt and old-fashioned boots. It was rare for her to even be conscious of her attire, but she knew Alexandra and her friends would be beautifully dressed...and appraising. With a deep sigh, she said, "Alright, dear. I'll go for you." But she truly dreaded it.

# 4

Anna was in a hurry to get to her mother's place, only because she wanted to get the obligatory visit over with as quickly as possible. As Hattie followed behind, she tried to keep up with Anna's car, but the young woman sped along. It made Hattie nervous to go so fast down the winding country lanes, so she maintained a safe speed and was soon left far behind.

*Just as well*, thought Hattie, *I'm in no rush to get there. I'll take my time and think about Annie.* Her old friend's face floated in front of her once again, looking as it had during Annie's sixteenth birthday party. She'd looked prettier than Hattie had ever seen her.

They'd had no secrets from each other, and Hattie had known for almost six months that Annie had had a serious crush on Hank Turner. Hank, a senior, was two years older than Hattie and Annie, and was much admired by all the girls at school. He lived in town, where his father was the only dentist. He often said he wanted to be a dentist, too.

That was an appealing prospect for most of the girls, who thought they were too sophisticated for farmers like their fathers, but that wasn't what Annie saw in him. Nor did she like him because he was a football hero. It wasn't even his handsome blond looks or deep blue eyes. She liked him because he was nice to everybody, so sincere.

Hank paid no more attention to Annie than he did to any of the other girls—less, really—but that didn't discourage Annie.

"I'm going to marry him one day," she told Hattie. "You just wait and see."

She invited him to her sixteenth birthday party, and he accepted. Her parents gave her a carefully chaperoned ice-skating party on the pond, followed by a sleigh ride. Afterward, they served hot chocolate, ice cream and cake in their spacious kitchen. Twelve youngsters had been invited, six boys and six girls. It was a wonderfully crisp, clear night, Hattie remembered with a smile, and everyone had a marvelous time.

She thought Hank was very nice, too, but, of course she didn't pay any extra attention to him, because she knew Annie's feelings toward him. The four other girls were under no such constraint, and they all but threw themselves shamelessly at Hank.

To Hattie's surprise, Annie didn't seem the least perturbed. In fact, she paid very little attention to Hank all evening. Hattie couldn't say that Annie actually ignored him, but she was equally friendly to everyone else at the party. She smiled and laughed and said cute things, and it was obvious that all the other boys were charmed by her.

Every once in awhile, Hattie saw Hank staring at Annie with an odd expression on his face, but nothing happened between them that she could see. That was why Hattie was so startled when, after everyone else had gone home, Annie whirled around and around the kitchen, giggling.

"He likes me! He likes me!"

Two years later, just after she had graduated from high school, Hank gave Annie a gold engagement ring with a pretty, half-carat diamond solitaire in a high Tiffany setting. Hank had graduated from college when he was twenty-two, then went to dental school for another four years.

They married—over the protests of both sets of parents, who felt they weren't ready—when Hank was in his first year of dental school and Annie was twenty. Hattie was her maid of honor.

By that time Hattie, an education major, was halfway through college and living away at school. Annie and Hank were living in a small apartment near the University of Pennsylvania, where he was in school. Though Annie and Hattie were separated by distance, they wrote to each other frequently. Hattie was thrilled when, almost a year after the wedding, she received a letter from Annie announcing that they were going to have a baby.

"And you will be the Godmother," it said, "if that's all right with you."

Annie's pregnancy had been extremely difficult, and when baby Douglas arrived a month early, she almost died. She hemorrhaged severely, drifting in and out of consciousness until only an emergency hysterectomy could save her.

Hattie skipped her classes for the rest of that week and the next, and took the first available train to Philadelphia to be with Annie, Hank and the baby.

How Annie had cried when she learned that she would never be able to have another child. Hank supported her with his usual tenderness and took excellent care of her and little Doug once they were home. With Hank, her parents and Hattie by her side—and the miracle of the new little life in her arms—Annie began to regain her former health and cheerfulness. Hattie returned to college with the comfort of knowing Annie was in good hands.

Hattie sighed deeply.

"Where did the time go?" she said aloud. "Annie was like a sister—closer than a sister."

For the first time in her life, and with Thanksgiving only ten days away, Hattie felt desperately lonely. She and Annie had spent every Thanksgiving of their lives together. It was a family tradition, full of love and fellowship. Even after the deaths of their parents and of Fred, Doug and Hank, they'd still cherished the custom. Now, Hattie would spend the holiday alone.

As she thought of all this, her eyes filled with tears and she could scarcely see to drive. She pulled her old station wagon off the road as soon as she found a safe spot.

"Silly old woman!" she muttered, scolding herself. "You're just being maudlin. You're not crying for Annie, you're crying for yourself. Stop it!"

She pulled a white linen handkerchief from her purse and wiped her eyes vigorously. After blowing her nose and taking several deep breaths, she veered back onto the road. She'd driven barely fifty yards when a dark green van rushed past, so fast and so close to the side of her car that it almost forced her off the road again.

Hattie slammed on the brakes, jerking her car to a rapid stop.

"Crazy driver!" she yelled. Shaken, she didn't start back down the road again until the van was well out of sight ahead of her.

Just moments later and a few miles down the road, a guard raised the gate to permit Anna to drive into the parking lot of her mother's fashionable condominium complex. The gate was barely closed when a dark green van headed for the entrance, then suddenly swerved away.

"Crazy driver!" exclaimed the guard, unwittingly echoing Hattie's words. He tried, but couldn't see the driver through the van's tinted windows. Shrugging his shoulders, he returned to the shelter of the little gatehouse.

A number of other cars were parked near the brick walkway leading to her mother's condominium, so Anna drove beyond them, parking beneath a big, old oak tree. She stood for a moment next to the car and looked up through the tree's bare branches to the heavy gray clouds. Raindrops began to fall, mixing with the tears on her cheeks. Except for a few remaining dry leaves rustling in the breeze and the soft splatter of the rain, there was no other sound.

Anna looked around to make sure she was alone, then very softly called, "Yoo-hoo! Are you home, Gram?"

She didn't expect an answer, and there was none, but just for an instant, the clouds parted and a ray of sunshine broke through. All at once, Anna was filled with an indescribable sense of peace and warmth.

"Yes, Gram, you *are* home. I know that now," she whispered. Wiping her eyes, and with a smile on her face, Anna walked over to the gate to wait for Hattie.

Betty Kerr Orlemann

# 5

Hattie shivered and drew her black cape tighter around her as she and Anna walked up the brick path to the entrance of Alexandra Turner MacArthur's condominium. She wanted to tell Anna about the close call with the van, but it seemed petty given the circumstances. She would wait till later.

Hattie didn't want to be here. Though she'd been fond of Doug, she had never liked his wife from the first moment the two had met. Alexandra—never Alex or Allie, or something equally as casual—Weston and Doug had met in college, where she had been Homecoming queen and he the king. She was undeniably beautiful, with naturally golden hair and cornflower-blue eyes fringed with the longest lashes Hattie had ever seen. Alexandra and Doug were both so remarkably good-looking that they turned heads wherever they went. But that's where the beauty ended.

Alexandra had come from a very wealthy family. An only child born to older parents, she'd been given everything she'd ever wanted from the time she was able to demand it, and demand she did.

"A spoiled rotten brat," was Hattie's opinion of Alexandra, but she shared that thought with no one. Though she believed she'd always been discreet about her disdain in front of Annie and Anna, they were aware of it.

Unlike his father, Doug wisely decided to finish dental college before he and Alexandra married, and she didn't like that one bit. She'd pouted for three years, or so it had seemed to Hattie. They were both twenty-four when the wedding took place. The ink hadn't had a chance to dry on his diploma before Alexandra marched her new dentist down the aisle, Hattie always thought uncharitably.

It was the biggest, most lavish wedding Hattie had ever attended. The reception, held in an enormous tent on the bride's parents' lawn, surpassed sumptuous. Alexandra was ravishing in her imported Parisian gown, and Doug was stunning in his white tuxedo. But Annie and Hank, though they had smiled broadly and participated in the festivities, didn't seem as happy as one might have expected.

Hattie, who knew them so well, was deeply concerned by their underlying sadness and wondered what on earth was bothering them.

The newlyweds embarked on a Mediterranean honeymoon cruise, courtesy of Alexandra's father. Two days after they'd left, Annie went to see Hattie.

"Is something wrong?" asked Hattie, knowing full well there was.

For a moment, Annie didn't speak. Then she looked into Hattie's eyes, with tears welling in her own

"Doug isn't going into practice with Hank, after all," she sobbed. "Alexandra doesn't want to live in Philadelphia, and her father has arranged a wonderful opportunity for Doug. He'll be going into a well-established practice on the Main Line, with an older cousin of Alexandra's." She wiped her eyes and tried to smile. "I feel just awful for Hank. He's dreamed of a partnership with Doug for years. You remember...Hank and his father had planned to practice together until his father's death ended that dream, too."

Hattie, greatly saddened by Annie's news, was also angry. It was far from the last time that she would be furious over Alexandra's selfish actions.

Anna's voice broke into her reverie.

"Well, here we are," she said, attempting cheerfulness.

They stood before the door of Alexandra's condominium. For a wild moment, Hattie considered turning and leaving, but Anna opened the door. Hattie stepped with her into a well-appointed entrance hall. A uniformed maid appeared, greeted Anna by name, and nodded politely to Hattie. She whisked Hattie's cape and Anna's coat away as soon as they had removed them, then disappeared.

Across the room, Alexandra glanced toward the door to see who had arrived. She started walking toward Hattie, when another guest plucked at her sleeve. Alexandra turned.

The woman whispered, none too softly, "My dear, what is that?" She nodded toward Hattie, her face bearing the disdainful expression of one with a bad taste in her mouth.

Anna, hearing the bad-mannered remark, tucked her arm protectively through Hattie's, as Alexandra made her dignified way across the thick white carpet.

"Hello, Hattie," she said in carefully modulated tones. A tight smile was betrayed by her eyes, which remained cool and aloof. "It was good of you to come."

She placed her limp right hand briefly in Hattie's.

"Do come in and have something to eat and drink," she urged, making no mention of Annie nor the reason they were gathered there.

"Anna, look out for Hattie, will you?" Alexandra said, for the first time acknowledging her daughter's presence. As she withdrew to talk to other guests, Hattie whispered to Anna.

"Your mother is just as beautiful as ever. At fifty-nine, she could almost pass for her late thirties." She nodded toward Alexandra. "And that blue dress exactly matches her eyes."

Anna laughed. She lowered her voice and confided, "Don't think that's accidental! And I probably shouldn't tell you this, but that smooth, youthful face has been helped along a bit by the surgeon's knife."

Hattie feigned shock while Anna just raised her eyebrows mischievously. Hattie looked around the room and nodded to several old mutual friends of hers and Annie's. She also recognized a group of Annie's city friends gathered at the far side of the room, but most of the guests were strangers to her. She supposed she should do the polite thing and greet those she knew, but felt like anything but interacting with anyone. At that fortuitous moment, Anna pulled her toward the den.

"Come, meet Cameron," she urged. "He's hiding out. He hates these things as much as we do."

Dr. Cameron MacArthur was comfortably ensconced in a leather chair, its back toward the door. In his hand was a copy of *Newsweek*. The *Wall Street Journal* lay unopened on a table next to the chair, awaiting his perusal.

"Hi, Cameron," Anna greeted her stepfather, with obvious fondness. "I want you to meet my favorite person in the world, Hattie Farwell."

Cameron closed his magazine and placed it on top of the paper on the table. He rose from his chair and nodded toward Hattie in a courtly manner. A slight smile played at the corners of his mouth. He was tall, gray-haired and pleasant looking. Hattie figured he was in his late sixties. His blue eyes were warm, and Hattie liked him immediately.

"Please accept my condolences, Miss Farwell, on the loss of your friend. It was a terrible accident. Anna tells me that you grew up together and were very close." Cameron spoke sincerely, looking with sympathy into Hattie's eyes. "I saw the Turners every once in a while with Doug, and I thought they were fine people."

"Yes, they were," Hattie answered, sadly. "The very finest."

"So, there you are!" said Alexandra from the doorway, a bit too perky for Hattie's taste. "I think it would be nice if you would spend a little time with our guests, don't you, dear?" Her words were directed toward her husband.

He turned at the sound of her voice , smiled pleasantly, sighed and walked toward the door. On his face was an expression of absolute adoration, which was not lost on Hattie or Anna.

"After ten years of marriage, he still worships the ground she walks on," said Anna, as the two walked back into the front room. "I believe there's nothing he wouldn't do for her." Anna picked up the magazine Cameron had been reading and glanced at the cover.

Pictured on it was one of the handsomest men she had ever seen. His glossy black hair held just enough wave to keep it in place without looking slick. His dark brown eyes stared straight into the camera. His chin jutted forward, but a confident smile turned up the corners of a sensual mouth, softening his intent expression.

"What has Senator DiRienzo done now, to get his picture on the cover of *Newsweek*?" asked Hattie.

"Where have you been, Aunt Hattie?" Anna chided. "Haven't you heard that he's thrown his hat into the presidential ring?"

"Well, no...I hadn't," Hattie admitted, "but I shouldn't really be surprised. That man has always been ambitious, and he's the consummate politician. He has the reputation of stopping at nothing to get what he wants. I shudder to imagine what would happen if he won his party's nomination and were elected president."

"Why, Aunt Hattie!" Anna laughed. "I'm surprised at your vehemence. You're usually the most charitable person I know. I've almost never heard you say a mean thing about anyone."

Alexandra reappeared in the doorway.

"Lunch is served," she said to Anna, clearly indicating that her daughter's presence was desired among the other guests. She didn't acknowledge Hattie before returning to the living room.

An elaborate buffet of sliced turkey and ham, chicken salad, shrimp, coleslaw, potato salad, aspic, deviled eggs, home-style rolls and fruit had been set up on the dining room table by the caterer. A few of the guests were just beginning to help themselves when Hattie and Anna walked into the room. Most of the other guests, however, remained in the living room, sipping cocktails and enjoying hors d'oeuvres. Their voices became louder the more they drank.

Hattie was no stranger to this practice following a funeral, but she had the sinking feeling that many of the people there were simply enjoying a party and really didn't care about the person whose death they were supposedly mourning.

Hattie and Anna carried their plates of food to the living room, where Alexandra was in the process of trying to shoo the cocktail drinkers into the dining room. At that moment, the outside door swung open and her younger daughter, Brooke, strode in.

It was obvious to anyone who saw her face that Alexandra was less than delighted to see her seventeen-year-old.

"Why...what are you doing here?" she demanded, almost harshly.

Anna stifled a giggle. "Look, Aunt Hattie," she choked, "I do believe you've started a new fashion trend!" She nodded toward Brooke, whose thick, dark hair was pulled into a bun at the nape of her neck. There was not the slightest hint of makeup on her face, and she was wearing a white blouse and a long black skirt. Like Hattie, she also wore black boots, but hers were Skechers instead of the pointed-toe lace-ups her "aunt" favored.

Brooke looked impishly across the room at Hattie.

"Why, Brooke!" Hattie called to her. "I'm not sure whether I should be flattered or insulted!" Everyone around them laughed, with the notable exception of Alexandra.

The girl walked over to Hattie and gave her a peck on the cheek. "Flattered, Aunt Hattie," she replied, with no further comment. She embraced her sister, and blew her mother a kiss across the room.

Alexandra shook her head and sighed. Brooke had always surprised her, from the moment she had realized another baby was on the way. From then on, her younger daughter had provided one unpredictable episode after another.

With her dark brown hair and brown eyes, Brooke stood out in a family of blonds. "She looks just like a portrait of my French great-grandfather," Alexandra commented frequently.

"How you've changed!" Hattie said to Brooke. "You've lost all your baby fat, and you look as if you've grown a foot since I last saw you."

Brooke smiled. "I almost have," she commented proudly. "I'm five feet nine, now, just like Mother."

Hattie observed that, except for her coloring, Brooke looked very much like her mother, too. She had the same high cheek bones, the same hairline and the same lovely slim figure. The biggest difference was her pleasant natural expression of openness and curiosity, as opposed to the critical and calculating look her mother often wore. She was five inches taller than her sister, and where Anna was very pretty, Brooke was truly beautiful.

Hattie was sorry the child had been away so much. She would have loved to have watched Brooke grow up as she had Anna, but with the near-thirteen-year difference in the girls' ages, the death of their father, and Alexandra's marriage to Cameron, other plans had been made for Brooke. She was only eight when Alexandra had sent her off to boarding school in New England.

Alexandra glided over and repeated, her lips barely moving, "What are you doing here? You're supposed to be in school!"

Brooke smiled, unconcerned at her mother's stern tone.

"A friend of mine drove me down from Massachusetts. I wanted to be here in time for Gram's funeral, but it just didn't work out that way." Her voice became sad when she mentioned Annie, but in a moment, she brightened. "Well, I'd better run outside and get my suitcase." She turned and hurried to the door, ignoring her mother's obvious expectation of further explanation.

Hattie had had enough of Alexandra. She made her way through the living room, greeting old friends and acquaintances, and nodding politely to strangers. She was anxious to leave, but didn't want to appear rude. She stayed for another fifteen minutes before thanking Alexandra and Cameron, kissing Anna and retrieving her cape to leave. She was approaching her car when Anna ran up behind her.

"Don't think I'm crazy, Aunt Hattie, but there's something I have to say to you." She paused a moment and continued, slowly, "I don't know anything for a fact, but I have a feeling Gram's death was no accident."

Hattie, shocked, stopped in her tracks and looked directly at Anna.

"Of course it was an accident. Why would you say such a thing, Anna?"

"Well, I've been turning that night over and over in my mind, and there are just some things that don't add up. First of all, the letter containing the concert tickets wasn't signed. Gram thought it was an oversight, but now I wonder. And remember, there was no return address on the envelope, either." Anna's face darkened. "Then there was the car. It absolutely raced out of Fifteenth Street, and drove straight at us. If Gram hadn't pushed me out of the way, we both would have been hit. She saved my life."

The young woman paused, collecting herself. "Maybe, if I hadn't been so terrified when I saw that car heading for us, she wouldn't have died. That thought haunts me, Aunt Hattie." Anna shivered.

"No, Anna. If whoever was driving that car was intent on killing one or both of you, he would have followed you up on the sidewalk, if necessary. No, you must never blame yourself for what happened. It was the fault of that driver and no one else!" Hattie was vehement. Even as she spoke, though, she was considering the unanswered questions Anna had posed. *Wait a minute*, Hattie thought. *Is it possible that Annie really was murdered? And if so, why?*

Aloud, she said, "Who'd want to kill Annie?" After a moment, she looked up at Anna and asked, "What did you do with the note that contained the orchestra tickets?"

"Oh, Gram threw it away," she answered. "There didn't seem to be any reason to keep it. She just figured that sooner or later she would learn who sent them and thank them then.

"Hmmm," mumbled Hattie. "What about the police? Have you told them of your suspicions?"

"No. They would have thought I had a head injury or something. There's really no pointed evidence to suggest such a thing, and I can't cite a single reason to think anyone would want to kill Gram. Everybody loved her."

Anna shook her head, perplexed. "But still..." her voice trailed off, then she added, "the police listed it as a hit-and-run accident."

# 6

After Anna had re-entered her mother's condominium, Hattie sat for some time in her car, thinking over what Anna had told her.

"Preposterous!" she mumbled, but the memory of the dark green van with tinted windows that had forced her off the road nagged at her. "That's ridiculous," she scolded herself. "What possible connection could there be?"

She started her engine and was pulling slowly toward the lot's exit when she became aware of a young couple locked in a lingering embrace in the far corner of the parking lot. The girl was unmistakably Brooke, but who was the boy? Apparently, it was the friend who had driven her down from her school in Massachusetts. Oblivious to the rain, they were leaning against a gray Honda of nondescript vintage, which Hattie surmised must belong to the boy.

Hattie sighed and shrugged her shoulders. As much as she wanted to go over and see Brooke, she didn't want to disturb them. Reluctant to leave, she was just turning into the exit, when she heard Brooke shouting to her. She stopped her car and turned to see the girl running across the wet pavement with her young man in tow. Hattie rolled down her window when they approached.

Brooke was radiant, more beautiful than ever.

"Aunt Hattie!" she squealed. "Guess what? We're engaged! Meet my fiancé." She turned to face him, playfully tugging on his hand, then back to Hattie. "This is Shawn O'Brien. He's a junior at Harvard."

Hattie extended her hand through the open window. "Congratulations, Shawn," she said, politely. "It's a pleasure to meet you. And my very best wishes to you, dear," she said to Brooke, thinking, *You'll need them when you tell your mother.*

Hattie looked up at the tall young man still holding her hand. Rain was dripping, apparently unnoticed, from a thick thatch of sandy hair and running down his freckled cheeks. His wide smile was infectious.

"Get into my car, kids," Hattie ordered in her best schoolmarm voice. "You'll catch your death standing out there in the rain!"

They both giggled and obediently climbed into the back seat, slamming the door. Shawn's green eyes twinkled when Hattie turned to look at him.

"You're the first to know," he said, flashing even, white teeth.

"I'm honored," Hattie said, "but I've no say in the matter. Brooke, I doubt if your mother will take this well."

"Let me practice on you, Aunt Hattie," pleaded Brooke. "You pretend to be my mother." She took hold of Shawn's hand and held it tightly.

Hattie sighed. "Okay," she agreed, somewhat reluctantly. She backed her car into a parking space and turned off the engine. Shifting sideways in her seat, she looked over the back at the eager young pair.

"Brooke, you're too young. You won't even be eighteen until February, and you won't graduate from school until May. What do you plan to do about college? How can you even think about marriage?" The irony was not lost on her that for once, she agreed with what Alexandra would likely be thinking.

"And Shawn," she continued, "what can you be thinking of? You have a year and a half left in college and then a career to worry about. How can you possibly support a wife—and maybe a family?" Harboring many of the same concerns herself, Hattie was really getting into the charade. "What will your parents say?"

Brooke and Shawn, still holding hands, were silent, so Hattie continued. "Where did you two meet? Brooke, have you met Shawn's family?"

"Wow, scary, Aunt Hattie! You do sound like Mother!" Brooke observed, somewhat taken aback. "We met at a party at Harvard a year ago and we've been dating ever since—except for summer vacation, when we emailed each other every day and talked on our cell phones whenever we could. Oh, Aunt Hattie, we're so much in love...can't you see?"

Hattie looked at the girl and sighed. She was so beautiful. So very young. So naive.

Shawn took over. "I've loved Brooke from the moment we met," he said seriously. "I'm a political science major, and I'm going to take off the spring and fall semesters to work for Senator Michael DiRienzo's presidential campaign. But I'll still have enough credits to graduate in two years. Then Brooke and I can plan our wedding. By then, I'll be almost twenty-three, and she'll be almost twenty. Who could object to that?"

He paused a moment, waiting for a reaction, but Hattie just listened patiently. He continued.

"If Michael is elected president, maybe he'll even give me a job in his administration." He smiled broadly. "As a matter of fact, Michael is going to be campaigning for the primary in Bucks County for the next four days, and Brooke and I have signed up to volunteer in his Doylestown headquarters."

Uncharacteristically, Hattie found herself unable to think of anything to say. She had met Michael DiRienzo only one time. Unlike his many adoring fans, she couldn't bring herself to like him.

When they'd met, she had to admit that he was handsome, very handsome. Tall, with a beautiful athletic build shown to advantage in his expensively tailored navy suit, he'd looked almost boyish with a lock of his black wavy hair curling as if by accident over the right side of his forehead.

The senator was articulate and charming. His frequent smiles displayed perfect white teeth. His dark brown eyes sparkled when he spoke, but Hattie felt no warmth from him, and she couldn't pinpoint the reason.

Their meeting had taken place at Annie's and Hank's home. Hattie recalled that Doug, Alexandra and Anna had moved in with Annie and Hank for a while, when Doug was in medical school. The vision of a very bored Alexandra floated into her mind.

During that time, Annie had been given responsibility for most of Anna's care. Alexandra, unmoored by her perceived drop in social status and Doug's constant absence, had apparently seen a place for herself in the charismatic politician's entourage. Always savvy about the art of social perception, she was drawn into the promotional end of things. She suddenly abandoned the family's traditional political party and threw herself into the DiRienzo campaign for reelection to Congress.

Hattie had met him when DiRienzo had dropped by the house to discuss brochures with Alexandra while Hattie was visiting Annie and Hank. It was obvious from the expressions on Annie's and Hank's faces when DiRienzo left the room that they didn't care for him, either.

Now, Hattie looked at the two eager faces staring at her from the back seat and thought, *Well, I'll give the*

*Senator the benefit of the doubt.* He did seem too polished, too sure of himself, too glib and insincere. But that was—what? Nineteen, twenty years ago? People can—and do—change. She smiled at Brooke and Shawn.

"What is there about Senator DiRienzo that has inspired such excitement in you two?"

Shawn leaned forward, but didn't drop Brooke's hand.

"Well," he began, "I grew up in South Philadelphia, not far from the DiRienzos. Michael had been a congressman since I was little, and I can remember how great he was to all us kids. He used to come to our school and speak to us, and one year he invited the whole fifth grade to visit him in Washington. He even paid our way! He said he was proud to have gone to our school, and was proud of us, too."

As he remembered Michael's words, Shawn's chest seemed to swell a bit. "All our parents pitched in to help him win his senate seat twelve years ago. They said he was a man who never forgot his roots. He even helped me get into Harvard."

A look of sheer adoration inhabited Shawn's face. The expression on Brooke's face mirrored Shawn's.

"We'll help him win the primary," she said with conviction, nodding her head for emphasis.

Teetering somewhere between amusement and concern, Hattie shook her head.

"Oh, Brooke, what will your mother say?" she asked with a sigh. "She'll be furious if you don't go back to school."

Brooke snuggled closer to Shawn. It was obvious she did not intend to leave him until she absolutely had to. She looked into Hattie's eyes with a touch of defiance in her own.

"I'll go back right after Thanksgiving vacation, I promise. I'm only taking a few days off now," she said, decisively.

Hattie gave the girl an affectionate smile. "I'm not the one you need to convince, dear," she said. "I have absolutely no say in the matter, you know."

Brooke ignored the comment.

"I can't wait to meet Michael DiRienzo," she said dreamily into Shawn's sleeve. "He's so handsome. He'll make a wonderful president."

"Is that what it takes to be a good president?" asked Hattie. "Just being handsome?" She teased Brooke, but not maliciously. "So, when are you going to meet this wonderful man?"

"Tomorrow, I hope," Shawn answered for Brooke. "He and his wife have been in Philadelphia for the past week visiting family and doing some campaigning during the legislative recess. They should be in Doylestown today, I think."

"What's his wife like?" asked Hattie with genuine interest. "I don't believe I've ever even seen a picture of her."

"She's okay, I guess," Shawn answered a trifle doubtfully. "She's kinda mousy, if you know what I mean. Her name is Maria. 'Maria Mouse,' all the office workers call her behind her back." He paused, seeming to search for a proper description.

"It's hard to describe her, really. She's little, about five feet two, and sorta plump. She looks up at Michael with puppy dog eyes and does anything he tells her to, but she prefers to stay in the background when she can. They've been married since before I can remember, but they have no children. I remember learning not too long ago that she'd had something like seven miscarriages. It was very hard on her physically and mentally, I heard. A huge disappointment to both of them."

"Poor thing," sighed Hattie. "It's funny, though, that Michael DiRienzo would pick a wife like that. She doesn't quite seem his type."

"My mother told me that Maria was a knock-out when they first met and married. Her eyes are still pretty, if you ever bother to look at them...a kind of deep, golden brown. Her hair is gray now, but my mother said it was a rich auburn when she was young. I guess she was slim, energetic and popular as a girl, but Mom said all of those miscarriages changed her. Now, you can stand right next to her and not even realize she's there. She's really quiet and shy, too. You can hardly hear her when she talks." Shawn looked right at Hattie and shrugged his shoulders as he finished his description.

"Poor thing," Hattie repeated.

Brooke, who'd been stealing glances at the door to her mother's condominium, emitted a tiny groan. "We'd better go in and face the music, I guess," she said, reluctantly. "The guests seem to be leaving, finally." They waited until a string of cars passed them and went through the exit gate. "I'll run over to Shawn's car and get my back pack."

"Stay in the car, I'll drive you over," Hattie offered. The rain was pouring down harder than ever when they reached Shawn's car. Hattie handed him her umbrella and he sloshed through puddles to retrieve Brooke's back pack. Then Hattie drove them as close to Alexandra's door as she could get.

"Keep your fingers crossed!" Brooke shouted as she and Shawn, carrying the back pack, jumped from the car and raced through the rain to her mother's door.

Hattie didn't wait for the explosion she knew was coming. She sat in the car just long enough to see Shawn and Brooke hug.

At that moment the door burst open and there stood Alexandra, staring them down. Without a word, she held the door wide open, and Hattie pulled away as the two young lovers ducked in out of the rain and into another kind of storm.

# 7

Rain, mud and all, this old farmhouse had been Hattie's home since her birth, and she loved it. She glanced at her watch. It was almost three-thirty p.m.

An enormous gray dog uncurled himself from a rug on the hearth when she turned her key in the lock. His plumed tail waved furiously as she pushed the door open and entered the room.

"Hi, Wolf!" she said to her beloved dog.

He forced his large head under her arm, begging her to love him up. She laughed and leaned over to hug him. He licked her face.

"You want to go out?" she asked, knowing what his reaction would be.

His front paws danced off the floor as he spun his great body toward the door, panting furiously.

"You can almost talk, can't you?" she asked, opening the door for him.

She watched with a smile as he bolted out, crossed the porch in a bound, dashed through the open gate and disappeared into a cedar forest across the lane. An unlikely mix of three-quarters Irish Wolfhound and one-quarter timberwolf, he was a giant of a beast, with the wolf's yellow eyes and the Wolfhound's rough, gray coat.

Hattie had found him in the woods three years ago where someone had abandoned him when legislation had been passed outlawing the keeping of wolf hybrids. He had been just a puppy, no more than two months old, and Hattie hadn't known then what his lineage was. He was starving—so skinny she could count his ribs—and sick with a cough and runny nose. When no one had claimed him, she'd kept him.

Because she'd found him in the wild, and because his eyes had something feral in them, she'd named him Wolf. She'd taken him immediately to the local veterinarian, who brought the dog back to health and, in time, identified his ancestry. Hattie begged the doctor not to reveal this to anyone, and the doctor, believing that the small amount of wild blood would have little influence on the animal's behavior, agreed. He knew Hattie, and thought it might even be an advantage for the old woman living alone in that house in the woods to have a dog with a bit of the ultra-loyal pack animal's blood running through its veins.

Hattie trained Wolf and was delighted to find he took well to instruction. She grew to love him mightily and, before long, decided that he was just about the best dog in the world. Not everyone agreed with this appraisal, though, as he grew to be an intimidating watchdog. But he'd never bitten anyone, and Hattie appreciated the protection.

Hattie removed her damp cape and hung it on a hook near the door before starting a blaze in the fireplace. The old-fashioned kitchen, with its walk-in fireplace, was her favorite room in the house.

She lowered herself with a sigh into an overstuffed armchair facing the fire. For a long time she just watched the dancing flames, not allowing herself to think about Annie, not allowing herself to feel the pain.

Sleep overtook her, and when she awoke, the fire had reduced itself to a few glowing embers. The room had grown chilly. Hattie rose stiffly from her chair and reached for her heavy cardigan, hanging on a wooden peg next to her cape.

She hunched herself into the sweater, enjoying its warmth. With the flick of a light switch by the door, a hanging lamp over an antique wooden table burst to life.

"That's better," she said aloud. "Now, for some more wood."

She walked out onto the covered porch and was relieved to find the rain had stopped. She stooped to pick up an armful of logs, but before re-entering the kitchen she peered toward the woods, looking for Wolf.

"Wolf!" she called. "Wolf! Don't you want your dinner? Come, Wolf! Come!" But the dog did not appear.

*No cause for concern*, she thought. Sometimes the dog ran far into the woods, even in the dark. She opened a can of dog food and scooped the contents into Wolf's dish. Then she added several scoops of dry food and placed the dish on the floor by the fireplace. It was after six p.m.

"Now," she murmured, "what'll I fix myself for supper?" She opened the refrigerator and finally decided on some vegetable soup she'd made the previous day. "This'll do just fine, especially after that big meal at Alexandra's."

❧

Back at Alexandra's, she and her daughters were not in the mood to eat. Shawn, who never let anything interfere with his appetite, helped himself to large portions of sliced ham and cheese, deviled eggs, shrimp and sauce, potato salad, coleslaw and kaiser rolls.

Alexandra regarded him with distaste, but Cameron kindly joined him, sitting next to Shawn at the table with his own plate piled high with leftovers from lunch.

Many years before, Alexandra had learned that temper tantrums no longer helped her get her own way. She'd developed a much better way to get her point across: She became coldly superior.

After pacing sedately in front of Brooke, she spun on her heel and confronted her, eye-to-eye.

"What utter nonsense!" she declared. "You are NOT going to get married! You are NOT going to stay home until after Thanksgiving! And above all, you are absolutely NOT going to work on the campaign of Michael DiRienzo!"

Brooke stood as straight as her mother and glared right back at her.

"Oh, yes, I am!" she shot back, through gritted teeth.

Cameron and Shawn, both with their forks poised in the air, turned and watched the scene unfolding before them. Cameron, who knew better than to ever interfere in an argument between Alexandra and her daughters, slowly resumed eating. Shawn followed his example, but inside he was becoming very uncomfortable.

Anna pulled out a chair at the table and sat opposite the two men. For something to do, she put a few shrimp on her plate and picked at them, but she really couldn't eat. She smiled across at Shawn, and he smiled back.

*He's really a nice-looking boy*, she thought, *and Mother is making his life miserable. Thank Heaven for Cameron.*

"Well," said Cameron, as if on cue, "tell me about yourself, Shawn."

Shawn, glancing nervously at Brooke and her mother from time to time, launched gratefully into the story of his life from South Philadelphia to Harvard. He described his family with genuine affection.

"There are eight of us," he said, smiling. "Besides my parents, I have three sisters and two brothers. I'm the baby." Then he told them about Michael DiRienzo, and why he was working for his campaign.

Anna and Cameron were both interested in what the boy was telling them, and even Alexandra glanced over and listened to him occasionally, despite the restrained but furious disagreement she was having with Brooke.

Finally, needing to reassert her control over the situation, Alexandra raised her voice.

"Brooke, it's getting much too late for company. We've all had a very trying day. Please send your guest home and go to bed."

"No way!" Brooke shouted. "In case you haven't noticed, I'm no longer a child! I've been deciding for quite some time what time to go to bed. Get a grip."

Not used to being challenged, especially by her own children, Alexandra was furious. "Young lady, you're in my home, and you will do as you're told. I do not have to put up with an impudent seventeen-year-old who thinks she's too grown up to show some respect!" Her face flushed crimson.

Shawn's glance darted back and forth between Brooke and Alexandra. Shrewdly sizing up the situation, he stood up and went over to Brooke. He wrapped his arms around her, and she burst into tears.

"Babe," he said quietly into her hair, "listen to your mom. Go on to your room now. You could use the rest. I'll see you in the morning." With that, he brushed Brooke's forehead with his lips, thanked Alexandra for her hospitality and told her he was sorry to have overstayed his welcome. He said good night to everyone and left.

As soon as he was gone, Brooke emitted a loud wail and ran from the room. Less than a moment later, a door slammed on the second floor. A ringing telephone interrupted the silence that followed.

Cameron walked to a table where the phone sat in the corner of the living room and answered it. A deep, hoarse, unrecognizable voice sobbed into his ear.

"Is Annie there?"

Cameron corrected, "ANNA is here. Would you like to speak to her?"

"No...no, that's okay," said the voice. "This is Hattie Farwell. Would you be kind enough to tell her that I really need her as soon as she can get here? Tell her to bring her overnight bag. Thank you so much." There was a click and the line went dead.

"That was Hattie," Cameron told Anna. "Her voice was strange. She sounds extremely upset...called you 'Annie.' She wants you to get over there as soon as you can." His eyes were filled with concern. He liked Hattie.

Anna was on her feet and halfway up the stairs before Cameron finished speaking. "Oh, and she said to bring your overnight bag!"

"It must be something awful!" Anna said, her voice full of worry. "Aunt Hattie is the calmest person I know. She must be taking Gram's death really hard. I'll go right away."

She heard her sister sobbing in her bedroom as she passed the closed door. She wanted to go in and comfort Brooke, but didn't feel she could afford the time. After all, Brooke was young and resilient. She wasn't so sure about Aunt Hattie in her fragile emotional state.

In her own bedroom, she literally threw some underwear, a nightgown, a few toiletries, a pair of jeans, a bright blue sweater and a blouse into her overnight bag. She was back on the first floor, putting on her jacket, in less than five minutes.

"What is the matter with that woman, anyhow?" asked Alexandra, clearly perturbed. "Why don't you call her and find out for yourself, instead of running all the way out there in this weather, for Heaven's sake."

Anna just shot her a look. She was through the door and running across the parking lot before her mother could say another word. Anna sped through the exit, returning the gateman's wave, and pressed her foot hard on the accelerator when she reached the road. She didn't see a dark green van with tinted windows pull out of a side road as she rushed past.

Betty Kerr Orlemann

# 8

For a while the van followed Anna at a distance, but as she turned onto one narrow, winding road after another, it drew closer. Anna was so concerned, though, about Hattie and getting to her as soon as possible, that she paid scant attention to the van behind her.

She was relieved that the rain had stopped, but the roads were still slick. She skidded as she took one turn, and forced herself to slow down. She now glanced into her rearview mirror, as the van's headlights grew larger and brighter.

The van was almost on top of her now; its high beams came on, threatening to blind her. The trees grew so close to the road on either side that there was no place for her to pull over. Why didn't that van just pass her, she wondered, reluctantly speeding up to put some distance between them.

The faster she went, however, the faster sped the car behind. Anna was becoming very nervous. This was getting dangerous, and there were no houses nearby, no driveways for her to turn into to get away.

The night was black. It hugged the woods and road, except for the bright path cast by her headlights on the shiny road ahead. The lights from the van were completely blinding her now. She pushed her rearview mirror up to avoid the reflection and drove faster, but the pursuing van stuck to her as if attached.

Anna realized as she hurtled down the road that she was nearing Hattie's private lane. What a relief!

She could end this dangerous game that the other driver seemed determined to play. Anna slowed and began looking for landmarks along the right side of the road, not wanting to miss her turn-off.

The van failed to slow, however. Suddenly, there was the horrifying sound of metal grinding against metal. Anna's car jerked violently, and she felt a sharp pain as her head was jolted into the headrest.

She tried to control her car, but it skidded to the right and off the road into the cedar forest. She felt her vehicle careening off trees and veering toward a wide swale. Her seat belt threatened to cut through her body, and her left shoulder and arm had lost all feeling.

Still she attempted to control the forward movement of her car, but to no avail. The left side wheels dipped into the rocky swale and the car began to sway, at first slowly and then rapidly, until it rolled over onto its roof. Her head again taking a blow as it slammed against the roof when she turned upside down, Anna lost consciousness.

The green van rushed past, made a U-turn and drove back to the spot where Anna's car had left the road. The driver pulled off the road as far as possible and tried to see Anna's car with the aid of the van's bright lights. There was no noise in the woods and the car was not visible from that angle.

The driver, dressed in a black knit cap, heavy sweater, and wool pants, climbed from the van, carrying a large flashlight and a hammer. The flashlight found the right front of the van and revealed a badly damaged bumper and crushed fender. The right headlamp was hanging loosely by its wires.

The driver impatiently turned the flashlight into the woods and followed the path of destruction caused by Anna's car until the wheels, still spinning slowly, could be clearly discerned in the circle of light. The car's battery lay useless on the ground, thrown from the engine compartment when the hood popped open as it flipped.

The van driver moved closer until the flashlight shone on Anna, curled in a fetal position on the car's collapsed ceiling. She was obviously unconscious, maybe dead. Hopefully dead, thought the black-clad figure. Anna's face was dark with rivulets of blood gushing from head wounds. All the car's windows were smashed and the driver's-side door had sprung open.

"Let's make sure you're dead, little girl," the driver snarled, moving as rapidly as possible down the rocky swale. The evil figure crouched over the still form in the car, hammer poised.

Suddenly, a ferocious growl startled the attacker, and a huge gray dog rushed through the woods toward the crippled car. For just the slightest instant, the flashlight shone on yellow eyes and large, vicious teeth. The driver scrambled back to the safety of the waiting van and sped away, the dog in hot pursuit.

❧

Hattie was becoming worried about Wolf. "He never stays out this late," she muttered aloud, a frown on her face. For at least the tenth time, she went out on the porch and called his name. "Where could he be?" she worried into the black of night. "He must be hungry. He hasn't even come back for his dinner." She called him again.

Knowing a search would probably be fruitless, Hattie nevertheless went back into the house to put on boots and retrieve her cape and a flashlight. She knew Wolf loved the woods, but he loved home more. She glanced at an antique steeple clock on the mantel above the fireplace. It was after ten p.m. He'd never stayed out this late before.

Hattie started her search on the opposite side of her lane, following a deer trail where she had last seen Wolf hours earlier. "Where would he have gone?" she asked herself. His activities in the forest were pretty much limited—as far as she knew—to running along the deer trails, sometimes chasing but never catching deer. He'd sometimes catch rabbits, pause to drink from a stream...all those things dogs do. But this extended absence was worrisome.

"Thank goodness for the mud, anyway," she murmured. Fresh, large pawprints led her on along the trail. "Wolf," she called. "Wolf!" Once in a while she found herself on a trail with no paw prints and had to retrace her steps until she found them again.

At first the prints seemed to be wandering aimlessly, sometimes crossing themselves, sometimes going in circles, but suddenly they became deeper and widely spaced. The great dog had obviously started to run.

Hattie followed them until they left the trail and vanished into a thicket. She pushed her way through brambles, which caught at her skirt and wrapped around her boots, threatening to trip her.

She shone her light at the ground, but the paw prints were no longer visible anywhere. Hattie continued to stumble forward, uncertain whether she was even heading in the right direction. "Wolf!" she cried again. "Wolf!" And then she heard a very faint whimper.

Hattie forgot about caution and started to run as best she could in the direction of the whimper. A small branch whipped across her forehead, and when she ducked she caught her right foot in the undergrowth and fell full length on the ground. A sob caught in her throat. "Silly old woman!" she scolded herself as she scrambled to her feet. Fortunately she was not hurt.

Another whimper sounded, this time closer. "Wolf!" she cried. The dog whimpered again. The sound was very near now. Hattie shone the light in the direction of the whine.

Then she saw it: Anna's car on its roof in the swale. Hattie hurried to the wreck and saw Anna, still bound by her seatbelt, curled up on the inside of the roof. Next to her, pressed as close as possible was Wolf, his heat warming her, keeping her alive.

"Anna!" Hattie gasped, "what are you doing here? What happened?" She knelt by the still form. Silly questions, she knew, but what was Anna doing here?

"Anna," Hattie said softly, and the girl fluttered her eyelids for an instant. "You'll be all right, dear, I'm going for help. Try not to move. Wolf will stay with you."

Hattie looked Anna over as best she could under the circumstances. She didn't find any heavy bleeding, and Anna's pulse was regular. That was a relief. She released Anna's seat belt, careful not to move the young woman in case she had back or neck injuries. Hattie removed her own cape, wrapping it around the girl.

"Stay here, Wolf," she commanded, and hurried home to phone for help. It was one time she questioned her decision not to get a cell phone.

The emergency call complete, Hattie threw on her cardigan and hurried back through the woods to Anna. Less than five minutes later, Hattie heard the sirens.

Two police cars, an ambulance and a fire engine arrived at the site of the accident. The first to get there was a police officer who saw the churned earth and damaged trees at the edge of the road. He followed the path of gouged trees to Anna's car and knelt to comfort her until the others arrived. Wolf refused to move, but seemed to realize help had come, because he did not threaten the policeman.

Hattie returned at the same time emergency personnel from the ambulance made their way through the woods. With a quiet, "Wolf, come," Hattie brought the great dog to her side, where he sat watching alertly.

"Are you the one who called 9-1-1?" the first police officer asked Hattie. When she murmured, "Yes," he continued to question her. She never took her eyes off Anna during his short inquisition.

He took out a small notebook, "May I have her name and your name and address, m'am?" he asked politely. She supplied the information numbly.

"Do you know what happened?" asked the officer.

Hattie shook her head. "No, I don't." She watched a paramedic take Anna's pulse.

"How did you happen to come across the accident?" persisted the officer.

Hattie told him about Wolf's disappearance and her search for him in the woods. She described how she had found the dog protecting Anna.

"Are you related to this young lady?" continued the officer.

"Not really," Hattie choked, "but she calls me her aunt. I've known her all her life."

"Where does she live?" He wrote in his notebook as Hattie supplied the information.

"Do you know what she was doing on the road there at this time of night?" he asked. "Was she coming to see you? Do you know if she drinks?"

"I don't know why she was here. I can only imagine she was on her way to my house, but I have no idea why." Hattie's eyes never left Anna. "No, she never drinks and drives. Not ever. She might have a glass of wine at a party, but that's all. And if she did, she wouldn't drive."

A paramedic told the officer, "There's no smell of alcohol."

The officer wrote that information in his notebook, too. "We'll still do a blood alcohol count at the hospital." he said.

As Hattie watched, the paramedics fastened a brace on Anna's neck, while one held her head firmly in place. Holding her carefully, they pulled her from the wreck, placed her on a stretcher, and applied a back brace.

"What's her name?" a young woman asked Hattie, who told her.

The paramedic said softly, "Anna? Anna, can you hear me? We're going to take you to the hospital. Do you hear me, Anna?"

Anna's eyelids fluttered again, but she did not speak.

In the meantime, the other two paramedics felt her arms and legs for broken bones. Hattie couldn't hear what they were saying to each other, but she saw them place a splint on Anna's left arm and strap it in place.

With great skill and care, they lifted Anna's stretcher and carried her through the woods to the waiting ambulance. Hattie followed as closely as possible and watched with a lump in her throat as Anna was driven away.

A police car, with siren wailing and lights flashing, led the ambulance, its own lights flashing and siren blaring. Hattie, with Wolf at her side, was hurrying back to her house when a tow truck arrived. *Not much left to tow*, she thought sadly.

She missed the arrival of a newspaper photographer who had heard the 9-1-1 call on his scanner.

Betty Kerr Orlemann

# 9

Back home, Hattie debated with herself about whether she should phone Cameron and Alexandra. It was nearly twelve-thirty a.m. and she feared they would be asleep. She also knew the hospital would call them. *Perhaps,* she thought, *it would be better to hear from someone they knew.*

She didn't want to waste any time before she left for the hospital, but in the end she did dial their number.

Cameron answered the phone. *Strange,* she thought, *how doctors always sound bright and alert when they answer the phone, even if they've been asleep.*

"Cameron," she started right in, "this is Hattie Farwell. I'm afraid I have some bad news. Anna has been in a serious automobile accident. Her car ran off the Old Pike Road. The ambulance just took her to the Valley Crisis Center."

"How did it happen?" Cameron asked in a calm tone. "What's her condition?"

"I don't know the answer to either question," Hattie stated. "When they were putting her in the ambulance, she seemed to regain consciousness for a moment, but I really know nothing. I'm on my way up there right now."

"Had she been to your house?" he asked.

"No. I only suspect that she was on her way here, because of the location of the accident. I haven't talked to her since I left your place this afternoon. Why would she be coming here?"

Cameron was clearly puzzled. "Didn't you call this evening and ask me to send her to you right away?"

"No, of course not," Hattie answered firmly. "Why would I do a thing like that? I know what a hard day it's been for her."

"This is indeed very strange," Cameron said. "Someone called, but I'm certain now that it was not your voice. Oh, Lord...what have I done?"

Hattie could hear Alexandra's sleepy voice in the background, questioning Cameron about the content of the phone call.

"I'll let you go, Cameron," Hattie told him. "Alexandra will need you, and I'm sure the hospital will be trying to reach you. I'll see you there. Goodbye."

"Goodbye, Hattie. Thank you for calling."

Hattie took off her muddy clothes. She quickly washed her face and hands, combed her hair and pulled it into a neat bun, and donned fresh clothes and dress boots. From its hook she pulled her old cape, since her good one was now part of the accident scene, secured by the police. She grabbed her purse and hurried out of the house. Wolf watched her from his spot by the hearth.

Anna was still in the emergency room when Hattie arrived at the hospital. No one could tell her anything. She gave her name to the receptionist, who told her kindly to just take a seat in the waiting room.

It was more than an hour before Alexandra, Cameron and Brooke burst into the waiting room. Alexandra and Brooke both looked as though they had been crying. Cameron was calm, but rapid speech and hand movements betrayed his anxiety.

He identified himself to the receptionist, asking if it would be possible for him to go back to see Anna and her physicians.

"Oh, Dr. MacArthur, it's a pleasure to meet you. I've heard so many good things about you." She rose from her chair behind the desk and held out her hand, which Cameron shook cordially. "I'll just run back and tell Dr. Fletcher you're here." She disappeared through a door down a hall.

In less than a minute, she reappeared.

"This way, Doctor," she said. "I'm so sorry about your stepdaughter."

Cameron stepped into a room with curtained cubicles on three sides. A curtain on the first cubicle to his right was pushed open as he entered the room. A middle-aged man—obviously a doctor, wearing a green scrub suit and cap with a mask dangling around his neck— stepped out to greet Cameron. Stitched on his shirt in blue thread was "Harold F. Fletcher, M.D."

Since Dr. Fletcher was wearing plastic gloves, Cameron did not offer his hand.

Dr Fletcher spoke rapidly, his tone somewhat brusque.

"I understand Anna Turner is your stepdaughter," he said. Cameron nodded. "She's in pretty bad shape," Dr. Fletcher said. "She has a ruptured spleen, a compound fracture of the left humerus, a severe concussion and various lacerations and contusions. She's just been X-Rayed and had a CAT scan. She hasn't regained consciousness. We have stabilized her and are taking her to the operating room right now. If you want to suit up, you're welcome to come up with her. My nurse will show you where, but first you'll probably want to see Anna." Fletcher raised his eyes in question.

Cameron nodded again.

"Yes, I would very much like to see her." He followed Dr. Fletcher into the cubicle where Anna lay, and stood back out of the way, his heart breaking.

Anna lay on a white gurney, her face drained of all color. Her long blonde hair had been pushed into a hospital cap, and her forehead and left cheek were bandaged. Her left eye was badly swollen, the skin around it turning purple and angry red—the only color on her face.

She was wearing a white hospital gown. Large cotton boots covered her feet and legs to above her knees. A nurse was in the process of covering her with a white cotton blanket and strapping her onto the gurney. Saline solution was dripping into her right arm from a plastic bag attached to a pole next to it.

"Anna," Cameron said softly.

She made no response. He stared at her still form and just shook his head sadly.

"Come this way, Dr. MacArthur," said a pretty nurse standing next to Dr. Fletcher.

"Thank you," said Cameron. "Will someone please keep my wife informed about what's going on? She's in the waiting room with our other daughter and a friend."

"Of course, Dr. MacArthur," the nurse responded. "We do that routinely."

She took him to the staff elevator, which they rode to the second floor. Cameron donned a sterile scrub suit in the prep room. He walked into the operating room wearing plastic boots over his shoes to avoid static electricity.

Anna was on the operating table. The large, round overhead light was shining on a bared area of her abdomen, which nurses were painting with antiseptic. An anesthesiologist sat at her head.

In a few minutes, the anesthesiologist nodded to Dr. Fletcher. A nurse handed him a scalpel, with which he made a fine line on Anna's abdomen. Blood flowed out along the incision, which the nurse blotted with sponges.

Cameron, so familiar with such a scene, found it difficult to watch. He knew that when the patient is someone you love, it's impossible to be impartial. He stood well out of the way and he found himself watching the busy figures surrounding the operating table. Every once in a while, Cameron glanced at Anna, but preferred to focus his attention elsewhere.

In his heart, he blamed himself for her accident. *No, not an accident*, he thought. *Someone did this to her deliberately. Someone wanted her dead. The same someone who killed Annie?* It must be, the situations were just too strange to be coincidental. He thought it must also be the same someone who'd called him on the phone last night, asked for "Annie" and said it was Hattie. *But who? Why? For Heaven's sake, why?*

Time passed while Cameron tortured himself with unanswerable questions. Finally, he was brought back to the present as Dr. Fletcher plopped Anna's ruptured spleen into a stainless steel basin.

"Stitch her up," he said cheerfully to a young woman standing next to him.

As the young resident began closing the incision, Dr. Fletcher pulled off his gloves and mask and walked across the room to Cameron.

"She did real well," he told his colleague. "As soon as we finish here, she'll go to Intensive Care. When she's able, we'll have an orthopod look at that broken arm."

Cameron thanked him warmly and left the room. He removed only the plastic boots from his shoes before he hurried down to the waiting room to give this piece of good news to Alexandra, Brooke and Hattie.

The instant they saw him, the three women stood up anxiously and moved toward him. Alexandra got to him first.

"How is she?" she asked, tears in her eyes.

Cameron took her in his arms.

"Her spleen was ruptured. I guess someone told you. It had to be removed. She came through surgery very well, though," he reported. "They're taking her to the Intensive Care Unit, where you can see her in about an hour.

"You must understand, though, Alexandra, she's still in critical condition. She never regained consciousness before surgery, and that's a worry. Also, she has a badly broken left arm. An orthopedic surgeon has been called in to look at that."

He saw that the women, particularly Alexandra, were exhausted.

"Don't you think you should go home to bed?" he asked her gently. "Anna won't be awake for some time, even in the best of circumstances. Turning his attention to his younger stepdaughter, Cameron addressed Brooke.

"Would you drive your mother home and see that she gets some rest?"

"No," Alexandra said firmly. "I can't leave until I at least see her."

Cameron glanced at the clock.

"Do you realize it's almost six o'clock in the morning? Please, promise me you won't give me any trouble about going home as soon as you've seen Anna. You've got to keep up your strength, Alexandra. She'll be needing you."

"Yes...yes," Alexandra sighed without conviction. "In the meantime, Brooke, will you please get me some more coffee?"

"Sure, Mom," answered Brooke. "How about you, Aunt Hattie, would you like some more, too? And how about you, Cameron?"

When everyone said yes, Brooke set out on her mission, returning in a few minutes with four foam cups of steaming, fresh coffee on a plastic tray.

Cameron sat close to Alexandra on a sofa, while Hattie and Brooke sat in overstuffed chairs situated at right angles to the sofa. Brooke sighed and rested her head against the back of her chair. Every so often she took a sip of coffee, but no one spoke.

Alexandra poured milk and artificial sweetener into her cup. She stirred slowly and aimlessly, staring into the liquid as she did. Absentmindedly, she drank a little of the coffee.

"Anna has always been such a thoughtful little thing," she said. "She's always been a good daughter to me...so considerate, always eager to please me. Oh, this is terrible! Why did this have to happen to me?"

Hattie and Brooke, as one, sat bolt upright in their chairs and stared at Alexandra as though not quite sure they'd heard her right. They glanced at each other with raised eyebrows before going back to sipping their coffee.

Cameron smiled indulgently at his wife. Her hair was awry, and her makeup, carefully applied even after she'd learned of Anna's accident, was smeared. He patted her paternally on the top of her head and pulled her closer to him.

A receptionist walked over to them. "Excuse me, Doctor," she said to Cameron. "In a few minutes, two of you will be permitted to see Anna. I think you'll be much better off if you go to the ICU waiting room. I think you know where that is. Someone there will direct you to Miss Turner's room."

They all rose rapidly and hurried to the elevator. Cameron spoke briefly to the nurse in Intensive Care.

She reported that Anna was holding her own, but had yet to regain consciousness.

The nurse led Alexandra and Brooke to Anna's bedside. Satisfied that his girls would be alright without him for a few minutes, Cameron went back down to the doctors' dressing room to pull on his own clothes.

Alexandra's reaction to Anna's appearance alarmed Brooke.

Her mother grabbed Brooke's arm in a vice-like hold and gasped, "Look at all those wires and tubes! Oh, she's getting blood. Look at those cuts and bruises on her poor, drained little face." Rapidly coming unglued, Alexandra leaned toward her other daughter. "Oh, Anna, it's me, Mother. Speak to me, Anna!" She burst into tears.

The nurse spoke quietly but sternly. "Mrs. MacArthur, please...try to calm yourself. You'll disturb the other patients."

Alexandra glanced around the room. At least eight other patients, all with wires and tubes, all being just as carefully monitored as Anna, lay in their beds on the other side of the glass walls that encased Anna. The constant "beep, beep" of cardiac monitors almost drove her crazy.

"I feel sick," she told Brooke. "I've got to get out of here."

"Mrs. MacArthur, just a word of warning," the nurse whispered. "Even though a person seems deeply unconscious or even in a coma, sometimes she can hear what you say. Please, use caution."

Alexandra looked at the nurse, put her nose in the air and fled from the room.

Anna didn't move. Brooke turned to the nurse, a pleasant-looking woman of about forty, with graying hair and striking green eyes.

"Please, don't think too poorly of my mother. She's very upset."

The nurse smiled.

"I know, dear," she said, patting Brooke's arm.

"How many minutes do I have left with my sister?" Brooke asked.

The nurse consulted her watch.

"Not quite five."

"Can I run out real quick and get our friend? She's been here all night. She kinda helped raise my sister."

"Of course, dear, but hurry. ICU visitation is pretty strictly enforced."

Hattie was sitting forlornly in the chair where Brooke had left her. She looked exhausted and very old. Alexandra was not in evidence.

"Aunt Hattie, hurry if you want to see Anna. Mother couldn't take it, so there's some time left for you."

Hattie rose stiffly and followed Brooke back into the unit where Anna lay. Anna looked so bad to her that she almost wept, but Hattie—being Hattie—refused to allow this emotion to show. Anna needed strength now, and she would be strong.

Hattie had such love in her face when she looked down at the battered girl that Brooke wanted to cry.

"We must just keep on praying for her, Brooke," Hattie said. Though she wasn't a particularly religious person, she had a strong faith in God. "There is only one who can help her pull through this." Hattie softly took hold of Anna's right hand with her left and bowed her head.

Brooke slipped her left hand into Hattie's right one and bowed her head, too. Very quietly, Hattie prayed for Anna's quick and complete recovery.

Betty Kerr Orlemann

# 10

After Alexandra fled from Anna's bedside, Cameron had no trouble convincing her to go home. He called Dr. Fletcher's office and left his name and phone number. The receptionist promised that Dr. Fletcher would call him with or without further news of Anna's condition.

"Mother," asked Brooke, "would you mind very much if I went home with Aunt Hattie? I'll be closer to the hospital if we should be needed, and Aunt Hattie could use my company, I know."

Alexandra answered in a voice clearly intended to be heard by Hattie. "Well, Brooke, I certainly can't imagine why you want to be with her. After all, this whole thing was her fault!"

Brooke gasped, and the normally reticent Cameron spoke angrily to his wife.

"You have absolutely no reason to say such a horrible thing, Alexandra! I told you that it wasn't Hattie who called us last night, saying she needed Anna."

"Oh, really?" spat Alexandra. "How can you be so sure of that?"

"I'll overlook that, Alexandra. You are clearly over-wrought," Cameron said through clenched teeth. "Come now, I'm taking you home." With that, he grabbed her arm forcefully and escorted her out of the hospital.

Brooke watched them go, then turned to Hattie. She wasn't surprised by the stunned look on the old woman's face.

"Oh, Aunt Hattie," she said, with a catch in her voice. "I'm so sorry. She knows better, I know she does. She's just so tired. She didn't mean to hurt you."

*Yes, she did,* Hattie thought, but she kept that to herself. Instead, she put her arm around Brooke.

"Let's go, honey. We must get some rest, and Wolf is waiting for us."

Before they went home, Brooke asked the green-eyed nurse if there had been any change in Anna's condition. The nurse shook her head.

"I'm sorry. We'll call you if there is."

Hattie wrote her phone number on a pad for the nurse, then she and Brooke left.

Wolf barked happily just inside the door as soon as he heard the car. Hattie and Brooke both hugged the huge dog when they entered the house before Hattie let him out. Now, home at last in her own kitchen, Hattie was once again in charge.

"Brooke, let's have a little bite to eat, then we can both lie down and try to get some sleep."

Brooke didn't argue.

Hattie pushed two slices of bread down in the toaster and poured dry cereal into bowls. When the toast popped up, she buttered it, then placed a pitcher of cream next to a sugar bowl on the table.

"Help yourself, dear," she said, placing paper napkins and spoons on the table. "Do you want any jam for your toast?"

Brooke, staring off into space, simply shook her head no.

As she poured milk on her cereal, Hattie looked hard at Brooke. The girl looked completely done in.

"I'm not making any coffee," Hattie told her. "We've had enough of that."

Brooke smiled wanly. She ate slowly and her movements

were almost robotic. Hattie, determined to salvage something pleasant from the day, persisted in chatting.

"I was glad to see you in blue jeans when you came into the hospital. Much more fitting attire for a girl your age. I liked your white turtleneck with that navy sweatshirt, too. That's your school crest on there, isn't it?"

Once again, Brooke nodded her head, but said nothing.

Though she recognized Brooke's fatigue, for some reason Hattie felt wide awake. She wanted to just rattle on, but controlled the impulse.

"I'll be right back, Brooke. You finish your cereal."

With that, she opened a door next to the fireplace, revealing a winding "piecrust" stairway. She quickly ascended the wedge-shaped treads of the tightly spiraling staircase to the second floor.

The room over the kitchen was hers, and had been since she was a baby. The only thing different about it from her childhood was the furniture, which had once been her parents'. Her grandfather had made it for them as a wedding gift. All the pieces were pine, including the four-poster double bed that Hattie loved.

Next to her room was a larger one, which sat above the dining room. She entered it through a door in the common wall. As with many older houses, there was no hall between the rooms.

This room, which she used for guests, was furnished with a mahogany double bed, a bureau and two bedside tables. Hattie went through another door into a hall, where she pulled sheets and pillowcases from a linen closet. She made the bed and placed a fluffy comforter over the sheets.

She took a flannel nightgown decorated with rosebuds from a drawer in the bureau and placed it on the bed. Then she hurried downstairs to get Brooke. When she walked back into the kitchen, Brooke was kneeling on the floor next to the fireplace with her arms around Wolf, crying into his fur.

"Come on, honey," Hattie said as she helped the girl to her feet. "Your bed is waiting for you."

In less than fifteen minutes, both women were in their beds and sound asleep. The antique steeple clock on the kitchen mantle struck nine, but no one heard it. They were barely aware that it was mid-morning.

**❧**

The morning paper lay folded and unread on the kitchen table. Neither of them had looked at it when Hattie picked it up from the porch. If they had unfolded it, they would have seen a story and an accompanying photo of Anna's crushed car on the front page. The headline read, "Prominent Physician's Stepdaughter in Critical Condition."

"Police are investigating circumstances leading to a serious one-car accident last night in Plumstead Township," the article began. "Twenty-nine-year-old Anna Turner, stepdaughter of Dr. Cameron MacArthur, famous children's facial reconstructionist and daughter of longtime civic activist Alexandra Turner MacArthur, was critically injured in the accident.

"For reasons unknown at press time, Turner's car crashed into the woods next to the Old Pike Road. Police theorize she was traveling at a high rate of speed and skidded off the wet road. Records state that no alcohol was involved. Turner is in intensive care in Valley Hospital. As of press time, no further information was available."

Shawn O'Brien, seated at a desk in Michael

DiRienzo's Doylestown headquarters, gasped when he read the article. He placed the paper on his desk, folded with the article in front of him, and re-read it.

Failing to pick up several phone calls while he repeatedly drummed his pencil on his desktop, Shawn's agitation was obvious to the half-dozen volunteer workers seated at desks near him. Even "Maria Mouse," as he always thought of Maria DiRienzo, stopped working at a nearby computer and stared at him.

"What's the matter, Shawn?" she asked sympathetically.

He held up the paper for her to read the headline. "This," he explained.

Did you see it? Anna Turner is my girlfriend's sister. She's been in an accident." He tossed the bad news on his desk, torn between his work responsibilities and his desire to make sure Brooke was okay. "Do you mind if I make a personal call?"

"No, of course not. Take as much time as you need," Maria answered. She retrieved the newspaper from Shawn's desk and scanned the account of Anna's accident.

Shawn pulled a cell phone from his pocket, on which he'd already entered Alexandra's phone number into speed dial, since Brooke would be staying there. Not considering that the family might still be asleep, he returned to his desk and dialed the number. As he listened to it ring on the other end, Maria spoke up.

"This is terrible, Shawn. Please, let us know how the poor girl is doing." She looked truly concerned.

❧

Cameron had given Alexandra a sleeping pill before he tucked her into her bed. When he was sure she was sound asleep, he disconnected her phone, closed her drapes and left the room, quietly closing the door behind him. He then went to bed in Brooke's room, where her phone extension was in easy reach on the nightstand.

When the phone rang at ten-fifteen, he was in a deep sleep. But to Shawn's ear on the other end of the line, the doctor sounded fully awake.

Cameron, much relieved that the call was not from the hospital, told Shawn all he knew, which was not much more than had been in the paper.

"It was necessary to remove Anna's spleen," he explained. "She came through surgery very well, Shawn, but hasn't regained consciousness yet."

"May I speak to Brooke?" Shawn asked, anxiously.

"I'm afraid she's not here, my boy," Cameron said. "And I'd be willing to bet she's sleeping. Like all of us, she was exhausted after a very long night at the hospital."

"Where is she?" Shawn persisted. "I'd like to see her, if I may."

Cameron didn't have to consider that request. He knew Alexandra would be wild if she thought he had sent Shawn to Brooke. Furthermore, he didn't want Brooke disturbed if she was sleeping.

"Shawn, Brooke really needs her rest, I'm sorry. But if you give me your phone number, I'll try to have her call you later on this afternoon."

Shawn, disappointed and upset, hung up the phone after giving Cameron the numbers of his phone at Michael's headquarters, at his parents' home in Philadelphia, and his cell. He rested his elbows on his desk and put his head in his hands.

He looked absolutely miserable, and Maria walked over to him, quietly placing his paper on the desk.

"Bad news?" she asked.

"Anna's still critical," he told her without looking up, "and Dr. MacArthur won't tell me where I can reach Brooke.

"Who's Brooke?" she asked, kindly.

"Brooke Turner," he answered. "She's Anna's sister." He finally raised his head and smiled weakly. "We're engaged."

"That's funny. I didn't know Alexandra had two daughters," Maria said. "I was surprised to read in your *Inquirer* this morning that Anna is twenty-nine. I saw her picture in the paper with her mother and stepfather a couple of weeks ago at some affair at The MacArthur Clinic. I thought she was a teenager."

"She'd love you for that," Shawn laughed. "You're right, she is very young-looking. It's Brooke, though, who's the teenager. She's seventeen, but she'll be eighteen soon," he added. "She goes to the Kendall School in Massachusetts, near Harvard."

"I knew Alexandra once, a long time ago," Maria said, softly. "She was very beautiful. Does Brooke look like her?"

"Very much," Shawn replied, a dreamy look on his freckled face. "She's the same height. Same features. They both have great figures." He sighed, then realized Maria had raised an eyebrow. "I mean...it's not like I check her out or anything, but you can hardly look at her and not notice!" he stammered. "The only difference is that Brooke has dark hair and brown eyes."

"She must be lovely," Maria said, smiling. "Congratulations, Shawn. I'd love to meet her sometime."

"Oh, you will, and very soon, Maria...as soon as her sister is better. She's promised to help with Michael's campaign."

"Well, wouldn't that be wonderful!" Maria smiled. "But Shawn, you mustn't push her. Her first consideration right now is her sister."

"Whose first consideration?" asked a deep voice behind them.

They both turned at once to find themselves looking into the handsome face of Michael DiRienzo. Maria's face lit up.

"Oh, no one you know, Michael," she answered. When Michael wasn't deterred, she continued, "We were just talking about Shawn's girlfriend."

"Well, Shawn!" Michael exclaimed, clapping the boy on the back. "Why haven't you told me about this better half?"

Shawn smiled.

"I had planned to today, actually. She wants to work on your campaign, and I was going to bring her over this morning. Unfortunately, her sister was in a bad car accident last night, and I'm sure Brooke wants to be with her."

Maria handed her husband the newspaper and he scanned the headline.

"Of course, of course," agreed Michael. "You just be sure to introduce her to me as soon as her sister is better."

Maria Mouse, understanding she'd been dismissed, scurried back to her desk and resumed working on her computer.

# 11

The phone at Alexandra's did not ring again until past two-thirty that afternoon. By that time Cameron was drifting in and out of wakefulness. "Hello," he answered immediately.

"Dr. MacArthur?" the voice was clipped and professional, and Cameron, now wide awake, knew at once that it was Dr. Fletcher, but he said only, "Yes."

Dr. Fletcher identified himself and said, "Your stepdaughter's vital signs are improving. However, she remains unconscious. It would seem that the blow to her head was more severe than we first realized. She has that concussion, and her CAT scan showed a hairline fracture of the skull. I'd say, however, that her injuries at this time don't appear life-threatening."

"I see," Cameron said. "Well, we can all be thankful for that. And thank you for calling me. I'll be coming back to the hospital soon to see her. Will you be around?"

"I will," Dr. Fletcher told Cameron, "and I'd like to see you again. Just ask the operator to find me when you arrive."

As soon as Cameron thanked Dr. Fletcher and hung up, he immediately dialed Hattie. Apparently she'd been awake, because she answered on the first ring.

"Hattie, this is Cameron. There has been little change in Anna's condition. I want to go back to the hospital this afternoon to see her in an hour or so. Would you and Brooke care to join me? I know she's gotten little sleep, but don't want her to feel left out."

"Certainly, but what about Alexandra?" Hattie hesitated. "My presence seems to upset her," Hattie said without resentment.

"Well, that's something we'll have to work on later," Cameron replied. "Right now, she's under the influence of prescription sleeping pills and probably won't wake up for several more hours. Will you please meet me in the ICU waiting room? There are some things on my mind I'd like to run past you. Of course, Brooke is welcome."

Hattie had tried to keep her voice down while she was talking to Cameron, but when she hung up after agreeing to meet him, a sleepy voice behind her asked, "Was that about Anna? Is she any better?"

Brooke was standing in the doorway to her room. She was still wearing the rosebud nightgown, her feet bare and her hair tousled. Except for her height, she looked like a little girl.

Hattie smiled at her tenderly. "That was Cameron," she told the girl. "Anna is holding her own, but she's still unconscious. However, he wants to meet us at the hospital as soon as we can get there. It's not an emergency; don't look so scared."

"Oh," Brooke sighed in obvious relief. "Aunt Hattie," she continued, "is there time for me to wash my hair?"

"Certainly, dear, you'll find shampoo and soap in the shower and a hair dryer on the shelf near the vanity. There are lots of towels in the linen closet. I put your clothes in the washer before I went to sleep. And when I woke up I put them in the dryer. They should be done by the time you're out of the shower."

"Thank you so much, Aunt Hattie," Brooke said. "Thank you, thank you, thank you for just everything." She smiled, turned and went back into her room.

Hattie was smiling as she descended the winding staircase to her kitchen. She took a can of tuna from the pantry and decided to heat up the leftover vegetable soup. While the soup was warming on the stove, Hattie prepared tuna salad and made two sandwiches. She covered the dish containing the remainder of the tuna fish and stored it in the refrigerator. There was enough left over for at least another half sandwich if Brooke wanted it. Then she made a pot of coffee and savored its aroma as the rich liquid dripped through the grounds.

The clothes dryer stopped, so she removed Brooke's clothes and dumped them into a basket. She had just taken them upstairs to place them on her bed, when there was a knock at the kitchen door. Wolf jumped to his feet from his usual spot next to the fireplace and raced, barking, to the door. Hattie hurried back downstairs.

The police officer to whom Hattie had spoken at the accident scene was standing on the porch holding a suitcase and a purse when she opened the door. He took a step backward when he saw the dog, but Hattie had a firm hold on Wolf's collar.

"Please, come in," she invited. Wolf did not move. "Sit, Wolf," she commanded, and the dog immediately sat down. "He won't hurt you," she told the officer. "He just looks scary."

The officer walked into the kitchen where Hattie offered him a seat at the table. "Would you like a cup of coffee? I just made it."

"Thanks, I don't mind if I do," he responded, taking the seat she indicated. She poured him a cup of coffee and one for herself. She offered him cream and sugar. "Black, please," he told her. "Me, too," she smiled. "I take mine black, too."

He put the suitcase and purse down next to the table. "These were in Anna Turner's car," he said. "The tow truck operator found them jammed against the back seat. Would you be able to identify them?" he asked.

Hattie snapped the suitcase latches open and pulled up the lid. Before she could comment on its contents, Brooke's voice from the bottom of the circular staircase claimed, "Yes. That's my sister's purse. That's her suitcase. Those are her clothes. I recognize everything."

"Who are you?" the officer asked Brooke.

"This is Brooke Turner," Hattie told him. "Anna's sister."

"Well, Miss Brooke Turner, will you take possession of your sister's purse, suitcase and clothing, and sign this release form, please?" He smiled reassuringly.

"Sure," Brooke responded, as she reached for the paper. He continued to smile at Brooke and turned to Hattie.

"Name's Jim Sawyer. I'm with the Plumstead Township Police department. I've been in touch with the hospital and was told that Anna Turner's condition has improved."

Brooke looked up from carefully examining her sister's things.

"Thank God she's better." With a last look over the items Officer Sawyer had handed her, she nodded. "I don't know what all she packed, of course, but all these things belong to Anna. I don't notice anything obviously missing, so I'll sign your release form." She took the proffered pen and did just that.

"Thanks," he said, taking the form and putting it inside his jacket.

"Welcome." Brooke took a seat at the table across from him.

Hattie poured Brooke a cup of coffee, into which the young woman added a generous amount of cream.

"We're about to have some late lunch. Would you care to join us, officer?" Hattie asked.

He smiled. "No thanks, I'll just drink my coffee. I do have something else to ask, though." He waited politely until Hattie had put soup and sandwiches on the table before proceeding. "First, do you think Miss Turner's well enough to answer any questions?"

"She's not," Brooke said. "She's still unconscious. You'll have to ask Dr. Fletcher when you can talk to her."

"Right." For a moment, he sat quietly while the two women ate, then took another swallow of his coffee. "Do either of you know whether Miss Turner had any kind of car accident recently, I mean before last night? Did she mention anything to either of you?"

"No," they answered in chorus.

"Why do you ask?" Hattie queried.

"Her car—what's left of it—is light blue. But there's a streak of dark green paint on the left rear bumper and some more on her left rear fender and trunk. We also found broken glass in the road that obviously came from a head-lamp. It would seem clear that another vehicle was involved in her accident. Any idea what might have happened?"

"No," stated Brooke. She looked puzzled. "Anna took great pride in that car, so it's not something that would have just been there. I just saw it yesterday afternoon, and I can tell you for sure that there was absolutely no mark on it then. And she didn't drive it after that until she left to come here."

"Her parents can attest to that," Hattie said.

He busily wrote their comments in his notebook.

"Now, here's the tough one," he said, swallowing and licking his lips nervously. "Um...do either of you know anyone who might want to see her hurt or...worse?" Officer Sawyer was clearly uncomfortable asking the question.

Hattie hesitated before answering. Finally, she stated, "I don't know of anyone who would want to hurt Anna, nor can I think of any reason why. But now that I think about it, something rather mysterious did happen, and I'd better tell you about it. It is possible that this was not an accident, that Anna was forced off the road deliberately.

"My best friend, Anna's and Brooke's grandmother, was killed four days ago by a hit-and-run driver in Philadelphia. Her funeral was yesterday. I was visiting her and Anna last Thursday when she received a strange little note in the mail. I noticed the envelope before she opened it. It bore no return address and it was addressed simply to 'Annie Turner'. No Mrs., Miss or even Ms."

"Excuse me, Miss Farwell," the officer interjected, "but is Anna Turner called 'Annie'?" He had his pen poised over his notebook.

"Oh, I'm sorry," Hattie responded, "I should have mentioned that Anna was named for her grandmother. Everyone called her grandmother 'Annie,' and Anna was always 'Anna.' I admit that it's caused some confusion over the years."

"Yes," he said. "Please tell me about the note."

"It contained two tickets to Saturday evening's Beethoven concert at the Kimmel Center. It said something like, 'Enclosed are two tickets to the Philadelphia Orchestra for Saturday night. I know how you love Beethoven,' and something like, 'We couldn't use them, so enjoy.' There was no signature. That's rather odd, don't you think? At the time, we just figured it was an oversight and that we'd eventually learn the name of the gift giver.

"Anyhow, Annie and Anna started out for the concert. They were walking, and when they were crossing Locust at Fifteenth, a car came out of Fifteenth...right toward them, according to Anna. Annie pushed Anna out of the way, but couldn't save herself. The car hit and killed her and drove away."

"Was anyone able to identify the driver or the car?" asked Sawyer. "Did anyone get the license plate number? What did the police who took the report say?"

"As I recall, Anna told me it was a burgundy-colored Chrysler with tinted windows. It all happened so fast, no one got the license plate number or a clear look at the driver," Hattie told him.

He sighed. "It looks like I'll have to wait until the doctor allows me to interview Anna. In the meantime, I'll see if I can get any further information from the Philadelphia Police Department on that accident scene. Is there anything else you can remember, Miss Farwell, that might be relevant?"

Brooke sat frozen to her chair. Much of this information was news to her, and she was completely dumbfounded. She said nothing, just listened to Hattie, her eyes wide and startled.

"Yes, there is, but this time you can interview Dr. Cameron MacArthur for his story. He told me that he, his wife and Anna were in their living room after we'd all left from the post-funeral gathering at their condominium, when the phone rang. Brooke had gone upstairs to her room. It was about seven o'clock yesterday evening.

"Anyway, whoever was calling identified herself to Cameron as me. The person sounded as though she'd been crying and was hoarse, he said. That person asked Cameron to send Anna to me at once. She—or he, who knows? It certainly wasn't me—said I needed her. Cameron said the person on the phone asked for 'Annie.' I never called Anna 'Annie.' Nobody did, that I know of. He thought it strange, but attributed it to me being upset by Annie's death."

Sawyer scribbled away in his notebook, looking up at Hattie when he'd finished. She continued.

"And about that dark green paint. A dark green van with tinted windows almost forced me off the road when I was going to Alexandra's from the cemetery after Annie's funeral. Anna was out of sight ahead of me. That van came from behind me, and almost took the paint off my car, it passed so close and so fast!" Hattie subtly shivered as she recalled the unsettling event.

"Hmmm," said Sawyer. "I take it you believe the van was pursuing Anna?"

"I didn't think anything about it at the time. Frankly, I was a bit distracted with my own thoughts. But now I believe that's a good possibility," Hattie admitted. She glanced nervously at the clock. "We really should be leaving for the hospital."

"I won't keep you much longer," said the officer. "But before I go, I have a few more questions about Miss Turner. She lives in Philadelphia, according to her driver's license. On Walnut Street. Correct?"

"Yeah," Brooke answered. "She lived with our grandmother."

"Does she have a job?"

"She teaches fifth grade at the Spruce Street Elementary School," Hattie contributed.

"Was she ever married? Engaged? Steady boyfriend?"

Hattie answered again. "She broke an engagement about a year ago. She and her young man were engaged for about three years, and the breakup was very traumatic. There has been nothing other than an occasional date since."

"What happened to the engagement? Was it a bitter parting? Where is this man now? What's his name?" Sawyer continued to take notes.

"He was an assistant principal at her school, but he quit his job and moved to Washington State when they broke up," Brooke said. "As far as we know he's still there, but she never heard from him after he left." Brooke scowled, clearly puzzled. "We really don't know why he left so fast, but I do know that Anna didn't want to leave our grandmother. She felt that Gram needed her. I think Larry wanted her to go with him. She said they fought over it."

"His name is Laurence Adams," Hattie said. "Everyone called him Larry. But I would never believe that he had any reason to want to hurt Anna."

"We'll look into it," he said. "Do you know of anyone else who might have it in for her? Does she have any enemies? What about the parents of any of her students?"

But Hattie and Brooke just shrugged their shoulders. "It is highly unlikely," Hattie told him.

"I'll ask around and see if anyone else saw that van," the officer said. "I appreciate your time and patience with my questions. Now I'll be on my way." He stood up and both women stood with him.

Hattie was surprised to see that he was not much taller than she—no more than five feet eight or nine.

Brooke, who looked down at him, noticed his height, too, but she was used to being taller than a lot of men. She saw that although he was stocky, he was muscular. She figured he worked out, and thought he would be a formidable opponent for any criminal who tried to give him trouble.

"Goodbye, Officer Sawyer," she said politely.

He apologized for keeping them and thanked them again for the interview.

When he was gone, Hattie let Wolf out for a few minutes, watching him closely so he wouldn't disappear again. When he came back into the house, she and Brooke left for the hospital.

Betty Kerr Orlemann

# 12

Cameron was waiting for them in the main lobby. He looked at his watch when they entered and shook his head. "What kept you so long?" he demanded.

"I'm sorry to have kept you waiting, Cameron," Hattie apologized. "We were being interviewed by a police officer."

"Oh," Cameron said simply. "Before we pursue that subject, let's go up to ICU. You'll be happy to know that Anna, though still not conscious, seems to be improving rapidly. They set her broken arm this morning and casted it. It should be okay."

"Thank heaven," Hattie sighed.

When they walked into the intensive care waiting room, the nurse in attendance told them that they had a fifteen-minute wait until they could see Anna. There were ten other people sitting around the room, some watching television.

Cameron found them three chairs off in a corner where they could talk without being overheard. He started the conversation. "This may not be a new idea to you, but I've been giving this accident much thought, and I'm pretty well convinced that it was not an accident at all.

"The person who phoned for Anna yesterday obviously wasn't you, Hattie. We all know that. I feel like such a fool for believing that it was. If I had only had Anna call you back, none of this would have happened. I should have been suspicious when the person called Anna, 'Annie.'

"Blaming yourself is foolish, Cameron. Why would you ever suspect anyone would impersonate me?" asked Hattie. "But while we're on that subject, the officer told us that there were streaks of green paint on the back of Anna's car, and broken glass from a headlight was found in the road.

"I didn't tell you that a dark green van almost forced me off the road it was in such a hurry to pass me. This happened on the way to your place from the cemetery. Anna was out of sight ahead of me, and I believe that the driver of the van was trying to get to Anna."

Cameron nodded and merely mumbled, "Hmm."

"There's more," Hattie continued. "I believe the driver of the car that killed Annie actually intended to kill Anna." She told him about the note addressed to 'Annie.'

"Oh my gosh!" Cameron exclaimed. He looked from Hattie to Brooke, but no one spoke. He'd suddenly remembered Shawn's phone call. "Brooke," he said, handing her the two phone numbers, "I'm sorry I forgot to give you this message earlier, but Shawn is most anxious to talk to you. He read about Anna's accident in this morning's *Inquirer* and called us up looking for you. He wants you to call him."

Brooke took the slip of paper with a barely audible "thanks" and hurried from the room to the hall, to call Shawn in privacy on her cell phone. She was still involved in an animated conversation when the nurse announced visiting time.

Hattie walked over to Brooke and tapped her on the shoulder. "Time to visit Anna," she whispered.

"Shawn, I've got to go see Anna now. Why don't you come over to Hattie's about eight tonight?" Brooke crooned into the phone.

"You bet I will!" Shawn's voice answered. "See you later. I love you, Brooke."

"You, too," she responded before flipping the phone shut. With a big smile on her face, she bounced into ICU behind Hattie and Cameron.

"Shh," the green-eyed nurse whispered to Brooke. She then cast her eyes at Cameron. "I suppose, doctor, we can make an exception to the two-visitors-at-a-time limit for you," she said, grinning.

"Thank you, uh..." he flashed her an appreciative smile while searching for her name tag.

"Terri," she offered.

"Thanks, Terri."

Hattie and Brooke were already in Anna's cubicle when he joined them. All three of them were staring at Anna, not certain whether to speak to her or not, when her eyelashes fluttered.

"Well," said Cameron, "your color is much better today."

Anna's eyes, discolored and swollen, opened for an instant. Then they closed again. She lay perfectly still for another minute, and her eyes opened once more. The three witnesses held their collective breath.

Cameron turned to alert the nurse that Anna was coming around when Anna called in a groggy voice, "Larry!"

Terri appeared at once.

"She seems to be regaining consciousness," Cameron stated.

"Larry," Anna repeated. Her eyes were staring at the wall.

"Why would she be calling Larry?" whispered Brooke. "She hasn't even mentioned his name once since they broke off their engagement."

Terri stood at Anna's bedside.

"Miss Turner, can you hear me? Can you see me?" she asked.

Slowly, almost painfully, Anna's eyes rolled toward the nurse.

"Yes," she answered, slowly closing her eyes again. Her breathing became regular.

"She's asleep," Terri advised them.

Cameron's face bore a broad smile.

"She'll be okay," he declared. "I'd better leave. I'm afraid Alexandra will be awake by now, and furious that I've left her behind!" He laughed. "But when I give her this good news, she'll calm down. See you all later!"

For another five minutes, Brooke and Hattie watched Anna sleep. Then, with ICU's shortened visiting time up, they returned to the waiting room.

"Aunt Hattie," Brooke said as they reseated themselves, "I've been thinking. You said Anna told you that Gram tossed out that note, the one with the orchestra tickets."

"Yes," Hattie agreed. "She did."

"Well, do you know if the trash has been picked up?" Brooke asked.

"Frankly, I'm not certain. I just assumed it had been. Maybe we'd better talk to the police," suggested Hattie.

"Something else," said Brooke. "What happened to the tickets? Wouldn't they have been in Gram's purse? Wouldn't her keys have been in her purse, too? Where's Gram's purse?"

"My word, Brooke, how brilliant of you! We've got to find that purse. If we had those tickets, maybe we could find out who purchased them!" Hattie was more excited than she had thought possible. "What if they were season tickets?"

Suddenly, a frightening thought entered her mind. "Brooke, I don't want to frighten you, but has it occurred to you that Anna is very possibly still in danger? If someone really is determined to kill her, won't he keep on trying until he's succeeded? And now someone might have the keys to her house!"

"Geez, Aunt Hattie! I wish she could talk to us. Maybe she knows where Gram's purse is." Brooke thought for a moment. "I think we should go down to Gram's house as soon as possible. It'll probably be a long time until Anna is well enough to go back, but if someone has the house key...that would be awful."

"Maybe you're right, Brooke. Maybe that envelope is still in a wastebasket in the upstairs sitting room," Hattie agreed. "And it might be an excellent idea for us to have the locks changed."

They were both silent for a few moments, lost in their own thoughts. Finally, Hattie spoke.

"Brooke, I'm a ninny! Here I am worried about Anna's life when she gets out of the hospital, but what about now? What if someone tries to kill her right here in her room?"

"Oh, Aunt Hattie, do you believe that would even be possible? She's under such close observation here," Brooke said.

"Yes," Hattie agreed, "but she won't be here much longer, judging from her rate of improvement. I wouldn't be surprised if they transferred her to another room tomorrow or Friday, at the latest. These beds are expensive. They don't keep patients in intensive care very long."

"How do you think we should handle this?" asked Brooke. "We don't want to scare her. Should we tell Cameron, do you think? What about Mother?"

"Or maybe," said Hattie, "it would be a good idea to ask Officer Sawyer for his opinion."

"Good idea!" said Brooke. "And we should tell Cameron what we think, too, but definitely not Mother!"

"No," agreed Hattie, and added with a laugh, "but don't you think she would notice a guard posted at Anna's door?"

Brooke giggled.

They decided to stay and wait until the next visiting period. Most of the people who'd been sitting in the waiting room earlier were waiting patiently again. Their faces mirrored concern.

When a nurse opened the door fifteen minutes later, they all hurried to their loved ones. Hattie was not surprised by her own anxiety. She fretted over the possibility that Anna was still in danger. She and Brooke both looked around covertly, each wondering how anyone could possibly attack Anna in this setting.

When they walked into her cubicle, they were astonished to see her looking at them.

"Hi," she said, in a weak voice.

"Anna!" Brooke whispered, keeping her voice low with difficulty.

"Oh, my dear," said Hattie. Tears formed in her eyes. She brushed them away impatiently.

"Where's Larry?" asked Anna. "What happened to me? Where am I? Why am I in a hospital?"

Hattie and Brooke looked at each other, perplexed.

"What's this about Larry again?" whispered Brooke to Hattie. "I don't get it."

"I have no idea," Hattie whispered back. "She's obviously very confused."

"What are you two whispering about?" Anna demanded. "Why don't you answer me?"

Hattie stood next to Anna's bed and took her right hand in her own.

"You're in the Valley Hospital's intensive care unit, dear," she said gently, deciding to be as honest as possible. "You were in an automobile accident last night on the Old Pike Road. Do you remember anything about that?"

Anna shook her head and immediately closed her eyes against the pain.

"Ouch!" she cried.

"Does your head hurt, dear?" asked Hattie, sympathetically.

"Yes," said Anna. Tears ran down her cheeks.

"Why was I on the Old Pike Road?" Anna wanted to know. "Was I alone, or was Larry with me?" She ran her right hand up and down the cast on her left arm, "Do I have a broken arm?"

"Yes, you have a broken arm," Brooke answered. "And why do you keep on talking about Larry?" Hattie gave Brooke a warning look and shook her head, effectively stopping her from saying anything more.

"Where's Gram?" Anna asked. "Isn't she coming to see me? Are Mother and Cameron coming?"

"Not only are they coming, they're here," Cameron informed her, stepping into her cubicle. Her mother followed right behind and hurried to her bedside. Alexandra's face was carefully made up, and her clothes perfectly coordinated. Navy slacks and shoes, a navy bag, white blouse and a navy sweater belied the uproar she'd been through in the past day. But although she frequently patted her hair and sought her reflection in the glass door, more than a few stray strands told of a restless night.

"We'll leave you two for a little while, dear," Hattie told Anna, stepping quickly toward the door to the waiting room. She gestured to Brooke to follow, and Brooke yanked at Cameron's sleeve. When he turned to face her, she put her finger to her lips and pointed to the waiting room.

Understanding Brooke's message at once, Cameron gave her a quick nod and said to Anna, "I'll leave you and your mother to have a nice little visit. I'll be right back." He leaned over and whispered into Alexandra's ear, "No matter what, just don't say anything to upset her."

"Of course not!" Alexandra's tone was one of wounded innocence.

In the waiting room, the trio returned to their quiet corner before Cameron spoke. "From what I heard when I was going in, she was asking for her grandmother. She's obviously blanked out the last several days."

"I'm afraid she's blanked out more than that," Hattie contributed. "She's been asking for Larry, too."

"Hmm," mumbled Cameron. "It's been almost a year since she broke their engagement, hasn't it? Has she seen him since? I thought he took a job in the state of Washington."

"You're absolutely right," Brooke told him. "She broke off with Larry between Thanksgiving and Christmas last year. She hasn't even mentioned his name since then, until now. I'm as sure as I can be that they have not been in touch with each other. I think she'd tell me that. And from what I heard, he did get a job in a Seattle school."

"Of course, we'll have to talk to Dr. Fletcher right away. He'll probably contact a specialist, but I'd say she has temporary amnesia. It's not unusual in head trauma cases. Hopefully, she'll have her memory back soon, but they'll need to keep a close eye on her.

"Speaking of which, your young Officer Sawyer questioned me today about the phone call for Anna/Annie yesterday afternoon. I told him everything I could remember, which was apparently just about what you had told him. He also asked when I thought he could interview Anna. I told him to call Dr. Fletcher, but now it seems he'll have to wait a bit longer."

"We have something else to talk to you about," said Brooke. "We're afraid that whoever has tried to kill Anna might try again."

"And," Hattie continued, "we think it's vitally important to find the purse Annie was carrying the night she was killed. Not only did it have the orchestra tickets in it, but it also had to contain her keys. We were saying a bit ago that it would be an excellent idea to have all of the locks on the house changed."

"What about Anna's purse?" asked Cameron. "Was that found?"

"Oh, yes," Hattie said. "She had it in her hand when Annie shoved her onto the sidewalk. She told me she found herself clutching it in a death grip. Annie was carrying the tickets and her house keys. All Anna had was tissues and some makeup. Her purse is at my place."

"Yes, the locks must be changed right away," Cameron agreed. "I'll see to it tomorrow. What really concerns me, though, is that if you're right, there is a possible murderer out there...somewhere who still wants Anna dead! If we only knew why. Does she know something the murderer is afraid she'll tell? What, for heaven's sake, could she know?"

"How can we protect her?' Brooke asked him. Her face was drained of all color, and she suddenly shivered from an intense fear of what she knew, as well as what she didn't.

Betty Kerr Orlemann

# 13

Alexandra pulled up a chair and sat next to her elder daughter's bed. She smiled at her through the railings in place on either side of Anna's mattress. "How do you feel, darling?" she asked in her most concerned motherly voice.

"Oh, Mother, I have the most dreadful headache," complained Anna uncharacteristically. "Do you think you could have them give me something for it?"

"Of course, darling. I know all too well what it's like to have a bad headache. You know, with all of my migraines. I had the mother of all headaches the day before Cameron and I left the Bahamas," Alexandra said. "I could have died, I was so sick.

"Cameron took such good care of me. He put ice packs on my head and gave me some kind of wonderful pills that simply knocked me out for hours."

"Mother," Anna protested, "please call the nurse for me."

"Certainly, darling." Alexandra pressed the button, which had slipped out of Anna's reach.

Terri, the green-eyed nurse, appeared almost instantly.

"My head is killing me," Anna sobbed.

The nurse assured her that she would get the doctor immediately and left.

After a brief silence, Anna rolled her eyes toward Alexandra.

"When were you and Cameron in the Bahamas?"

"Why darling, you know that we just got home this week. Right before Annie's funeral," Alexandra recounted in a concerned tone.

"What do you mean, Annie's funeral?" Anna almost shouted. "Mother, what do you mean? Gram is fine, I know it. What do you mean, her funeral?" She put her right hand on her head and began to sob.

Alexandra stared at her daughter in alarm.

"Anna, what are you saying? You must remember that your grandmother was killed by a hit-and-run driver in Philadelphia on Saturday night. You were with her."

"That's not true! It can't be true!" Anna wailed. "Mother, why would you say such a thing?"

"Anna, darling, you've had serious trauma to your head. You can't remember things right now, but you'll get well, don't worry," Alexandra said soothingly, masking an unfamiliar maternal concern she rarely felt.

"Is Larry here?" Anna, still very agitated, asked.

"You're just confused, darling," Alexandra said. "You and Larry broke up almost a year ago, and you haven't seen him since. He went to Seattle, I believe."

"No! No! No!" cried Anna. She pressed her head harder and closed her eyes. "I feel as if I'm going crazy!"

The nurse and Cameron rushed into the room at the same time. Anna was sobbing, almost hysterically.

"What happened? What did you say to upset her so?" Cameron demanded of his wife.

"I didn't say anything," Alexandra protested. "She's very confused. She doesn't even know her grandmother is dead, and she thinks Larry is coming to see her!"

"And I suppose you straightened her out on both counts?" Cameron asked sarcastically, under his breath as he turned his attention to Anna.

The nurse looked accusingly at Alexandra.

"Dr. Fletcher is on his way in right now. I think it would be better if you waited in the other room." She turned back to Anna and placed a cool compress on her head.

"Absolutely," agreed Cameron. His flushed face showed his obvious embarrassment. He put his hand on Alexandra's arm and led her none too gently to the waiting room.

"You don't have to be so rough," complained Alexandra. "I have no idea what made you so angry."

From their chairs in the corner, Brooke and Hattie watched the little scene unfolding between Alexandra and Cameron.

"What could she have done this time?" Brooke whispered in alarm. "I've never seen Cameron so angry. He's having a tough time controlling himself, isn't he?"

Hattie didn't answer. She silently prayed that whatever had happened had not set Anna's recovery back.

At that moment, Dr. Fletcher hurried into the waiting room. He took in the anger of the couple before him, nodded quickly to Cameron and walked directly in to see Anna. Once at the girl's bedside, he checked the pupils of her eyes. "What's the matter, Miss Anna?" he asked gently.

"Who are you?" she asked with an air of confusion. "Am I supposed to know you? I don't seem to be able to remember much of anything."

He smiled at her kindly and patted her right hand. "I'm Dr. Fletcher," he told her, "and although I saw you, you didn't see me because you were unconscious."

"What's wrong with me?" she implored weakly.

"Well, I suppose you know you were in an accident last night," he said.

"Yes, they told me I was, but I can't remember a thing about it," Anna sighed.

"You mustn't worry about that," Dr. Fletcher comforted her. "That's perfectly normal after a bad blow to the head. You'll get over it." He smiled warmly at her. "Did they tell you also that I had to remove your spleen last night? It had been ruptured in the accident. Don't worry, though, you can live just fine without it."

"Oh," Anna's eyes were wide. "Oh, my. No wonder my stomach hurts, too."

Dr. Fletcher smiled.

"You're going to be okay before you know it."

"But Doctor, can't you do something about this dreadful headache and the pain in my abdomen?" Anna begged.

He wrote on her chart as he told her, "I'll order Demoral for the pain. It should relax you very pleasantly. I'll come back to see you before I leave tonight, but if you want me before that, just tell the nurse."

Anna, her head still pounding, watched him leave. Nurse Terri was back with the Demoral the doctor had ordered. Anna soon dozed comfortably, her headache relieved. She felt as though she were floating on a cloud, just floating gently. It was a wonderful feeling. No pain. No worry. Just floating and floating.

She opened her eyes drowsily and looked into Larry's concerned brown eyes. His light-brown hair looked as if he hadn't bothered to comb it. He was wearing a navy sweatshirt and blue jeans. She tried to smile at him, but her face didn't seem to respond to her message. She kept on floating, trying to keep her eyes fastened on Larry's familiar, strong face.

"I had to see you, Annie, my darling," he said softly. "I'll come back when you're better, if you'll let me." Then he left the room.

Terri appeared beside her and began straightening her bedding.

"Are you feeling better, Anna?" she asked. Anna tried to nod her head, but she simply floated away.

The nurse smiled at her. "I'm happy that you're so much better. I've been taking care of you all along, but you didn't know that. My name is Terri. If you need anything, just push your button and ask for me."

Betty Kerr Orlemann

# 14

Hattie and Brooke followed Cameron and Alexandra from the hospital, but at a distance.

"Aunt Hattie," asked Brooke when they were walking across the parking lot, "what do you think happened?"

"Just from the little I overheard, Brooke, I believe that your mother said something that upset Anna quite a bit. I can only guess that perhaps she told her about your grandmother's death," Hattie answered. "Anyway, Dr. Fletcher said he prescribed Demoral. She's sound asleep now. She should be much better tomorrow."

"Well, I know how upset Mother is. She never even told me to go home with her instead of staying at your house. She sure would have if she'd known Shawn was coming over tonight, wouldn't she?" Brooke said with a wide smile.

"Brooke Turner," Hattie scolded through a thinly-disguised grin, "you are making a co-conspirator out of me!"

When they arrived at Hattie's house, Brooke insisted on cooking hamburgers for supper. Hattie took frozen hamburgers from the freezer. "There are rolls in the bread box," she told Brooke. "I'll make a salad. Do you want anything else?"

"No, I'm not that hungry. Do you?" Brooke asked.

Hattie shook her head. She finished ripping lettuce into pieces. "While you're cooking, I'll take Wolf for a walk. I need the fresh air." Wolf, hearing his name and the word "walk," jumped to his feet and trotted to the door. Hattie flicked two switches by the door; one illuminated the porch and the other lit four spotlights fastened at the corners of the eaves. The lights bathed the lawn and set the shrubs and trees into sharp relief, but beyond that the world was pitch black.

She walked down the flagstone path, opened the gate, and was forced to turn on her flashlight as she strode from her driveway into her lane. Suddenly, Wolf emitted a deep growl. Hattie reached down and felt his hackles rise under her hand. Wolf was staring toward the barn, his entire body alert. Hattie felt a cold chill creep up her spine.

Wolf growled and barked sharply. Hattie shone her flashlight on the barn. The side door squeaked and cracked open a trifle. She saw the glow of another flashlight. A figure moved toward her.

"Who's there?" she called out into the night.

"I'm sorry if I scared you, Miss Farwell. It's only me, Shawn." He shone the light on his face. I got here early and was just kind of looking around. I dig your old barn. Very historical. I hope you don't mind."

Wolf growled again, still protective.

"It's okay, Wolf," Hattie told him soothingly. "Come over here, Shawn." She sounded much like the schoolteacher she had been. "We'll go into the house now." Wolf ran into the woods for a few minutes on his own mission, and they stood waiting for him.

When he returned, Hattie took hold of his collar as Shawn approached, but the great dog did not growl again.

"Where did you park?" she asked.

Shawn pointed his flashlight to a spot in front of the barn, and Hattie could just make out the gleam of a bumper.

Once on the kitchen porch, Wolf decided that Shawn was not a threat to the household and wagged his tail at him.

"This is absolutely the biggest dog I've ever seen," Shawn commented in awe, as he patted Wolf's head.

Brooke heard their voices on the porch and didn't wait for them to come inside. She flung the door open and rushed into Shawn's arms with a squeal of utter delight. After a quick "Hi" and a longer, welcoming kiss, she took his hand and led him into the house.

In the kitchen, she fixed a place for him next to hers at the table and offered to cook him a hamburger.

"I've had my dinner," he said, nevertheless eyeballing the cooking burgers. "But how can I refuse an offer from such a mesmerizing cook?" he added, with a grin.

While they were eating, Hattie and Brooke took turns telling him about Anna, her regaining consciousness and her amnesia.

"We're really afraid for her," Brooke said. "We're afraid she was the intended victim of the hit-and-run car that killed our grandmother, and we believe her accident was no accident at all. Someone deliberately tried to kill Anna!"

Shawn frowned.

"Couldn't it all be a coincidence?" he proposed. "Why would anyone want to kill Anna...or, for that matter, your grandmother?"

"We haven't the foggiest notion," Hattie told him. "But on looking back at Annie's death, it does seem that it was planned." She told him about the orchestra tickets and the note.

"Wow!" said Shawn. "If you're right, Anna is still in danger, like you thought. Have you told anyone? What's going to be done to protect her?"

"Actually, we've told a police officer. He agrees with us. Of course, we've also told Dr. MacArthur, and he agrees with us, too," Hattie replied.

"I think they're going to put a guard at her door at the hospital," said Brooke. "So she'll be safe there, anyhow."

"Because of her amnesia, no one can question her about either accident, unfortunately," Hattie explained. "As we told you, she remembers absolutely nothing."

"That's scary," Shawn said, finishing his hamburger and digging into his salad.

Brooke watched him solemnly.

"You're going to be expensive to keep," she observed. "How much would you eat if you hadn't already had your dinner?"

They all laughed. "You know I didn't come here to eat," he chuckled. "Actually, Brooke, I wanted to talk to you about Michael's campaign. When do you think you can come to headquarters and give us some help with phoning and mailing and stuff?"

"It all depends on Anna," Brooke responded. "Maybe, if I could work part time, I could go in tomorrow morning. Then I would still be able to see Anna in the afternoon and evening." She looked over at Hattie for guidance. "What do you think, Aunt Hattie?"

Hattie would have preferred to be left out of this conversation. What she really thought was that Brooke should not work on Michael DiRienzo's campaign at all, but of course, she couldn't say that. Anyway, she told herself, her assessment of the man might be entirely wrong.

She looked at the two young people so eagerly awaiting her answer. "Cameron promised to call us early in the morning with an update on Anna's condition," she said. "If she's better, or at least holding her own, I don't see why you couldn't go in just for the morning."

"Good," stated Brooke. She put her hand on Shawn's arm, "Then that's what I'll do." He gave her a one-armed hug.

"I'd better go home now. It's a long ride to South Philadelphia." He stood up and started for the door. He pulled Brooke into both arms and kissed her firmly. He turned to hug Hattie when she stopped him.

"I wish you would spare yourself that trip," she said. "There are a couple of extra rooms upstairs, and you're welcome to spend the night here."

"Oh, that's a great idea!" Brooke agreed. "I'll make his bed for him, Aunt Hattie."

Shawn hesitated, but only briefly, before accepting Hattie's invitation. "I guess I could do that. Thanks, Miss Farwell. By the way, would you like it if Brooke and I took the dog out for a few minutes before we go up to our bedrooms?"

"Thanks," said Hattie. "Don't go to bed too late. Brooke hasn't gotten much sleep." She watched as they left with Wolf, then she went up the back stairs to her own bedroom.

After Hattie had snuggled into her bed, she heard the clock on the kitchen mantle strike nine times before she fell asleep. She slept soundly and dreamed about the farm, when the cedar forest across the lane had been just a pasture and the lane, a cowpath. She was a child in her dream, and she and Annie were jumping in the barn's hayloft. Annie giggled and giggled, and suddenly Hattie woke up. The giggling was real.

In an instant, she was wide awake. Hattie saw by the illuminated dial on her clock that the time was ten-forty. She grabbed her robe from the foot of the bed, and not bothering to put on slippers, hurried across the room to the connecting door to Brooke's room.

She knocked on the door and the giggling stopped. There was a scrambling sound in the room, and Hattie opened the door to see Shawn rushing toward the facing door to the hall. He stopped dead in his tracks when he saw Hattie, and Brooke sat bolt upright. For a moment neither spoke, and then Brooke said weakly, "We were just talking about the campaign, Aunt Hattie."

Hattie was kind enough not to flick on the lights, but she could tell even in the semi-darkness that Brooke's hair was disheveled and her bedding was in disarray.

Once she could get past her surprise, Hattie finally spoke.

"If Shawn is to stay in this house, he will sleep in his own bedroom, and you will sleep in yours. There will be no more sneaking back and forth, even to discuss the campaign—understood?"

"Yes, Aunt Hattie," Brooke said, meekly.

"I'm sorry, Miss Farwell," Shawn said, genuinely contrite. "It won't happen again."

Shawn left the room, quietly shutting the door behind him. Brooke lay down and pulled the covers up around her neck. Hattie turned back to her own room, leaving the adjoining door open. Hattie was far from shocked, but she didn't want Brooke to know that. She returned to her bed and slept like the proverbial log.

The next morning, Brooke was still sleeping when Hattie arose. Hattie used her bathroom and dressed quietly but didn't close the door between the rooms. She was surprised to find that Shawn had used the main staircase and was in the kitchen when she descended the winding stairs from her room.

"Good morning, Miss Farwell," Shawn said politely. "I'm just making coffee."

"So I see," Hattie observed.

"About last night," he blurted. "I'm sorry. We didn't do anything, honest."

"I hope not," Hattie replied sternly. "Remember, Shawn, Brooke is only seventeen. I know she's a mature seventeen, but she's seventeen, just the same."

The steeple clock struck seven.

"Should I get her up?" he asked. "We ought to leave here by eight-thirty at the latest."

"Let her sleep another half-hour," Hattie suggested. "She should be able to get ready in an hour."

"Miss Farwell, I know what you're thinking, but you need to know that I love Brooke. I love her so much and would never hurt her. I'd never want her to do anything she might regret later."

Hattie looked at his serious face and smiled.

"Or that you might regret, given that she's still a minor."

He blanched, and she decided she'd made her point.

"I believe you, Shawn. As a matter of fact, I think you're a fine young man. Brooke is a very lucky girl." Shawn returned her smile, relief written all over his face.

Hattie was creaming chipped dried beef in an iron frying pan when Brooke came down the circular staircase into the kitchen. She was wearing the same blue jeans and navy sweatshirt she wore the day before. Her hair was loose around her face. She looked absolutely beautiful.

"I hope this outfit will be okay for Senator DiRienzo's campaign headquarters," she said with a worried frown. "It's all I have. Maybe we could drive by my mother's place on the way, and I could pick up some more clothes," she suggested to Shawn.

"You look amazing," replied her love-struck boyfriend. "You won't be on display, anyway, but if it's really necessary, I can drive you to your mother's on the way home, okay?" From the expression on his face, it was obvious that Shawn was not anxious to go to Alexandra's. Not then, not any time.

It was nearly eight-thirty when they finished their breakfast and said goodbye to Hattie. Shawn and Brooke were running toward the front of the barn for his car when they were startled by a shotgun blast coming from the woods.

"What the...!" shouted Shawn. He grabbed Brooke and shouted to Hattie. "What was that?"

She was standing on the kitchen porch, staring into the woods. She had a firm grip on Wolf's collar, but the great dog was pulling in the same direction, poised to charge. No one was in sight. She watched the kids start to climb into Shawn's car and called to them.

"Small game hunting season began this week, and it seems that someone is poaching in my woods. It happens more than it should, and I'm going to call the game warden. That shot was illegally close to the house, as well as being fired on my private property.

Brooke and Shawn agreed that the shooter should be reported. They drove past Hattie as she picked up the morning paper. They all waved goodbye and Hattie returned to the kitchen, still holding firmly to Wolf's collar. Annoyed at the gunshot, she was on her way to call the Game Commission when the phone rang.

"Oh," she said aloud. "That's probably Cameron. I forgot about him." She lifted the receiver. "Good morning."

"Good morning yourself, Hattie," chuckled Cameron's voice. "And a very good morning it is! I've just talked with Dr. Fletcher, and Anna is much improved. Her head doesn't hurt as much as it did yesterday, and she says she is feeling much better. She still has no recollection of the accident, but that should correct itself when the swelling goes down. If she continues to progress as well as she has, she should be out of intensive care tomorrow or the next day at the latest."

"Thank heaven," Hattie sighed. "But Cameron, have you given any more thought to her protection once she is in a regular room?"

"I discussed that with Dr. Fletcher," said Cameron. "We agree that she should have police protection around the clock, at least until a perpetrator is found."

After they'd hung up, Hattie lit a fire in the fireplace, poured herself another cup of coffee and sat in her rocking chair. She was still annoyed that a shotgun had been fired in her woods, but with Cameron's news, she now wondered whether she should call the game warden or Officer Sawyer.

Her problem was solved for her when the phone rang again. This time it was Officer Sawyer.

"I've done some asking around about that green van," he told her. "It seems that the gate attendant at the MacArthurs' condominium complex saw a van fitting that description on Wednesday afternoon. He said Anna Turner had driven in, and he'd just closed the gate when a dark green van with tinted windows came reeling down the road from the same direction Anna had come from.

"The driver had turned the van into the drive before noticing the gate. He stopped, made a quick three-point turn and drove away. The guard said he didn't see the driver or the license plate. I haven't found anyone else who saw the van."

"Well," Hattie said thoughtfully, "that's very interesting. It would seem my assumption that the van was following Anna was correct."

"Yes, it would," said the officer. "I've also talked to the lieutenant of the Philadelphia Police Department's squad whose precinct includes Fifteenth and Locust Streets. They're still calling Annie Turner's death a hit-and-run accident, but they haven't closed their investigation.

According to their official report, an old homeless man who haunts that corner swears up and down that the maroon car was waiting on Fifteenth Street until the two women came along. He says they were crossing Locust with a green light, when the car started up and drove right at them.

"The man found the older woman's purse lying in the gutter some time after she was hit. He gave it to the police, but when they got it, there were no keys or money or orchestra tickets in it. It contained only a handkerchief and a pair of broken reading glasses. They'll need someone to go to headquarters and identify the purse and its contents. Of course, they can't give it to you until the case is no longer under investigation, but as evidence, it needs to be identified, if you don't mind."

"Yes, I'll get down there as soon as I can," Hattie replied. "In the meantime, something happened this morning that really annoyed me." She told him about the shotgun blast within feet of her kitchen. She also told him of their fears for Anna when she would be removed from intensive care, and the fact that the doctor would be arranging round-the-clock protection for her.

"I'll drop by in an hour or so, if that fits your schedule," Sawyer said. "I want to look around the area where the shotgun blast came from, so don't let your dog go in there, okay?"

"Okay," Hattie agreed. "But do you really think this has anything to do with Anna? How could it?"

"I'm not sure, but it's an ongoing investigation. We have to pursue all possibilities."

They hung up, and while she waited for him to arrive, Hattie puttered around the kitchen, looking out every so often to see if anyone was in the woods. Finally, feeling restless, she hooked Wolf to his leash and walked him down the lane toward the Old Pike Road to wait until Jim Sawyer drove in.

# 15

Brooke brought all of her feminine wiles into play as soon as she and Shawn drove onto the Pike Road.

"Shawn," she cooed, running her fingers up and down his right arm, "I desperately need another outfit, I really do. I know it's a terrible imposition, but couldn't we go to Mother's real quick, before we go to Senator DiRienzo's? Please?" She gazed beseechingly into his face.

"Stop that!" he ordered, smiling as he said it. "You know I can't deny you anything. We'll be late to headquarters, and it'll be all your fault!" Nonetheless, he turned into the road that would take them to the MacArthur place.

The guard, recognizing Brooke, opened the gate and waved them through. Shawn elected to wait in the car while Brooke ran into the condominium to collect some clothing. He had no desire for another encounter with Alexandra.

Brooke ran up the brick walk and used her key to open the front door. She tiptoed into the foyer, and when she didn't hear anything, walked quietly up the stairs to her second floor bedroom. Cameron's and Alexandra's bedroom door was closed, and she hoped they were still sleeping.

She pulled her suitcase from her closet and began throwing her things into it. The more of her clothes she took to Hattie's, the better, she thought. While she packed her suitcase, she looked for something to wear that day.

In one of her bureau drawers she found a cashmere sweater in a gorgeous shade of cherry red—her favorite color. Although she didn't recognize it, it was her size, so she laid it on the bed, along with a white turtleneck blouse and a pair of cream wool slacks.

Brooke dressed rapidly and stepped into a pair of cream pumps. Her image, as reflected in a full-length mirror on the back of her door, pleased her.

"Lookin' good!" she whispered, as she ran a comb through her hair and smiled at her reflection with the confidence allowed only the young.

Brooke grabbed her jacket from the bed where she'd tossed it and put it on, then picked up her suitcase and left the room. The second floor was still quiet and the door to Alexandra's and Cameron's room remained closed. She descended the staircase noiselessly and was about to tiptoe to the front door, when she saw Cameron standing in the foyer. Startled, she jumped.

"Aren't you being a little sneaky?" he asked in a hushed tone. "Where do you think you're going with that suitcase?"

"Come outside with me," Brooke whispered. "I'll explain everything to you."

Her stepfather followed her through the door and across the parking lot to Shawn's car. When Shawn saw him, he stepped from the driver's seat and shook Cameron's hand.

"Good morning, Doctor," he said trying to sound matter-of-fact.

Cameron noticed a slight blush on Shawn's fair cheeks.

"Good morning, Shawn," he responded cordially, "Do you two mind telling me what's going on?"

Suddenly, Brooke burst into laughter.

"Ohmigod!" she choked out. "You thought we were eloping, didn't you, Cameron? Tell the truth. You did, didn't you?" she teased.

Now it was Cameron's turn to be embarrassed.

"W-well," he stammered, "it did cross my mind."

"Oh, Cameron," she said seriously, "I'm disappointed that you have so little faith in me."

"Please accept my apologies, Brooke. I'm sorry, but what do you think your sneaking into the house and packing your suitcase looked like?"

"Well, I'll tell you the truth," said Brooke. "I'm going to help Shawn out at Michael DiRienzo's headquarters this morning, and I didn't have a thing to wear."

"You sound exactly like your mother!" Cameron chuckled. "But why did you pack your whole suitcase?"

"Well, since we're being so honest, I didn't want to keep coming back for more clothes, and I definitely want to stay at Aunt Hattie's," Brooke admitted. "And," she continued, "nothing against Mother, but you know how she is. If I told her face to face that I wasn't coming home to stay, she'd have a fit, and we'd wind up in another big argument no one would win."

Cameron smiled and nodded.

"I'll pretend I never saw you. But you'll have to confront her sooner or later, and it should really be sooner. It should be today." He picked up her suitcase. Shawn popped the trunk lid open, and Cameron put the suitcase inside.

"Thanks, Cameron," she said, hugging him. "You're a peach!"

They didn't arrive at campaign headquarters until a few minutes after nine-thirty. Maria looked pointedly at her watch when Shawn walked through the door.

"Where've you been? You're more than a half-hour late," she scolded.

Shawn walked to her desk, leaned over and kissed her cheek.

"Forgive me, me darlin'," he said, with an exaggerated Irish brogue. "And now let me introduce ye to me lassie." He held out his hand to Brooke.

Smiling, Brooke walked over to them.

"Maria," said Shawn, "meet Brooke Turner, the woman who has agreed to be my wife some day."

Brooke held out her hand, but for a long moment Maria didn't move. She just stared at the girl. Then she seemed to shake her head as if to clear it, and regained her composure. She stood and shook Brooke's outstretched hand.

"This is indeed a pleasure, Brooke. I can't tell you how happy I am to meet you, and how happy I am that you've chosen this young man to marry." Smiling broadly, she continued. "I hope you'll pardon me for staring at you like that, but you look exactly like your mother! It's like history repeating itself. Imagine two generations of the same family helping out with Michael's campaigns. How is your mother, anyway? I haven't seen her in years." Maria had a very soft voice. "That, by the way, is a lovely sweater."

"Thanks," Brooke said, glad she had insisted on the change of outfit. She was making a good impression with Shawn's boss. She assured Maria that her mother was fine and living with her husband, Dr. Cameron MacArthur, in a condominium near New Hope.

"I was sorry when I read that your father had died. He was a fine man," Maria sighed. "But that was many years ago. I'm happy Alexandra found herself another good man." She saw the newspaper still lying on Shawn's desk from the day before. "Pardon me for not asking sooner, but how is your sister? Shawn showed me the article in yesterday's paper about her accident."

"Thanks for asking, Mrs. DiRienzo...."

"No, no, no, no," Maria interrupted. "My name is Maria. Please, call me Maria. Now tell me about your sister."

"She's in Valley Hospital in intensive care. She was unconscious for almost a whole day, but finally came to last evening. Unfortunately, she has amnesia. She can't remember anything about the accident. She can't remember lots of things," Brooke explained. "Her memory of our grandmother's death last Saturday is gone, and she can't even remember breaking up with her fiancé last year."

"How awful!" Maria commiserated. "Will she ever get her memory back?"

"I don't know," Brooke said sadly. "The doctor said she probably will when the swelling in her head goes down, but there's no guarantee."

"Hey!" Shawn interrupted. "Are we here to work or gab?"

The women laughed.

"But," continued Shawn, "before you give Brooke a job, Maria, I want to introduce her to the others." He looked around the office, where seven volunteers sat at desks talking on telephones or working on computers.

"That's fine," Maria agreed. "As soon as she has met what staff is here, bring her right back to me, okay?"

"You got it," said Shawn with a grin. He was impatient to show off Brooke.

The volunteers, two retired men and five women of various ages, were friendly and welcomed Brooke warmly. The men congratulated Shawn on his good taste.

As the couple walked back to Maria's office, Brooke said, "I'm going to like it here. These are nice people, but when will I meet the great man himself?"

Shawn smiled. "Who knows?" he replied. "He pops in and out as his schedule allows. Even Maria doesn't know where he is half the time, but we figure he's campaigning.

And on days when his campaign manager Howard Cole, his legislative aide and his public relations people have speeches scheduled for him, he appears everywhere he's supposed to be, like clockwork.

"The press will be waiting for him at each stop, you can count on that. Reporters, news photographers, television crews. These P.R. guys are pros. They know just what they're doing, and Michael obeys them without question. He knows the press can make or break a candidate."

Brooke frowned, "What about Maria?" she asked. "Is it usual for a candidate's wife to work on his campaign? I always thought the wives appeared everywhere their husbands did, especially when they were making speeches. I always thought their job was to just look at their husbands adoringly."

"Michael's just getting started, officially," Shawn explained. "His advisors will be working with Maria soon. She's very shy, you know. She'd much rather work here at headquarters than be out in front of crowds of people. I believe the very thought of making a speech herself terrifies her.

"Up until this campaign, she's managed to stay in the background pretty much. Once in awhile when Michael was a congressman and then a senator she had to appear in pictures with him or at the podium, but that was basically it."

Maria stood up at her desk. "Shawn," she said in as commanding a tone as she was capable of, "will you please get Brooke over here? I want to put her to work." Immediately Shawn left Brooke with Maria and went off to his own desk to work.

"Brooke," Maria said sweetly, "do you see that tiny cubicle over in the corner? There are lots of papers on the desk there bearing the names of contributors. What

I need you to do is transfer those names, addresses and phone numbers into the computer. Can you do that?"

"I believe I can," Brooke answered. "I'm pretty good with a computer."

"Good," said Maria, "and, I forgot, please add the amounts of their contributions, too."

"I'm on it," said Brooke. As she walked back to her corner, she was unaware of the appreciative stares that followed her.

The chair at her desk had its back to the room. She felt almost isolated despite the busy office behind her. She could hardly see anything going on. She couldn't even see Shawn at his desk. She attempted to move the computer so she could reposition her chair, but its short cords kept it solidly where it stood. At any rate, her little cubicle was obviously a former closet and very inconvenient. Clearly, this office was set up for maximum productivity and little else.

*Oh well,* she thought, *this isn't supposed to be a social affair. I'm here to work so I'd better get started.* She sorted slips of paper that had come with donations in the mail and put them in alphabetical order. Then she typed the names and required information into the computer. It was a very boring job, but she knew someone had to do it.

She was well into her work, when an electric charge seemed to fill the room. She turned her head to see the best-looking man she'd ever laid eyes on. He was even more handsome than his pictures, she thought—at least at this distance.

Despite the fact he was all the way over on the other side of the room, she could sense his personal magnetism. The workers rose from their desks as one and circled around him.

Suddenly, Shawn appeared at his side, having actually pushed his way to Michael. He pointed to Brooke's dark little corner. Brooke couldn't hear their conversation, but Shawn was obviously anxious for Michael to meet her.

What Shawn said was, "Michael, I want you to meet the most beautiful girl in the world," and he pointed to Brooke. "But don't get too friendly," he laughed. "She's mine!"

Michael squinted and looked toward Brooke, but he couldn't see her well.

"C'mon, Shawn," he coaxed with a smile. "Aren't you going to take me over to meet her?"

Maria, in her own quiet way, had edged herself next to her husband.

"Not now, Michael," she said. "You'll have to postpone meeting Shawn's pretty little friend. I have a million papers here that require your attention, and there are an equal number of phone calls from big contributors that you should return right away."

"Yes, dear." Michael gave an exaggerated sigh, winking at Shawn before following Maria to his office. "I'll have to meet your girl later, I'm afraid," he called back to Shawn over his shoulder.

Brooke was disappointed and let down. She'd been dying to meet Michael DiRienzo for some time. She wanted to see him up close and shake his hand. The other girls at school would be so jealous. *Oh, well*, she thought. *Maybe tomorrow*.

She glanced at her watch. It was nearly noon, and she really had to leave if she wanted to eat lunch before going to the hospital. She piled the contribution papers neatly and in order on her desk and went to find Shawn.

He was coming out of Michael's office when she spotted him. He saw her at the same time and went to her at once. "I know," he smiled, "it's time to leave. Will you have time for lunch before I take you back to Miss Farwell's?"

"You've been reading my mind," she smiled back at him. "Give me a sec to get my things together and I'll be right with you."

"Oh, leaving all ready?" Maria asked as she was leaving Michael's office. "But that's right, you have to go see your sister, don't you? I hope she's feeling better, poor thing.

"Thanks, Maria. I'll see you first thing tomorrow morning," Brooke told her. Maria merely nodded.

They were about to go out when Maria stopped them. "Just one minute, please, Brooke," she called in her soft voice. It was amazing, Brooke thought, how Maria's voice carried despite its softness. Brooke followed Maria to her desk, where she saw that her morning's work had been called up on the computer. Maria was studying it carefully.

"This is very nice, Brooke," Maria said with a smile, "but it isn't exactly what I wanted."

Brooke frowned, "How does it differ from what you asked me to do?" she asked, puzzled and a bit hurt.

"It should be in columns," Maria answered with a long-suffering sigh. After years of campaign work, she was used to answering such questions, but they did become tedious. "First the name and address and business address, if appropriate, and the phone numbers. The second column should contain the amount of the contribution. The third column should register the pledge, if any, and the fourth column is for any previous contributions to the senator's other campaigns. Didn't I make that clear?"

"No, no you didn't," Brooke responded in a small voice. "I'm sorry if I misunderstood you."

"That's all right," Maria said sweetly. "Don't let it upset you. You can do the whole thing over tomorrow. That will be fine."

Brooke found herself clenching her jaw. She relaxed with effort, took a deep breath, smiled at Maria and nodded.

"Yes," she said simply. "See you tomorrow." and she turned and left with the waiting Shawn.

"You know, Shawn," she said over a cheeseburger at a local diner, "I don't think Maria is a mouse at all. I think she's a pretty tough lady, and I don't think she likes me."

"Don't be silly," Shawn argued. "Why wouldn't she like you? She doesn't even know you. Don't let your imagination run away with you just because Maria wants you to do your work over.

"Let me tell you, and I've known that lady all of my life and she's is a perfectionist. You should see her house. It sparkles. When she's not working for Michael she's cleaning and polishing everything in sight."

"Okay," Brooke said doubtfully, "but I have the feeling that if I quit working for the campaign she wouldn't miss me a bit!"

"I shouldn't tell you this," Shawn said, "but Michael has the reputation of being something of a ladies' man. Maybe she's jealous of you because you're so young and beautiful, especially in that red sweater. "

"Be on with ye, Shawn O'Brien. You're full of blarney," she laughed.

# 16

Officer Jim Sawyer stopped his patrol car and gave Hattie a cheery greeting. Wolf turned his great head toward the policeman but did not move from his spot next to Hattie.

"As you requested," Hattie said, "we haven't gone into the woods at all."

"Good, I'll just drive up ahead and park. Do you think you can show me the spot where the gun was fired?"

"I'm pretty sure of the location," Hattie responded. "You park in my driveway, and I'll come up and show you." She tightened her grip on Wolf's leash, and they walked back to the house.

"Are you certain it was a shotgun you heard?" Sawyer asked behind her.

"As sure as I can be," Hattie answered. She showed him the spot across the lane from the barn where the blast of a shotgun seemed to originate. He walked carefully as he entered the woods, inspecting the ground for some sign of disturbance.

He had walked less than 45 feet when he found a fresh shotgun shell casing on the ground, behind a fallen cedar tree. "Here's the shell," he called out to Hattie, "and here are some deep impressions beneath the oak leaves and evergreen needles that look like footprints.

"Where would this person have parked, Miss Farwell?"

"It's possible that someone could park on up the lane out of sight of the house and barn. Every once in awhile a hunter poaches in my woods, and once I walked up the lane and found a pick-up truck parked on the side. I'm always afraid to let Wolf run during hunting season."

"Yes, I don't blame you," Sawyer agreed. "Where does this lane go?"

"It's an old cowpath that winds its way up to what was once our upper pasture. There are over 100 acres up there. It used to be a truly beautiful spot." Hattie sighed.

"What happened to it?" Sawyer wanted to know.

"I had to sell it," she told him. "It's now in the process of becoming a housing development. Most of the roads are in, and the houses are going up almost overnight."

He looked surprised. "What are they calling it?" he asked.

"They've named it Brookside Farms," Hattie said with a deep sigh.

"Brookside Farms? What a dope I am!" stated Sawyer. "Of course, I know that. I just didn't realize that it had been part of your farm. I'm all turned around, I guess."

"It was probably the lane that confused you," Hattie explained. "As I said, it was a cowpath, and the cows took the easiest route to their pasture, not necessarily the quickest. This old lane just meanders around bends and up and down hills until it gets to where it's going. There's nothing straight about a cowpath."

Sawyer smiled. "Well then, I can figure where a hunter might park. If not on your cowpath lane where he might be seen, he could always park somewhere in Brookside Farms. It's doubtful that any of the workmen there would even question another parked car."

"I guess there's nothing we can do about poachers unless we're lucky enough to catch one," she said. "It's not that I dislike hunters, but they have no business trespassing on my land. Here we are again at the beginning of the season starting with small game, and archery season, and gobblers, then deer—buck and doe separately. Maybe I'm just getting old and grouchy, but I've grown to hate the sound of a shotgun. Archery season frightens me even more, because I can't hear anything, and I have to wonder if anyone is out there.

"Of course, I know that no one would shoot a dog or a human deliberately, but I'm afraid not only for Wolf but for me. I love long walks in the woods, especially in autumn, but I don't go in there anymore when there might be people hunting."

"You're smart, Miss Farwell, and I'm very sorry to say so. I guess there are just too many people in Bucks County these days. It used to be that you could give permission to hunters to use your land if you wanted to; now it seems many people just use it whether you want them to or not.

"I've noticed just from the little distance I walked into your woods, that there are many dense cedar thickets in there. They may be great for the deer, birds and other animals, but they also make super hiding places for hunters. So you must be careful. And call me if you see anyone trespassing in there." Officer Sawyer most decidedly did not cheer Hattie up. As a matter of fact, she was quite depressed after he said goodbye and drove off.

Back in her kitchen Hattie fixed herself a grilled cheese sandwich for lunch and had just finished eating it when she heard Shawn and Brooke drive up. She went out on the porch to greet them, and looking at their happy faces made her feel better. *They're such a cute couple*, she thought, *but so very young*.

The two greeted her with bright smiles and a "Hi!" Hattie returned the greeting and watched as Shawn opened his trunk and took Brooke's suitcase from it.

**127**

He brought it up onto the porch and into the kitchen with Brooke following happily behind him.

"So, Brooke, "Hattie said as she walked into the kitchen after them, "I see you convinced your folks to let you stay here with me. I'm so glad!"

"Well," said Brooke, "not exactly 'my folks.' Actually I convinced Cameron that I should stay here. Mother was still sleeping when we were there."

"Poor Cameron," laughed Hattie. "I wonder what your mother had to say to him."

"I hope she got it out of her system," Brooke stated. "I'm kinda dreading seeing her at the hospital this afternoon."

"As much as I hate to leave you two, I've got to get back to work," Shawn said. "I hope you find Anna much better. Please, tell her I send my best—that is, if she remembers me." Hattie followed Shawn and Brooke as far as the kitchen door, where she asked Shawn if he could come back for dinner that evening.

"I don't even have to think that over, Miss Farwell," Shawn responded with a quick grin. "I'd love to come back for dinner. Thank you."

"Come any time you can. We probably won't sit down to eat until seven, but the earlier you get here the more time we'll have to chat," Hattie told him. She closed the door behind them and went upstairs to freshen up before leaving for the hospital. She heard Shawn's car drive off and Brooke return to the kitchen about five minutes later.

When she and Brooke arrived at the hospital, they found that Anna was still in intensive care. There were some new faces in the waiting room as well as some they'd seen before. Almost as soon as Hattie and Brooke found seats, a nurse announced that it was visiting time, and they all filed into the other room.

"There's no doubt about it, Anna," Brooke gushed at her sister. "You are the healthiest person in here, even if you do look like a cute panda with your two black eyes."

Anna smiled, "That's what they tell me. As a matter of fact, I'm to be moved into a private room upstairs this afternoon. Isn't that wonderful?"

"Oh, Anna, I'm so glad!" cried Brooke. "Now we can see you anytime we like for as long as we like, and we won't have to wait in the waiting room any more."

"Don't worry, dear," Hattie directed her remarks to Anna, "I won't let her tire you out. Tell me, how do you feel? Is your head any better? How's your arm?" She wanted to ask if her memory had returned, but she was afraid of upsetting her again.

"I feel much better. My abdomen still hurts where Dr. Fletcher took out my spleen, but its not as bad. My arm really doesn't bother me as long as I keep it still, and Dr. Fletcher says the swelling in my head has gone down a lot. They give me pain medicine when I need it."

For a moment no one spoke. Then Anna asked, "Has either of you seen Larry? He was here last night."

"He was?" Brooke fought to keep her voice down.

"Did he talk to you, dear?" Hattie asked.

"Not really," Anna said. "He just looked down at me with the loveliest expression on his face. He did say he just had to see me and that he would be back, and he left."

"What time was that?" Hattie asked.

"I don't know," said Anna. "It was after everyone had left and the nurse had given me a shot for the pain. I was getting pretty drowsy and didn't say anything to him."

"Oh, I see," said Hattie raising her eyebrows at Brooke.

"No, I don't think you do see, Aunt Hattie," said Anna with a catch in her voice. "I can tell you don't believe he was really here, but he was. I know he was!"

"Don't get excited, please Anna," begged Brooke. "If you saw him, then he was here. We didn't say he wasn't."

"Well, he was!" Anna replied. "He was wearing blue slacks and a navy sweatshirt. His hair was kind of messy, as if he'd rushed here from someplace. And he said something else to me."

"He did? What was it he said?" asked Hattie.

"What he said exactly was, 'I had to see you, Annie my darling. I'll come back when you're better if you let me.' That's all. That's everything." Anna had lifted her head off the pillow as if to emphasize the importance of what she was saying. She let her head fall back and looked exhausted from the small effort of talking.

"Are you sure he called you 'Annie?'" Brooke asked.

"Of course he called me 'Annie.' Didn't I just say that?" Anna was becoming testy and tears threatened to spill. She sighed deeply. "Larry calls me 'Annie' a lot when we're alone. Often 'Annie me darlin'. Didn't you ever know that, either of you? Gram knows it."

Brooke cast a quick glance at Hattie, her eyes wide.

Hattie tried to change the subject. "Let Brooke tell you about her new volunteer job," she suggested.

"Where is that, at school?" Anna asked, switching her focus to Brooke.

"No," said Brooke. "It's here in Doylestown. I'm working on the campaign of Michael DiRienzo. He's testing the waters to see if he has enough support to run in the primaries for his party's nomination for president."

"Who?" Anna was clearly puzzled. "Why aren't you in school?"

Brooke looked at Hattie, who only shrugged her shoulders. "Anna, we must be going for a while," Hattie said gently. "We'll be back later. I hope you'll be in your private room very soon. That will be lovely for you." The women exchanged hugs and cheek kisses, and Hattie and Brooke shut the door quietly behind them.

They went down to the soda shop on the first floor. Neither of them was thirsty, but they ordered Cokes for something to do. "She's even more confused than I thought she would be," Brooke said with concern. "Do you think Larry was really here last night?"

Hattie shook her head. After she paid for the drinks, she stripped the paper off her straw and stuck it into her Coke can. "Oh, Brooke, I don't know what to say. Maybe it would be a good idea if we asked around tonight to see if anyone saw a man in ICU who fit the description Anna gave us of Larry. I tend to think she was dreaming, but maybe she wasn't."

"You know what bothers me?" asked Brooke. "She insists he called her, 'Annie,' that he always did. And on top of that, she still doesn't know that Gram is dead. This is really terrible, Aunt Hattie." She took a tiny sip of her Coke.

"Brooke," Hattie asked, "how well did you know Larry? Do you think...I mean, would it be possible that he might have a reason to want her dead? What happened to make her break their engagement? Did she ever talk to you about it?"

"I wish she had, Aunt Hattie, but she never said a word to me about him after they broke up. You know something, though? I really liked him."

"I felt the same way," Hattie recounted. "I thought he was an extremely nice, intelligent man, and it seemed so obvious to me that he was deeply in love with Anna. Your grandmother thought so, too, and he was in her home a great deal of the time."

"Did Anna uncover some dark, hidden secret, do you suppose?" Brooke guessed. "Something so terrible that he couldn't afford for anyone to know about it?"

In spite of the seriousness of the conversation, Hattie could not help laughing. "Oh, Brooke, I don't think so. I really don't think so. Of course, those things do happen. You read about them in the paper more and more. But Larry and Anna went together for years, and he was well liked and respected at the Spruce Street School."

"Well," Brooke observed, "if everything was so hunky dory at the Spruce Street School, why did he leave at the beginning of the second semester and run away to Seattle?"

"The whole thing is a mystery," agreed Hattie. "It really is, and I honestly don't believe that your grandmother had any idea why Anna broke the engagement. As you said, Anna would never talk about it. She never even mentioned his name once they parted ways."

# 17

Twenty minutes later, Hattie and Brooke returned to Anna's bedside only to find her sound asleep. They decided to go grocery shopping and come back later in the afternoon. They picked up their jackets and carried them from the room.

While walking across the lobby on their way to the door, Alexandra and Cameron came in. "Uh-oh," groaned Brooke when she spotted them.

Alexandra was wearing carefully creased apple green slacks, a matching turtleneck sweater and an apple green and cream plaid blazer. Gold and jade pierced earrings hung below her chin. "You look gorgeous as usual, Mother," Brooke told her sincerely.

"Thank you, Brooke," Alexandra replied cooly. "You look gorgeous yourself. Tell me, where did you get that lovely sweater?"

Brooke had the good grace to look embarrassed, "Oh, is it yours, Mother? I found it in a drawer in my bureau."

"Yes, I know where it was. I put it there. Did you remove the price tag before you put it on, or is it still on it?" Alexandra's manicured hand darted out to the sweater and turned the bottom of the left side up. There, sticking out of the seam, was a price tag.

"I was wondering what was scratching me," declared Brooke with an embarrassed grin.

"You might have asked me, Brooke. It's obviously brand new, and you had to know it was mine. I was planning to wear it today," Alexandra was clearly annoyed.

Brooke stroked the cherry red cashmere sweater fondly. "I really like it," she stated, "and don't you think it goes better with my dark hair than with your blond?"

Alexandra sighed, "Brooke, you are hopeless. I want you to take off that sweater as soon as you get home."

"I'm not going home, Mother," Brooke said patiently. "Didn't Cameron tell you? I'm going to stay with Aunt Hattie for at least a few more days."

"He told me," Alexandra said looking at Cameron. "I did not agree."

Cameron simply shook his head at Brooke.

"When do you plan to go back to school? You are so obviously running your own life." Sarcasm dripped from Alexandra's mouth.

As usual, Brooke was not intimidated. "I," she said, "am not going back until after Thanksgiving. I am not going back until I'm sure that Anna is going to be okay. I don't think that's unreasonable."

Hattie watched the verbal sparring with a touch of amusement. Those two tall, beautiful women glaring at one another, neither giving an inch. They were so much alike in appearance and yet so entirely different in personality.

Alexandra sighed, shrugged her shoulders and acted as if she had just noticed Hattie. "Oh," she said with mock politeness. "How are you, Hattie?"

Hattie nodded somewhat stiffly in response. "And you?" she rejoined.

Alexandra turned back to Brooke, "We shall discuss all of this later. In the meantime, if you insist on staying at Hattie's, we'll stop there on our way home and pick up my sweater." She turned on her heel and followed Cameron to the elevator.

Cameron turned to smile at Hattie and Brooke.

"We'll see you later," he said.

"Phew!" exclaimed Brooke as she and Hattie left the hospital.

At the supermarket Brooke commandeered a shopping cart by the door. "You throw in anything you need for everyday, Aunt Hattie, but, please let me buy the food for our dinner tonight, okay?"

"That wasn't what I had in mind when I asked Shawn to dinner," Hattie said.

"Aunt Hattie, I want to buy everything and to cook it, too. Please, agree," pleaded Brooke.

"I guess so," Hattie said, understanding the need to feel useful.

Brooke hummed as she pushed the cart from aisle to aisle. She hesitated at the meat counter looking at the filet mignon. "I can't eat more than one," she said.

"Neither can I," Hattie stated. Brooke picked up a package of four.

While Hattie filled the cart with essentials, Brooke continued to concentrate on Shawn's dinner. She bought baking potatoes, sour cream and chives, salad fixings, rolls, green beans and almonds, and ice cream. "Do you think I've forgotten anything?" she asked.

"Good heavens, no!" said Hattie. "You're going to prepare a meal fit for a king."

Brooke's eyes danced and her face beamed. "Shawn is a king, Aunt Hattie," she sighed.

Back in Hattie's kitchen they finished putting the groceries away just as the steeple clock on the mantle struck four times. "If we leave for the hospital right away, we can be back in plenty of time to start cooking dinner," Hattie said.

"And," Brooke added, "we'll be sure to be here when Shawn arrives."

Driving back up Pike Road toward the hospital, Hattie was almost blinded by the brilliance of the late afternoon sun. Even the sun visor couldn't cut the glare completely. "This is terrible," she complained, trying to shade her eyes with one hand. It wasn't long, however, until they turned onto the main highway, and the sunlight was no longer a problem.

Hattie glanced over at Brooke, "Do you think you'll be able to take tomorrow off from your volunteer job to go to Philadelphia with me? I really think we should get to your grandmother's house as soon as possible."

"Remind me to ask Shawn tonight if he thinks I can get away. We'll have to find out if Cameron has had the locks changed yet. If not, I still have my own keys."

They parked in the hospital lot and were walking toward the lobby door when they saw Cameron and Alexandra coming out. Brooke walked over to them and said to her mother, "I didn't think you'd be leaving so soon." She pulled open her coat. "I forgot to take your sweater off."

"Oh, Brooke, for heaven's sake," spat Alexandra. "Don't lie to me! We both know you did not forget to take off that sweater. But I'm not going to let you get away with it. Cameron and I are going to the Bon Ton. They're having a sale, and there are a few things I need. We'll stop at Hattie's at about six, and you'd better have that sweater ready for me!"

"Yes, Mother," Brooke said, the barest hint of defeat in her voice.

Cameron interrupted. "I have good news for you both," he said. "Anna has been moved to a private room on the third floor. Number 326. It's at the end of the hall—a nice corner room. We've provided round-the-clock nurses for her." He winked at Hattie behind Alexandra's back and mouthed the word "security."

Alexandra plucked at his coat sleeve, "Come, Cameron, we don't want to miss that sale." She looked pointedly at her daughter, "Six o'clock, Brooke. No excuses."

As Alexandra walked toward the parking lot, Brooke asked him quietly, "Have Gram's locks been changed yet?" He shook his head, "Not until Monday," he said.

Before he could get away, Hattie asked, "Did Anna say anything to you about Larry?"

"No," Cameron answered. "Is she still talking about him?"

"She even says she saw him," Brooke told him.

"When?" asked Cameron.

"Last night after we all left," Hattie said.

"And she says he called her 'Annie.' That he often does," Brooke added.

"No!" Cameron exclaimed. "Do you think she was dreaming?"

"We don't know," Hattie said.

"Cameron!" Alexandra called. "Let's go!" He laughed and shrugged his shoulders. "I'll talk to you later," he said to them a trifle apologetically and left with his wife.

Finding room 326 was no problem. The door was closed, and when Hattie rapped softly, it was opened almost immediately by a young woman in flower-patterned medical scrubs, similar to the outfits worn by many of the nurses.

"Would you please identify yourselves?" she asked politely.

"I'm Anna Turner's sister, Brooke, and this is our Aunt Hattie Farwell," Brooke said. She looked the young nurse over curiously. She was no more than five feet, four inches and slight. Her shoulder-length brown hair hung loosely around a face filled with unremarkable features and hazel eyes. Altogether, she could be described as 'cute' rather than pretty. Brooke wondered how such a petite woman could protect Anna against an attacker.

Hattie wondered the same thing, but she noticed as the young woman led them across the room to Anna's bed that she moved with the grace of an athlete.

"I'm Terri," she introduced herself, not bothering to give a last name. "I'll be here every day from three till eleven. You might remember me. I was assigned to Anna's care in ICU. Shirley Grant will be her night nurse and Amy Franz will be here from seven till three."

The top of Anna's bed had been maneuvered into a sitting position. Anna was wearing a blue nightgown. Her hair had been combed and she was smiling cheerfully at them.

"I'm so glad to see you. Isn't this room nice? It's so great to be out of ICU."

"Anna!" they said together and laughed.

"You look wonderful," Hattie told her. "How do you feel now?"

"Even better than I did earlier when you were in," she chuckled. "How do you like this nightgown? Mother bought it for me. She and Cameron brought it in for me this afternoon." Without giving Hattie a chance to answer, she continued. "Is it warm out? From here it looks like a beautiful, sunny day."

"It is a beautiful day," Hattie said. "But that sun was so bright that it almost blinded me as I drove up Pike Road."

"Blinded by the bright light," Anna said in a monotone. "I was blinded by a bright light. I remember that. Why can't I remember any more?" Hattie and Brooke looked at each other. Should they say anything? No, that would be a mistake. They both looked at Terri.

"I'll tell the doctor," she said, and left the room.

Hattie and Brooke pulled chairs close to Anna's bed. "How is your arm?" asked Brooke, not knowing what to say.

"Good," Anna answered flatly.

"Good," said Brooke, "is your head feeling better?"

"I guess so," Anna sighed. "It really doesn't hurt so much anymore. It's just so frustrating! I get some kind of hazy memory, and just when I think I'll be able to remember what happened, the memory vanishes. It's driving me crazy! It's like trying to catch smoke. Do you think my memory will ever come back to me?" Anna's concern was written all over her face.

"Oh, I do believe it will, darling," Hattie assured her. "You must be patient and try not to force it. Since we're going over all of your problems, how's your abdomen?"

"It still hurts, but the medicine really helps. When do you think I can get out of the hospital? Has the doctor said anything to you? He won't tell me."

"Be patient, for cryin' out loud," Brooke scolded. "You just got out of intensive care. You're pretty beat up, you know."

Anna smiled. "You sound like the big sister. Pardon me for being a baby." She yawned and pressed the button to lower her head. "I've been upright for long enough," she stated.

When the bed was flat, she rolled onto her right side and stared at them, but none of them could think of a thing to say. Anna's eyes grew heavy and finally closed, and within a few moments she was sleeping.

Brooke and Hattie stayed for several minutes more, watching Anna sleep. "This is silly," Hattie whispered. "I think we'd better go." She turned to Terri, the nurse-guard who had come back to the room after she had talked to Anna's doctor. "Will you please tell Anna that we'll be back late tomorrow afternoon or early evening?"

Brooke turned to Hattie as they left, "Anna will get well, won't she Aunt Hattie? She does seem better, don't you think?"

"Oh yes, I do think so," Hattie responded. "We just have to be patient."

"It was hard talking to her, wasn't it? I mean, it was hard trying to be cheerful and pretend that nothing is wrong, wasn't it?"

"Yes it was, darling, but just concentrate on how much better she is every time we see her. Now I think we should talk about our trip to Philadelphia tomorrow."

As they walked down the hall from Anna's room, Brooke looked worried.

"Aunt Hattie, you're taking for granted that I can leave my volunteer job tomorrow, aren't you? But I've only been working on the campaign for one morning, and apparently not doing a very good job at that.

"What do you mean, not doing a very good job?" Hattie asked, in surprise.

Brooke told her about everything that had happened that morning.

"I told Shawn that I really don't believe Maria DiRienzo likes me. She didn't tell me exactly how she wanted me to enter the contributions into the computer until I had finished the whole pile of papers. Then she said my spreadsheet was all wrong and explained in much detail just how it should be done. It's bad enough I have to do the whole thing over, but Maria's exaggerated patience made me feel like an idiot."

"What did Shawn say?" Hattie asked. She pushed the "down" button for the elevator.

"Oh, he thought I was imagining the whole thing. He says Maria is a perfectionist about everything. There is no reason she wouldn't like me, he said, and then he kidded me by saying she was probably jealous because her husband has a reputation for being something of a ladies' man."

"I see," Hattie said, noncommittally.

The elevator doors slid open, and Brooke and Hattie stepped in. They turned their backs to five other people already inside and silently watched the floor indicator over the door as they descended to the main floor.

Betty Kerr Orlemann

# 18

They were surprised when they drove up the lane to find Officer Sawyer's patrol car parked in Hattie's driveway. They could see him at the edge of the woods, but when they drove up, he walked over to greet them.

"Hi, ladies," he called cheerfully.

"Hi, Officer Sawyer," Hattie called back. "Is there something wrong?"

"No, not at all," he responded. "And please call me Jim. 'Officer Sawyer' is much too formal. I'm here because I thought it would be a good idea to look a bit farther through the woods to see if I could find anything else that might indicate a hunter had been in there, especially near the house."

"Did you find anything?" Hattie asked.

"No, nothing," he responded. "I also drove up your cowpath lane and through the Brookside development, and I didn't see any strange cars or pick-up trucks parked anywhere up there. I asked a couple of workmen who were finishing up for the day, and they said they hadn't seen any strange vehicles or people."

"Good," stated Hattie. "Maybe it was just a one-time thing. I'm afraid I overreacted."

"No, I don't think you did, Miss Farwell," Jim Sawyer argued. "Someone who should not have been in your woods fired a shotgun too near your house. You acted appropriately."

He started to get into his car, but Brooke stopped him.

"My sister claims she saw her former fiance last night," she said.

"Yes, but we aren't sure she wasn't dreaming," Hattie interjected. "Won't you come in out of the dark?" she added.

"Thank you. Now tell me about the fiancé," Jim Sawyer ordered as he followed them inside.

"Anna was in a lot of pain, and the nurse had given her some heavy medication for it. Anna admits she was getting drowsy when she saw Larry leaning over her bed," Brooke said.

"Yes," Hattie agreed and added. "She told us he called her 'Annie,' and said he often did. She also told us that he said he would be back when she was feeling better. She's been moved out of intensive care and is now in room 326 with round-the-clock nurse-security guards. There has been no further talk of Larry, to whom, by the way, she still believes she's engaged," Hattie told him.

"So," mused Jim Sawyer. "I take it she has not regained her memory yet."

"No, she hasn't," Brooke said. "But something maybe hopeful happened this afternoon. Aunt Hattie told her how the bright sunlight almost blinded her when she was driving up Pike Road on the way to the hospital, and Anna said, 'Blinded by the bright light, I was blinded by the bright light. I remember that. Why can't I remember any more?' Doesn't that seem hopeful?"

"To tell the truth, I haven't any idea how the mind works, but I guess some memory—even if it is clouded—is better than none at all," Jim Sawyer answered. He pulled his notebook from his pocket and read. "Laurence Adams, that's the name of Anna Turner's former fiancé, right?"

"Yes," the women answered in unison.

"According to my records, he lived in center city Philadelphia near the Spruce Street School where he was the assistant principal until last December, when he suddenly left his position and moved to Seattle, Washington. He worked at the Spruce Street School for almost five years, my records state."

Hattie added, "He and Anna met at the school where she taught fifth grade. They went together for several years before becoming engaged. We all liked Larry and, as I said before, we have no idea why Anna broke off their engagement. They seemed to be so much in love."

"I'm waiting for some information on him from Seattle. His background seems clean. He grew up in Philadelphia, went to public schools and Temple University, where he graduated with honors from the undergraduate school...majored in education. He also earned his masters and PhD degrees at Temple. His parents were hardworking, decent folks from what I was told. His father owned a hardware store on Chestnut Street. His mother was a housewife who sometimes helped out at the store. Laurence helped earn his way through college by working for his father. The whole family was popular in the community. Laurence's younger sister Corinne is married and living in South Jersey with her husband and baby. Mr. and Mrs. Adams are retired and still living in the same house on Pine Street. There's nothing to indicate that Laurence might have been mixed up in anything sordid." Sawyer flipped the cover shut on his little notebook and returned it to his pocket.

"That's reassuring," Hattie said. "Anna's vision of him was probably a dream. By the way, did he have his own apartment on Spruce Street when he was at the school?"

"Yes, he did. As a matter of fact, he lost a month's rent when he moved away so suddenly. It seems he had a number of good friends at the school, and I've talked to some of them. No one can figure out why the engagement was broken, or why he left town the way he did. From what they tell me there was no one else for him or for Anna."

"Thanks, Jim, for sharing all of your research with us. The information is very interesting. And mysterious," Hattie said.

"I'm happy to help," Jim replied. "I really enjoy detective work and I'm pleased that the chief has allowed me to work on this case."

Brooke had been looking at him with interest. She thought he was very bright and would help solve Anna's case.

"I have to run upstairs and change my sweater, but when I come down, tell me how you became a cop," she said.

She was back in an instant, wearing a green sweater and carrying the red one. "Okay," she said. "Now tell me how you became a cop."

He looked her over appreciatively before answering, "This will sound crazy to you, but I originally majored in archaeology in college," he laughed. "After fooling with that for my freshman year, I decided there was no future in it for me. So I started looking around for something I would like better. The more I thought about criminal work the more it appealed to me, so I switched my major to criminology. After graduation, I heard that there was an opening on the force here and applied. The rest is history." The officer paused. "Now I believe that eventually I'd like to be a lawyer, probably a prosecutor. So when I have enough money saved for tuition, I'll go back to school—law school this time."

"You know," Brooke said solemnly, "that's really impressive. A mid-life career change and back to school? Not an easy thing."

"Nah, not really," Jim said with an embarrassed smile. "And what do you mean by mid-life?"

Hattie laughed to herself. Jim couldn't be much older than thirty.

She glanced at the clock. It was nearly six. Without saying anything, she turned on the oven and began washing the baking potatoes. She smiled to herself. She knew she was absolutely unnecessary in the conversation taking place between Jim and Brooke. Jim was clearly attracted, but Hattie knew Brooke had eyes only for Shawn.

Still unnoticed, Hattie placed the potatoes in the oven. Wolf poked her arm with his nose, indicating he wanted to go out. Hattie patted the massive head.

"Poor Wolf," she said softly. "I've been ignoring you, haven't I?"

She took her sweater and the dog's leash from their hooks by the door, turned on the porch light and spotlights, and slipped out, not wanting to interrupt the friendly banter. It was cool, crisp and clear outside, and a full moon made a flashlight unnecessary.

Somewhere nearby a barn owl hooted and was soon answered by another off in the woods. Hattie took a deep breath, stretched and smiled. There was something about a moonlit night that was magic.

She didn't bother to hook Wolf's leash onto his collar. He trotted along beside her, taking only short jaunts off to the side of the lane. They strolled together up the lane for a while and had turned to go back into the house when Hattie saw headlights coming toward them from the Pike Road.

She walked up onto the porch holding Wolf's collar. The car parked next to the police car. She had been so sure that it was Shawn arriving that for an instant she was startled to see Cameron and Alexandra, whom she'd forgotten about, getting out of the car.

**147**

"Good evening, Hattie," Cameron greeted her in his usual courteous manner.

"Hello, Hattie," Alexandra said cooly.

"Good evening to you both. Won't you come in?" Hattie said as she held the door open for them.

"We can't stay," Alexandra stated. "We have to meet some friends for dinner, and I must hurry home and dress."

"What," asked Cameron with a note of concern in his voice, "is a police car doing here?"

"Oh, Officer Sawyer is just checking on a complaint of a poacher in the woods," Hattie stated in an offhand way.

Brooke greeted them near the kitchen door with her mother's red cashmere sweater in her hand. Wolf went over to sniff it.

"Don't let that beast drool all over my good sweater!" Alexandra exclaimed. She grabbed the sweater from Brooke. "Now I'll have to take it to the cleaner's before I can wear it, and it was brand new!"

"Wolf didn't drool on the sweater, Mother," Brooke stated. "Look at it. It's still like new."

"Didn't you wear it all day?" Alexandra demanded in her haughtiest of tones. For the first time she acknowledged the presence of Jim Sawyer and gave a slight nod in his direction. "Hello," she said. "Hattie told us there was a poacher in the woods."

Brooke stepped in. "Mother, this is Officer Jim Sawyer. Jim this is my mother, Alexandra MacArthur and my stepfather, Dr. Cameron MacArthur."

Jim shook hands with Cameron. Alexandra made no move to shake his hand so he simply smiled at her and said. "There can be no doubt that you and Brooke are closely related, but you honestly look more like her sister than her mother."

For the first time since her arrival Alexandra smiled. "That's what some people tell me," she said immodestly. Cameron took hold of her arm. "We'd better leave, dear," he told her. "You said yourself that we have to change before dinner."

They were crossing the porch when Shawn's car roared up the lane and came to a rapid stop in front of the barn. He jumped from the car and ran across the lawn. It wasn't until he was almost to the porch that he saw Alexandra and Cameron.

"Dr. and Mrs. MacArthur," he greeted them with his usual wide, friendly smile. "It's good to see you again."

Cameron said. "It's good to see you again too, Shawn," and shook his hand firmly. Alexandra gave him the slightest of smiles and simply said. "Good evening, Shawn."

Brooke, who had been standing in the doorway, rushed forward and embraced him. "Hi," she said. "I'm cooking your dinner. I've planned the whole thing, and you'd better like it."

"You know I will," he responded. "I love everything you do."

Cameron was smiling as he helped Alexandra into the car, but she sucked her teeth and emitted a small disgusted noise. "Ach!"

Jim stepped onto the porch behind Hattie. Both had been observing the little scene, Hattie with amusement, Jim with confusion.

"Oh, Jim," Brooke said. "I want you to meet my fiancé. This is Shawn O'Brien. Shawn, this is Officer Jim Sawyer. He's been working with us on Anna's accident-that-might-not-be-an-accident."

The men shook hands. Shawn, who was at least six inches taller than Jim, looked down at him with a smile, but he put his left arm possessively around Brooke as he did.

"What brings you here this evening?" Shawn demanded somewhat suspiciously.

"Nothing, really," Hattie jumped in. "He came after I told him about that gunshot this morning."

"Oh, yes," Shawn said, remembering. "It came from right near the barn. Scared us quite a bit, I must say. Did you find anything?"

"I found a shotgun shell in the woods about 50 feet from the barn. Nothing else," Jim said. His eyes appraised Shawn. "I should go," he said to Hattie.

"I'll walk with you to your car," Hattie offered.

"Goodbye everybody," Jim said.

"So long, Jim. It was fun talking to you," said Brooke.

"It was nice meeting you," said Shawn, putting his arm around Brooke's waist as they walked into the kitchen.

"Who's that?" Jim asked Hattie when he was sure he couldn't be overheard.

"They say they're engaged," Hattie told him. "They met a year ago at a party at Harvard, where Shawn is a student. Brooke, if she hasn't told you, is a senior at a boarding school nearby. "She's very young, Jim, and very naive in the ways of the world. She's not even eighteen yet."

"You're kidding!" Jim exclaimed. "I thought she was at least twenty. She's very mature in how she carries herself, isn't she?"

Hattie nodded. "She's a very bright girl."

As Jim was driving away Hattie could have sworn that she heard him mutter, "Damn!"

# 19

Shawn again spent the night at Hattie's, and Hattie once more slept with the door between her room and Brooke's wide open.

It wasn't that she didn't really trust the young people. Despite the fact that she had never married, she knew all about raging hormones and youth, and she didn't want to feel responsible for anything that happened to Brooke on her watch. She cared deeply about Brooke, and was, she admitted, a bit intimidated by Alexandra, who had so reluctantly permitted Brooke to stay with her.

She went to sleep with moonlight illuminating her room and barn owls calling to one another in the woods. She awoke to a gray predawn haze and the honking of Canada Geese as they flew over her house on their way to the Delaware River.

A quick peek into Brooke's room showed her sleeping soundly. "Good," thought Hattie. "I can enjoy a little time to myself." She descended the winding stairs to the kitchen, started a generous pot of coffee and built a fire in the walk-in fireplace.

Wolf pranced at the door while she worked. Hattie put on her sweater and grabbed his leash. Before she even had the door completely open, wolf ran across the porch, through the gate and disappeared into the woods on the opposite side of the lane.

"No, Wolf, no!" she called after him. "Come back!"

Terrified that the poacher might be back, she ran into the woods after the dog.

"Wolf!" she called. "Wo-olf!" If it weren't for the heavy mist, she could have seen a short distance between the bare deciduous trees and beneath the browse line of the cedars and other evergreens. As it was the mist would probably not lift until the sun was fully up.

The hazy form of a white-tailed doe leapt gracefully over a fallen tree not twenty feet from where Hattie stood. Behind her two more deer leapt over the same tree and disappeared after the lead doe into the fog. They paid no attention to Hattie. There was no sound from Wolf, and she knew he'd be right behind the deer if he were anywhere close. Where could he be? Hattie continued into the fog.

A red-tailed hawk screeched unseen in the sky above. The day was brightening. Hattie walked a little farther down the trail. Suddenly, she saw the shadowy figure of a man coming toward her. She caught her breath and stood still.

"Who's there?" the shadow called, nervously. "Who is it?"

She recognized Shawn's voice. "It's Hattie, Shawn," she responded quickly. When she spoke, Wolf bounded up to her from a spot on the trail right behind Shawn.

"Thank God, it's you," breathed a visibly relieved Shawn. "I was afraid you were the poacher. I went deeper into the woods than I had intended, and then I got all turned around and wasn't sure which way was back to your house. If Wolf hadn't come to my rescue, I don't know what I would have done."

"What were you doing up and out in the woods so early?" she wanted to know.

They came to the lane and walked side-by-side back to the house. Shawn explained, "I woke up and couldn't get back to sleep, so I went over to look out of my window. Everything was foggy, of course, but I saw a movement on the ground at the edge of the woods and realized that I was looking at a flock of wild turkeys—maybe eight or ten of them. I'd never seen anything like that before, so I decided to get dressed and go for a walk. Maybe there would be more of them. It was really very exciting."

"Yes, it is exciting to see wild animals in their natural habitat," Hattie agreed. "Nature is thrilling. Did you see any more turkeys?"

They walked through the gate and up the flagstone walk to the porch. "No more turkeys," Shawn said. "But I did see some deer. Growing up in the city, the only wild animals I ever saw were pigeons, sparrows, squirrels in the park and occasionally rats and mice, except for the zoo, of course."

In the kitchen he sniffed deeply. "Boy, that coffee smells good!" he exclaimed.

They were drinking their coffee when Brooke came down the winding stairs looking bright-eyed and rested. Shawn stood up and gave her a big hug. Brooke helped herself to a mug of coffee and poured cream into it. While Hattie scrambled eggs, Brooke made and buttered toast. She poured more coffee into everyone's mug before she sat down for breakfast.

While they were eating she broached the subject of going to Philadelphia with Hattie instead of working on the campaign that day. To her amazement, Shawn was annoyed, even angry. "Why do you have to go to Philadelphia today?" he demanded. "You have a ton of work to do for Maria. You know that."

Brooke found herself angry, too. "I am only a volunteer, you know. I guess if I want to take a day off I can. What is Maria going to do? Fire me?"

Hattie spoke calmly. "It is only one day, Shawn, and we really want to see if the purse the police have was Annie's. And we want to see if we can find anything in hers and Anna's house that points to the killer. The locks

**153**

are to be changed on Monday, Cameron said, so we have to go in while our keys still work."

"Tomorrow's Saturday," Shawn said to Brooke. With barely disguised sarcasm, he asked, "Can you bring yourself to work on a Saturday?"

Brooke found herself irritated by his tone and his sarcasm. "Maybe I'll never bring myself to work on the stupid campaign ever again!" she yelled, sounding every bit like the seventeen-year-old she was.

Shawn's face turned red. "This campaign is very important. Petty self-interests are completely out of place!" He glared at Brooke. "Do you know how much I care about Michael? How much I appreciate all he has done for me? You can be a bigger help than you realize. I was counting on you."

"Are you suggesting that going to my grandmother's house to look for clues to her murder is petty self-interest?" Brooke asked through clenched teeth.

"When a person commits to something, she should follow through!" Shawn growled. "November might seem early to the uninitiated, but Michael has a lot of work to do to get ready for the spring primaries. The work Maria gave you is important and ongoing, and you just can't take days off when you feel like it!"

"I can't believe you!" Brooke shouted. "You have no consideration at all for what I'm going through, have you?" She stood with her hands on her hips and glared at him with an anger he had never seen in her before.

He matched it with his own.

"I told you that Michael's campaign needs you—needs everyone it can recruit. You promised me, and I promised Maria, and she is counting on you. Why can't you and Miss Farwell go to Philadelphia on Sunday? Miss Farwell said the locks won't be changed until Monday."

"Because," shouted Brooke, "we are going today! You can just tell your precious Maria Mouse that!"

"The hell I will!" Shawn shouted back. "Here," he said, scribbling on a piece of paper. "Here is Maria's number. You call her yourself!" He slammed the paper down on the table and turned and stormed out of the house.

Hattie sighed deeply and Brooke burst into tears.

"We really don't have to go into the city today, dear," Hattie said softly as she patted Brooke's shoulder. "Please, don't be so upset. If you want to work on the campaign, I'll understand. Shawn was right, we could go on Sunday."

"Well, we won't!" Brooke said firmly, her chin jutting forward. "You said yourself that the killer probably has Gram's keys, and the sooner we get there the better."

Brooke ran upstairs to wash her face and apply her makeup while Hattie cleaned up the kitchen. She scraped the leftover scrambled eggs into Wolf's dish with regret. It had started out to be such a nice breakfast, she thought. She had been a trifle surprised at the degree of Shawn's anger and hoped he would get his temper under control if his romance with Brooke were to lead to marriage.

Fifteen minutes later, they were ready to leave for the train station.

"Brooke, dear, I really think it would be courteous if you called Mrs. DiRienzo before we go," Hattie suggested.

"You're right, I suppose," Brooke sighed, reaching for the paper with Maria's number on it. It was still early, and Brooke was secretly wishing that Maria would not yet be at campaign headquarters. She was disappointed when she answered the phone.

To Brooke's surprise, Maria didn't seem the least bit annoyed that she was taking the day off.

"Oh, I'm sorry that you can't come in today, Brooke," Maria said casually. "I hope your sister isn't worse."

"No, as a matter of fact, she's better, and in a private room," Brooke told her. "Actually, she's so much better that I'm going with an old friend to my grandmother's house in Philadelphia. She's the one who was killed last Saturday night, you know, and we want to see if there is anything in her house which might lead to her killer."

"Hasn't your sister regained her memory, yet?" Maria wanted to know. "Maybe she could tell you something."

"No, I'm sorry to say," Brooke said regretfully. "As I told you yesterday, the doctor isn't sure she will."

"That's a terrible shame," Maria commiserated. "Well, you just take the day off and do whatever you have to do. It's best to get your problems off your mind before you attempt to concentrate on your job here. And, I must add, we are very grateful to you for volunteering your time to my husband's campaign." In what seemed an afterthought, she added. "Do you think you could possibly come in tomorrow? I know it's a Saturday, so if you can't, we'll all understand."

Grateful for the chance to prove her dedication, Brooke gladly agreed.

"Yes, I'll be there," Brooke said. "Would nine o'clock be okay? And, Maria, thank you for being so understanding."

"Nine o'clock will be fine," Maria said. "Maybe I'll even take some time off today myself. My windows need washing."

After Brooke had hung up she laughed. "That woman is a nut about cleaning her house. Shawn told me she is forever cleaning or polishing something."

"Was she mad at you?" Hattie asked.

"Not at all," Brooke responded. "She was as sweet as pie. So phooey to Mr. Shawn O'Brien!"

# 20

They parked in what seemed to be the last parking place at the Doylestown SEPTA Station and had only a few minutes to wait before the four-car electric train pulled up to the platform.

Once seated on the train and headed for Philadelphia, Brooke turned her gaze from the passing scene beyond the window and looked at Hattie.

"I've been wondering," she remarked, "why Shawn was so absolutely furious at me this morning. It didn't seem like him at all. I've never even seen him mad before."

"I've been thinking about that," Hattie replied. "I believe the primary reason for his explosion was the fact that he had been looking forward to taking you to the office with him and spending the day with you. I think he was just very disappointed."

"That's awfully childish, isn't it?" asked Brooke. "It seems to me there must be another reason. After all, it's not like I quit or anything."

"Well, it was kind of controlling. But he is very invested in Michael DiRienzo's campaign and wants everything to go just right. Mostly, though, I think he wanted to show you off to Mr. DiRienzo and perhaps some other people. He's very proud of you, you know. You are a very beautiful young woman, Brooke."

"Oh, Aunt Hattie!" Brooke exclaimed. "That's terrible! You make it sound as if Shawn looks at me like a thing—a possession!"

"Don't be angry, Brooke, but it is a possibility. He wouldn't be the first man to think that way. And you really don't know him very well."

"But we met a whole year ago!'

Hattie smiled indulgently.

"Honey, your time with him has been spent at parties and fun things, not doing serious activities like political campaigns. And last summer, you didn't see one another at all. I know to you a year seems like a long time, but you really don't know much about Shawn. You've never met his family or seen their home. I'm sorry, dear, but I believe you should get to know him and everything you can about him, before you commit your life to him."

"Don't you like Shawn, Aunt Hattie?" Brooke asked with a worried frown.

"I like what I've seen—except for that temper—but I hardly know the boy."

"Mother doesn't like him," Brooke stated with some distaste, "but that's probably because she thinks we're better than he is."

"You're so young, Brooke. You should be dating lots of boys. And frankly, Shawn should be seeing other girls, too." She didn't miss the look of alarm that passed across Brooke's face. "You could keep on seeing each other if that's what you want, but maybe not so seriously."

"Oh," replied Brooke flatly. She turned and shifted her gaze out the window again. Hattie thought at first that Brooke would give her an argument, but then she was afraid that she had overstepped her bounds and made Brooke angry.

Neither spoke for a while.

Finally Brooke, without taking her eyes from the window, said, "Thank you, Aunt Hattie. I know you're just concerned. I appreciate your thoughts."

Hattie reached over and patted Brooke's hand.

Again they lapsed into silence. Eventually Brooke changed the subject, "Aunt Hattie, next Thursday is Thanksgiving. What plans have you made?"

Hattie turned her head and looked at the girl's profile. "I haven't made any plans, Brooke. With all that's happened recently, I just haven't thought that far ahead."

"That's what I thought," Brooke answered, "and I think that's a big mistake. We've always celebrated Thanksgiving together at your house. The hard thing will be that Gram won't be with us, but if we don't do it this year, maybe we won't ever do it again. I don't know about you, but I think we need this ritual. We should celebrate Thanksgiving at your house again."

It was Hattie's turn to stare outside. The train rounded a curve and a weak shaft of sunlight penetrated the dirty film on the window. They were nearing the city now. Fields and forests had long since given way to housing developments and suburban scenes. Now the train was passing closed-up factories and row houses. Soon they would reach Suburban Station.

"It won't be Thanksgiving without your grandmother," Hattie stated.

"Nothing will ever be the same without Gram," Brooke agreed. "But we can't pretend that holidays don't exist. We have to go on without her. That's what she would want us to do."

"You are a wise child," Hattie turned and smiled at Brooke. "And I know you're right. But what about your mother? Won't she want to take you someplace as she always has for the holiday?"

"I doubt it," Brooke answered. "Don't forget that Anna might be home, and I don't think she will be able to travel anyplace. Nor would she want to, I'm sure. And if she is still in the hospital, Mother probably wouldn't want to go away and leave her."

"Of course not," Hattie said and fell silent once more.

"Brooke," Hattie said suddenly, "would you think me crazy if I invited your mother and Cameron to Thanksgiving dinner? Do you think they'd come?"

"Only one way to find out!" Brooke said. Flush with victory, she was elated. "On top of everything else I feel, I just love the tradition. Do you realize," she continued, "that you have a perfect house for Thanksgiving? It's so old and cozy and early American."

"Here we are," Hattie observed. She stood up before the train had fully stopped and started for the exit with Brooke right behind her. When they were on the sidewalk in front of the station, she hailed a cab to take them to the police station Jim had told them to go to.

They stayed just long enough to identify themselves and look through Annie's purse. It contained a pair of broken reading glasses and a hanky. Her wallet was gone, as was her comb, a pen and a box of cough drops. Hattie signed an affidavit identifying it as having belonged to Annie. She and Brooke were both silent during the cab ride to Annie's house.

Hattie brought up the subject of Thanksgiving again as they rode to Walnut Street.

"We'll serve dinner in the dining room as we always did," she said. "When we get home I'll call Alexandra and Cameron. Then tomorrow I'll order a turkey from the butcher."

"I'll help you with the shopping and everything," Brooke offered enthusiastically. "I'll make the stuffing with you and help cook all of the vegetables and bake the pie. Oh, Aunt Hattie, it will be fun."

"Yes," Hattie responded. But when they pulled up in front of Annie's house, she wasn't sure that it would be fun at all. She knew all too well that she was no favorite of Alexandra's. And on the off chance the MacArthurs did accept her invitation, Hattie wondered if the atmosphere would be tense.

The keys slipped into the regular lock and the deadbolt with ease. They opened the door and found a pile of mail lying on the floor where it had been pushed through the slot as if everything were normal. Hattie scooped it up and placed it on the mahogany table next to the wall.

"We'll have to take that home with us," Brooke observed. There could be some mail for Gram that needs attention from her executor or lawyer."

"Of course," Hattie answered. "Let's remember before we leave to get a bag for it from the pantry."

Hattie put her cape—and Brooke, her jacket—on a chair in the hall. Brooke started to go into Anna's apartment, but Hattie stopped her.

"We can go in there later," she said. "I think we should look in your grandmother's sitting room first."

Brooke followed Hattie up the stairs. She stopped just inside the door to the sitting room, and swallowed a lump in her throat.

"Everything looks and smells just the same," she said, with tears in her eyes. "It's as if Gram were just in another room."

"That's where she is, darling, just in another room," Hattie said softly, her own eyes full of tears. She tried unsuccessfully to make her voice sound calm and firm. "Well, let's get started."

They searched through Annie's desk for anything that might have to do with the fatal night, but they found nothing. At last Hattie dumped the contents of the

**161**

wastebasket onto the flat surface of the desk, and they began to paw through the discarded papers. Most were crumpled up and some were torn into small pieces.

"I believe I've found the letter!" Hattie cried, holding a wadded piece of cream-colored notepaper out for Brooke to see. Very carefully she pressed it on the desk.

"Annie, dear," Hattie read aloud, "I know how much you enjoy Beethoven so am enclosing two Philadelphia Orchestra tickets for Saturday evening..."

"That's interesting," Brooke interrupted. "I didn't know Gram was such a Beethoven fan. I always knew Anna loved Beethoven, though. I wonder how the person who sent the tickets knew Gram did, too?"

"Hmmm, what makes you believe that Anna loves Beethoven?" asked Hattie.

"Well," Brooke said, "when she and Larry were going together, even before they were engaged, they went to every Beethoven concert they could get to. Sometimes they took Gram with them. Anna used to tell me all about it in her letters."

"Hmmm," Hattie repeated. "That is interesting."

Brooke continued to look through the contents of the wastepaper basket. "Aunt Hattie, look!" she cried. "Here's the envelope, and it's just like you said. It's written in the same shaky handwriting as the note, and there is no return address."

Hattie took the envelope and placed it and the note in her purse. "Unfortunately, I'm not sure if it's too late to find the sender's fingerprints on either of these, but I'm sure Jim will be interested in seeing them anyhow." They found nothing else of interest in the sitting room or elsewhere on the second floor so decided to go to the first floor to look through Anna's apartment.

"We mustn't be too nosy here, or Anna will be very upset with us when she gets well," Hattie said. "However, if her life is at stake, there just might be something here to tell us why."

In the living room they looked through the papers in Anna's desk, but found nothing other than school-related items. There was nothing of significance in her bedroom, and since the only other room in her apartment, besides the bathroom, was the tiny kitchen, their search was soon over.

Back in the entrance hall they both looked quickly over the mail. "Mostly bills it seems," observed Brooke. "I'll run back to the pantry to get a plastic bag for them."

She disappeared down the hall toward the back of the house while Hattie was putting on her cape. Suddenly she heard Brooke scream followed by the terrible clatter of someone falling down a flight of wooden stairs.

Hattie dropped her purse, the plastic bag containing Annie's purse and her cape and ran toward the cellar stairs. The coat closet door was open, but Hattie was so alarmed about Brooke that the fact did not register with her. Too late, she realized that someone was hiding behind the door. Before she could react, she was shoved into the closet and the door was slammed shut.

Hattie fumbled in the dark for the door knob. During her frantic groping she heard the front door close noisily. When she finally released herself from the closet, there was no one in sight.

She ran back to the cellar stairs in time to see a dazed Brooke stumbling from the top step into the pantry. "Did you fall down the stairs? Or did someone push you? Do you need a doctor?" Hattie cried.

"I'm not hurt," said Brooke. "And I didn't see anyone, but someone did push me down the stairs. And no, I don't need a doctor. It just scared me half to death. I found the plastic bags stuffed onto a shelf at the top of the stairs, and I was leaning over to pull one out, when I felt a mighty shove and fell down the stairs. Luckily I grabbed the railing before I hit bottom, or it could have been serious. I'll have some nasty bruises, but I'm not hurt, thank goodness."

"Well, we'll just look you over. I'm so relieved you're not seriously injured. It scared the life out of me, too," said Hattie. "It would seem that the same person—and we must assume it was the murderer, pushed me into the hall coat closet and slammed the door. By the time I found the door knob and got out, that person was gone."

They walked back into Anna's kitchen where Hattie helped Brooke look herself over. There was no blood, but bruises were already forming. Brooke wet a paper towel under the spigot and wiped her face. "There," she said. "Good as new," but Hattie noticed her hands were shaking.

Hattie called for a taxi. She helped Brooke on with her coat, and picked up her cape and put it on. It was then that she noticed that her purse and the plastic bag containing Annie's purse had been hidden under the cape. She looked through her purse quickly and found with relief that everything, including the envelope and note to Annie, were where she had put them. They put the mail into a plastic bag.

Brooke leaned against the back of her seat on the train and closed her eyes. Hattie looked at her with concern but said nothing. She realized that she herself was pretty shaken, so followed Brooke's example and leaned back in her seat to rest her eyes.

The gentle movement of the train and the clack of its wheels were soporific, and soon Hattie dozed off. Somewhere in the relaxed state between sleep and consciousness she saw the open closet door. There was someone hiding behind the door. Who was it? Why push Brooke down the cellar stairs? Why shove Hattie into the closet? Was it someone who meant them great harm?

*No*, thought Hattie. *Nobody tried to hurt her, just wanted her out of the way in order to escape from the house. Was it the killer? Had Brooke been in the way, too—or was it something more sinister?*

She re-created the scene in her mind, but try as she would, she could not see the person who shoved her. All she remembered was that it was someone strong, but she had no idea if it was a big or small individual.

It had to be the killer. The person who deliberately ran down Annie and tried to kill Anna. The same person who went back to Fifteenth and Locust Streets and found Annie's purse lying against the curb and took it, because the purse contained two orchestra tickets and the keys to Annie's house. Obviously the killer had used the keys to get into the house today.

Hattie believed she and Brooke had arrived when the killer was searching Anna's apartment. *The mail,* she thought, *was there anything important there? Someone could easily have searched through the mail and taken a letter. Did that happen?* How would they ever know? There had to be a reason someone would inflict all this pain and apprehension on other people. What could it be? Who was filled with such hate?

Hattie opened her eyes and found Brooke staring at her. "Were you asleep, Aunt Hattie?" she asked.

"No, not really," Hattie told her. "I was just trying to fathom why anyone would want to do such terrible things to your family. It makes no sense at all."

"I was thinking about everything, too," Brooke said. "One thing I do remember is that the closet door was wide open when I went down the hall to the pantry, but it was closed when we first went into the house."

"You know, I thought it was closed, too, but I just couldn't remember for sure," Hattie concurred. "But now I do remember. It was definitely closed when we got there. You're right."

"That means," Brooke stated, "that someone—I guess it was the killer—was hiding in the closet all the time we were in Anna's apartment. He must have hidden in there when we came downstairs."

"I guess we came out of Anna's sooner than expected," Hattie surmised. "The killer ran from the closet to the back of the house. So did you, so you had to be pushed down the stairs to get you out of the way. The same thing with me in the closet."

A thought suddenly occurred to Brooke. "Aunt Hattie, do you suppose it's someone we know?"

"I don't know, Brooke. I just don't know. I certainly hope not." A chill ran down Hattie's spine.

# 21

The two women drove directly to the hospital from the station. To their delighted surprise Anna was sitting up in an armchair when Terri admitted them to her room.

"Anna, you look wonderful!" Brooke told her sister. "How do you feel?" She kissed her softly on her cheek.

Anna smiled brightly at them both and happily accepted a peck on the cheek from Hattie as well. "I'm so much better," she told them. "I even walked down the hall this morning."

"That's just terrific," Brooke exclaimed. "You should be out of here real soon."

"Dr. Fletcher told me I might be well enough to go home for Thanksgiving. The trouble is, I don't know what plans have been made for Thanksgiving. Mother hasn't mentioned it."

"I want to have Thanksgiving dinner at my house," Hattie said. "Brooke has promised to help me. Of course, I want you there, and I plan to invite your mother and Cameron."

"How nice of you, Aunt Hattie," Anna said. "Would it be okay if Larry came, too?"

Brooke and Hattie glanced at one another. Neither spoke.

Anna looked from one woman to the other. "Well? Would you mind inviting Larry?" Anna persisted. I mean, it is your house, after all."

"No, darling, I wouldn't mind inviting Larry," Hattie said. "I'll see if he can come as soon as we get home. It's getting late now, so I'll call him as soon as we get home, before we eat dinner." She shot a warning glance at Brooke and shrugged her shoulders.

Alexandra and Cameron chose that precise moment to enter the room, and Hattie was actually glad to see both of them. Now the subject would be changed, thank goodness. Alexandra rushed to Anna and kissed her on the forehead.

"You look marvelous, darling!" she exclaimed. "Are they treating you well?"

"They're wonderful to me, Mother," Anna said. "But still, I'm getting ready to leave here."

"Don't rush things," Cameron warned. "It's only three days since your accident and all that went along with it." He leaned over and kissed her cheek.

Hattie cleared her throat.

"Alexandra," she began tentatively, "I would like to have Thanksgiving dinner at my house, and I'd very much like to have you and Cameron and the girls there, too."

To her surprise, Alexandra accepted immediately.

"Hattie, that would be lovely. We'd be happy to join you, and I'm grateful you thought to include us."

"Yes, indeed," Cameron agreed. "Thank you, Hattie." He smiled and bowed slightly toward Hattie.

"Well, it's settled, then," Hattie said, with a smile. "I'm delighted you'll be coming.

"Would you like us to bring a pumpkin pie?" Alexandra offered. "I have a wonderful baker in New Hope. How about rolls, too?"

"That would be perfect," Hattie said, trying to conceal her surprise. "That's very thoughtful of you. Of course, I'll see you before Thursday, but two o'clock would be a good time for me, if it's convenient for you."

They all agreed on the time.

Anna said. "I hope I'll be there, too. I'm recovering

very quickly. I really want to be there, and I've asked Aunt Hattie if she'll ask Larry to come, too."

"Larry?" Alexandra said in surprise. "Why Anna, don't you remember..."

Cameron interrupted her before she could finish her sentence. "I've been talking to Dr. Fletcher every day, and he tells me he's amazed at the speed of your recovery. But it's a little too early for you to make any plans for Thanksgiving until he says so. Let's just take this one day at a time, alright, my dear?"

"Dr. Fletcher told me I might be able to go home for Thanksgiving," Anna said, not quite pouting. "I already told Aunt Hattie and Brooke that."

Alexandra was staring at Anna's face. "When does that bandage come off?" she asked.

"I don't know," Anna answered with a puzzled frown. "Why do you ask?"

"Oh, I guess it's silly of me," Alexandra said with a little shrug. "But I was just hoping you won't have a scar. Your eyes are still all black and blue, you know, but I know they'll clear up after awhile. I was worried about a permanent scar, that's all. Of course you could always have plastic surgery."

"Alexandra, for heaven's sake!" scolded Cameron. "What would make you say such a thing? Don't you think Anna has enough to worry her, without your adding to her troubles?"

To everyone's surprise, Anna laughed.

"Don't worry about me, Cameron," she said. "We should all be used to Mother. She didn't mean to scare me, and she didn't. She just says whatever comes into her mind at the moment." She smiled indulgently at her mother, as if she were the parent and Alexandra the child.

A moment's uncomfortable silence was followed by a loud crash in the hall near Anna's door. Cameron jumped to his feet and was in the hall in an instant, followed closely by Terri. Brooke started to follow them, but Hattie grabbed her arm.

"We'd better stay here with Anna," she whispered.

Brooke nodded knowingly.

Alexandra remained in her chair, staring at the door.

"Oh!" she gasped, her right hand pressed to her chest. "What in the world was that? It scared the life out of me."

"It was probably just a clumsy person knocking something off one of the many carts left in that hallway," Hattie assured her.

Nevertheless, Alexandra wasn't the only one clearly startled by the loud noise. Anna's face around her bruises was white, her eyes as wide as the swelling would permit. Then a knowing look crept into those eyes. She was remembering something.

"A...a car...followed me," she said, "when I was going to your house, Aunt Hattie. I remember everything now." She blinked rapidly. "I can't describe the car because it was so dark, but it clung to my rear bumper. Its headlights were so bright, I was almost blinded."

She swallowed and stared into space. In a voice completely void of emotion, she continued reliving her nightmare.

"I tried to adjust my rearview mirrors to get the light out of my eyes, but I was driving so fast I was afraid to take my hand off the wheel. I knew I shouldn't let the other car push me faster and faster like that, but I was so scared. I wanted to get away from it."

She sat forward in her chair, still staring.

"I finally pushed the overhead mirror out of the way, but the side mirrors were still reflecting that piercing light into my eyes. I was on the Pike Road and getting close to your lane, Aunt Hattie. I had to slow down. It was so dark and I was afraid I'd miss it.

"I tapped my brakes to warn the car behind me, but it kept on coming. I tapped my brakes again, and when I slowed down, that car plowed into the rear of my car with a loud crash...that one in the hallway just brought it back.

"I ran off the road. I remember trying to control the car as it ripped through the woods, but I couldn't. It lurched to one side and then the other. I cracked my head on the side window and back into the head rest. The last thing I remember is hitting my head with tremendous force, and the car starting to roll over."

Cameron had re-entered the room during Anna's recounting of her ordeal. He stood looking at her as she spoke. Terri was behind him, carrying a medicine tray. He turned to face her.

"I think we'd better get this young lady back into bed," he suggested.

Terri placed the tray on a table, nodded her head in agreement and moved immediately to Anna's chair. Between them, they carefully transported Anna back into her bed, where she leaned back and shut her eyes in obvious relief. She seemed completely drained of energy.

"I also remember little snippets of other things," she said, without opening her eyes.

"Such as?" Cameron gently coaxed.

"Wolf," said Anna. "Wolf licked my face, I remember that. I came to one time and he was lying next to me. He was so warm." Eyes still closed, she lay trying to remember something else.

"Don't strain, Anna," Cameron told her. "It will come on its own—in its own time—from here on in."

Hattie was relieved to note that Anna's color was returning. She turned to Cameron.

"What was that dreadful noise in the hall?" she asked.

"Some clumsy soul knocked over the medication rack," he said in disgust. "Like all hospitals these days, we're understaffed, and things don't get put away as they should. Someone must have hit the rack trying to avoid all the carts and gurneys sitting around. Nurses, volunteers and aides were all scrambling to put things back in order. You can't leave prescription medications lying around, you know," he added with a tight smile.

"You mean it was all over the floor?" Brooke asked.

"Some of it was, and now it's all fouled," Terri said. "It will all have to be destroyed. Some of the trays were still intact, though. Anna's didn't seem to have been disturbed at all."

She returned to the tray and picked up a little paper cup containing two small, white pills. "And speaking of your medication," she said to Anna, who was now lying with her eyes wide open, "it's time for yours." But instead of handing Anna the pills, she tucked them into her pocket. "I'm going to have these tested. I'll go get you some others." She left the room immediately.

"What's going on?" Alexandra asked, with obvious confusion.

"Nothing, dear," Cameron answered soothingly. "It apparently occurred to Terri that the pills might have gotten mixed up in the accident. She's just going to check."

"Well, she's a nurse, isn't she? Doesn't she know what Anna's pills look like?"

"Of course, dear," Cameron said quietly. "But many pills look alike sometimes. It's just a precaution."

"But how would the pills get mixed up?" asked Alexandra. "Terri said that Anna's tray wasn't disturbed."

Cameron was spared a reply when, at that moment, Terri re-entered the room carrying a white paper cup containing two pills.

"Here you are, Anna," she said cheerfully, handing them to Anna.

"Well, were they?" Alexandra turned to Terri.

Terri gave Cameron a quick look that indicated the pills had been switched. She didn't know how to answer Alexandra, but knew she had to say something fast to allay her suspicions. She had seen Alexandra's histrionics before and didn't want a replay.

"The pills were fine," she lied.

"See, dear? Nothing for you to worry about," Cameron assured his wife.

"Good," she said. The whole matter clearly behind her, Alexandra was finished with the hospital for the day. "We must go now," she told her husband. "Let's stop at that new restaurant in New Hope for dinner. I've been told it's very good."

"Fine," Cameron said with some relief. As Alexandra went to Anna's bed to say goodbye, he beckoned Terri to follow him into the hall. When the door to Anna's room was safely closed, he turned to Terri.

"Well?"

"Digitalis. The police are already looking into it."

"Dear God! Digitalis would have killed Anna. Who could have switched the pills?"

Terri couldn't answer.

"I'll do my best to find out," she said earnestly. She hesitated before she spoke again. "Please, Doctor, share this with no one; but as well as being a registered nurse, I'm also a detective with the Philadelphia Police force. Jim Sawyer is the only other one who knows.

Cameron nodded, and watched her walk back down

the hall to Anna's room. He felt better knowing this sharp guardian would be watching over her.

# 22

Cameron went back into Anna's room. He kissed Anna gently on the cheek, and watched as Alexandra finished her goodbyes. As she left the room, he whispered the truth to Hattie.

"It was digitalis," he told her. "Do you know what that is?"

"I know the name, that's about all," Hattie confessed. "I believe it's used for heart patients?"

"Yes, especially in the treatment of those with congestive heart failure," Cameron explained. "It's a powerful cardiac stimulant. If Anna had taken those pills they could very likely have been lethal for her."

"What was in the pills she did take?" asked Hattie.

"Just a common painkiller, nothing dangerous," Cameron assured.

Hattie shivered and hugged herself.

"Oh, how dreadful. How very, very dreadful. Have you any idea how this happened?"

"Hattie, I have to believe this was no mistake. Yes, the hallway was crowded, but someone deliberately pushed over that cart, and during the ensuing commotion simply switched the pills. It wouldn't be hard for anyone to find out who is taking digitalis if they put their mind to it. But the question is, who made the switch?"

"Yes, who?" echoed Hattie.

"Cameron, will you please hurry up?" Alexandra opened the door. "We want to get to the restaurant before it gets too crowded. As it is we might not get a table," she said petulantly.

Cameron smiled indulgently at Alexandra and winked at Hattie.

"We'll be in touch," he told her. "The important thing is to be even more diligent from now on," he said to Terri.

"Yes, Doctor," she said, with a visible sigh of relief. "Thank you."

Hattie went to stand by Anna's bed and thought of what might have happened. She looked down at her and gently stroked her good arm.

"Your color has come back, thank goodness." She took hold of Anna's right hand and held it gently for a few moments.

Terri came to stand beside her.

"It's almost time for Anna's dinner," the nurse said. "Shall I have them bring you and Brooke each a tray, too? They usually need prior notice for guest trays, but in seeing you're Dr. MacArthur's family, I don't think we'll have a problem."

Hattie looked at Brooke.

"Well, we did skip lunch today. I'm really hungry. It sounds like a very good idea to me, Brooke. How about you?"

"Sure does," Brooke agreed. Even hospital food sounded good right now. "Thank you, Terri. We'd love to have dinner here."

"Good," Terri said. "I can't promise what you'll get, but it will be nourishing. It will be nice for Anna to have some dinner company, too."

"Oh, yes, it really will," Anna chimed in, with a smile.

Terri picked up the phone and placed the dinner order.

Hattie beckoned to Terri to join her on the other side of the room.

"What about her meals?" she whispered, when she was sure she would not be overheard. "Isn't there a danger that her food might be tampered with?"

"All her meals have been specially prepared since I've been with her. The person who prepares them never takes her eyes off Anna's trays until she delivers them to me," Terri said.

"Good," sighed Hattie. "Oh, one more thing: I noticed that you used the phone. I thought it had been disconnected."

"No incoming calls," Terri assured her. "But we can call out."

"Aunt Hattie," Anna called. "What are you two whispering about? I hate secrets, and everything is creepy enough right now."

"I'm sorry, dear." Hattie said. "Actually, I was asking Terri about your phone. She said you are not allowed incoming calls yet."

"Why not?" Anna asked.

"A reasonable question," Terri answered. "You may be feeling better, but you still need your sleep. We don't want you disturbed, that's all."

"What if Larry has been trying to reach me?" Anna asked.

"Anyone who wants you can call the desk, and someone there will bring you the message," Terri said.

"Oh," said Anna, sounding disappointed.

The women chatted for about twenty minutes when a knock on the door announced the arrival of the trays. Because of Terri's official position, she was not able to go out to eat, even to the cafeteria, so there were four identical trays on a cart being pushed in by a young woman.

"What's for dinner tonight?" Anna called.

Terri lifted up one of the tray covers.

"Baked chicken, mashed potatoes, green beans and gravy," she answered. "With rolls, butter, tea and rice pudding for dessert. Are you hungry?"

"Yes, a little bit," Anna answered.

"Good," Terri said, handing out the trays.

Anna was unusually preoccupied while they were eating. She spent most of the time simply staring at her food, taking a bite every now and then but not seeming to notice what she ate. When Hattie and Brooke attempted to initiate a conversation, Anna answered in mono-syllables.

"I thought you said you were a little hungry," Brooke scolded. "Why aren't you eating more?" Noticing her sister's eyes narrow, she added, "What are you thinking about, anyway?"

"There was a person there...at the accident," Anna said haltingly.

"You remember a person?" Hattie asked in surprise.

"Yes," Anna said. "I remember someone looking at me. I remember things in quick flashes, not in a smooth, drawn out way. Do you know what I mean?"

"I think I do," Brooke said. "Like a quick slide show, not a movie. Click-click-click."

"That's right," Anna was relieved. "That's just how it is."

"I was lying in the car. My head was killing me, my arm hurt something awful and I was freezing cold. I heard someone coming through the woods and I was happy about that. Someone was coming to help me, I thought.

"I must have passed out again, because I came to with a light shining in my face. I closed my eyes, or maybe they were closed, I don't know, but there was that bright light. I guess I drifted off again, because suddenly some-one was crouched over me. It was someone coming at me menacingly. Someone who meant to harm me, not help me.

"All I saw was black. The person was dressed all in black, I'm sure, and there was a hammer raised in the air. I thought I was going to be killed. I must have passed out again. The next thing I remember Wolf was licking my face, and the person was gone, but I heard a car start and drive away fast."

"Can you remember the person's face?" asked Brooke.

Anna thought for a moment. "No," she answered. "I don't think I saw a face. A blur of white, perhaps. No features."

Terri, unseen by Anna, was sitting back from the other side of her bed, taking notes.

Suddenly, Anna said, "I know Gram is dead."

Tears welled in her eyes and rolled down her cheeks. "I've really known for maybe a day, but I couldn't bring myself to face it. Or to say the words out loud. I don't remember much, but I remember the car, how hard it hit her." She buried her face in her covers and sobbed like her heart would break.

Hattie, tears running down her own cheeks, hurried to Anna's side.

"Oh, darling," she said, patting the girl's good shoulder. She simply didn't know what else to do. Experience told her that sometimes, it's enough just to have another person near.

When Anna had calmed down, Hattie said softly, "Anna?" When the young woman looked up, she continued, "There's a very nice young policeman who wants to ask you some questions. His name is Jim Sawyer, and he's been waiting patiently for your memory to return. Do you think you'd be able to talk to him tomorrow?"

"Yes," was all Anna said. She didn't feel like talking about any of this, to anyone.

Betty Kerr Orlemann

Betty Kerr Orlemann

# 23

The first thing the women noticed when they pulled from the lane into Hattie's driveway was Shawn's car parked, as usual, in front of the barn.

"What does he want?" mumbled Brooke. Seeing his car reminded her of the morning's scene.

They were scarcely out of Hattie's car when Shawn stepped from his own and strode over to Brooke. "I have to talk to you," he said.

Hattie walked on to the house. "Perhaps you'd better talk inside where it's warm," she suggested. "I'll be outside walking Wolf."

She entered the kitchen and turned on the overhead lamp as well as a converted kerosene lamp on one of the wide window sills. Then she flicked the switches for the porch and other outside lights, took Wolf's leash from its peg and hooked him onto it. She passed Brooke and Shawn as they were going in.

"I had to come," she heard him say before the door closed. "Please, Brooke, don't be mad at me. I've been miserable all day. Forgive me for being hard on you. I am sorry. Maybe I'm so wrapped up in Michael's campaign that I'm seeing things a little lopsided. Please, honey," Shawn begged.

Brooke walked over to a chair by the fireplace and sat down. "Why don't you get some wood and start a fire?" she suggested.

Encouraged because at least she hadn't thrown him out, Shawn went out to the porch and gathered an armful

**181**

of cut logs. He was almost cheerful when he returned to the kitchen. He built up some of the logs and kindling in the fireplace, stuffed newspaper under them and poked a lighted match into the paper. Soon he had a fire.

"Is the flue open?" she asked when smoke began to fill the room.

"Ah, geez!" he yelled. He grabbed some potholders and a poker and pulled at the damper until it opened and the smoke went up the chimney. "You must think I'm the biggest jerk in the world," he said contritely. "A jerk AND an idiot."

He looked so miserable and so much like a little boy that Brooke, try as she would, couldn't stay angry with him. She began to laugh, and in another moment Shawn joined in.

He leaned over her, pulled her to her feet and they threw their arms around each other, still laughing. "I forgive you," she gasped, and he kissed her.

That was how Hattie found them when she and Wolf returned to the kitchen. Her cough could hardly have been described as discreet. Brooke and Shawn sprang apart and looked at Hattie in embarrassment.

Hattie laughed. "I wasn't trying to tell you anything," she said, and coughed again. It was the smoke." She flung the door wide open despite the cold outside. "Someone forgot to open the flue," she observed with amusement.

"I'm sorry," Shawn apologized. "It was me."

"No damage done," Hattie replied. The smoke dissipated rapidly. "See, it's almost gone." She crossed the room to where Shawn was standing. "How long were you out there waiting for us?"

"Almost two hours," he looked sheepishly at Brooke. "I didn't want us to stay mad at each other. Our stupid fight worried me all day."

"Have you had anything to eat?" Hattie asked, certain that he hadn't.

"Not since lunch," Shawn replied, "and not very much of that."

Hattie walked over to the refrigerator and examined its contents. She pulled from it a carton of milk and a jar of mayonnaise. She placed those items on the table and went back to the refrigerator for a tomato and some lettuce. Then she took a loaf of bread from the bread box, a glass and plate from the cupboard, and a knife and fork from a drawer.

Shawn watched her while Brooke went over to help. "Goodness, Aunt Hattie," she said, "let me make Shawn's supper." She turned to Shawn. "Do you want bread or toast for your sandwiches?"

He looked embarrassed. "Bread is fine. Am I the only one eating?" he wanted to know.

"We had dinner with Anna," Brooke said. "But that's okay." She opened a fresh can of tuna, made him two sandwiches and poured him a glass of milk. She poured one for herself, too, and sat next to him at the table.

"It's been a busy day," Hattie said, "and I am going to bed. Shawn, if you would like to spend the night here again, you are most welcome." She turned and ascended the winding piecrust stairs in the back to her bedroom, where once again, she left the door open between hers and Brooke's rooms.

Still downstairs, Brooke told Shawn all about the return of Anna's memory. She described in detail everything Anna had told her about the accident and the strange figure dressed all in black. After that, she recounted their day in Philadelphia and the stranger who had been in Annie's house who had pushed her down the cellar stairs and Hattie into the hall closet.

"It was really scary," she admitted.

"Brooke! That's terrible! You could've been killed!" Shawn yelled. "I'm going to spend tonight here, and every other night, too, if Miss Farwell will let me. You two need protecting." He was furious and frightened at the same time, but the idea of protecting his beloved Brooke calmed him.

"Thanks, Shawn. I think that's a great idea," Brooke said gratefully. "I, for one, will feel much better knowing you're here," She put her arms around his neck and kissed him on the cheek.

"Couldn't you do better than that?" Shawn smiled.

He stood up, took her in his arms and kissed her passionately. She returned his kiss with ardor. He picked her up and carried her to the couch in the living room, where their kisses became more intense. He unbuttoned Brooke's blouse and slid his hand under her bra. She moaned with pleasure. He kissed her throat and her chest to her cleavage. His fingers unfastened her bra and he began to fondle and kiss her naked breasts. She moaned again.

"You are so beautiful," he said into her skin. "I love you so much."

Brooke's arms tightened around him.

"I love you, too," she said, breathily.

He slid the zipper down on her slacks and caressed her abdomen, gently pulling her pants down as he did so. He kissed her mouth again, harder this time, more demanding. He moved his hand farther down. She was his now, he knew.

Suddenly, she pulled away from him and sat up.

"Shawn, no!" she said, quietly but firmly. "I do love you, but I'm not ready for that." She tugged at her slacks and underpants until they were back in place, then fastened her bra and buttoned her blouse.

His breath was ragged, and Brooke could see that he was distressed, but he didn't argue. Finally, he helped her straighten out her blouse, then pulled her to him and kissed her softly.

"I'm sorry," he said. "Besides, I promised Aunt Hattie I wouldn't make you do anything you might regret."

Brooke, too, was breathing hard. She clung to him, tears welling in her eyes.

"It's not that I don't want to."

"I know...I know," he said, soothingly. "And you'd better believe I want to. But we're going to be together forever. We'll have plenty of time." He kissed her again, and felt himself becoming aroused all over again. "But for now," he said, pushing her gently away, "you'd better get off to bed. I have used up all my willpower."

"Thank you," she said, with a shy smile. As she ran up the main staircase to her bedroom, and he stood watching her, she said softly, "I love you."

Betty Kerr Orlemann

# 24

The next morning, Hattie arose at six-thirty, dressed in her usual attire and went downstairs to take Wolf for his walk. When he heard her, he danced over to the foot of the back staircase and greeted her joyfully as she opened the door.

"You'll have to wait another few minutes, old boy," she said, "while I make a pot of coffee." With that done, and the aroma of fresh brewed coffee filling the kitchen, she put the dog on his leash, took her cape from its hook and left the house.

The day was crisp and clear, and although it was still dark out, the setting moon was bright enough to light the way. Hattie decided to take a long walk, all the way up the lane into the new Brookside Farms development.

As usual, Hattie stepped out rapidly, the great dog keeping pace beside her. She breathed deeply and enjoyed the early morning quiet and the cool air. By the time she reached Brookside Farms, the sky was brightening and a rising red sun was peeking through fuzzy pink clouds on the horizon. Directly above, the sky was a deep blue.

She walked down one street and up another, looking with interest at the different stages of construction development. Some of the roads were paved with sidewalks in place and others were rutted dirt. She tried to remember the way it used to be when it was their upper pasture. She couldn't see any familiar landmarks, with the exception of the clumps of trees at the head of her lane.

There was no one around, nor were there any cars. "At least there are no poachers here yet," she said to Wolf. He looked up at her lovingly and wagged his tail as if in agreement. Hattie returned to her lane. She was almost half way home when she heard a car coming from the development behind them.

Wolf moved to the side of the lane without her encouragement as the car approached. Hattie turned and was delighted to recognize Jim Sawyer behind the wheel.

She told him about Annie's purse and finding the letter that had contained the orchestra tickets. She also told him about the unseen person who had pushed Brooke down the cellar stairs and her into the closet.

"I was going to call you today," she said, "because Anna has regained much, if not all, of her memory. She's willing to talk to you today if you have the time."

"You bet I'll have the time," he said with a smile. "I've been hoping to talk to Miss Turner ever since her accident. What can you tell me about her memories?"

"If you have time to come down to the house for a cup of coffee, Brooke and I will tell you what Anna told us yesterday."

"You don't have to ask me twice," he said. "Would you like a ride home?"

"Thank you, Jim. Wolf and I would like that, but it's not that far, and we both need the exercise." She waved as he drove slowly past.

Back in Hattie's kitchen, they all sat around her table drinking coffee and munching on bagels and cream cheese. Jim hadn't been overjoyed to see Shawn, and the feeling was clearly mutual, but they managed a reluctant cordiality.

Hattie produced Annie's purse and the handwritten letter. As they'd suspected, Jim said he didn't hold out much hope for any information being found on the letter or envelope, but he would take them to the police lab anyhow. The same held true for the purse.

"Maybe a handwriting expert can be of some help," he said, referring to the letter. "Did you know that even when a person tries to disguise his handwriting, there are still characteristics in it which might help to identify him?"

"That's very interesting," Hattie said. "Let's hope it's true in this case."

Brooke and Hattie between them supplied Jim with every bit of information they could remember, from the stranger in Annie's house to Anna's restored memory.

"She even remembers that Gram is dead," Brooke said. "And she can describe the car that killed her."

"The only thing of which we're not certain," Hattie said, "is whether or not she remembers that she broke her engagement to Larry last year. The other day she asked me to invite him here for Thanksgiving, but the subject has not come up again."

"And there is something else, but you may have heard about it already," Brooke contributed. "Someone apparently substituted digitalis for Anna's pain killer. It could have killed her if she'd taken it."

"Wow!" said Jim.

"I have something to ask you," Hattie said to Jim. "Do you often drive around Brookside Farms?"

"Lately more than usual," he admitted. "I do patrol it, but since you reported a poacher in your woods, I have been going through there much more frequently. So far I haven't seen any suspicious cars, but you haven't heard any more gunshots, either. I also drive around the perimeter of your woods, but I really can't think of a place for anyone to park that wouldn't be difficult and very obvious."

"Thank you," said Hattie. "It makes me feel safer knowing that you're around."

"You know what makes me feel safer, too?" Brooke asked, looking fondly at Shawn. "Shawn has offered to stay here with us until the killer is found."

"Great," said Jim with no particular pleasure.

"Well, Shawn, if that's the case, would you be able to spend Thanksgiving with us? Would your family object?" Hattie asked.

"I'm sure my parents would understand," Shawn answered. "Anyway, as far as I know they're going to my sister's, and she would probably be happy to have one less mouth to feed. In other words, I would love to spend Thanksgiving here." He gave Brooke a lingering look.

Hattie glanced at Jim. "What are your plans for Thanksgiving, Jim?"

"I haven't made any, yet," he answered. "But I will be off duty."

So Hattie added two more names to her Thanksgiving dinner list. She was actually beginning to look forward to it after all.

Then she remembered Anna's request for her to invite Larry. For all she knew, Larry had never left Seattle, but she felt she'd better try to find him if she could.

"Jim," she said, turning to face him, "do you have any phone numbers for Laurence Adams? Would you mind if I called him?"

"Of course, I wouldn't mind. He isn't a suspect yet," Jim pulled out his notebook and read aloud the phone numbers of Larry's parents, his sister in New Jersey and his home in Seattle. "So far I have been unable to contact him, but if you reach him before I do, will you please give him my number and ask him to call me?"

"Certainly," Hattie agreed as she wrote down the three numbers.

"C'mon, Brooke," urged Shawn. "Hurry up and get

ready. We should be getting off to campaign headquarters right now."

"Got it. Give me five," Brooke said as she pushed her chair back from the table and ran up the circular stairs behind the door. She was back in less than five minutes with combed hair and wearing fresh lipstick. "Okay," she said to Shawn. "Let's go!"

She grabbed his hand, and they ran out to his car laughing. "See you this afternoon, Aunt Hattie," she called back. "'Bye, Jim." "Good bye," Shawn echoed.

"So long," Jim said in barely audible tones. His forehead furrowed, his smile arced downward in a formidable frown. Hattie went to the door and waved to them as they drove past. She deliberately kept her back to Jim so he wouldn't see her smile.

He left almost immediately. *After all*, Hattie thought, *there is nothing to keep him here any longer.* She smiled again to herself.

She went to the phone and dialed the Philadelphia number Jim had given her for Larry's parents, but there was no answer and no answering machine. She was about to try his sister's number when the phone rang.

She lifted the receiver immediately and to her amazement heard Anna's voice. "What were you doing, Aunt Hattie, sitting on the phone?"

"Anna! How wonderful!" Hattie exclaimed.

"Yup," laughed Anna. "And I'm calling to ask you for a special favor. They're letting me come home for Thanksgiving! Would you mind very much inviting Terri to come, too?"

"Not at all, dear," Hattie answered. "How wonderful that you'll be here! It would be very nice to include Terri."

"Good, I'll tell her when she comes in this afternoon. She doesn't have anybody around here, you know."

"No, I didn't know, but she will be most welcome," Hattie assured Anna.

"You can't call me here, Aunt Hattie, they've fixed my phone so I can call out but no one can call in. Did you know that?"

"Yes, as a matter of fact Terri told me that yesterday, but in my excitement just now, I forgot. I think that's a good idea, don't you? You can get more rest without being bothered by phone calls." Hattie said.

"That's what Terri says," Anna said. "It's good to talk to you, Aunt Hattie. Will you and Brooke be in this afternoon?"

"Well, I'll be there. Brooke will probably be there late. And by the way, Officer Jim Sawyer will also be in sometime today to chat with you. You'll like him."

"Okay," said Anna. "I'd better hang up now. See you later, Aunt Hattie, and thank you very much."

"You're very welcome. Goodbye, dear," Hattie said and wondered why Anna hadn't said anything more about Larry.

She decided not to try again to reach him, at least not for the time being. Maybe it wouldn't be necessary.

# 25

When Brooke and Shawn entered the DiRienzo campaign headquarters Maria was already there and waiting
for them. "Good morning, you two," she said with a
smile. "I've outlined a pretty busy day for both of you.
Shawn, if you'll go into my office with Howard, I'm
afraid we have a little damage control to work on."

As she spoke a tall older man approached them. "Hi,
Shawn," he said. "This must be your beautiful young
lady." Before Shawn could introduce them he held out
his hand to Brooke. "I'm Howard Cole, Michael's
campaign manager."

She smiled politely. "Good morning, Mr. Cole, I'm
Brooke Turner."

"Please, call me Howard," he said. He clapped his right
arm around Shawn's shoulders. "C'mon boy," he ordered,
"You and I have a little work to do." They walked across
the room to Maria's cubicle and disappeared inside.

"Don't look so concerned, Brooke," Maria advised.
"It's nothing, really. I guess you didn't see the morning
paper, but some Associated Press photographer snapped
a picture of Michael in what looks like an embrace with
an Eagles cheerleader. I'm sure it's a phony. The camera
angle makes it look like something it isn't, that's all.

"Now, let me show you your new office," Maria
continued. She led Brooke back past her own cubicle
to a door, which she opened to reveal the cellar stairs.
"Come on down," she said enthusiastically. "You have
all the space in the world down here. Come see."

Brooke hesitated at the top of the stairs as Maria went ahead of her into the cellar. "Do I have to work down there?" she asked in a small voice, one she hoped didn't make her trepidation transparent.

"Come on down," Maria ordered. "It's really very nice down here. Come see for yourself."

Brooke reached for the railing and reluctantly descended the straight flight of wooden stairs. Her ordeal of the day before was foremost in her mind, but she didn't want to share the experience with Maria.

Maria was acting like a delighted child.

"Look, Brooke, isn't this terrific?" She had walked to the back of the cellar, where there was indeed an office. She stood holding the door open for Brooke, her face awash in smiles.

Brooke hadn't been expecting much, but the room was actually very nice. It had plasterboard walls painted a pale green; a darker green rug covered the cement floor. The desk, computer table and filing cabinet were made of mahogany. Two windows looked out on the rear alley. A closed door stood between them. Photographs of Michael as a congressman and senator lined the walls. Venetian blinds, their slats slanted partially open, covered the windows.

"You should be able to work here in peace," Maria said with a happy smile. "Only one thing, though, be sure to keep the back door locked at all times." She indicated the door between the two windows.

"If you feel for some reason that you have to go out that way, please, ask me first."

"Okay," said Brooke. "This is really very nice. Would you mind telling me who used to have this office?"

"It was mine," Maria said. "Michael had it fixed up just for me. However, I really thought I should be more in the thick of things, so I moved upstairs. I never knew when

Michael came in and out. I never knew anything that went on in the office, and I thought that was a big mistake. In your case, though, it won't make any difference."

"Yes, I see," Brooke answered. She hoped her disappointment wouldn't show. This wasn't going to be at all what she had dreamed it would be. She had pictured herself working side-by-side with Shawn and the other volunteers, chatting with Michael, having an entirely different involvement with the campaign.

She walked around the office looking at all the photographs. All were of Michael, some giving speeches, some with Maria and some with other people. Brooke recognized the governor, other legislators and even the President. "These are great!" she exclaimed, impressed. She continued to look at the pictures.

There was one with a slim, young Maria in it as well as two dark, good-looking men. Michael had his arm around Maria and they were all laughing. A large sign behind them read "BERTOLINO MOTORS."

"How pretty you were," Brooke said without thinking. "Where was this taken?"

Maria looked at the picture soberly, her spark gone. "Thank you, Brooke, I guess I was pretty once, wasn't I? That was taken in front of my family's business in South Philadelphia. Michael and I were newly married. The two men are my brothers. They still run the business. Those were truly happy days," she said with a sigh. "To tell you the truth, it was all of my family's contacts that helped get Michael elected to congress and then the senate. I almost wish they didn't know so many powerful people," she added a trifle wistfully. Her voice was so low, Brooke could hardly hear her.

"Now, let's discuss you and your family. How is your sister? And was your trip to Philadelphia yesterday successful?

Maria looked directly into Brooke's eyes, her own large, amber eyes showing sincere interest. Brooke told her all about Anna's memory coming back. Maria smiled sympathetically and said how happy she was for them all. "It must be an awful thing to lose your memory," she added.

"Yes," Brooke said, "but thank goodness Anna's is so much better now. As a matter of fact, she's better in every way. We're hoping her doctor will let her come to Aunt Hattie's house for Thanksgiving. Wouldn't that be wonderful?"

"Yes, it certainly would," Maria agreed in her soft voice. "Now tell me how everything went in Philadelphia yesterday."

"Pretty well," Brooke answered. "We identified my grandmother's purse at police headquarters, but it really didn't have anything important in it. Then we went to her house where we didn't find much, either, except a note someone had sent her with the Philadelphia Orchestra tickets. The note was in her waste basket, and the tickets were not there, of course. We don't know what happened to them." She shrugged her shoulders and said no more about the day.

"Well, we've been gossiping much too long," Maria was suddenly all business. "Let me show you what I want you to do today."

She sat at Brooke's computer and pulled up lists of names of contributors. "What we need as well as money are volunteers. They can make a campaign. Never underestimate their importance.

"We must send out thousands of letters to Michael's supporters first and then to party members all over Pennsylvania. Of course, we will ask for donations, but this time we'll downplay the money a trifle and emphasize volunteering. Then we can re-format the work you did the other day, but more about that later. For now, we'll flatter the most active supporters by giving them important roles to play in the campaign; emphasize our need for their talents and time. We'll tell them why we need them, and why they need Michael. We'll list all his ideas and outstanding achievements since he's been serving the people, first as a congressman and particularly as a senator.

"Howard has written a fine first draft of this letter. What I want you to do is clarify it to his liking, remembering all the things I just told you. Your main job is to go over the lists of contributors and print out their names and addresses as we discussed on Thursday. Don't worry about the other work now. We can concentrate on the contributor spreadsheet with the names, addresses and everything we discussed the other day when this is completed. Any questions?" Maria asked brightly.

"No, I don't think so," Brooke said. "But before I get too far into this, could I please take up some of your time to look it over so I don't have to repeat everything again?" She was a trifle shocked at her own temerity.

Maria's eyebrows shot up for a brief instant, but she covered her annoyance with a pleasant smile.

"You can ask my assistance any time you need it," she said sweetly. With that, she left the office, and mere seconds later Brooke heard the door close at the top of the cellar stairs.

Brooke was decidedly unhappy with the present arrangement, but she consoled herself by remembering that she had only three days to work next week before Thanksgiving, and then only two more until she had to return to school. She was convinced Maria really didn't like her, and she wondered what she could possibly have done to estrange the older woman. She could only surmise that Shawn was right and Maria was jealous of her looks and youth. Even thinking such a thing embarrassed her.

Then, however, she remembered what Maria had told her about the newspaper photo of Michael and the beautiful young cheerleader. Michael had a reputation of being a ladies' man; Shawn had told her as much. Perhaps, as he suggested, Maria was trying to keep Michael away from Brooke.

"It figures," Brooke mumbled softly. "I really want to meet the man. On the other hand, I don't want him coming on to me. That would be disgusting. Maybe if Shawn could be with me and introduce me to Michael, that would be safe."

She stared into space for a few moments. "Well, I'd better get to boring work," she said louder. "Maria will undoubtedly be checking her computer for my progress." She didn't fool herself that the work she was doing was really important. *Just grunt work,* she thought as she began retyping lists into her computer.

Upstairs in Maria's cubicle Howard, Maria and Shawn sat in a tight little group around her desk. They spoke in low voices. It would not be wise to allow anyone, even loyal volunteers to overhear their conversation.

It might have seemed difficult for anyone who knew what was going on to understand why Maria would confide in a twenty-year-old like Shawn. His loyalty, however, could not be denied. Nor could his intelligence.

Howard Cole understood that. He'd grown up in South Philadelphia with Michael DiRienzo. They had been inseparable friends since babyhood. He'd also known the O'Briens and the Bertolinos all of his life, and there was no doubt in his mind that Shawn would give his life for Michael if necessary.

"We must make it clear to the press and thus the general populous that someone is out to get Michael," Maria said firmly. "There is undoubtedly a conspiracy against him by

198

people who want to damage his reputation. That picture is a set-up. As far as the current young woman is concerned, does either of you know anything about her?"

"Not at the moment," said Howard. "But we can certainly find out everything in short order. I have some connections with Eagles' management." He leaned over and put his hand on Maria's phone. "May I?" he asked.

"Of course," she said. She beckoned to Shawn to follow her out of the area. "It's better that we don't know what's being said," she whispered conspiratorially.

In less than ten minutes, Howard signaled to them from the entrance to the cubicle, and they returned. "Her name is Stacey Tyburn. She's twenty-one years old and lives in an apartment on South Street with another cheerleader named Jane Flynn, also twenty-one.

"Stacey grew up in Harleysville. Her parents and younger sister still live in the same house. She attended a junior college in New Jersey. Her health is good. She does not have a steady boyfriend, but is rumored to have been having an affair with Michael on and off since last summer." Howard reported this last bit of information with obvious hesitation and not a little embarrassment.

Maria looked pained. "I should be used to this by now," she sighed, "but I'm not."

"Just because he has been getting away with this kind of behavior for years doesn't mean he won't get caught now that he's going for the brass ring," complained Howard. "Lord knows we've warned him a million times, but he thinks he's smarter than anyone else."

"What do you want to do about this one?" Shawn asked.

"Get to know her, Shawn," Maria ordered. "Pour on all of your boyish charm. Make sure she won't do anything to damage Michael. Make sure she won't see him again."

"How can I do that? And what about Brooke?" Shawn asked uncomfortably. "What can I tell her?"

"Don't worry about Brooke," Maria answered with assurance. "I'll keep her busy."

"There's an Eagles game tomorrow, Shawn. I'll arrange for a ticket for you and an introduction to Stacey Tyburn. Someone from management will contact you," Howard said. "Good luck."

"I'd better tell you that I'll be staying at Hattie Farwell's for at least the next week," Shawn said. "Brooke is staying there, too. I've no idea how I'm gonna pull this off."

"You'll think of something," Howard said. "Just make sure that Stacey woman stays away from Michael. This shouldn't keep you away from your girl too long."

"If Stacey Tyburn is stubborn, if she seems inclined to meet Michael anyway or to talk to the press, let us know right away. You might not have to see her again after tomorrow," Maria said.

# 26

Visiting hours started at noon, and Hattie was anxious to spend as much time with Anna as she could. She counted in her head the number of people coming for Thanksgiving. *Eight at least,* she thought, and called the butcher to order a 12-pound hen turkey. "It's always good to have leftovers," she told herself. Keeping her eye on the clock, she spent the rest of the morning dusting and straightening up.

At noon promptly, her head still filled with Thanksgiving plans, Hattie entered Anna's room. Anna was seated in her easy chair, eating her lunch.

"Do you want one?" she offered Hattie one of her dessert cookies.

Hattie declined politely and launched into her plans for Thanksgiving. "Do you know, Anna, I'm really beginning to look forward to it. A few days ago I wouldn't have thought that possible."

"I know," Anna responded. "It simply won't be the same without Gram, but you know something, Aunt Hattie, I believe that in some way she'll be with us."

"Yes," Hattie nodded her head in agreement and turned to Terri, who was pouring fresh ice water from a carafe into Anna's glass. "By the way, Terri, I hope Anna invited you to join us. We would really enjoy your company."

"Thank you so much, Miss Farwell. I would love to be there. Anna and I have been talking about it and your lovely old farmhouse."

Hattie laughed.

"Well, I can't say how lovely it is, but it certainly is an old farmhouse, and I love it."

"Who all's coming, Aunt Hattie?" Anna asked. There was no mention of Larry.

"Well, let's see, besides you, Brooke, your mother and Cameron, Terri, of course, Brooke's friend, Shawn, and Officer Jim Sawyer. Including me that makes eight," said Hattie. "I've ordered a 12-pound turkey, so we should have lots of leftovers. But maybe not, considering the way Shawn eats!"

They were laughing when there was a knock on the door. Terri went to the door at once and opened it a crack. "Yes?" she asked. A deep male voice could be heard from the hall as Jim identified himself as Officer James Sawyer. He held out his identification for Terri to read. She stepped back and allowed him to enter.

He was neatly dressed in tan slacks, a light blue shirt and a navy jacket. His tie was red, white and blue regimental stripes.

"Don't you look nice!" Hattie observed.

"Thanks, Miss Farwell," he answered. "I felt it would be better if I didn't wear my uniform." He smiled at Anna.

"Jim," Hattie said, "this young lady, as must be obvious, is Anna Turner. Anna this is Officer Jim Sawyer."

"Aunt Hattie has told me a lot about you," offered Anna with a wide smile. "It's a pleasure to meet you." she held out her right hand for him to shake.

He returned her smile as they shook hands. "And it's a pleasure to meet you." He observed a young woman who was wearing her casted left arm in a blue sling. *She was probably pretty*, he thought, *when her eyes were not black and blue and the left side of her face was not bandaged.* She reminded him of a little, wounded animal.

*Poor thing*, he thought, *why would anyone want to kill her?* He wanted desperately to find out. "As you know," he said gently to Anna. "I'm here to ask you some questions, if you're up to it." He pulled out his notebook.

"Excuse me," said Hattie. She rose from her chair and left the room.

After she'd gone, Jim turned to Terri. "That woman really impresses me," he stated.

"Me too," Terri agreed.

Jim asked Anna to tell him everything she could remember about her grandmother's death. She was able to repeat in exact detail the events of the day when the strange note arrived with the Orchestra tickets.

"Good," Jim said. "Now I'll ask you to try to remember what seats the tickets were for. You said they were in the orchestra section. Do you remember the row? Can you remember the seat numbers?"

Anna closed her eyes. She was silent for some time. Finally she said, "I remember that they were in the center section of the orchestra. I think they were in row nine, but I'm not sure. I do remember that they were great seats."

"Good," Jim said again. "Now try to remember the seat numbers. Take your time."

She shut her eyes once more. She frowned and screwed up her face, but she could not remember. "I'm so sorry," she apologized. "I simply can't remember."

"Don't worry about it. You've really been a big help. You might be surprised, if you don't try to remember, maybe the numbers will come to you some time. The trick is to relax." He gave her a kind smile.

"Now, I need to ask you about the night of the concert. I know how painful this will be for you, so please tell me if it becomes too difficult for you to recount what happened." He looked at her with deep concern.

"Gram and I," Anna began, "were walking to the Kimmel Center. It was a pleasant evening, and there were not too many people around. We were chatting about nothing in particular, but Gram and I were never at a loss for words..." Her voice trailed off, and her eyes filled with tears.

They were all silent for a few minutes. Anna continued. "We were both really looking forward to the concert. I love Beethoven. I have CDs of just about every work of his which has ever been recorded. I often played them for Gram."

"Excuse me for interrupting," Jim broke in. "But did you say you love Beethoven and played your CDs for your grandmother? Did your grandmother love Beethoven, too?"

"She was really a Bach lover, but I kind of turned her onto Beethoven, too." Anna replied with a grin.

"Do you any idea which of her friends knew that she had been listening to Beethoven with you?" Jim asked.

"No," said Anna with a frown. "It was nothing she would be bothering to discuss with anyone unless for some reason music came up, and I don't know any of her friends who were really that interested in classical music. I've been scouring my brain to try to think who would have sent her those tickets in the first place."

"What about you, Miss Turner," Jim continued, "which of your friends knew that you liked Beethoven?"

"Well, besides Larry, maybe one or two of the teachers at school. I'm not sure. I never made a big deal of it." Anna answered. She was clearly puzzled.

Jim feigned ignorance. "Who's Larry?" he asked.

"Laurence Adams. We were engaged for three years," Anna answered. "He was the assistant principal at the Spruce Street School where I teach fifth grade."

"You're no longer engaged?" he asked.

"No," Anna sighed. "I broke up with him last year.

After that he accepted a position in a school in Seattle, Washington. He left Philadelphia almost right after we broke up."

"Have you seen or heard from him since?" Jim inquired.

Anna hesitated. "I'm not certain," she replied.

"What do you mean, you're not certain?" Jim probed.

"Most likely I dreamed I saw him. I had been given Demoral for abdominal pain, and I had a terrible headache. I felt as if I were floating from my bed, I opened my eyes and saw Larry leaning over me. He looked very concerned. I couldn't talk because I was too weak. But Larry said, 'I had to see you, Annie my darling.' He said something about seeing me again, I'm not sure...He never came back."

"Did he often call you 'Annie'?" asked Jim.

"Yes, he did when we were alone. I don't remember that he ever called me 'Annie' when we were with other people, but it's possible."

"You said that you were the one who broke off the engagement, is that right?"

Anna sighed again. "Yes," she answered quietly, clearly wishing she did not have to have this discussion.

"Why?" asked Jim. "Why did you break your engagement?"

"It was be...be-because I, he...Oh, I just can't talk about it. I'm sorry." Anna was clearly flustered, and Jim didn't want to push her, so he steered her in another direction.

"Did he ever threaten or hurt you in any way?" Jim persisted.

"No! Oh no. Nothing like that." Anna was vehement.

"Did you discover something about him which made it impossible for you to marry him?" Jim needed this information, and while he was willing to try different interviewing strategies, he wasn't about to give up.

"No," Anna answered.

Jim continued. "Was there someone else? Either for him or you?"

"Heavens no!" Anna was annoyed. "Please, I can't talk about it now."

"Okay," Jim said. "You were telling me about the night your grandmother was killed." He glanced at his notebook in which he had been writing since he had begun to question Anna. "You were walking to the Kimmel Center," he prompted.

"Yes," said Anna. Her voice dropped. "We got to the corner of Fifteenth and Locust Streets. There was a red light, so we waited on the curb until it turned green." She stared into space, remembering, trying to picture the scene. "I think we were the only ones waiting for the light to change at that time. I can't remember seeing..." She stopped talking. "There was an old man on the far corner. He was looking at a maroon car that was speeding toward the corner. He yelled a warning, but we were in the street –crossing the street...That car just sped around the corner and aimed right at us. It meant to hit us, I know it did!

"Gram yelled, 'Get out of the way, Anna!' but I was frozen. She pushed me hard. I fell on the sidewalk, and I heard the thud, that horrible thud when Gram was hit." Anna burst into uncontrollable sobs. Terri rushed to comfort her.

Jim felt awful that he had led her to this. He said nothing until the sobs subsided. "I'm so sorry," he told her gently. He waited for her to blow her nose and wipe the tears from her eyes until he continued his questioning.

"I have to do this," he was apologetic, his voice low.

"I know," she replied. "Go ahead." She took a deep breath.

"Can you remember anything distinctive about that car? Did you see anything of the driver? Could you tell if there were any passengers inside? Did it have a Pennsylvania license plate, could you tell?"

Anna frowned deeply and put her right hand to her head. She closed her eyes and tried to force a memory. Finally she said, "I'm almost certain that it had a Pennsylvania license plate. I'm sure that there was no plate on the front of the car as it came rushing toward us, but when it was speeding away I have just the vaguest impression that I saw a Pennsylvania license plate. I can't remember a number.

"As far as occupants are concerned, I couldn't see anyone. The windows were tinted. The car was a late-model sedan. It could have been a Chrysler." She shook her head. "That's all I can tell you."

"That's very good," he complimented her. "Now let's talk about the night of your so-called accident."

"I've written down all of that," Terri told him in a semi-whisper. "Perhaps you would like to read it before you ask her to go through it again." She handed him her notebook.

"Thanks," he said to Terri as he accepted the book.

To Anna he said. "Why don't you just take it easy for a bit? I'll go over this information, and then if I have any questions, I'll ask them, Okay?"

"Would you mind if I went back to bed?" she asked. "I'm sort of tired."

"Please, go ahead. I'll leave you alone for a few minutes. I'm sorry if I wore you out." Jim said. He walked briskly across the room to the door and left, taking Terri's notebook with him.

Terri helped Anna to her feet and into bed.

Betty Kerr Orlemann

# 27

Jim found Hattie sitting in a waiting room down the hall. He was glad to see she was alone. "Hi," he greeted her. "Time out for Anna to get some rest."

Hattie put down the magazine she'd been reading and welcomed him with a smile. "How did the questioning go?" she asked.

"Oh, I don't know," he sighed. "I doubt if I learned much more than I already knew. Anna did say the car that killed her grandmother was a Chrysler, or so she thought. She couldn't see any occupants. She's pretty certain it had a Pennsylvania plate. That could be helpful.

"Anna also believed that the orchestra seats were in the ninth row, in the center section. She couldn't remember the numbers. She also remembers that she broke her engagement to Laurence Adams last year, that he often called her 'Annie,' and that he has since moved to Seattle. She remembers why they broke up, too, but she won't reveal the reason."

He glanced through Terri's notebook. "I have here some copious notes made by Officer Terri Mason. Apparently Anna gave a detailed description of the events she remembered of her so-called accident."

"Yes," Hattie told him. "Brooke and I were there."

"Well, I'll just read them over." He sat at the end of a sofa and began to study Terri's notes. "By the way, isn't Terri here early today?" he asked. "I thought she was on the three to eleven shift."

"She's been pulling double shifts lately. The woman who usually works from seven to three is ill," Hattie informed him. "This change actually makes Anna very happy. Terri is far and away her favorite. And, by the way, Terri will be with us on Thanksgiving, too."

"Good," he said and went back to reading the notes.

Hattie picked up her magazine again but failed to find it interesting. She stood up, walked to the window and gazed absently out at the parking lot. Without giving them any thought, she watched cars park and people get out and walk toward the building. The entrance doors were out of sight under a wide roof, but it was obvious that the people were heading toward them.

She began playing a game with herself: A happy-looking man who appeared to be in his late twenties almost bounced from his car and trotted toward the doors, carrying a teddy bear. A new father, Hattie surmised. An older woman walked slowly in the direction of the building, her shoulders hunched. Her husband is dying, Hattie guessed. He probably doesn't recognize her anymore.

She continued to play her game as Jim read the notes and added some more of his own. A young man Hattie figured was in his early thirties was carrying an arrangement of fall flowers in a basket. He stepped slowly from his car. He glanced around as if looking for someone he might recognize, then walked rapidly toward the entrance doors.

Hattie gasped. Jim looked up quickly from his notes. "What's wrong?"

Hattie's eyes were still on the spot where the young man had disappeared under the roof.

"That was Larry! He just entered the building. I'm almost positive it's Larry!"

Jim shoved the notes into his jacket pocket and hurried down the hall to Anna's room.

Hattie remained in the waiting room until she heard the elevator doors close, followed by quick footsteps in the hall. She stood out of sight of the hallway until the footsteps passed. When she poked her head through the doorway, she saw the man from the parking lot walking toward Anna's room. The bouquet in his arms appeared even larger than it had from the window. She was convinced the man was Larry. She followed him at a distance, walking slowly. He did not turn around.

Larry knocked softly on Anna's door and was surprised when a man opened it. He found himself starting to stammer.

"Is-is this Anna T-Turner's room?" he asked.

"Yes, it is," said the other man. "May I ask who you are?"

"M-My n-name is L-Larry Adams. M-may I come in, p-please?" He was furious at himself. He hadn't really stuttered like this since childhood. It was just nerves, he knew, and he tried to force himself to calm down. He took a deep breath while he waited for the stranger to deliver his message to Anna.

It was Anna who called to him.

"Larry, is that really you? Please, come in right away!"

He felt himself relax, but entered the room uncertainly.

"These are for you," he said unnecessarily, placing the flower arrangement on her bedside table. He looked around the room and chuckled. "I guess my gift is a little redundant. Look at all of those flowers!"

Arrangements containing flowers of many hues were sitting across the room on Anna's bureau and on her windowsills. She reached over and pulled Larry's basket to her.

"These are the loveliest," she told him.

Just as Hattie entered the room, Anna began to cough. She grabbed a tissue and sneezed four times in quick succession. Her eyes filled with tears that spilled over and ran down her cheeks. She began to wheeze. Terri grabbed the flower basket and carried it into the hall. When she returned, Anna was gasping for breath. Terri turned and ran out of the room, returning in less than a minute with an inhaler. She placed it in Anna's mouth.

"Breathe slowly, now. That's it, try to relax."

Larry looked panic-stricken. The door opened and Alexandra and Cameron came in. One glance told Cameron exactly what had happened. He hurried to Anna's bed, but saw that Terri had the situation under control.

"Oh, this is my fault!" Larry moaned. "It was my flowers. She had a terrible allergic reaction to the flowers I brought her."

Alexandra strode over to him, a perplexed look on her face.

"Larry, where on earth did you come from? I thought you were in Seattle."

"I was, but a couple of people from the Spruce Street School called to tell me about Annie's accident. I came as soon as I could."

"Larry, did you bring Anna those autumn flowers in the hall?" she demanded.

"Y-yes."

"How could you? She's allergic to most autumn flowers! You should remember that, for heaven's sake! How stupid of you! Don't you remember the time she almost died at the Philadelphia Flower Show when someone handed her some mums?"

Larry had turned deathly pale. He didn't answer Alexandra, but simply stared at the ground like a scolded child.

Anna was breathing quietly on her own. Cameron stood watch over her, but he could see she was out of danger.

Jim gestured to Terri to follow him to the other side of the room. Alexandra and Hattie went to Anna's side. Larry looked as if he wanted to run away.

Jim, who up until this moment had stayed on the periphery, looked at Terri.

"Did you hear him refer to her as 'Annie'?"

She nodded.

Jim continued, "Do you believe he brought her that huge bunch of flowers by mistake?"

"I don't know," Terri answered. "Another thing I'd like to know is when he came back to this area? If someone from the Spruce Street School really did call him, he must have jetted right in. That is, if Anna didn't dream he was with her in intensive care the evening following the so-called accident." She paused, thinking. "Then again, what if he was here before the accident? Say, at least a week before?"

Jim looked across the room to where Larry was standing, looking absolutely miserable. "Certainly doesn't look the part, does he?"

"No, but you and I both know that's no a reliable measure," Terri chided.

"Right," Jim agreed. "I'll check airline reservations from Seattle."

"And we'll have to keep him under surveillance, but not so that he gets suspicious," Terri added.

Anna turned her head to look at Larry.

"Please, Larry, don't look so stricken. I know you didn't mean to cause my allergic reaction. Come on over here and talk to me."

Larry forced a weak smile and walked over to Anna. Hattie and Cameron backed out of the way to let him near her, but Alexandra stayed right where she was.

"Why did you come here, anyway?" she demanded of him. "It seems to me that Anna sent you on your way a year ago."

"She did," he answered sadly. He looked directly at Anna, dismissing Alexandra. "How do you feel?" he inquired. "I've been very worried about you. I called the hospital several times asking about you, but no one would give me any information. I was only able to get your room number this morning by following your family up here."

"I'm sorry. Things are a bit...strange. But I'm getting better every day," Anna answered with a pained little grin. "It was so good of you to come all the way from Seattle just to see me."

"Could we talk sometime?" Larry begged. "Alone?" He looked pointedly at Alexandra, who still hadn't moved away.

"Maybe on Thanksgiving," Anna suggested. "Aunt Hattie is having dinner at her house, and the doctor told me I could go." She looked at Hattie. "You said Larry could come, too, didn't you, Aunt Hattie?"

Hattie glanced quickly at Jim, who nodded almost imperceptibly. "Of course you're invited, Larry," she said with conviction.

"Thanks a lot, Miss Farwell, I'd love to come." Larry smiled for the first time since he'd arrived. "I'm really glad to see you, and will look forward to being in your wonderful old farmhouse again. By the way, how is Wolf?"

"He's just fine, thanks. You'll be seeing him on Thanksgiving, too."

"What about your own family?" Alexandra snapped. "You'd think they'd want you with them, after you've been living away so long."

"I believe my parents will understand," Larry said quietly. "They'll be with my sister and her family, anyway. Besides,

I've been staying with them since I came home. They've seen too much of me already, I'm sure!"

"It's all settled, Mother," Anna said firmly. "Larry will be having Thanksgiving with us."

Jim and Terri exchanged a quick glance. "Something else to look into," he whispered. "When did he show up at his parents' house?"

Alexandra gave a disdainful "Hmph" and walked over to Cameron. "I think we'd better go now," she said. The tone of her voice left no doubt that her ego was bruised. Before Cameron could answer, there was a knock on the door.

Terri opened it the usual crack to see Brooke and Shawn standing outside. She swung the door open to admit them.

"Hi!" Brooke addressed everyone. She looked around the room until her gaze fell on Larry. "Larry, wow! When did you get here?" She took Shawn's hand and led him to Larry. "It's really nice to see you again," she said. "I want you to meet my fiancé, Shawn O'Brien. Shawn, this is Larry Adams, an old friend of Anna's."

The men shook hands.

Jim went over to introduce himself to Larry, too.

"I think I owe you an apology," he said. "My name is Jim Sawyer. You might say I'm a friend of the family." He shot a warning glance at the others.

To Hattie's relief, Alexandra was too busy licking her wounds to blurt out that Jim was a police officer working on Anna's accident investigations.

"Brooke," Larry observed. "You are more beautiful than ever. What are you up to these days?"

"I'm still in boarding school, but I'm going to graduate this spring, thank goodness," she replied. "Right now, I'm home until after Thanksgiving. I have to go back to school next Sunday, but in the meantime I'm working with Shawn on Michael DiRienzo's pre-campaign for the presidential primaries in the spring."

"How interesting," Larry said, without much conviction.

"Say, speaking of your boy," Cameron added, "did you see his picture in the *Inquirer*? He was all over that Eagle's football team cheerleader."

"That wasn't what it looked like," Shawn said with a dismissive gesture. "You know how Michael is always hugging people. It didn't mean a thing, but you know how the media are always blowing things up. Hey, speaking of the Eagles," he said, turning to Brooke, "I forgot to tell you that Howard gave me a ticket for tomorrow's game. Isn't that super?"

Brooke looked surprised. "Didn't he give you one for me, too?"

"Since when have you liked football?" he teased, laughing. "Anyhow, he only had one ticket. They're hard to come by. I'm sorry."

"Yeah, you look sorry," she snapped.

"Now the shoe's on the other foot, isn't it?" he whispered in her ear, referring to his annoyance when she'd insisted on going to Philadelphia with Hattie instead of accompanying him to campaign headquarters.

# 28

Hattie was dressing for church when Brooke knocked on the door between their rooms. "Come in, dear," Hattie called, and Brooke, wearing a beige sweater and skirt, entered the room.

"I'd like to go to church with you this morning," Brooke stated. "I haven't been too good about attending and today I'd really like to go. They'll probably pray for Gram, won't they?"

"Yes, I'm sure they will," Hattie replied, "especially since her funeral was only five days ago. It will mean a lot to me to have you there, Brooke."

They didn't have much time to chat during the brief car ride to the church, but Brooke repeated her former assessment of Larry. "He is a nice person, Aunt Hattie, I'm sure he is. I'm positive he would never do anything to harm Anna. I believe he's still in love with her."

"I think so, too, Brooke. I'd hate to think that he deliberately brought those autumn flowers to Anna knowing of her allergy. He seemed so genuinely stricken. You didn't see him until afterward, of course, but he looked dreadful when she had that asthma attack."

"I believe that," Brooke said. "Mother was terrible to him, wasn't she?"

"Yes," Hattie answered. "You didn't hear everything she said to him, but she was terrible, and I don't know why."

"She was glad when Anna broke off their engagement," Brooke said. "There was something about Larry she just didn't like. To tell you the truth, I always thought it was his parents. His father owned a hardware store in the city, as you might know. He and Larry's mother both worked there. They were honest, hardworking people, and frankly, I always enjoyed their company. But Mother thought Anna could do better.

"I hate to say it, but Mother is the worst snob I've ever known. She wants us both to marry 'well.' That means wealthy professional men. She is already giving me a bad time about Shawn."

They were pulling into the church parking lot. Hattie kept to herself the fact that she agreed wholeheartedly with everything Brooke had just said. Still, she gave Alexandra the benefit of the doubt as the girls' mother.

"Your mother really loves you girls," Hattie said. "She wants what she thinks is best for you both. You must understand that."

They walked past the cemetery on their way to the door of the church. The great bell in the steeple began to toll, and Hattie swallowed a lump in her throat.

Being in the church was a comfort to Hattie, and having Brooke sitting next to her gave her solace. This church was where she had belonged all of her life, where she had rejoiced at so many weddings and so many baptisms, and grieved at so many funerals.

For some reason, everything was in sharper focus today than usual. The music was more beautiful, the prayers more heartfelt and the sermon more spiritual. A candle had been lit for Annie, and perhaps the focus on Annie was the reason for the unusual intensity. The candle, the prayers for her immortal soul and for all of her loved ones. Hattie was aware of a feeling of renewed strength, in herself and those around her.

"I'm so glad I came, Aunt Hattie. I feel uplifted," Brooke told her after the service.

They walked over to Annie's grave and stared at it silently for some time. They both saw just a pile of dirt with flowers dying on top of it.

"Gram's not here, is she?" Brooke asked softly.

"No, not at all. The body is like a winter coat. You wear it when the weather is cold, but in the summer, you simply don't need it any more. Your Gram doesn't need her body now."

"I feel so much better," Brooke confessed.

"Yes, dear, so do I," Hattie said, giving Brooke's hand a squeeze.

Brooke and Hattie were still on church grounds when Shawn left for the Eagles game in Philadelphia. Brooke had written a quick note to him saying where she had gone and left it on the kitchen table where he was sure to find it. He simply turned it over and wrote that he was leaving for the game and would be back as soon as it was over.

Characteristically, he did not leave hungry. Before heading out, he fixed himself three scrambled eggs, two pieces of toast with butter and strawberry jam and helped himself to coffee from the coffee maker left on by a thoughtful Hattie.

The weather forecast had predicted a cold day, so Shawn wore a heavy sweater under his fleece-lined leather jacket. He knew how cold it could be in the stadium stands, so he also took a knit cap and gloves.

He smiled at his image in a mirror next to the door. Girls had always been drawn to him, and he didn't expect to have a problem with Stacey Tyburn. He was cocky in his belief that he could convince her to listen to reason. "That wee lad could charm the thorns off a rose," his Irish grandmother used to say.

As he drove down Interstate-95 on his way to the stadium, that charming lad, now grown, felt a mounting excitement. This was his first really important assignment for the DiRienzo campaign. Granted, Michael would be furious if he knew what they had cooked up behind his back, but there was no doubt in Shawn's mind that this was the right thing to do for the senator's career. Someone had to reign in that man's libido; he clearly couldn't—or wouldn't—do it himself.

Before stepping from his car in the vast parking lot of the stadium, he pulled the newspaper photo of Michael and Stacey from his pocket and stared at her picture again. Fortunately her features could be clearly seen next to Michael's shoulder, and unfortunately Michael's distinctive profile was undeniably recognizable as he smiled down at her.

"She's a real looker, all right," Shawn observed aloud. He found himself looking forward more than he should have to the task before him.

As promised by Howard Cole, there was a ticket awaiting Shawn at the ticket booth. To his delight it was in the lower section on the 50-yard-line.

He had ample time during the game to watch Stacey Tyburn, and he found her something to watch. Sometimes it was hard to take his eyes from her slim, shapely body and legs, to say nothing of her face. *Michael really had excellent taste*, he thought.

Shawn enjoyed himself tremendously. He loved football, he loved the Eagles, and when they won the game 21 to 14 in the last few minutes of play, Shawn shouted as loud as any fan there.

He watched with no thought of Brooke as Stacey and the other cheerleaders leapt into the air and turned cartwheels. Then suddenly, the players and the cheerleaders had run from the field, the fans were making their way from the stands, and Shawn started to wonder what would happen next. How was he supposed to meet Stacey? Howard had said he would make the arrangements, but what were they?

He remained at his seat feeling a bit foolish. *What now?* He wondered. Did he forget some instructions Howard had given him? He went over their entire conversation in his mind, but he couldn't remember anything specific.

The crowd was thinning out when a young man approached him. "Are you Shawn O'Brien?" he asked. When Shawn answered in the affirmative, the young man introduced himself as Paul Patterson. "Howard Cole told me to find you," he said.

He handed Shawn a bulky plain white envelope. "I'll take you to Stacey Tyburn," he said. "She should be dressed by now. Come this way," and he led him to the cheerleaders' dressing room.

"About that envelope," Paul Patterson instructed. "If Stacey gives you any trouble, I mean if she refuses to do what you ask her to do, offer her what's inside the envelope. If she still refuses, call Howard at his phone in the campaign headquarters. Got it?"

"Got it," Shawn answered. He was beginning to feel really important. He stuffed the envelope into his right pants' pocket.

Stacey was even more striking up close than she had been on the field. Her hair was a thick auburn, which her brown eyes complemented well. Her skin was like ivory—smooth and flawless.

She was not as tall as Brooke. Probably at least two inches shorter, he figured, and she was not as strictly beautiful. Where Brooke had perfect features, Stacey's were somewhat irregular, but that just added to her charm.

"It's nice to meet you, Shawn," she said in a husky voice. "Paul tells me you are a friend of Michael's."

*Lord! She's sexy!* Shawn thought—even her voice. Out loud he said, "Thanks, Stacey, it's nice to meet you, too. I was watching you out there during the game. You really are good at what you do. And yes, I am a friend of Michael's. I've known him all my life."

"He is wonderful, isn't he?" she said, and Shawn couldn't miss the glow in her eyes. "And thanks for the compliment," she added as an afterthought.

"Would you like to go somewhere and talk?" she suggested. "My roommate drove me here today. She's a cheerleader, too. Anyway, if you have a car here, maybe we could go get a cup of coffee someplace and then you could drive me home. If you don't mind, that is. I mean, if that's okay with you, I'll go tell her. She won't mind going home without me. It's not that far."

Shawn laughed. "All that in one breath!" he exclaimed. "Sounds great to me. You can be my navigator."

They drove through territory very familiar to Shawn, but he made no suggestions about a place to eat. It would be wiser, he thought, to allow Stacey to take the lead.

"So," he said, "Where are you from? How'd you get to be an Eagles cheerleader? Do you really like being a cheerleader?" What do your folks think of having a famous Eagles cheerleader in the family?"

Stacey's lips parted in a very appealing, slightly crooked smile. "Aren't you the curious one?" she asked. "Well, let's see...I grew up in Harleysville. I have a nineteen-year-old sister who's in college. She thinks it's cool that I'm a cheerleader, but my parents are a little old-fashioned. They're not crazy about it. I think my dad worries that guys might hassle me. As far as how I got the position, I tried out like everyone else. I had a lot of experience. I was a cheerleader in school from seventh grade right on through junior college. Most of the time I really love it. I get to travel a lot, meet a lot of nice, interesting people."

Stacey looked at Shawn as he steered the car through the old city's narrow streets. She saw a clean-cut, lightly freckled face beneath a thatch of sandy hair and a muscular build. Aware that he was being observed, Shawn turned his head briefly and looked directly at her. He smiled and she was impressed by the twinkle in his eye and his overall warmth. She returned his smile sincerely.

"Turn right at the next corner," she directed. "There's a little soda shop halfway down the block."

"A soda shop?" he was surprised. "I thought you'd take me to a bar, or a club."

"No," she said simply. "I don't drink. Are you disappointed?"

"Surprised," he admitted, "but not in the least disappointed." He had expected her to be sophisticated, a woman of the world, but she wasn't. She was more like the girl next door, and he found her appealing. It was easy to understand how she might be a breath of fresh air for Michael.

Betty Kerr Orlemann

# 29

Hattie and Brooke ate cold ham sandwiches for Sunday lunch and were about to leave for the hospital when the phone rang. Hattie picked up the receiver and was surprised to find that Maria DiRienzo was calling Brooke.

She covered the mouthpiece and whispered the identity of the caller to Brooke.

The girl took the phone and was slightly annoyed when she heard Maria say in her quiet voice. "I'm truly sorry to bother you on a Sunday, Brooke, but there are a few things which need correction in the work you did yesterday. Can you come to headquarters this afternoon?"

"Maria," Brooke said firmly, "I was just leaving for the hospital to see my sister. Can't it wait until tomorrow?"

"I'm afraid not," Maria said. "Can you come in right now?"

"I don't see how, Maria," said Brooke. "I don't have a car, and Miss Farwell is going to the hospital to visit Anna. Since campaign headquarters would be out of the way, I really don't want to ask her to take me there. I'm sure you understand. You probably know that Shawn always takes me to headquarters, and he's driven down to the Eagles game. So that leaves me without a ride. I'm sorry."

"Well, if that's your only problem," Maria told her sweetly, "I'll just drive over and pick you up. How do I get there from here? I'm at headquarters."

"Here," Brooke said in resignation. "I'll let Miss Farwell give you the directions." She handed the phone to Hattie with a whispered. "She's coming to get me." She made a sour face.

After she'd hung up the phone, Hattie commented. "That is one very persistent lady. Her voice is so soft that I could hardly hear what she was saying, but she obviously has a very strong will."

"You know, Aunt Hattie, if I hadn't committed myself to this campaign, I'd be a much happier person. I had my own idea of what the work would be like, and nothing has turned out as I imagined."

Hattie smiled, but had to admit to herself that she would be a happier person, too, if Brooke had never become involved with anything to do with Michael DiRienzo.

"I believe I'll just wait until Mrs. DiRienzo arrives," she said. "I'd be very interested in meeting the person who might one day be our First Lady."

Less than half an hour later, they heard a car in the lane. Brooke looked through the window in the kitchen door and announced that Maria had arrived and was backing into the driveway.

"I should go right out," she said, "but I do so hate to be bossed around. I think I'll wait until she blows the horn or something." She stood back away from the door so Maria couldn't see her looking out. "Oh great!" she exclaimed sarcastically. "She's coming in!"

Wolf had roused himself from his spot by the fireplace when he heard the car approaching. He walked over to the door where Hattie took a firm grip on his collar.

"You sit, boy," she commanded. "Some people don't like dogs—especially such big ones."

Brooke opened the door as Maria reached the porch.

"Hi!" she said, sounding perkier than she felt. "I'm all ready. First, though, I'd like you to meet Miss Farwell. Aunt Hattie, this is Maria DiRienzo."

Hattie was just about to invite Maria in, when Wolf snarled viciously and lunged at the senator's wife. Maria screamed and ran back toward her car.

"Wolf, no!" What's gotten into you?" Hattie reprimanded, grabbing Wolf's collar and shoving him back into the kitchen. She and Brooke both stepped out onto the porch, carefully closing the door behind them. Hattie was full of apologies when she went to Maria's car to meet her.

"I don't know what possessed him to behave like that," Hattie said. "He's usually as gentle as a pussycat. I'm so sorry, Mrs. DiRienzo."

"That's the story of my life," said Maria, still visibly shaken. "I must have a funny smell or something, but dogs just don't like me. To tell you the truth, they scare the life out of me."

"I've often heard that animals can smell fear," Hattie said. "It certainly seems that Wolf knew how frightened you were of him."

"I have nightmares about dogs," Maria admitted, "and that is the biggest dog I have ever seen. He's really terrifying." She took a deep breath and closed her eyes in an effort to control her shaking. "Does he run loose?" she asked when she was calmer.

"Not any more," Hattie responded. "He always did, but recently there was a poacher in the woods, and I was afraid he might get shot."

Maria didn't speak, but it was obvious from her expression that she thought it wouldn't be a bad idea if someone had shot Wolf.

"I'm fine now, Brooke," Maria said. "Hop in. We have a lot work ahead of us."

Before Brooke realized what Maria was doing, she turned the car left into the lane and headed toward the Brookside Farms development.

"You're going the wrong way, Maria," she said.

"Oh, Lord," said Maria. "I guess I'm still upset. Can I get out if I keep going this way?"

"Well, yes," Brooke said hesitantly. "We're heading toward a new development. Not all of the roads are paved, though, and it will take us a little longer to get to headquarters.

"There doesn't seem to be any place to turn around, so I'll keep going this way," Maria said. "You'll have to excuse me for being such a fool."

The only other person at campaign headquarters was Howard Cole. He was busily working on his computer when Maria and Brooke walked in. He barely nodded to acknowledge their presence as they passed his desk.

Reluctantly, Brooke walked down the cellar stairs to her workstation, and Maria followed her. Maria sat at the computer and brought up Brooke's lists of the day before. She immediately began to point out errors in them. Brooke fought back anger at the constant criticism of her work by this precise, mousy little woman.

Trying to sound calm, she said, "Oh, Maria, this is like a repeat of the other day. These issues you're pointing out seem kind of picky. Honestly, I can't see what I did wrong. I may have done things differently than you would have, but the work got done. And it's accurate."

Maria, mindful that nearly all the office staff were volunteers, was very much in control as she patiently showed Brooke the exact changes she expected to be made.

Brooke took several deep breaths before she was able to be cordial, but in the end she agreed to do everything Maria told her to.

"That's a dear girl," Maria consoled. "I know it's not much fun to make endless lists, but there's an established system to how we enter data. There has to be, when so many different people are using it. What you're doing is vitally important to Michael's campaign, and we are both very grateful to you."

Somewhat mollified, Brooke settled herself at the computer. Maria walked quietly—mousily, thought Brooke—from the office. Brooke heard her soft footsteps on the stairs and the closing of the door at the top.

Small shafts of sunlight worked their way through the Venetian blinds and across the green rug as Brooke typed away at her lists.

"This is so boring!" she said aloud, after about an hour of rewriting her old lists.

She pushed back her chair, stood up and stretched. With a deep sigh, she walked around the office and looked once again at the countless pictures of Michael that adorned the walls.

"You are handsome," she told a photograph, in which he sat staring directly into the camera. "I just hope you're worth all this work."

The splotches of sunlight slid further along the rug, but Brooke was not aware of the passage of time as she resumed concentrating on her work. This time, she thought, it had to be right. There was nothing worse than going over and over the same thing.

Finally she was finished. After checking and rechecking her work, she was convinced that this time she had done everything the exact way that Maria wanted. She slid out of her chair and ascended the stairs to consult with Maria and hopefully get a ride back to Hattie's. The door at the top of the stairs wouldn't open. Brooke shook the doorknob and pushed the door, but nothing happened.

There was no sound from the first floor. Brooke yelled for help.

"Maria," she called. "MARIA!" There was no response. "Howard! HOWARD!" she cried, but still no one came. She pounded on the door, and was greeted by silence.

*How odd*, she thought, annoyed. The cellar below her was growing dark. She flicked the electric switch and was relieved to see the lights come on. She tried the door once more, but with no success. "This is ridiculous!" she said aloud. "I am not going to panic."

She ran down the stairs and back into her office, where she tried to open the back door to the alley, with no luck. Pulling the blind aside, she clearly saw the reason: The door was fastened with a deadbolt, and there was no key in evidence.

"That's why Maria told me to come to her before I use this door," she reminded herself, aloud. She was certain Maria had the key, but began to search her desk for it anyway. When that proved unproductive, she ran from bookshelf to bookshelf, flinging books to the floor as she looked behind them. No key anywhere. "I will not panic," she repeated.

She listened in vain for footsteps overhead, but there was no sound.

"The windows!" she said, but when she opened the blinds, there were bars on the outside, and the sills were nailed shut.

"The phone," she cried, chiding herself. "Duh! Why didn't I think of that before?"

She rushed to her desk and lifted the receiver, but the line was dead. She quickly rummaged through her purse, but realized that in all the uproar with Wolf when she left with Maria, she'd left her cell phone on Hattie's kitchen counter.

Finally, despite her resolve, Brooke gave in to fear and burst into tears.

"What'll I do?" she sobbed. "I must be calm. I can't think if I panic." She sat down and closed her eyes, taking deep breaths until her breathing slowed. "Think. Think," she told herself.

Just then, she thought she heard footsteps above her. She held her breath and listened. Yes, those were definitely footsteps. She ran to the stairs, shouting, "Help!" all the way up. When she reached the door at the top, she pounded on it with both fists. "Help! Help! HELP!" she cried.

The door was flung open, and she fell into the arms of Senator Michael DiRienzo.

Betty Kerr Orlemann

232

# 30

Shawn helped Stacey off with her coat, a soft, fleece-lined denim that exactly matched her jeans, he noticed. Sort of a casual elegance, he thought. She was wearing a white turtleneck sweater, and looked very cute and perky.

They smiled at each other.

*We could be friends*, Shawn thought.

As Stacey slid into a booth, Shawn hung her coat and his own on hooks on a post and sat opposite her.

"What would you like?" he asked.

Again, she surprised him.

"A chocolate soda, thanks."

"Chocolate soda?" he repeated. "How do you keep that girlish figure?" he asked, in a parody of some bad commercial.

For a moment, she was embarrassed. "I really never had a problem with my weight," she confessed. "I guess it's all the exercise."

"I'll have a chocolate soda, too," he decided. "And how about a hamburger?"

"No, thanks. I'm going to meet Michael for dinner at seven-thirty, and I don't want to spoil my appetite."

"Really?" he asked. "Where are you meeting him...if you don't mind my asking?"

She hesitated. Michael had been adamant about keeping their relationship a secret, but this guy was with his campaign. He wouldn't do anything to hurt Michael.

"Oh, there's a little out-of-the-way restaurant on south 13th Street, this side of Pine," she answered vaguely.

"Would you like me to drive you there?" he offered.

"Oh...no, thanks. You can drive me home after we drink our sodas, though, if you don't mind. I want to change my clothes. I'll just take the subway up Broad Street."

The waitress appeared, pad in hand, and Shawn ordered the sodas and a hamburger for himself. After she was gone, Stacey asked, "Why did you want to see me, Shawn? Did Michael send you for some reason?"

"No, he didn't," Shawn answered truthfully. "He actually doesn't even know I'm with you."

"Oh?" The smile ran away from Stacey's face.

Shawn patted the fat envelope in his pants pocket, making sure it was still there.

"Stacey," he began, not knowing quite what to say. "Stacey..." he tried again. "You know that Michael is married, don't you?"

"Yes."

"And you know he has his eye on the White House, right?" Shawn continued.

"Yes."

"And that a picture of you in his arms was in yesterday's paper?"

"Yes..."

"Well, not to be indelicate, but...don't you realize that his relationship with you would be very difficult to explain to the media if it continues? It could ruin his chance to be president."

"We've talked about that." Stacey was very serious. "He says if we're very careful from now on, nobody will have to know. He also says that when the proper time comes, he will divorce his wife and marry me." Her beautiful eyes sparkled.

"Stacey," Shawn said. "I hate to be the one to tell you this, but Michael has had many girls to whom he has made that same promise." He felt sorry as he watched her face fall, but continued. This was an important duty, and he had been entrusted with it. "He doesn't intend to marry you, Stacey…not ever. He will never divorce Maria."

"How can you say that to me?" she nearly yelled. "You don't have the slightest idea how we feel about each other! His wife is…well, she's a bitch. He's told me all about how awful she is. Things will work out between us. I know they will!'

Shawn, though he thought Maria something of a doormat, felt protective of her. "His wife is not a bitch," he protested. "She's devoted to him and works very hard on his campaign. She has stuck by him through many others like you." He saw tears rise in the girl's eyes. "Please, Stacey," he pleaded, reaching across the table to take her hand, which she snatched away. "I'm not trying to hurt you, but listen to reason! You're unfortunately not the first, and you probably won't be the last woman he has been involved with outside his marriage. Aside from being unfair to Maria, it's no way for you to live, either. You're a beautiful, sweet girl, who lots of guys would die to be with."

Stacey choked back tears. "You don't know how it is with Michael and me. I love him so much, and he loves me. He wouldn't say so if it weren't true."

"Yes, he probably does love you…now. The trouble with Michael is that he falls in love too easily—and right back out again, too." Shawn felt sorry for her; he hated adding to her misery. "Besides," he added, "He's old enough to be your father."

"So what?" Stacey challenged him.

The waitress arrived with their order, then left. Neither spoke for a short time. Dreading what he was about to do next, Shawn pulled the envelope from his pocket and handed it to Stacey.

"This is for you," he said. "All you have to do is stop seeing Michael—forever."

She opened it just enough to see what was inside, closed it immediately and pushed it back across the table to him.

"I don't want it!" she said, a bit too loudly. Shawn visibly flinched and looked around to make sure no one was watching.

"That envelope," he said slowly, painfully, "contains ten thousand dollars. I counted it. Certainly, you can use that kind of money."

"No," she said. "I won't take it." She began to cry.

"Stacey," Shawn said gently, "forget the money. Just please...stop seeing Michael. Your relationship could cause irreparable damage to his chances of ever being president! Do you want to ruin his career?"

"Stop it! Of course not. But I can't stop seeing him," she sobbed. "I love him too much."

Not knowing how to respond, Shawn took a large bite out of his hamburger. He stared at Stacey thoughtfully. "If you really love him, you won't want to see him lose his life's dream. Think of what's best for him!" Shawn was desperate. "I know it'll cause you terrible grief, but it will be a very brave thing for you to do, believe me. And Stacey, I don't want you to get hurt, honestly, but if you persist in seeing Michael, I'm afraid you face much worse pain in the future."

Shawn looked at her sadly for a long moment. She was so vulnerable. He wanted to take her in his arms, to comfort her. Instead, all he could do was eat his burger.

Stacey dabbed at her eyes and blew her nose with a tissue. She sat for some time, deep in thought. Finally, she spoke.

"I've decided what to do. I'm going to meet Michael tonight as planned. We'll discuss his future, and then I'll know what I should do."

"Oh, Stacey," Shawn sighed. "He is so convincing. Please, remember what I've told you. He's weak. When it comes to women he has the morals of a rabbit."

"Would you mind taking me home, now?" she asked, angrily. "I need to get dressed to go see Michael." She pushed her untouched soda aside, dabbed at her eyes once more and rose to put on her coat. Shawn took a long final draft of his soda and finished his hamburger. It tasted like sawdust.

"All right, I'll take you home. But just excuse me a minute, will you?" he asked. He paid at the counter for their food, and walked quickly to the back of the store where the restrooms were. But it wasn't a restroom he wanted. He pulled out his cell phone.

Stacey had sat down again, her view of the back of the store blocked by the booth. She sat lost in her own miserable thoughts, waiting for Shawn to return.

Howard Cole answered the phone on his desk on the first ring—or in his case, the first chirp. He hated loud phones.

"Howard, it's Shawn. I'm afraid I've failed."

"Talk."

Shawn told him about his meeting with Stacey. He described her and told Howard what a really great girl she was. He explained how she'd refused to even look at the money, and that she planned to meet Michael that evening in spite of every argument he'd made.

Howard's voice was calm and businesslike. He'd been through this before, many times.

"Where are they meeting?" he asked.

"She wouldn't say exactly," Shawn answered in frustration. "She said it was a little out-of-the-way restaurant someplace on 13th Street south of Pine."

"Okay." Howard sounded bored. "What time are they supposed to meet?"

"Seven-thirty."

"Where is she now?"

"We're in a soda shop. Right now she's in a booth, but she's anxious to leave and get ready for their date. I told her I'd drive her home."

"Why don't you drive her to the restaurant to meet Michael?"

"I offered, but she refused. She said she'd take the Broad Street subway."

"Okay. Shawn, thanks. You've done the best you could." Howard glanced at his watch. "It's almost five-fifteen. You'd better get going."

When Shawn dropped Stacey off at her apartment, she suddenly turned to him.

"Shawn, is there anyone special in your life?"

"Yeah."

"Are you in love with her?"

"Yes, very much," he admitted.

"Would you take ten thousand dollars to give her up? Would you give her up for anything?"

Shawn didn't hesitate. "No, of course not!"

"That's how I feel about Michael."

She looked at him very directly for a beat, then got out of the car. She strode across the sidewalk and through the door without turning around again.

Shawn stared after her helplessly.

"She didn't get it," he mumbled. "She doesn't understand that she has to give him up for his own sake."

# 31

As soon as Howard hung up the phone, Maria came from her desk to his. "I heard the whole conversation," she said. "I listened in on my phone."

"Why doesn't that surprise me, Maria?" he asked sarcastically.

"I'd like to wring Michael's sexy neck!" she snapped. "I've been reasonable with him. I've yelled at him, I've even hit him, but to what good? You'd think now that he's working toward the presidency he'd have better sense."

Howard suppressed an amused grin at the idea of tiny Maria actually hitting the 6-foot, 3-inch, muscular Michael. *He probably never felt it*, he thought, but he spoke gently to Maria. "You know how often I've tried to talk sense into Michael. He's charmed so many people that now he thinks he can get away with anything he wants to and nobody will think poorly of him. He's arrogant, Maria, and you know it. He's spoiled and selfish and self-indulgent. I don't know why we stick by him."

"Because we love him," Maria said sadly. All at once she put her hands to her stomach and doubled over.

"Maria!" cried Howard in alarm. "What's the matter?"

She was pale and in great distress. "It's my damned ulcer!" she gasped. "Give me a minute, I'll be better."

Howard had seen these attacks before, and they always worried him. "Can't I do something for you?"

"My purse. In my desk. I have antacid pills there." Still doubled over and clutching her midriff she pointed toward her cubicle.

Howard ran to Maria's desk and grabbed her purse. He was back in half a minute. She popped several antacid tablets into her mouth and chewed them slowly.

In a few minutes she was able to stand upright and force a small smile. "It's better, now," she said, a defeated edge in her voice. "But I think I should go home."

Howard took Maria's arm and walked her to her car. "I could strangle Mike for doing this to you," he growled. With great concern he watched her drive off.

It was right then that he decided to drive downtown and confront Michael and Stacey in their little restaurant. He'd find it if he had to search every hidden eatery on 13th Street. He turned out the lights and locked the door behind him.

❧

Maria and Howard apologized to Brooke the next day, explaining that they had both been so preoccupied that they'd completely forgotten she was in her basement office.

Michael DiRienzo had spent most of the afternoon in his party's headquarters in Doylestown, trying to convince the party leaders to support him in the spring primaries. He left feeling buoyant and confident. Things had gone well.

He felt in his pocket for his reading glasses. Vanity had kept him from wearing them in public, but he knew he would need them for the restaurant this evening. His spirits soared when he thought of Stacey. He could hardly wait to see her.

The glasses weren't there. That meant a side-trip to his own headquarters to look for them. This was something he did not look forward to. He wasn't in the mood to face Maria and more of her accusations about that unfortunate picture in yesterday's paper.

He used his key to unlock the door and had scarcely walked into the building, when he heard a woman's voice yelling for help and someone pounding on the cellar door. The door seemed to be stuck, and when he wrenched it open he was completely amazed when a beautiful girl fell into his arms.

He held her at arms length to get a better look at her. Despite her moist red eyes, tear-stained cheeks and mussed hair, she was a knock-out. "You must be Shawn's girl," he surmised, "the only person around here whom I have not yet met. As I remember Shawn told me your name is Brooke.

Brooke gave him a weak smile and nodded her head. "That's who I am, Senator." She was clearly embarrassed. "This is not the shape I had planned to be in when I met you."

"And just why are you in this shape?" he asked.

"Maria wanted me to do some extra work today, so she drove me over here and sent me down to the basement office. That's where I'm supposed to work. I worked there yesterday, too." She felt as though she were rattling. This was so embarrassing.

He smiled down at her. "And the door got stuck when you tried to get out, didn't it? Then you discovered that there was no way to get out through the back door, and the windows had bars, and you didn't hear anyone up here until I came in. Am I right?"

She nodded her head again. "Yes, and on top of that, the telephone was dead and I didn't have my cell with me."

"Let's go down and see about that," he said, and pushing the cellar door wide open to prevent further sticking, he led the way down the stairs.

Once in the office he went directly to the phone. "It is indeed dead," he acknowledged. He knelt on the floor and held up the connecting wire. "It was simply unplugged," he said. "You must have tripped over it or something." He plugged it in.

"Now try it," he ordered.

Brooke put the phone to her ear, and with a sheepish grin she said. "It's working. I can hear the dial tone."

"Good. Now, can you tell me where everyone is?"

"I haven't the vaguest idea," she said. "Shawn usually brings me in and takes me home, but he went to the Eagles game. Howard Cole and Maria were both here earlier, but I don't know what happened to them. I wonder how I'll get home... What time is it?"

"He looked at his watch. "Uh-oh!" he said. "It's almost six. I have a dinner date in Philadelphia at seven-thirty, so I'd better not hang around here too long. Let's close up shop, and then I'll drive you home."

"Oh, I hate to put you out, but that's very kind of you," she said. "I was trying to figure out how I would get there. Shawn should have been back by now."

"So Shawn went to the Eagles game, huh?" Michael said, thoughtfully. Something about that bothered him.

"I'll wait if you want to go wash your face," Michael offered. "I have to get something in my office, anyway."

By the time his glasses were safely tucked away in his pocket, Brooke came out of the lady's room looking fresh and well-scrubbed. Her hair was combed and pulled back in a pony tail.

Michael stared at her, shocked. "Brooke," he kept his voice calm. "What is your last name?"

"Turner," she answered.

"Is your mother Alexandra Turner?"

"Yes, but it hasn't been Turner for years. My father died when I was five, and when I was about six-and-a-half, Mother married Dr. Cameron MacArthur. You've

242

probably heard of him."

"I certainly have," he said indifferently. "But did you know that a couple of decades ago your mother worked for my campaign for Congress? Isn't that a coincidence?"

"That's what Maria told me," Brooke said.

"Did Maria also tell you that you look exactly like your mother except for your coloring? The resemblance is astounding." He put his arm casually around her waist and escorted her through the door, turning to lock it behind them when they were on the sidewalk outside.

"How is your mother?" he asked as they walked to his Lincoln Continental.

"Mother is just fine, thank you. She's enjoying all of the finer things in life such as traveling, shopping, dining out, decorating and redecorating their townhouse, entertaining and being entertained, you know."

He helped her into the car. "Cool car," she said casually.

"Thanks," he laughed. "Most people are a little more impressed by it."

"I guess," she answered. "One of the many differences between Mother and me is that I don't care about 'stuff.'" His laugh was contagious, and though she wasn't sure why, Brooke joined in the hilarity.

"How is your sister?" he asked. "Shawn has told me all about her accident. What a terrible experience for her, for you all." Brooke gave him directions to Hattie's place before she answered him. The car purred along as if its wheels weren't touching the macadam.

"Anna is much better, thanks," she said. "In fact, we're hoping she'll be home from the hospital for Thanksgiving. Aunt Hattie is having dinner at her house."

"Aunt Hattie?" he asked in a "who-is-she" tone.

"Hattie Farwell, she says she met you years ago at my grandparents' house in Philadelphia. I'm staying with her."

He frowned, trying to remember. "Maybe I'll recognize her when I see her. Tell me about you, now. How old are you? Are you still in school? What do you want to do with your life?"

"I'm seventeen, but I'll be eighteen in February. I'm going to graduate from the Kendall School in May, barring any disasters. I've applied to several colleges but haven't heard from any of them yet. I'm thinking of majoring in political science," she told him.

He smiled. "That," he stated, "would be Shawn's influence. Tell me, when did you start going to boarding school?"

"When I was eight," she said with a shrug.

"Why so young?" he wanted to know.

"I always believed it was to get me out of the way," she answered simply. There was neither anger nor self-pity in her tone. Fact is fact.

"Oh, come on now," he chided. "The Kendall School has a wonderful reputation. I'm sure your mother just wanted what was best for you."

"Then why didn't she send my sister away to school? Didn't she want what was best for her, too?"

Michael kept his eyes on the road. There was no answer to her question. Apparently Alexandra wanted to have a good time with her new husband, and little Brooke had been in the way. By the time Brooke had been sent off to Massachusetts, her sister was halfway through college and well out of the way on her own, he thought.

He glanced at Brooke out of the corner of his eye and felt an almost tender sympathy for her. "It must have been lonely for you sometimes," he observed. "You were such a little girl, so far from home."

"Yeah, it was. But they were good to me there, and I had friends."

They both fell silent.

Several moments later, Brooke said, "There's Aunt Hattie's lane, up ahead on the right." He slowed to turn in, and at Brooke's instructions parked in Hattie's driveway.

"How gallant!" she chuckled when he stepped from the car and walked around to her side to open the door for her. "Thanks more than I can say, Senator. How very, very lucky for me that you came along this afternoon."

"Call me Michael," he instructed. "And let me tell you that it was very lucky for me that I met you." Smiling he leaned over and gave her a peck on the cheek.

At that exact moment, Shawn drove up the lane. He was already feeling sorry for Stacey, and when he saw Michael kissing Brooke, his jealousy and quick temper got the best of him. He spun his car to a stop next to Michael's and jumped out.

"What's going on here?"

Shawn balled his hands into fists, and Brooke was terrified that he was about to strike Michael.

"Shawn, geez!" she screamed. "Michael wasn't doing anything!"

The senator looked at his protegé and smiled, remember what it was like to be nineteen.

"Take it easy, my boy," he said. "Your girlfriend was stranded at headquarters and I simply drove her home. The little peck on her cheek meant nothing to either of us. Calm down."

Hattie, who'd come out onto the kitchen porch when she heard the commotion, stepped across to the driveway. By the time she reached them, Shawn had backed off and, embarrassed, apologized to Michael.

Hattie, of course, recognized Michael instantly, but waited for Brooke to introduce them. Michael beamed at her as though she were the only person in the world he wanted to greet. As they shook hands he told her, "It's very good to see you again, Miss Farwell. It must be what...nineteen, twenty years...since we met at the Turners' home in Philadelphia?"

"What a wonderful memory you have for names and faces, Senator," Hattie complimented. She was obviously impressed. Brooke covered her mouth with her hand to hide a smile. She was learning about politics.

# 32

Michael drove as fast as possible down Interstate 95 to the Center City exit. He looked frequently at the clock, and was relieved to see that it was only seven-fifteen when he reached town. His mind was on nothing but his meeting with Stacey.

To his delight, he had no trouble finding a parking spot and was in their favorite booth in the restaurant eight minutes early. By design, their booth was in the very rear of the restaurant, where its occupants were sheltered from unwanted attention.

Rather than seats on opposite sides of the table, as in more conventional booths, theirs had a curved bench so its occupants sat side-by-side, facing out over the table in front of them. It was private and intimate and they felt safe from prying eyes there.

The only inconvenience with this arrangement was that Michael could not see out of the booth without sliding around to the edge and poking his head out. Even then, it was difficult for him to see the front of the little café, and the door was out of his line of vision. He sat uncomfortably for almost fifteen minutes, straining to see Stacey when she came in.

Their usual waitress came to the table.

"Hi!" she greeted Michael, cheerfully. "May I bring your usual drinks?" She lit the candle in its amber glass holder in the center of the table. It flickered wildly at first, drawing strange patterns on her face.

He squinted at his watch in the semi-darkness. It was seven thirty-eight.

"Yes, I guess so." A worried frown creased his brow. "She's a little late this evening, but she should be here any minute."

"A glass of dry red wine and a Shirley Temple, right?"

"Right," he said with a smile.

A few minutes later the waitress brought their drinks, but Stacey still hadn't arrived. Michael vacillated between anger and fear. By now, he was literally hanging out of the booth, his eyes glued to the front of the restaurant. To his alarm, he saw Howard Cole come into view. Michael quickly pulled his head back into the booth, but too late. Howard had seen him.

"Well, well, Michael," Howard gloated, sliding into the booth next to Michael. "I've finally found you. You can't imagine how many little out-of-the-way restaurants there are on south 13th Street.

"What the hell are you doing here?" Michael growled. "And how did you know where to look for me?"

"That's a long story which I am not prepared to share with you, at least not now. Where's your girlfriend?" He gave a questioning look toward the restrooms.

"She's not here. I'm eating alone," Michael lied.

Howard looked at the glass of red wine and then at the Shirley Temple, its ice cubes nearly melted. He picked up the latter and sipped it. "Since when do you use Shirley Temples as chasers?"

"Shut up, Howard! And get lost!" Michael was clearly perturbed. "Did you have anything to do with this? Did you say anything to Stacey to keep her away from me? Or did Shawn?"

Howard was the picture of innocence.

"Whatever do you mean, Michael? I don't have any idea what you're talking about. What does Shawn have to do with your love life?"

Michael glared at Howard.

"I understand that he was at the Eagles game this afternoon. I'm curious as to where he obtained a ticket."

Howard smiled and leaned back comfortably, but he didn't answer the question.

Michael didn't have to be told what had happened.

"Does Maria know? Was she in on this latest 'save Michael' campaign, too?" He was very angry, but years in politics had taught him how to control his rage. "Did you buy her off?" he questioned through his teeth. When there was still no response, he continued. "No! I know her too well to believe that. She would never take a bribe for anything. She's the most decent woman I have ever known. It was Shawn, wasn't it? He talked her into giving me up for my own good. He told her that our relationship would ruin my career. Wasn't that it? He shamed her for having an affair with a married man. He must have been real good to convince her to stay away from here tonight."

Howard sighed and shook his head.

"Michael, Michael, how many times do I have to tell you how dangerous it is for you to keep getting involved with these young beauties? Some eager member of the press will catch on some day soon, and your career will be ruined. That picture in the paper wasn't good, not good at all, and it upset poor Maria more than you know."

"I know," sighed Michael. "I could have killed that damned photographer."

"If you hadn't been fooling around again, there wouldn't have been a photographer," Howard scolded. "You do understand that, don't you, Mike? It was your own fault. There's no one else to blame. Your business is the paparazzi's business."

"I didn't want Maria to know. How did she take it?"

Howard sighed. "She had another attack. The pain doubled her up. She thinks it's an ulcer, you know, and she thinks she can treat it herself with antacid tablets."

"I'm sorry about that," Michael said. "I really am." He looked almost contrite, then changed the subject abruptly. "Did you know that you turned off the lights, left the office and locked the door while Shawn's young friend, Brooke, was stuck in the basement?"

"Oh, damn!" Howard cursed. "When Maria got sick, I completely forgot the kid. What do you mean, 'stuck'?"

"The door at the top of the stairs wouldn't open. She was yelling for help when I went in. The poor girl was scared to death. She said she had been banging at the door and calling for help for a long time."

"Lucky thing for her that you went to the office," Howard said. "We didn't know you were coming or I would have waited for you. I wish I had. Then I'd have heard Brooke banging on the door and released her."

"I didn't plan to go back, that's what's so lucky about it." Michael said. "I'd forgotten my reading glasses. They were in my office. Brooke would have been trapped down there all night if I hadn't shown up."

The waitress came back to the booth.

"Hello," she said cordially, if a tad surprised to see Howard instead of Stacey. "Can I get you anything?"

"A vodka martini with an olive, please—up. How about you, Mike? Another Chianti?"

Michael considered his answer, then snorted softly. "Why not?"

The waitress placed two menus in front of them and left to retrieve their drinks. Michael picked up his menu and looked it over with disinterest.

"Excuse me a minute, Howard, I have to make a phone call." He pulled a cell phone from his pocket.

"Excuse me," he said more pointedly. Howard left the table and headed toward the men's room. When Howard was safely out of sight, Michael dialed Stacey's number.

Her roommate, Jane Flynn, answered on the second ring. "Crazy House, this is Jane!"

Michael couldn't help smiling at the carefree, chipper voice.

"Hi, Jane, this is Michael. How's everything with you?"

"Just fine, Senator. You?" She sounded surprised to hear his voice.

"May I speak to Stacey, please?" He failed to mask the concern in his voice.

"Stacey?" Jane repeated. "Michael, she left to see you, a few minutes before seven."

"She did what?" Michael almost yelled. He forced himself to lower his voice.

"Did she seem okay?"

"Well, now that you mention it... She'd been crying earlier, but she seemed to work out whatever was bothering her. By the time she was dressed and ready to leave, she seemed okay."

"She never showed up here. I've been waiting for over an hour. Do you know what upset her earlier? Why she'd been crying?" He really didn't need an answer. He blamed Shawn and Howard, and maybe even Maria.

"She was concerned that her relationship with you might hurt your career. However, she made the decision to meet with you tonight and discuss everything. Her problem is, Michael, that she loves you too much."

"Is there any doubt in your mind, Jane, that she would go anywhere but here?" he asked. Fear gripped his heart.

"None at all, Michael. She was definitely on her way to see you, and she should have been there almost an hour ago."

"How was she coming?" he asked.

"She was planning to take the Broad Street subway, like she always does."

He gave Jane his cell number. "Promise to call me if you hear anything."

"I will. And will you call me, please, if you hear anything first?" she begged.

The senator agreed and they hung up.

When Howard returned to the booth, Michael was standing in front of it, putting on his overcoat. He hurriedly repeated his conversation with Jane, and announced. "I'm going to see if I can find Stacey."

The waitress walked back to the booth with two drinks on a cork-lined tray, but Michael was already halfway out of the café.

"Here," said Howard, placing a twenty-dollar bill on the tray. "Sorry. On second thought, I will take this." He picked up the martini and downed it in one gulp before he sped after Michael.

"Wait, Mike," he called after his boss' departing back. "I'll go with you!"

# 33

Stacey had been feeling pretty sure of herself when she said good night to Jane and started walking to the subway stop on Broad Street. Try as she would, she hadn't been able to decide what to do about her relationship with Michael, but she had made up her mind to talk to him about it. Between the two of them maybe they could solve the problems inherent in such a situation.

*The heck with it. I'm just going to enjoy my evening with him*, she thought. She was wearing a brand new expensive wool suit in a sapphire blue that she had bought on sale. She was quite proud of herself for that, and she thought Michael would be proud of her, too. Around her neck she wore a sapphire and diamond pendant—a gift from Michael. It matched the suit exactly. Her coat was a classic camel's hair.

Stacey floated down the subway steps, not noticing the dirty concrete or the pervasive smell of urine. She put her coins in the turnstile and pushed her way through to the train platform. She was vaguely aware that there were very few people scattered along the platform waiting for the next train. In the tradition of city dwellers, they didn't spare her a glance when she joined them. The train could be heard roaring toward them, and all eyes turned to the tunnel, watching for it to burst into the opening.

Stacey stepped closer to the tracks. Suddenly she felt a violent shove from behind her. She stumbled to the edge of the platform and fell full force under the wheels of the approaching train.

No one heard her scream over the deafening rumble around them. For only the briefest moment, the figure of the young woman falling in front of the train was caught in the bright glow of its headlights, but the only one who saw her fall was the engineer. Although he was in the process of slowing the train down, he slammed the brakes on hard when he saw the falling figure in front of him.

Passengers standing at the doors of the cars were thrown to the floor as the train screeched to a premature halt. Half-way between panic and nausea, the engineer called for emergency help.

While Stacey's attacker escaped the platform unnoticed, police cars and an ambulance soon jammed Broad Street at the subway entrance. Below, officers looked helplessly at spattered blood and scraps of sapphire blue wool and camel's hair scattered along the tracks down in the subway pit.

All trains were stopped from that point south. Police units had cordoned off the area where forensics teams had arrived to process the scene. Subway workers stood by to help remove Stacey's lifeless body and clean up when the detectives said they were finished. However, the body was trapped under the wheels, and it was going to be a sensitive process to remove it. They were waiting on a special extraction team, and nothing much could be done at this point.

News reporters and photographers began to crowd the platform.

"Did anyone here see what happened?" a policeman asked the gathering crowd.

Another officer questioned the engineer, who was close to shock.

"I saw a figure falling in front of the train. That's all I know," answered the badly shaken man. "I believe it was a woman, but I can't be sure. I really can't tell if she jumped or fell. I just don't know. I just don't know." An emergency medical technician led him quietly away, shooing newspeople out of their path as they made their way up the stairs to the ambulance.

Michael and Howard arrived on the scene in the midst of all the confusion. Howard had talked Michael out of taking the subway south to find Stacey. Instead he had suggested, forcefully, that they drive down Broad Street and attempt to retrace Stacey's steps from her apartment to the subway.

They took Howard's car and found themselves blocked from further travel at the subway stop that Stacey had used. Michael jumped from the car and headed blindly toward the stairs, red and white lights flashing all around him.

Howard yelled after him, but Michael paid no attention. Howard pulled his car into a "no parking" zone and raced after Michael. A police officer stopped Michael at the head of the stairs. "I'm sorry sir, there's been an accident. The trains aren't running, and no one is permitted down there."

Howard caught up to him in time to hear what the officer was saying. "What happened?" he asked.

"I'm really not sure, sir," the officer answered politely. "But I believe someone fell onto the tracks in front of a train."

A large crowd was forming around them. Howard took hold of Michael's arm. "You'd better get out of here," he advised.

They saw a television crew pull up in its familiar white van. "Michael, let's move. You cannot afford to have your picture smeared all over the networks and tabloids. Not here. Not at this place."

Michael numbly let Howard lead him away. "My God, Howard. Was it Stacey? Oh, God, please...no! Don't let it be Stacey!" Michael cried. Howard bundled the senator into the passenger seat of his car, ran around to the other side and drove back up Broad Street. All he could think of doing was driving around until Michael had regained his composure.

Michael sat for some time with his hands over his face. He rocked back and forth as much as his seat belt would allow, moaning. "Don't let it be Stacey. Oh, God, please don't let it be Stacey."

After a while, Howard said quietly, "Mike, maybe she got caught in the crowd down there. Maybe the police are questioning her to find out what, if anything, she saw. Maybe she's been calling the restaurant trying to get hold of you. Let's not jump to any conclusions."

Finally Michael calmed down. "Let's go back to the restaurant," he suggested. "You're right, maybe she's been trying to reach me." He checked his cell phone, but there were no messages. When they reached the restaurant, they learned there had been no calls left for him there, either.

Michael had, however, recovered much of his composure and decided on his own that the best thing for him to do was drive his own car home. Howard, still concerned, followed him all the way to his house. He didn't care whether or not Michael was aware he was there.

Michael parked his car and sat for a few minutes, trying to look as normal as possible. Inside he was terrified for Stacey, but he certainly couldn't let Maria know anything about his conflict. He sighed deeply and walked into the house. Maria was not downstairs, where only a small lamp on the desk was illuminating the darkness.

He thought of staying down there, but decided to go up to their bedroom where he could hear the sound of the television. He glanced at the reflection of his face when he passed a mirror in the hall. The image looked pale, he admitted, but he didn't look upset. He forced a smile.

Maria was sitting up in their king-size bed, propped against pillows in pastel-flowered cases. She was staring at a movie on television.

"Hi," he said more buoyantly than he had believed he could.

"Hi, yourself!" she responded, smiling up at him cheerfully.

"Howard said you had another of your attacks this afternoon." He drew his brows together in a concerned frown. "Are you better now? I think you should see a doctor."

"When did you see Howard?" she asked, ignoring his question about her health.

"Oh, we had a few drinks together up-town."

"Did you have your dinner? Do you want anything to eat?"

*Always the dutiful wife*, he thought with a tinge of guilt. "We ate," he lied. "But what about you?" he persisted. "Do you think you have an ulcer? You really should see a doctor about that." He sat on the edge of the bed, a solicitous husband.

Maria smiled and stretched over to take hold of his hand. "Thanks for caring so much, Michael," she said softly, "but I'm okay. I can handle this thing."

He shook his head, but didn't argue with her. Getting up from the bed, he walked to his chest of drawers across the room and removed a pair of maroon silk pajamas that she had given him for his birthday.

He threw them on the end of the bed, and was starting to undress when the eleven o'clock news came on. They watched together as various commentators took them through events around the world. Then it was time for the local news. Michael held his breath when a newscaster described a death in the subway.

He clenched his fists so hard that the nails bit into his palms when the newscaster described the body of a young woman—"as yet unidentified"—that had been excavated from beneath the wheels of a northbound train.

"The body was so badly mauled," explained the reporter, "that a spokesperson for the coroner's office states that physical identification is impossible. Police do not know whether the woman fell or jumped in front of the train." There were shots of emergency vehicles blocking Broad Street and even one of the stalled train surrounded by police.

"That's just horrible, isn't it?" Maria observed quietly. "What a grisly way to commit suicide."

"Yes." he answered, equally quietly. He felt the bile rise in his throat. *Did she commit suicide because of him? No. No*, he thought, *Stacey would never kill herself. But how could she fall?*

He'd started buttoning his pajama tops when Maria gave a little cough. He looked over to see her slipping her nightgown up over her head.

*Oh, no!* he thought. *Oh, God…please, no. Not tonight!*

# 34

As usual Hattie arose early the next morning. Reluctantly, she hooked Wolf's leash to his collar.

"Poor Wolf," she said to him. "You should be running free. Darn poacher."

Wolf wagged his tail as together they headed across the porch and up the lane. Hattie looked up at leaden clouds between the branches of the trees and wished for clear weather for Thanksgiving. She had a lot of work to do, and rainless days would be a big help this week.

When she and Wolf returned from their walk, Brooke and Shawn were both in the kitchen. They had a fire burning in the fireplace and the room was filled with the aroma of fresh coffee.

"This is nice," she exclaimed. "How will I make out when you are both gone, and I'm all alone again?"

They laughed politely. "You probably can't wait to see the end of us," Brooke said as she poured orange juice into three glasses and placed them on the table.

"Not true," said Hattie. "Would you like oatmeal this morning?" When the young people nodded their heads in the affirmative, Hattie started mixing the porridge. She turned on a small countertop radio as she worked.

The news reported the death of a young woman, as yet unidentified, whose body was removed from beneath the wheels of a subway train the night before. It made them all recoil. Shawn felt a strong uneasiness when he heard the location of the tragedy and the time of its occurrence.

Brooke and Shawn left immediately after breakfast and arrived at campaign headquarters a few minutes earlier than usual, but Howard was already there to greet them as soon as they entered. "Shawn, may I see you in Maria's cubicle, please?" He looked pale and drawn as if he had not slept well, if at all.

"Brooke," he said, "Michael told me what happened to you yesterday, and I'm very sorry. From now on whenever you are down in your office, we'll leave the basement door wide open until it's fixed."

"Thanks, Howard," she responded. "I really was kind of freaked out."

"Before you go down now, there's a pile of papers on my desk that you can work on. Oh, and Michael called. He was invited to speak at a Chamber of Commerce breakfast this morning, and miracle of miracles, Maria agreed to go with him, so they'll be in a little late."

Brooke picked up the papers from Howard's desk and, making sure the door at the top of the basement stairs would not swing shut, she descended with them to her office.

Howard watched her go and then led Shawn to Maria's desk. He looked around the office, but no one was nearby. When they were both seated, he said. "Did you hear about the young woman who died in the subway last evening?

"We heard it on the radio this morning," Shawn said uneasily.

"I have good reason to believe that the young woman was Stacey Tyburn. I realize that the body has yet to be identified, but I think it was Stacey."

The color drained from Shawn's face.

"Oh, my God!" he exclaimed. "I've been so afraid that it was. The woman fell in front of the train at the subway station that Stacey uses, for one thing, and it was at about the same time that she would have been there."

"I hate to ask you this, Shawn, but did you say anything to the girl that would have made her want to take her own life?" Howard looked directly into Shawn's eyes.

"I only said what you and Maria told me to say." Shawn looked as if he might cry.

"I told her that her relationship with Michael could ruin his chances of becoming president. I told her that she should give him up for his own good." He looked guiltily at Howard and confessed. "I also told her that she was just one of many young women who Michael has had affairs with."

Howard raised an eyebrow.

"She told me Michael wanted to divorce Maria and marry her when the time was right, and God help me, I told her that Michael would never divorce Maria."

"How did she react to all of this?" Howard asked.

"She cried," Shawn said in a low voice. "She was so upset that she didn't even drink the soda I bought her. But she did argue with me. She protested a lot. Michael was in love with her, she said, she was sure of it, and of course, she was very much in love with him. At the end she decided she was going to see him last night no matter what anybody said. At least that was my interpretation."

"Of course, you didn't really know her, but from your conversation with her, do you believe that she was so distraught that she threw herself under that subway train on purpose?"

"No, I don't believe that. Not for a second," Shawn said vehemently.

"Think of it this way," Howard counseled. "She was very young. Michael was probably the first man she had ever truly loved. He was everything to her. She believed him when he said they would marry some day, and she was very happy. Suddenly, you tell her things about Michael that—no matter how aggressively she denied them—made her think. He would never leave his wife, you said. She was just one of many lovers. Even if that wasn't true, if she permitted him to keep on seeing her, she could ruin his chances of ever becoming president. She couldn't imagine her life without him, but she couldn't be the cause of his losing his life's dream. What could she do? There was only one answer..."

"For cryin' out loud, Howard! You make me feel responsible for her death!" Shawn was nearly beside himself. "I only did what you told me to do. I told her what you told me to say. I didn't deliberately go out of my way to hurt Stacey! I liked her. I liked her a lot. I feel horrible!" Shawn was on the verge of tears, but he was also angry at what Howard seemed to be implying.

"Now, now, boy," Howard said patronizingly. "Don't take it personally. You're right. You were following orders. I didn't mean to be so hard on you."

Shawn was more shaken than Howard had anticipated. They sat in silence until Shawn finally asked. "Howard, does Michael know I saw Stacey? Will he blame me, too? Howard, what will Michael do to me? What will this do to our relationship?" The tragedy had not only shocked Shawn, but the prospect of facing Michael with his guilt terrified him.

Howard sat staring thoughtfully at Shawn for a long time. At last he suggested, "Why don't you take the rest of the day off? Take Brooke with you. Go to the hospital and see her sister or something. Give Michael another day to come to grips with his loss...to grieve. Anyway," he brightened a little, "we don't know for certain that the dead woman is Stacey."

"Thanks, Howard," Shawn said gratefully. He jumped to his feet and ran down the basement stairs to get Brooke. Howard leaned back in his chair.

"Whew!" he said. He was not in the mood to face Michael if Shawn were to tell him about his and Maria's role in all of this. Michael had already guessed some of it, but if knew the full extent, God only knew what he would do. Perhaps Shawn should stay away for the rest of the week.

P. 253

# 35

Hattie pulled out her good silver, her "once-a-year silver," she called it now, and placed it on newspapers on her kitchen table. With a clean flannel rag torn from an old nightgown, she began to apply silver polish to the pieces.

The little radio on the counter was playing soft music; Hattie sang along in a slightly off-key alto. After Annie's death she had thought she could never again look forward to Thanksgiving, but she was. If she could not be here in person, Annie would at least be present in her darling granddaughters.

Every hour on the hour, the radio blared its five-minute newscast. Though the subway tragedy of the previous evening was mentioned each time, the identity of the dead young woman was still either not known or not disclosed, and the story remained essentially the same.

*Does her family know yet?* Hattie wondered. *Was it someone so disconsolate that she had to kill herself? Poor soul. Who was she? Was it an accident?*

Wolf's ruff went up and he stared at the door before Hattie had even heard a car in the lane. In a matter of seconds, the great dog walked to the door and began wagging his tail. "A friend is it, Wolf?" Hattie said just as she heard the sound of footsteps on the porch followed by a polite knock on the door.

She attempted in vain to wipe the black residue from the silver polish from her hands before she went to the door. Grabbing a clean flannel rag, she opened the door with that, attempting not to get black fingerprints on the curtains or woodwork.

Jim Sawyer stood outside. "Come in, come in," she said. "As soon as I wash my hands, we can have a cup of coffee. Please, sit over there." She gestured to a chair on the far side of the table.

After they were both seated and drinking their coffee, Jim said, "I might have some news for you. Anna remembered the license number of the maroon Chrysler that killed her grandmother. She told Terri late yesterday.

"The Philadelphia police traced it and discovered that it belonged to a car stolen from a couple in Upper Merion. However, the car which they reported missing two days before Mrs. Turner was killed was a blue '98 Buick."

"But that's not the car that killed Annie," Hattie protested. "There must be a mistake."

"No," Jim smiled at her. "In the stolen car business, one of the first things a thief will do is change a license plate to complicate things. In this case, the Philadelphia detectives called Upper Merion police, who went to the home of the couple affiliated with the license plate. Of course, they explained that the plate had been fastened on their blue Buick, which they had reported missing."

"And," Hattie added, "all that created much unnecessary work."

"Yes," Jim agreed. "The research was time-consuming and under normal circumstances, could delay an arrest. Although in this case that didn't apply, because Anna remembered the numbers on the plate long after the fact."

"I assume you've not found the car that hit Annie."

"No, but the day before the hit-and-run, a Chrysler fitting that description was reported stolen from a home in Ambler. Also, a day or so later, a green van with tinted windows was reported missing by a man in Plymouth

Meeting. He said he had parked it at the mall for a 'few minutes' and had neglected to lock it."

"I suppose," Hattie said thoughtfully, "that it would be impossible to stop every green van or maroon Chrysler on the road. But," she mused, "wouldn't some mechanic report the types of damage done to each of those cars? I would surmise that no one would be driving them around, but I'm sure the police had flyers out on both of them, especially the Chrysler. They'd have to be somewhere, wouldn't they?"

"Yes and no," Jim told her cryptically. He finished his coffee, put the cup on the counter and picked up a piece of flannel cloth from the table. "Let me help you polish the silver," he offered. "But before I get started, I'd better call headquarters." He left to make the call from his patrol car.

"Has there been any word on the identity of the woman who died in the subway?" Hattie asked him when he returned.

"They haven't released her name yet," he said. "I believe they are trying to reach her next of kin."

"Oh, that's so horrible," Hattie sighed and changed the subject. "Jim, getting back to those stolen cars, why did you say 'yes and no' when I said the cars had to be somewhere?"

"Have you ever heard of a chop-shop, Miss Farwell?"

"Hattie," she corrected, "and the answer is no, I've never heard of a 'chop-shop.' Tell me about it."

He picked up a cream pitcher and began to spread silver polish on it. "Well, do you remember when I said, 'stolen car business'? That's what it is, a business. There are actually stolen car rings in which some people steal cars and sell them to a 'shop,' often with a legitimate front. At these shops, mechanics sometimes take the cars apart and reuse what's salvageable. Or they change the number on the engine, paint the car a different color, change the upholstery and resell the vehicle. As far as the vehicle identification numbers are concerned, changing them is easy as pie."

Hattie buffed a teapot. "What is your opinion of the car that killed Annie? Do you think it was stolen by a car theft ring? Would the killer be in that?"

Jim placed the gleaming cream pitcher on the table and picked up a sugar bowl. "My opinion—and that's all it is, an opinion—is that the person who took the car used it because it was available. A fast car was necessary in the plan to kill Anna, and it's my guess that there might always be one available one way or the other."

"Hmmm," Hattie mused. "I've been thinking about this whole thing ever since Annie died, and there is no doubt in my mind that the killer did some considerable research into Anna's life. Either he knew her personally or somehow learned a great deal about her.

"Much deliberate planning went into that night. The killer knew that Anna liked Beethoven and either knew or took a chance on the fact that she was free that Saturday evening. He knew the way she would walk to the Academy of Music. Had he been spying on her? Or had he walked that way with her? He didn't realize that Anna's grandmother was called 'Annie' apparently, so when he wrote the note to 'Annie,' he actually intended it for Anna. Then when the wrong 'Annie' was killed, he went after Anna, determined for some unknown reason, to kill her."

"That's excellent sleuthing!" Jim was impressed. "I'd say there isn't much you missed, but you didn't finish. The killer had possession of the keys to Mrs. Turner's house, which he'd taken from her purse. He happened to be searching for something in it the day that you and

Brooke went there. Fearing identification, he pushed Brooke down the cellar stairs and you into the closet and fled. But what was he looking for?"

"Do you suppose it was the note addressed to 'Annie'? The one I found in the wastepaper basket and gave to you?"

"That is a possibility," he said with a frown. "He might have feared that somehow we could trace him through that note. So far, incidentally, we've had no luck on that score, but it's a good thing to have, anyway."

"But the question keeps going through my head, over and over," Hattie stated.

"Why would anyone want to kill Anna?"

"As I've said—as we've all said—she must have some information which would be very damaging to him. But what? She doesn't seem to know...or won't say..." Jim let his voice trail off. "Once again," he said more decisively, "it seems to come back to this Laurence Adams, doesn't it?"

"You just can't imagine how I hate to think such a thing," Hattie said sadly. "I've always liked Larry, but, yes, things do seem to point in his direction."

They continued to polish the silver, each lost in thought.

It was shortly after ten when the door burst open and Brooke and Shawn strode in. "Hi," said Brooke. "Howard sent us home. Isn't that awesome?"

Hattie's eyebrows shot up.

"Why'd he do that?" she asked in surprise. She remembered Maria's forceful request that Brooke work on a Sunday, so to be sent home on a weekday seemed suspicious.

"I dunno," Brooke answered. "It seems Michael and Maria are going to lots of meetings and stuff, and there just isn't enough work at the office for us right now."

Hattie thought Shawn was unusually quiet, but she questioned no further.

"Well, Brooke," she said, "I must admit I'm delighted to have you here to help with the Thanksgiving preparations. If you feel like it, you can always go back to work for Michael in the spring when the primaries have heated up."

"I guess," Brooke replied. She turned to Jim. "Hi! What brings you here this morning?"

"Oh, I was just in the neighborhood and thought that I'd drop in on Miss Hattie. When I saw her polishing her silver, I offered to help."

"Well, no reason we can't help, too," said Brooke. She and Shawn picked up some flannel cloths and joined the others at the table.

Jim and Hattie both glanced at Shawn from time to time. Something was obviously bothering him deeply.

# 36

Tuesday dawned cold and damp. A freezing north wind blew up the lane pushing an icy drizzle before it. It was a morning when Hattie had to force herself from bed and out for her walk with Wolf. The outing, which she usually found so enjoyable, was a trial for her. The muddy lane, covered with dead leaves, was slippery under her feet, and the cold rain pelted her face.

In addition Wolf seemed uneasy. He pulled on his leash and dragged Hattie along behind him precariously, causing her to reprimand him numerous times. "What is the matter with you, Wolf?" she demanded as she skidded along in the mud.

Furthermore, she was vaguely apprehensive. Annie's death followed by the whole business with Anna had made her a trifle edgy, but there was something else bothering her now. Some nameless fear she just couldn't put her finger on. There was something she just...knew. Or felt, rather. Something not quite right.

The wind blew harder and whipped the rain into icy crystals that tormented and stung her skin. As soon as Wolf remembered his purpose for being outside, Hattie turned around and hurried him back to the warmth of the house. She'd planned to pick up her turkey right after breakfast, but the weather would change those plans. Darn, what a nuisance! Her sense of foreboding increased.

As they entered the kitchen, Hattie heard the furnace kick on and relished the almost instant warm air pouring from a register near the door. But the kitchen was dark and empty.

"The kids must be sleeping in this morning," she said out loud. She felt guilty for being disappointed. After all, why should they come down early every day, especially when they were no longer working?

With a sigh she started a fire in the fireplace, made a pot of coffee and fried several slices of scrapple for herself. The rain had turned to ice altogether now. She could hear its clatter against the porch roof. She turned on the radio and sipped a glass of orange juice while the scrapple fried.

The weatherman did not have a good report for the day. The bitter cold storm sweeping across the Delaware Valley was predicted to continue until late afternoon. The roads were already coated with a dangerous ice. A travel advisory was issued.

"There have been numerous fender-benders on many of the local roads, and although the major highways are being salted, they're still treacherous," reported the weatherman. "Emergency personnel are warning everyone not go out unless it is an absolute necessity."

Hattie had gone with Brooke and Shawn to see Anna the afternoon before, and Hattie was glad that she had. Anna was getting better every day and could hardly wait to come to Hattie's.

Hattie could hardly wait until Anna came, either. That's what she told her...but was that entirely true? She looked at the cheerful fire and around her cozy kitchen and she told herself that being here would be wonderful for Anna...but would it?

Would Anna really be safe here even with Terri, a policewoman, guarding her night and day? So many things could go wrong. She thought of the digitalis and of the bouquet of flowers that Larry had brought to Anna, both of which could have killed her.

Was this why she felt so uneasy? Was it because of Anna? As if reading her mind, Anna phoned Hattie at that moment. "Hi, Aunt Hattie, I just felt like talking to someone," she said.

"Where's Terri?" Hattie was alarmed.

Anna chuckled. "She's right here," she said. "Kind of in and out, but always right here, and always busy."

"It will be nice for her when you are both here for Thanksgiving. She'll have a welcome break," Hattie said, and wondered if Anna had called just for small talk.

"The weather is horrible," Anna stated unnecessarily. "I guess no one will be able to come see me today." Hattie smiled to herself. *This is a good sign*, she thought. *Anna is getting edgy, perhaps feeling a little sorry for herself. She's really better, thank Heaven.*

"No, darling, I'm sorry, but the weatherman says the roads are treacherous; a travel advisory has been issued. I doubt if conditions will improve by this afternoon, but if they do, we'll be there."

"I haven't seen Larry since Saturday evening," Anna said. She sounded close to tears.

"Why not?" asked Hattie. "Hasn't he even called you?"

"Oh, yes, he called me yesterday. He went to Philadelphia Saturday night, and he says he won't be able to come out here again until Thanksgiving. He says he has some business to attend to. He says it's important."

"Even on Sunday?" Hattie asked. "What kind of business, did he say?"

"No. He intimated it had something to do with his family. That's fine, really. I had hoped to see him, that's all."

Hattie was still confounded by Anna's sudden reattachment to Larry. *Why*, she wondered, *did she break her*

*engagement to him and now act as if that never happened?*
Anna started to say something else when Hattie shushed
her. There was news on the radio about the woman who
had died in the subway.

"The identity of a young woman who died beneath
the wheels of a northbound subway train Sunday
evening has been established through her fingerprints. A
spokesperson for the coroner's office said that the next
of kin has been notified.

"The body is said to be that of an Eagles cheerleader,
twenty-one-year-old Stacey Tyburn. Her parents, Philip
and Dora Tyburn of Harleysville, were scheduled to
come to the coroner's office today to positively identify
the body, but are being held up by the icy roads."

"What's the matter, Aunt Hattie?" Anna's worried
voice came over the phone.

"Oh...nothing, darling. Something on the news just
captured my attention for a moment," Hattie soothed.

"There's one more thing before I hang up, Aunt
Hattie," Anna said. "I'm coming to your house tomorrow
morning, if that's okay with you. Dr. Fletcher told me that
I'm to be discharged before eleven. Isn't that wonderful?
I was going to save that information to tell you when you
came to see me today. I wanted to see your face."

*It's a lucky thing that didn't happen,* Hattie thought
after she had hung up. *I'm not certain my face would be
as delighted-looking as Anna imagines.* Her unease, she
now realized, was about Anna's safety. Anna would be
coming to her house, and Hattie somehow felt responsible
for her. But was there something else?

At that moment, she realized Shawn was standing in
the doorway to the dining room. He was so white that
his freckles seemed to be floating above the surface of
his skin.

"Shawn!" she exclaimed. "What's wrong? You look awful, are you sick?"

"The news," he said vaguely, waving toward the radio. "It's definite, then. The body was Stacey's!"

"You knew the woman who was run over by the subway train?" she asked.

"I-I'd met her once," he stammered.

Brooke's footsteps could be heard coming down the winding staircase. Hattie led Shawn to the table and made him sit down. Before she could pour him a cup of coffee, the door at the bottom of the stairs opened and Brooke burst into the kitchen. "Good morning, everybody!" she said with her usual enthusiasm.

When nobody answered, she looked at Shawn and was shocked by his appearance. "What's wrong?" she cried. "What's happened? Is it Anna?"

"No," Hattie soothed. "Shawn just heard on the radio that the young woman who was killed by the train was an acquaintance of his."

Shawn sipped miserably at his coffee. "It's my fault she died," he said in a voice so low that they had to lean forward to hear him.

"Your fault?" gasped Brooke. "How could that be?"

"I-I can't talk about it," he sobbed and put his head on his arms on the table and wept.

"Let's all take our coffee and go into the living room where the chairs are more comfortable," Hattie suggested sympathetically. When Shawn rose from the table she took his arm and together, with Brooke following, they walked through the dining room, through the formal entrance hall and into the living room.

To her surprise, as soon as they entered the room Shawn turned on the television set, tuning it to the all-news station. He then sat rigidly waiting for more information about Stacey. His eyes never left the screen.

Brooke and Hattie, seated on the sofa, also found themselves glued to the set. In less than two minutes, the picture of Stacey in Michael's arms filled the screen.

"Oh, no!" Shawn groaned.

"Twenty-one-year-old Stacey Tyburn, an Eagles cheerleader, has been positively identified as the young woman who either fell or jumped under a northbound Broad Street subway last Sunday evening. She is pictured here with Senator Michael DiRienzo with whom she is rumored to have been having an affair since summer. DiRienzo, who is married, has been unavailable for comment.

"Miss Tyburn's parents, of Harleysville, were to have identified their daughter's remains today but have been held up by the ice storm."

"Oh, God help me!" Shawn cried.

Brooke and Hattie looked at Shawn helplessly. "Is there anything I can do?" Brooke asked him, but he simply shook his head.

"Do you want to be alone for awhile?" Hattie asked.

When Shawn nodded, they both got up and walked quietly back to the kitchen. The sound of his sobs followed them. "I don't get it. Aunt Hattie, what can he possibly mean? How could it be his fault? He wasn't anywhere near Philadelphia when she was killed." Brooke poured herself another cup of coffee, stirred in cream and sat disconsolately at the table.

After a while she asked in a small voice. "Do you believe Michael was having an affair with her?" The thought shocked her. "She was beautiful, wasn't she?"

"Yes," Hattie answered her second question first. "She was very beautiful. As to the alleged affair, only Michael knows whether or not that is true."

The nameless fear seemed to grip Hattie's heart with icy fingers, but the reason for it still eluded her. *What is it? What is it?* she thought in frustration. *There's something so near the surface that I can almost grasp it, but it keeps on vanishing.*

The sudden ringing of the phone broke into her thoughts. Jim Sawyer was calling to say he'd had had a rough time getting to police headquarters and did not intend to leave except in the direst emergency.

"I was coming out today, but now I won't. I want to look over your second floor. It's important to me to know which room Anna will be sleeping in. Terri, who also had the devil's own time getting to work this morning, just called to say that she and Anna will be leaving the hospital tomorrow morning, weather permitting.

"Tell everybody to keep this quiet. It will be much safer for Anna," he cautioned. "By the way, is there a cot or something in Anna's room for Terri?"

"Fortunately, it's the only bedroom I have with twin beds, so that will work out very well," said Hattie.

"Good," Jim approved. "I'll get there as soon as the roads permit."

Shawn entered the room. His gait could be described more accurately as a shuffle than a walk. He looked worse than ever.

"Who was that on the phone?" he asked with alarm.

Hattie looked at him hard. "Sit down, Shawn," she ordered. When he was seated she explained, "It was just Jim Sawyer to say he wouldn't be coming here today unless the roads cleared up. Who did you think it might be?"

"I was afraid it was either Howard or Michael," he admitted in some relief.

"Shawn, please tell us what's wrong," pleaded Brooke.

"Why would you be afraid of Howard or Michael? Why do you think that you had anything to do with that poor girl's death?"

Shawn put his head in his hands. "It's because of what I said to her," he mumbled into his palms. "Oh my God!" he wailed. "I have to tell someone, I can't stand this any more."

And then he told them the whole story. How Howard and Maria were afraid that if news people followed up on the published picture of Michael and Stacey, and Stacey kept on seeing Michael, he would lose his chance at the presidency.

He told them about Howard's getting him a ticket to the Eagles game so that he could meet Stacey. He told them how he took her to a soda fountain because she didn't drink. He told them about the ten thousand dollars in the envelope and how she spurned it. And with downcast eyes, he told them what he said to her about Michael and other women, and how he would never leave Maria.

"She cried," he sobbed. "She said she could never give Michael up, because she loved him too much. I said something like, if she really loved him, she'd give him up for his own sake. Oh my God!" he wailed. "I think she committed suicide, and it was all my fault!"

He was oblivious to Brooke's murmured reassurances. "Oh, no. It wasn't your fault. You can't blame yourself."

Hattie said. "She might not have killed herself. It could have been something as simple as her tripping and falling by accident. Please, Shawn, give that possibility more thought."

Then the awful realization came to her that someone could have deliberately pushed Stacey in front of the train, but she kept that suspicion to herself.

# 37

By late afternoon, the temperature had started to warm up and the ice was beginning to melt. A heavy rain had been falling for about two hours, increasing the amount of mud in the lane, and Hattie felt that a trip out in the car was still out of the question.

"It looks as though we'll have to wait until early tomorrow morning to pick up the turkey," she told Brooke as they were preparing a ground beef casserole for dinner. The radio on the counter was playing soft music just minutes before the five p.m. news was due to come on.

The trio had spent the day cleaning the house and setting the dining room table for Thanksgiving dinner. Shawn, who was now helping to set the kitchen table for dinner that evening, had been a big help with the vacuum cleaner, and the activity had seemed to brighten his mood. Although he said nothing about it, he was very relieved there had been no phone call from either Howard or Michael.

The clock on the mantel began to strike the hour when Shawn walked over to the radio to listen attentively to the newscaster, waiting for anything new on the death of Stacey. Nothing new was announced except that a reporter had phoned Jane Flynn, Stacey's roommate. A recording of his conversation with her followed.

Jane, obviously in tears, had nothing to add to the story. "She was my best friend," she sobbed, "and I know in my heart that she would never, ever kill herself. It just wasn't in her character."

"Why was she in the subway?" the persistent reporter demanded. "Where was she going? You must know, you were her best friend and her roommate."

"She was going out for dinner, that's all," Jane sniffed.

"By herself?" the reporter asked incredulously.

Shawn's face turned red. "SHUT UP!" he yelled at the radio.

"She was planning to meet a friend," Jane said in a small voice.

"A friend, eh?" the reporter seemed to be on to something. "Would that friend have been United States Senator Michael DiRienzo, by chance?"

Michael, sitting in his den, was listening to the same newscast. His face turned white as he followed the conversation between the reporter and Jane Flynn. *Oh, Lord, why did Stacey have to tell Jane about me?* he thought. He waited, subconsciously holding his breath, for Jane's answer.

Jane seemed to regain her composure.

"Senator DiRienzo?" she asked in amazement. "Why, she barely knew him!" Michael released his breath, but the reporter was a bulldog.

"Now, Miss Flynn," he said, patronizingly, "didn't you see their picture together in the paper? They certainly didn't look like strangers in that, did they?"

"Maybe not," she said defiantly, "but pictures can lie. People see what they want to see." She abruptly hung up the phone.

"Bless her, bless her," Michael whispered.

Upstairs in her dressing room, Maria had been rigid with apprehension. She nearly cried when she heard Jane's statement. Howard Cole, who had been glued to the radio in his study, also sighed with relief. And in Harleysville, Stacey's parents nodded in approval. They never believed their daughter was having an affair in the first place.

In Hattie's kitchen, Brooke turned to Shawn.

"Did you hear that, Shawn? Stacey's roommate said that Stacey would never, ever commit suicide! You see, it was just a horrible accident, like I said."

"You don't know how much I want to believe that," he replied, but he thought, *Jane also said that Stacey barely knew Michael.*

And Hattie continued to wonder how Stacey really died.

By the following morning, the temperature had risen to nearly fifty degrees. The rain had stopped during the night, and the ice of the previous day was nothing more than a miserable memory.

Shortly before the mantel clock struck eight, Hattie, Brooke and Shawn were in Shawn's car heading for the grocery store. Hattie picked up some fresh celery and an extra can of coffee, while Shawn placed the turkey in the cart. "There's nothing else I need," she told them as they rolled the cart to a check-out lane.

Her mind was on the chores ahead. She was planning to make the stuffing today, stuff the turkey tomorrow, and make a molded cranberry ring today. Mashed potatoes, peas and creamed onions would wait for tomorrow. Thank goodness Alexandra would be bringing the pumpkin pies and rolls.

Then there was Anna. She sighed deeply as they walked to Shawn's car.

"Is something wrong, Aunt Hattie?" Brooke asked with concern.

Hattie smiled. "I was thinking about all of the things that must be done before two tomorrow afternoon."

"We're here to help you, don't worry," Brooke said. But it wasn't really the work that worried Hattie.

They were in the process of frying onions and celery for the stuffing when Jim Sawyer arrived. "What a great

smell," he remarked as Brooke held the door open for him.
"I'm here for a tour," he told Hattie. She wiped her
hands on her apron, asked Brooke to keep her eyes on
the frying pan, and led Jim through the dining room to
the hall and up the main flight of stairs. Wolf followed
silently behind.

"I really love this place," he stated. He looked around
with appreciation at beamed ceilings, plaster walls, deep
windowsills. "It's a wonderful house."

Hattie smiled. "If you like old houses," she observed,
then added, "I love it, too. The portion we're in now
was built almost a century after the original house. As
you can see, this part has higher ceilings and a more formal appearance. That's the Victorian influence."

"This will be Anna's room," she said as she led him
into a large bedroom in the rear corner. As she had told
him, it had twin beds. White fluffy curtains hung at the
windows. Perky floral bedspreads covered the beds, and
pastel throw rugs were scattered around on the random-
width, pumpkin pine floor.

"What a beautiful room. Anna should love it," he said
with enthusiasm. He strode to each of the windows, two in
the back and one on the side, and looked out. "It seems
safe enough—nice and high." He flung open the sash on a
back window and poked his head out. "Looks good," he
said and then did the same thing at the side window.

She showed him the main bathroom across the hall,
Shawn's bedroom in the front corner, and Brooke's
bedroom next to the bathroom. She led him through
Brooke's room to her own, showed him her bathroom
and took him down the back stairs to the kitchen.
"That's it," she said.

"Everything should be fine," he assured her. "This is
a fabulous home, Miss Farwell..."

"Hattie!" she corrected.

"Hattie," he corrected himself once again. "Anyway, as I was saying, this is a fabulous home, but isn't it awfully big for just you alone?"

"Yes," she answered soberly. "I suppose it is, but it's been home to me all my life, and I don't plan to leave it until I'm carried out feet first!" They descended the back staircase to the kitchen.

Jim walked over to the stove to observe what Brooke was cooking. Shawn sat at the kitchen table chopping onions. He glared at Jim through teary eyes. In his opinion the man was standing too close to Brooke. However, he made no move to get up. He simply kept glaring—though the glare lost some of its intensity as tears spilled onto Shawn's cheeks.

Only Hattie noticed Shawn's displeasure. "Jim," she said, "there's a basement, too. Do you want to see it?" He agreed that he did and followed Hattie to a door next to the one at the bottom of the piecrust stairs. Behind it was an identical flight of circular stairs that led to the basement.

Hattie led Jim down into a damp, low-ceilinged room with small, dirty windows set high in the walls. A single light bulb hanging in the middle of the room failed to lend it much light. Shelves on the far wall held cans of paint and brushes.

It smelled old and dank. At the end of the room, next to the heater, was a short flight of concrete steps leading up to an old-fashioned wooden cellar door. He checked it to make sure that the wooden bolt was fastened. "My grandfather had a cellar door like this," he said. "I used to slide down it when I was little."

"And I used to slide down this one," Hattie laughed.

Satisfied that everything was as it should be, Jim and

Hattie began climbing back up the stairs. The phone rang, but by the time they reached the kitchen, Brooke had answered it. From the expression on her face, Hattie assumed that it was not someone she'd wanted to hear from.

"But Maria," Brooke was saying into the instrument, "Howard sent us home on Monday, and it was my clear impression that he really didn't want me back right now. I came away with the opinion that there was no more work for me until spring or summer."

"Well, I wish you'd called me sooner," Brooke said after a pause. "I cannot come in today, and I'm leaving to go back to school on Sunday. If you are desperate, I could come in on Friday, I suppose."

There was another, longer pause, during which Brooke kept shaking her head, her mouth set in a stubborn straight line. "No, I'm very sorry, but I can't come in today. My sister is coming home from the hospital and I have to be here to help her and to help Aunt Hattie get ready for our Thanksgiving dinner. I'm sorry."

"Yes, Shawn is here," she said and handed the phone to him.

Shawn was all sugar when he spoke to Maria. He truly liked the little woman, and he always felt sorry for her, although he tried not to convey that feeling. "Sorry, Maria," he kidded her. "This is one time you won't get your way. We were told to leave and let things rest a while."

He listened for some time, and then he merely answered, "Yes, it's a big relief to me, too. You can't imagine how I've been feeling. I'm sorry about Brooke, but we can both come in Friday. Certainly at Thanksgiving there isn't that much urgency."

He smiled into the phone as if she could see his charming face. "Thanks, and you and Michael have a great Thanksgiving, too. Where will you be going? To your brother's, as usual?"

"Great," he said heartily after a brief pause. "Tell Michael when he gets home tonight that I said Happy Thanksgiving to everyone. Take care," and he hung up.

"That lady has a tendency to try to push me around," Brooke commented with a frown.

Shawn laughed. "That's because there's no one else she can boss." He put his arm around her waist and hugged her. "Michael's making some speeches in Philadelphia today and won't be back until very late, so Maria thought she could get some work done while he was gone. That's why she called you."

"So I take it that she's not cooking a Thanksgiving dinner," Brooke observed.

"Actually, she never has," Shawn said. "They always go to the Bertolino's every year. It's a big family thing. I'm sure she always takes a couple of dishes, though," he added defensively.

"That's not the same," Brooke observed.

"No, it isn't," Hattie volunteered. "Was Maria's maiden name Bertolino?" she asked. "The name sounds familiar."

"Yes, it was," Shawn answered. "Her family owns Bertolino Motors. You've probably seen it advertised on television and in the papers."

"That must be it," said Hattie.

The phone rang again. This time it was Hattie who answered it. Terri was calling from the hospital. "We'll be ready to leave in about an hour," she said. "Is Jim there?"

Hattie handed the phone to Jim. "Anna's almost ready to leave," she said. Jim took the phone, and after a quick "Hi," simply said, "I'm on my way." He hurried out to his car and seemed to be out of sight in seconds.

"That was quick," Brooke laughed. "Let's hurry and finish making this filling before Anna gets here."

Betty Kerr Orlemann

# 38

Anna's homecoming, though hectic, was uneventful. Brooke and Hattie both rushed to hug and kiss her as soon as she'd climbed the three steps to the front wrap-around porch. At Hattie's suggestion, Terri had parked her car in a pull-off next to the gate that opened onto a flagstone walk leading to the porch. It was an easier walk for Anna. Jim, who had parked next to Terri, followed them into the house.

"I've never had such attention in all my life," laughed Anna. "Terri drove as though she thought I would break, and Jim rode in the rear!"

They put her suitcase and Terri's at the foot of the main staircase, and everyone went into the living room. Anna settled herself gingerly into an overstuffed armchair, and the others sat all around her. "I feel like a queen," she said, a trifle embarrassed.

"Are Mother and Cameron coming?" she asked and quickly added, "Of course, there is no reason why they should. They'll be here tomorrow." Just then the ringing of the doorbell announced their arrival.

Brooke opened the door for them, and they came in carrying five white boxes, which Cameron carefully placed on a hall table. They both hurried into the living room to greet Anna. "Darling!" Alexandra cried as Hattie took her coat. "It's so good to see you out of the hospital and dressed in your own clothes. You've lost weight, haven't you? How do you feel?"

"I'm feeling pretty well, thanks, Mother. And don't

worry, I'll put that weight back on whether I want to or not." She absent-mindedly rubbed the sling on her left arm.

Alexandra nodded to everyone in the room then turned to Terri. "It's good that you could come with her," she said in the condescending tone she reserved for domestic help. "It makes me feel better to know my daughter's in such good hands."

"Thank you, Mrs. MacArthur," Terri responded in the most dignified tone she could muster. She gave Jim a sideways glance when no one was looking and actually stuck her tongue out at Alexandra. It was a bit of professional colleagues letting their hair down, and Jim smothered an outburst of laughter just as Alexandra turned her superior gaze in his direction.

"Why are you here, Officer?" she demanded. "Is there something you wanted to ask Anna?"

"I believe that has all been taken care of," he answered politely. Alexandra gave his uniform a disdainful glance. "Well, then, why are you here?" she demanded.

"Really, Alexandra!" Cameron scolded. "Jim's presence here is none of our business, is it?"

She sniffed. It was perfectly clear she felt public servants had no business joining in family gatherings. She turned to Hattie.

"There are three pumpkin pies and two dozen rolls in those boxes in the hall. We stopped at the bakery on the way over. I thought we'd just bring them to you today."

"Thank you very much, Alexandra. That's very kind of you," Hattie replied.

"Is there anything you need, Anna?" Alexandra asked. "Anything else I can bring you when we come tomorrow?"

Anna smiled. "No thanks, Mother. It will just be nice having you and Cameron here."

"Well then, we must be off," Alexandra stated. "I have an appointment to have my hair and nails done." She held her slim and shapely hands out in front of her and inspected her fingertips. "Come, Cameron, I don't want to be late."

Both kissed Anna, said goodbye to the others and breezed out just as quickly as they'd come in.

"It's nice to be noticed," Brooke grumbled after they were gone.

"Oh, you know Mother," Anna said gently. "She didn't mean to snub you. That's just the way she is."

Hattie noticed that Anna looked exhausted. "Anna, why don't you go upstairs and take a nap?" she suggested. "You're looking a bit tired."

Terri agreed, and with Jim's help, she took Anna to her room. Shawn followed them with the suitcases, and Hattie, Brooke and Wolf trailed behind them.

"Oh, Aunt Hattie, this is the most beautiful, peaceful room in the world!" Anna stated.

"A slight exaggeration," laughed Hattie, "but well received. Now we'll leave you to get some sleep."

"Can we have dinner in the kitchen tonight? Anna asked as they were going out. "I love that cozy kitchen. Do you know, I've even been dreaming about it?"

"That's where we always eat," said Brooke. "And anyway, the dining room table is set for tomorrow's feast."

"Good," they heard Anna say as they were closing the door behind them.

Before Jim left to return to headquarters, he patrolled the grounds outside the house. He checked the double cellar doors to make certain they were locked shut, and he did the same with every window on the first floor, particularly those which opened onto the wrap-around porch. "Make sure all of the doors are locked tonight," he said quietly to Terri. "You know how to reach me at any time." She nodded her head, and after bidding everyone goodbye, he was gone.

It was nearly eight that evening by the time they finished dinner, and it was obvious that Anna was fatigued and ready for bed. Hattie walked with her and Terri to the hall and watched them ascend the stairs before she returned to the kitchen.

Shawn and Brooke were busily cleaning up when she reentered the room. "You two are a blessing," she said, realizing how tired she was herself. They were all in bed by nine.

Hattie snuggled under her down comforter and relaxed pleasantly as she listened to the familiar sounds of the old house. The furnace rumbled into activity, a tree limb brushed the siding, the floor boards creaked and groaned softly. It was a lullaby to Hattie, and she sank into a deep sleep.

It was almost two hours later when she awoke. Something was wrong. Then she became acutely aware of the shrill blare of the kitchen smoke alarm. Her heart beat rapidly as she pushed her covers down and swung her legs over the side of the bed.

She turned on the lamp by her bed. The steeple clock on the kitchen mantel struck eleven as she started down the back stairs. Wolf yowled a vicious, primitive sound she'd never heard before.

Before she could speak to him, she smelled kerosene, and Wolf began to bark ferociously. He raced between the cellar door and the door to the kitchen porch. When he saw Hattie, he seemed to be trying to tell her something with his actions. He sniffed around the cellar door, his ruff up, then ran again to the porch door, barking. Suddenly, she saw the orange flicker of flames through the window.

"FIRE!!" she yelled, before running out onto the porch.

The woodpile was on fire. Flames licked at the window frame and at the side of the house and grew more active as she watched. She feared that in minutes they would set the ceiling afire.

Mindless of the cold night air permeating her nightgown and gripping her bare feet, she ran back into the kitchen for a bucket of water. "FIRE!!" she yelled again as she dialed 9-1-1. Holding the phone to her ear she commenced to fill the bucket with cold water from the tap in the sink. The operator repeated her address and said she'd notify the fire department at once.

Hattie ran back out onto the porch lugging the full bucket of water. Getting as close to the fire as the heat would permit, she flung the water over the logs. When she started back for another bucket of water, Shawn came running into the kitchen. "The log pile is on fire!" Hattie cried as she rushed back to the sink.

"Here, let me do that!" Shawn said and grabbed the bucket from her.

"I've called 9-1-1," Hattie told him. "The fire department should be on its way."

Terri, wearing pajamas and a bathrobe, ran through the gate and up the flagstone path to the porch just as Shawn was carrying the second bucketful of water out. Wolf continued to bark at the cellar door, but nobody paid any attention to him.

"I heard the commotion and looked through the window in the second floor hall," she stated. "I didn't see the fire, but I could see a man running away from the house up the lane. I ran downstairs and out through the front door and raced up the lane in the direction in which he had gone, but when I rounded the bend up there." Breathlessly, she pointed in the direction she had run. "I was too late. The only thing I saw was a pair of red taillights zooming away. I couldn't see the license plate or even determine the make of the car. I must call Jim right away." She ran past them into the kitchen to the phone.

The fire in the log pile continued to burn, but the water was reducing its potency.

Shawn kept throwing one bucketful of water after another on the still blazing wood, racing in and out of the house for refills.

He sighed with relief when he heard the sound of approaching sirens. As the fire trucks pulled up outside, Hattie grabbed Wolf's collar and opened the cellar door intending to put him downstairs. Smoke suddenly poured from the cellar into the kitchen. She rushed to the porch. "There's a fire in the cellar, too!" she called to the firemen. The smoke was filling the kitchen. The smoke alarm continued wailing.

Two men in protective gear and wearing gas masks rushed across the floor and down the winding stairs. Outside, other firefighters quickly extinguished the blaze in the wood pile with the powerful spray of water from their hose.

One of the men who'd gone to the basement called for help. Dragging the heavy hose with them, three of the men from the porch crossed the kitchen floor and struggled with it down the winding cellar steps, their heavy boots hampering their speed.

At that moment Jim ran into the kitchen. He barely glanced at a fireman on the porch who was carefully separating soggy charred logs and scattering their ashes.

"Hattie! Is everyone okay?" he cried as he quickly took assessment of the room. "Where's Brooke? Who is with Anna?"

Shawn and Hattie were standing side-by-side, slightly damp but otherwise obviously fine. "Everyone's okay,"

Hattie told him. "Terri has gone back up to be with Anna, and although it seems hard to believe, I think Brooke must still be asleep!"

"Didn't anyone tell you to get out of the house?" Jim yelled. "None of you should be inside!" He was angry. He hurried down the cellar stairs, half tripping over the fire hose as he did.

Hattie and Shawn looked at each other. The smoke in the kitchen had abated, and everything was clearly under control. "I'm going upstairs to dress," Hattie stated, and Shawn added a quick, "Me, too."

From her bedroom Hattie looked through the open door into Brooke's room. To her surprise, the bed was empty. She hurried through Brooke's bedroom, across the hall and into Anna's room. There she found Brooke, Anna and Terri deep in conversation.

"You are well enough, Anna, to know the truth," Terri was saying. "I'm a nurse, it's true, but I'm also a Philadelphia police officer assigned to guard you. Ever since your grandmother was killed and you nearly lost your life in that accident, we've assumed someone wants you dead for some reason.

"You've regained your memory, now, and you must know something that someone is afraid you will tell. Please, try to think what it might be. I'm certain someone deliberately set the fire tonight. Someone who wanted you out of the way and didn't care how many others went with you.

"I saw a man running up the lane, away from the house. I grabbed my flashlight and gun and rushed downstairs and through the front door. By the time I reached the lane, though, he had a big lead on me. I yelled at him to stop, but he ran faster, jumped into a car around the bend and drove off as though all the imps of Hell were after him. There was no point in shooting at his car; he was too far away."

"So," said Jim's voice from the doorway. "You've told Anna. I've been listening to everything you've been telling her, and believe me, Terri, I think you had no choice at this point but to let her in on the truth."

The three young women, still in their nightclothes, were sitting cross-legged on the beds—Anna on her own, farthest from the door, and the other two on Terri's bed.

Hattie's first thought upon entering the room was that if it weren't for the seriousness of the fire and the events leading up to it, they might have been at a pajama party. She was relieved when she heard Terri finally telling Anna the truth.

Jim walked into the room. He looked directly at Anna. "Now that you know, there are two things I want you to do. First, and most important, don't stand in front of any windows. If you see anyone outside or on the porch whom you don't know, get out of sight as fast as you can.

Second, try to think of something—some piece of information—you know that might have placed you in this danger. It could be anything. Even if you think it's silly, please tell Terri or me."

Anna looked shocked. She shook her head. "There is nothing. I can't think of anything I've heard or seen, or that anyone has told me that would hurt anybody. This is crazy! I can't believe what you are saying. Who in the world would want to kill me? This is the scariest thing that has ever happened to me!"

"You all should know," said Jim, looking around at each of them, "our suspicions that the fire was set deliberately are well-founded."

Shawn, fully dressed in blue jeans and a sweatshirt, joined them.

"You saying the fire was arson?"

"Not only did someone set fire to the wood on the porch, he doused the logs with kerosene first," Jim said. "But worse than that, he poured kerosene around the cellar, too, especially on the wooden shelves containing the paints. He set fire to that, too, but fortunately most of it didn't ignite...or, if it did, the fire went out. That's puzzling." He paused a moment to let the news sink in, then added, "My guess is that the dog scared him off before he could get a good blaze going."

"But how did he get into the cellar?" Hattie asked. "We were very careful about locking the outside doors. The windows are too small, and they don't open, anyhow. The only other way to get into the cellar is through the kitchen, and Wolf would never have permitted that."

"It was the outside doors," Jim said. "The wood is old, some of the boards were rotten, and he just ripped them apart. Probably a child could have done it. I'm sorry, Hattie, I didn't realize what bad condition they were in. We'll have metal doors installed for you as soon as possible.

"Terri," he continued, "can you tell me anything about the man you chased?"

"It was too dark to see him properly, even with my flashlight. I'm sorry. From what I could tell, though, he was tall and seemed to be slim. I really couldn't see him. I don't know if I could recognize him if I saw him again. Damn!" Terri was mad at herself.

"Hey!" Jim scolded. "It wasn't your fault. You aren't a wizard, you know. I think you did the best job possible, and I mean it. By the way, everyone, the firefighters are cleaning up the mess in the cellar. They'll put a safe, temporary cover on the outside cellar stairs before they leave. I suggest you all go back to bed. I'll check on things before heading out."

Betty Kerr Orlemann

*Scrapple*

# 39

Hattie hadn't expected she'd be able to go back to sleep, but to her surprise she found herself awakening four and one-half hours after she sunk her head into the pillow.

A hurried look at her bedside clock told her that it was six thirty. She arose quickly and washed and dressed. She had a million things to do in preparation for the holiday feast.

Before she went down to the kitchen, she peeked into Brooke's room and saw that she was sleeping soundly. She looked like such a little girl when she was asleep, Hattie thought tenderly.

She descended the back stairs quietly and was astounded when she opened the door at the bottom to find Terri cleaning the range with a damp cloth. The coffeemaker was gurgling and sending the scent of fresh coffee throughout the room. The kitchen, however, stank of stale smoke, a horrible smell.

"I think I have a cleaning job to do," Hattie sighed. "Terri, how long have you been up? You should be getting your sleep, like everyone else."

Terri laughed. "I've only been up since five," she said. "Really, I couldn't sleep any longer, and I knew there was a lot to do today. Happy Thanksgiving, by the way. And don't worry, I'll help you clean up."

Her kind smile strengthened Hattie's fortitude.

"And a happy Thanksgiving to you, too," she said. "We really do have much to be thankful for today, fire notwithstanding. It's chilling to think that the whole house could have gone up in flames, and us with it!"

She looked over at Wolf lying in his usual spot by the fireplace. "You were a wonderful watchdog last night. Thank goodness for you, too!"

They were contemplating the methods they would use to clean up the smoke residue in the kitchen when a man knocked on the door.

"Hattie Farwell?"

"Yes..."

"Hank Smith. Jim Sawyer sent me to clean up the smoke smell in your house. My company does this all the time for the fire department and police." He sniffed the air in the kitchen. "This isn't bad at all. With a little ozone and some professional room deodorizer, it won't take me any time to make it good as new!"

Hattie was cheered by this information, and silently blessed Jim for his foresight in sending Hank over.

Wolf strolled over and sniffed the newcomer.

"Whoa! Giant dog!" Hank observed. He held out his hand, palm up, for Wolf to sniff. When the imposing creature seemed satisfied the stranger meant no harm, Hank patted Wolf. The great dog wagged his tail.

"Thank you, Mr. Smith," said Hattie. "You're a lifesaver. Now, if you'll both excuse me, I'm going to take Wolf out for his morning stroll," Hattie said. She put on her heavy cape and a knit cap and picked up her flashlight. "The only thing I don't care for this time of year is the dark mornings."

She didn't bother hooking Wolf's leash to his collar. She looked over to Terri.

"There's no hunting allowed on Thanksgiving, so he'll be safe even if he does wander into the woods," Hattie explained. "What a relief not to have to worry about that today!"

Terri followed her to the kitchen porch.

"Jim replaced your woodpile, see?" She pointed to the wrought iron holder, which was once again full of logs. "He worked hard last night while we all slept. You'll have to replace a number of floorboards, though."

"I imagine so," Hattie agreed. "But Jim shouldn't have done all that." She felt guilty for worrying about so superficial a thing as where the logs would come from for the living room fireplace.

Instead of walking the lane as she usually did, Hattie decided to patrol the outside of the house. The firemen had done a good job pounding solid wooden boards over the cellar steps. She would be glad when metal doors were installed, but in the meantime no one could get in.

The same questions kept nagging at her. *Who? Why? The killer must be insane,* she thought. She didn't keep Wolf out any longer than necessary. There was so much to do.

When she returned to the kitchen the coffee was made, and Terri had already helped herself to a cup. She poured one for Hattie as soon as she took off her cape.

"Mmmm, that's good," Hattie murmured. "I needed that."

She opened the refrigerator door. "What would you like for breakfast, Terri? We have eggs, bacon, toast, English muffins, bagels, cereal..."

"All I want is a bowl of dry cereal, and I am perfectly capable of fixing it for myself," she smiled. "Let me fix you something for a change." So they both ate dry cereal with milk and sugar while plans for the day whirled around in their heads.

Afterward Terri helped Hattie stuff the turkey. They boiled potatoes to mash, creamed little boiled onions, made coleslaw and put the giblets in water over a low flame to simmer all day for the gravy.

It wasn't until after the preparations had been made and the turkey was in the oven that Brooke came down the piecrust stairs, rubbing sleep from her eyes.

"It smells much better down here, this morning," she observed, even though it still couldn't be described as smelling good.

"You can thank Terri and Jim for that," Hattie told her. "They worked hard scrubbing the fire smell away as much as they could, and Jim sent a professional cleaner over. He will have the place smelling just fine by the time our guests get here."

"Where's Jim?" Brooke wanted to know. She poured herself a cup of coffee.

"I sent him home for some much needed sleep," Terri said. "We can call him if we need him, but otherwise he said he'd come back at about one-thirty this afternoon."

"Good," Hattie said, "he should get some rest, and so should you, Terri. Why don't you go back to bed when you take Anna's breakfast up to her?"

"You know, Hattie, that's a good idea!" Terri agreed.

While Brooke poured herself a bowl of cereal and covered it with sugar and cream, Hattie started a fire in the kitchen fireplace. When it was blazing nicely, she sat in her overstuffed chair and stared into it, thinking about the fires last night.

"Puzzling," she mumbled.

"What's puzzling?" Terri asked as she buttered an English muffin for Anna.

"I was thinking about what Jim said about the fire in the basement. 'Puzzling' was the word he used." Brooke and Terri peered at her closely.

"Why?" they said in unison.

"Because," said Hattie, "the fire should have been blazing. The arsonist poured kerosene over the wooden shelves and the floor before setting fire to them. The shelves contained cans of combustible material—paints, paint thinner and turpentine. Everything should have gone up...*kaboom!* Why didn't it? Puzzling," she repeated.

"As I recall," Terri said as she poured cream into Anna's coffee. "Jim gave credit to Wolf for scaring the attacker away. Didn't he say the fire hadn't ignited, or if it had, most of it went out on its own?"

"Yes, that's what he thought," Hattie agreed. Strange, though, she wondered, why would the fire go out? But she didn't beleaguer the point. She had enough other things to focus on. By mid-morning everything was under control. The whole house was bathed in the redolence of roasting turkey, and the other dishes had been prepared.

Hattie, who hated to give in to her age, decided that she would function much better when her guests gathered if she'd lie down for just a bit now.

Shawn came into the kitchen from the dining room, where he'd been placing chairs at the table. He saw her starting up the back staircase. He'd been wandering around the property and especially in the old barn, which he found fascinating, before coming back into the house to help himself to coffee and cereal.

"Where are you going?" he asked. "Is everything okay?"

"Nosey, aren't you?" she kidded him. "Yes, dear, everything is okay. I'm tired, that's all, and decided to lie down for a little while."

"Hattie, before you go, I have something odd to show you. When I got up this morning I took a short walk before breakfast. As I like to do, I poked my head into the barn. You know how much I like that old building."

"Yes," she encouraged him. "Did you see something besides the barn cats?"

"Come with me, I'll show you." He took his jacket from the hook and she her heavy cape, and they walked together across the kitchen porch, down the flagstone path, through the gate in the picket fence, across the driveway and into a side door of the barn. It still bore the scent of hay, although not much was left. What few piles remained served only to shelter cats and the mice on which they feasted.

Hattie looked at cattle stalls, now empty, and way up through the haze past heavy, hand-hewn oak beams and empty haylofts to the inside of the cupola. She remembered with a lump in her throat the days when this sturdy building and a silo beside it had been bustling with activity.

Shawn's voice broke into her reverie. "Earth to Hattie! Earth to Hattie! Come in!" She laughed as he took her arm and led her to the double front doors, which were open onto a bank that led down to her lane. There, just inside the doors, bundled up as if thrown down in a rush, was an old blanket.

She leaned over and picked up one end of it. Once it had been pale green, but now it would be difficult to determine the color. Most of the blanket was charred black. Some of it had been burned away, and it bore the faint but unmistakable smell of kerosene.

"Do you think," mused Shawn, "that someone was setting fire to the barn, and was frightened off?"

Hattie considered the blanket for some time. Finally she said, "No, I don't believe anyone was trying to set fire to the barn." She studied the blanket some more before adding, "This was the blanket I kept in the basement for Wolf to lay on when I put him down there. Sometimes that was necessary when one of our guests was afraid of him."

"You digress," Shawn said pointedly. "How do you think it got over here in that condition if nobody was trying to use it to start a fire here? What if the man who started the fires at the house found this blanket in the basement and decided to use it to set fire to the barn? I still think that's what happened."

Hattie shrugged her shoulders. "That could be what happened, Shawn," she said vaguely, but she thought that although somehow the blanket had obviously been used in the basement, someone had deliberately carried it to the barn. It clearly had something to do with the cellar fire, but she didn't believe anyone had tried to set the barn afire. If so, its ancient wood would have gone up like tinder. She pushed the blanket aside with her foot and said, "I'd like Jim and Terri to see this. Let's see if they agree with you."

They walked through the front doors to the lane.

"Are these doors often kept open?" Shawn asked. "They were both wide open when I came in this morning."

"No, not often," answered Hattie. "But sometimes they blow open if they aren't properly latched. I don't remember that kind of wind last night, though. I wonder if they were opened and, if so, by whom. I don't remember Jim saying anything about them, do you?"

"No. I think I would remember if he had." Shawn scratched his head, clearly puzzled.

They walked on down the lane to the kitchen gate. Shawn took off his jacket.

"It sure has gotten warm, hasn't it?"

"Yes, very warm for this time of year," Hattie answered, but her mind was far away, working on this new mystery.

When she and Shawn returned to the house, Hattie decided to finally lie down for an hour or so before it was time to take her bath and dress for dinner. She closed the door between her room and Brooke's, and stripped to her slip before pulling down her covers and climbing into bed. This time, she didn't sleep but lay uncomfortably, turning all the events surrounding Anna and Annie over and over again in her mind. Hattie was an extremely practical person, and although the fires in her house were disturbing, once they'd been put out and the smoke smell cleaned out, she accepted the situation calmly and tried to analyze everything that had occurred.

As she lay there, she focused on who was responsible. Who would want to set her house on fire? There was no doubt in her mind that it was the same person who had killed Annie and tried to kill Anna. Nothing else made much sense. She considered a different explanation. Did Annie, she wondered, have some information that would have been injurious to somebody if it were out in the open?

If that were the case, she surmised, Anna might not, as she had said, know anything. What if it were Annie, after all, who was the target, and she was killed deliberately? What if the killer went after Anna on the assumption that Annie had given her the secret information? But what could Annie have known?

"Ohhhhh..." Hattie groaned quietly. She placed her palms on her spinning head. The more Hattie thought about it, the more preposterous the idea became. Who had the opportunity to kill Annie, cause Anna's accident, exchange Anna's pills, search Annie's house and set fire to her own? Who had access to all these things and places? And what was the motive? There simply had to be some connection between it all.

She closed her eyes and pondered the situation from the beginning. The beginning, the beginning, the beginning...When was the beginning?

The same disturbing thought that had been on the fringe of her consciousness for several days now came back to nag at her. *There's something I'm not seeing, some-*

*thing I should notice,* she thought. She kept her eyes closed and went over everything again in her mind.

Suddenly, she sat bolt upright in her bed. She was sure she knew who the killer was!

*But why?* She wondered. *Why? The motive is right there in front of me, and I simply can't see it.* She decided to keep her revelation to herself for a while. Maybe this afternoon, she would share it with Jim and Terri, but meanwhile, the killer might do something incriminating to lock the case up tight. And now that Hattie knew who it was, she was no longer frightened.

The more she thought about it, the more certain she was of the killer's identity, the only person it could be. The one person with the ability and opportunity…but why?

That question kept running through her head like a mantra. It repeated itself over and over while she took her bath and dressed. It followed her down the piecrust stairs to the kitchen. She was fairly certain that neither Annie nor Anna knew, or had ever met, the killer, because she knew most of the people in both their lives. What was the motive?

Jim arrived at one o'clock in the afternoon, looking handsome in a dark gray suit. Hattie was the first one to tell him so.

Shawn, who was walking into the kitchen from the dining room at that moment, was wearing slacks and an open-necked shirt. When he saw Jim, he turned at once and ran upstairs to put on a tie. No way was he going to be outdone.

"Hi!" he said to Jim upon his return, "and Happy Thanksgiving." Shawn offered his hand.

"Hi. Same to you," Jim responded pleasantly, accepting the boy's handshake.

"We have something to show you in the barn," Shawn said. "Where's Terri?"

"Helping Anna dress, I expect," Hattie said. "Perhaps we could take Jim without her this time."

On the way to the barn, while Shawn hurried on ahead of them, Hattie asked Jim if he'd come through the Brookside Farms development. When he said he had, she asked if he had seen any cars up there.

"No," he answered. "Do you have any particular reason for asking?"

"Maybe. I'll let you know."

"Here, Jim," Shawn called from the barn door. He pointed to the charred blanket that lay bundled up where Hattie had pushed it with her foot earlier.

"This blanket has definitely been on fire," Jim said. "How long has it been here?" He sniffed it. "It smells of kerosene, too."

"I found it there this morning," Shawn explained. "I know it wasn't here yesterday, because I would have seen it." He hesitated a moment, feeling a trifle embarrassed. "I like to come in here and just poke around. It's such a neat building. Hattie knows."

"Do you know where the blanket came from?" Jim asked.

"It was in the basement. I kept it down there for the dog," Hattie said.

"So," said Jim, "you both believe that someone brought it here last night?"

"Absolutely," stated Shawn. "I think it was the killer, and that he was trying to set fire to the barn. I guess Terri chased him away. Hattie's not so sure."

"No?" Jim looked at Hattie. "How come?"

"I'll explain my deductions later," she said. "But right now, I've got guests coming. I'd better get back to the house."

Jim picked up the blanket and awkwardly attempted to fold it without getting his good suit dirty. "Would you have a bag for this?" he asked.

"I'll bring one back to you," Shawn volunteered, and he and Hattie walked back to the house. However, when they walked into the kitchen, Brooke had come downstairs, and Shawn had no compunction about leaving Jim standing in the barn while he made a fuss over Brooke. She was dressed in what she fondly called her "Aunt Hattie" outfit, the black skirt and white blouse she'd worn the day of her grandmother's funeral. As before, her hair was pulled back into a bun just as Hattie's was.

"I think you look great dressed like that," Shawn told her.

Hattie handed Shawn a large, dark green trash bag. "Here's the bag for Jim. You know he's waiting for it." She smiled as she spoke, and he gave her an impish grin back. He was in no hurry to get to Jim, but he trudged off obediently, bag in hand.

Anna and Terri came downstairs shortly before two. Anna was wearing a soft blue wool dress and looked lovely. Terri had changed the sling on her broken left arm to a blue one to match her outfit. Her black eye had faded nicely, and Terri had combed her hair as much as possible over the angry, dark red scar on her forehead. "Am I presentable?" she asked.

Hattie and Brooke met them at the bottom of the main staircase. "Oh, darling, you're much more than that!" exclaimed Hattie. "You don't know how good you look to me."

Terri was dressed in a tailored burnt orange wool dress, and she looked more attractive than Hattie had ever seen her.

"You look great, Terri!" Brooke complimented her. "I like that dress."

"My thoughts exactly," Hattie added.

Terri and Anna went into the living room, where Shawn was starting a fire in the fireplace. They sat on the sofa and watched him set wadded newspapers under the grate. Soon the logs were blazing merrily.

Hattie and Brooke were still in the hall when the doorbell rang. Hattie opened the door to find Larry standing there. "Hi, Larry!" she said heartily. "Welcome, and happy Thanksgiving! Go on into the living room, we'll all be in there shortly." She smiled to herself. Larry, she was certain, didn't care who else would be in the living room as long as Anna was there.

Hattie left the front door wide open but the glass storm door closed. It was exactly two when she and Brooke saw Cameron's car drive into the pull-off. Brooke stepped out onto the porch and watched Cameron help her mother from the car. Alexandra was wearing the red cashmere sweater that had caused so much consternation, a multi-colored silk scarf around her neck and a long gray skirt. She looked, Brooke had to admit, absolutely gorgeous.

They both looked up at the figure standing on the porch and smiled politely. "Happy Thanksgiving, Ha—," Alexandra began before realizing the figure on the porch was Brooke. "Brooke!" she exclaimed. "I thought you were Hattie! Honestly, why did you have to wear that outfit again?"

Cameron and Brooke both laughed. "You fooled me, too, for a few minutes," Cameron acknowledged.

When Alexandra was passing Brooke to enter the house, Brooke whispered to her. "You look lovely in my red sweater!" This time, Alexandra had the grace to laugh, too.

# 40

Hattie gazed down the dinner table, and her heart was full. It was almost as if Annie were there after all. The spirit of conviviality moved her deeply. She was happy to see that even Alexandra was laughing and enjoying herself.

*It was because of Anna,* Hattie thought. After those first terrible days of fear that they would lose her, followed by tiring hospital visits and continued concern, now here she was. Hattie smiled lovingly at Anna. Cameron was seated at the opposite end of the table from Hattie, where he had insisted on carving the turkey. Anna sat to his right, and she seemed to simply glow.

The reason for her happiness was seated to her right. Larry cut her meat for her and almost literally hovered over her. Occasionally he whispered something into her ear which brought a blush to her cheeks.

To his right sat Brooke, with Shawn to her right and Hattie's left. On the opposite side of the table, Alexandra was seated to Hattie's right with Jim seated between her and Terri. Hattie had not been alone in worrying about Alexandra's acceptance of Jim and Terri—and Shawn in particular—but she found her fears were groundless.

"What's gotten into Mother?" Brooke leaned across Shawn to whisper to Hattie. "She's certainly in an unusually good mood. She's even being nice to Shawn."

They both looked at Alexandra, who had been listening attentively to Jim's detailed plans for attending law school the following year. "I think that's very admirable, Jim," she was saying. "I think you'll make a fine lawyer."

Next to Jim, Terri and Cameron were chatting quietly. Every so often Hattie noticed one then the other cast a quick appraising glance at Larry. *Anna's safe here,* Hattie thought with relief, *no one can hurt her now with all those protectors.*

Again the haunting question—what was the motive?—began coursing through her mind. She was convinced that she knew who the killer was, but she still didn't know why. Perhaps after dinner she'd find time to talk to Jim when the others were otherwise occupied. She felt as though she'd run up against a brick wall. *The reason should be obvious,* she thought. It was right there in front of her and she couldn't see it.

"I'll clear the table, Aunt Hattie," Brooke's voice broke into her thoughts and brought her back to the present. Hattie started to get up when Terri pushed her gently back into her seat.

"I'll help, too, Hattie," she offered. "You just sit there and enjoy yourself."

The girls soon had the table cleared. The sound of their voices drifted in from the kitchen. "This is so nice," Hattie said to everyone in general.

"Your dinner was excellent, Hattie," Cameron stated heartily. "That was about the best stuffing I've ever eaten, and the turkey was out of this world. So was everything else. Thank you so very much for including us."

"Yes, Hattie," Alexandra agreed, "we so much appreciate your inviting us."

Once they had cleared the table, Brooke and Terri brought in an antique china coffee pot and matching cups on a tray, and while Hattie poured, they brought in the pumpkin pies.

The only one who didn't worry aloud about where to put another bite was Shawn, who managed to devour two good-sized pieces after eating more dinner than anyone else there. Alexandra alone refused dessert. "Are you still watching your figure, Mom?" teased Brooke.

"If she doesn't, I won't either!" quipped Cameron. Everyone laughed.

"Not very original, dear," Alexandra told him, "but cute!"

"Let's go sit in the living room by the fire," Hattie suggested. "I'll bring the coffee pot in case anyone would care for another cup."

Shawn helped Brooke clear the dessert dishes from the table. When Terri started to join them, he shooed her away. "No thanks, Terri," he said, "we're just fine. You go join the others by the fire."

He and Brooke filled and started the dishwasher. They rinsed more dishes and piled them on the counter, and Shawn washed the counters and sink.

"Very good!" complimented Brooke. "Your mother raised you right!"

He laughed and pulled her into his arms.

"Let's go out for a walk, okay?"

"Sure," she responded, giving him a big squeeze. He kissed her lingeringly.

Afterward, when she had caught her breath, she suggested taking Wolf with them. The great dog was making it obvious that he wanted to go out. They barely had him on his leash and the door open before he pushed his way past them. Wolf loped across the porch, through the gate and across the lane into the woods, with Brooke holding his leash and Shawn behind them. Just looking for some time alone, they didn't tell the others they were leaving.

The peaceful, contented mood continued in the living room. Cameron beamed at Anna. "We have a great deal to be thankful for today," he remarked. "Anna, your recovery has been remarkable. It's wonderful to have you here with all of us."

"Thanks, Cameron," Anna said, "and let me tell you how wonderful it is for me to be here." Larry covered her hand with his and smiled at her lovingly.

"We have an announcement to make," Anna continued. "Larry and I are re-engaged! We want to be married in the spring—as soon as my doctor tells me I'm in the clear."

"That's just marvelous, Darling!" Hattie exclaimed. "I wish you both all of the happiness in the world!"

Alexandra and Cameron both crossed the room to the sofa where Anna and Larry sat. Alexandra leaned over and kissed Anna. "I really am very happy for you both," she said. "But why did you break off your engagement in the first place?" Larry had stood up, and Alexandra stood on tiptoe to kiss his cheek. He didn't answer her question but looked at Anna.

Cameron kissed Anna, too, and shook hands with Larry. "It will be great having you in the family," he told him. "I need another man around." He hesitated. "Or will you be around? I expect you'll both be going off to Seattle, won't you?"

"No, I don't think so," Larry said. "I'm hoping to get a job as assistant principal at a suburban high school in the area. I've been interviewed twice for the job and feel pretty good about my chances." He turned to Anna. "That's where I've been."

"Great, great," Cameron said with enthusiasm. "I wish you all the best."

As soon as Alexandra and Cameron moved aside a bit, Hattie went over to kiss Anna and hug Larry. Across the room, Jim and Terri looked on with skepticism. "I think he has some questions to answer before I congratulate him," Jim whispered.

"You bet!" Terri responded. "I have no intentions of leaving him alone with Anna. Not until I'm satisfied that he had nothing to do with the so-called accidents."

Anna looked over at Terri. "No congratulations, Terri?" she asked.

Terri smiled. "You know I want what is best for you, Anna," she said. "I want to see you happy more than anything."

"That's not what I wanted to hear from you," Anna complained. "I want you to be happy for me right now. I'm very happy, really I am."

Suddenly Anna realized that Brooke was not in the room. "Where's Brooke?" she demanded. "Don't tell me she didn't hear our announcement! She'll kill me when she finds out that everyone else knew before she did."

Terri felt miserable. She wanted to congratulate Larry and wish Anna the best, but there was still that nagging feeling that Larry was somehow involved in the attacks on Annie and Anna. She stood at the front window looking out at the lane and feeling totally inadequate.

Suddenly she saw a tall thin man walk rapidly out of the woods and up the lane in the direction of the barn. Her heart seemed to jump when she saw him, particularly from the back. There was little doubt in her mind that he was the same man she had chased up the lane the night before.

She cast an anguished look at Jim before hurrying into the hall and out the front door. He knew she'd seen something suspicious and, trying to appear casual, followed her out.

Terri approached the lane cautiously. The man did not turn around, but walked rapidly to the barn. The front doors were still standing open, and he ducked inside. Moving as quietly and as fast as she could, Terri reached the barn. She flattened herself against the siding and inched herself slowly to the door, removing her .38 pistol from her shoulder holster as she did. Jim was right behind her, gun in hand.

When she reached the door, she chanced a careful peek into the dim interior. The man was standing no more than 15 feet away. His back was to her, and he seemed to be searching for someone. He walked around casting furtive glances into the stalls, up ladders and around corners. She heard him sigh in frustration.

"Police!" she yelled. "Put your hands in the air and turn around slowly."

The man jumped perceptibly when he heard her voice. He immediately placed his hands over his head and turned to face her. At almost the same moment, Terri and Jim saw that both of the man's hands were wrapped in thick gauze bandages.

Jim, who was now squatting next to the door opposite Terri, moved to the man. Both kept him covered with their guns. Jim patted the man down for a weapon despite the fact that it would have been impossible for anyone with such bandaged hands to handle a gun. Satisfied that the man posed no danger, Jim and Terri replaced their own revolvers in their holsters.

"May I have your name, please, sir?" Jim asked, professionally polite as he placed his hand on the man's right arm and led him from the barn.

"My name is Howard Cole," the man answered in a sheepish voice.

"Are you a friend of Miss Farwell's?" asked Terri.

"And what brings you here on Thanksgiving Day?" demanded Jim.

Howard did not answer.

"Where do you live, Mr. Cole?" Terri asked. Howard gave her his address in South Philadelphia, while Jim examined his bandaged hands.

"What happened to your hands?" Jim asked.

Howard didn't answer.

"Want me to Mirandize him, or do you want the honor?" Jim asked Terri.

"Go ahead," she answered.

"You have the right to remain silent..." Jim began, but Howard interrupted him.

"Am I being arrested?" he asked in alarm.

"You are," Terri said.

"Please, don't do that," he begged. "I'll answer your questions."

"Were you involved in a fire here last night?" Terri asked.

"Yes," Howard answered, "but I didn't start it."

"What's wrong with your hands?" Jim asked.

"They're burned," Howard said quietly.

"This is like pulling teeth," Terri grumbled, looking imploringly at Jim.

"How did you burn your hands, Mr. Cole?" Jim persisted.

"I burned my hands..." Howard straightened up a bit and his voice became louder, more confident. "I burned my hands trying to put out a fire in the basement of the house."

Jim wasn't surprised. This solved one mystery, anyhow— why the fire in the basement didn't consume everything. Why it went out despite the presence of the kerosene.

"Tell me about it," Jim coaxed.

"The fire had been started with kerosene, like the one on the porch. There was a shelf full of paints and paint thinner and turpentine—stuff like that. I was sure that it would all go up, and the house with it. There was an old blanket lying on the floor, in the corner. I picked it up and started beating and beating at the flames. I managed to smother most of them before the smoke and fumes got to me.

"I thought it was almost out, but I had to leave. I was choking. So I ran up the cellar steps, outside, around the house and up the lane. As I ran, I realized I was still carrying the blanket.

"Someone was chasing me. I guess it was you," he nodded toward Terri. "I ran to my car, which was parked around the bend up there," he nodded toward the bend in the lane. "On the way, I threw the blanket into the barn. That's all, and it's the truth."

"That's fine, as far as it goes," Terri said. "But there is still much you haven't told us. Why were you here in the first place? How did you know about the fire in the cellar if you didn't start it yourself? And if you did start the fires, why?"

"I didn't start any fires, I swear," Howard stated, automatically putting his right hand in the air.

"We'll get back to your involvement in a minute," Jim said, "but first, who bandaged your hands?"

"They were beginning to hurt a lot as I drove home. At first I didn't feel anything. I didn't even know I was burned, but my skin started sticking to the steering wheel as I drove, and I was beginning to feel sick to my stomach," Howard admitted. "So I went to the emergency room at Saint Agnes Hospital and they took care of me."

"I want to know who you were looking for in the barn just now," Terri said. "But let's go back to the house and finish our questioning there."

Though it was only four o'clock when they started walking back to the house, the sky was already darkening and a stiff breeze had begun to blow down the lane. They were crossing the kitchen porch, when a Lincoln Continental roared up the lane and spun to a dirt-spewing halt in the driveway.

"Michael!" Howard gasped. They all gawked as Michael DiRienzo jumped from the car and ran up the flagstone path toward them.

"Where's Brooke?" he yelled. Then his eyes widened. "Howard! What the hell are you doing here?" Without waiting for an answer, Michael pushed ahead of them and ran into the kitchen. Finding no one there, he ran on into the dining room and across the entrance hall to the living room. Terri, Jim and Howard followed closely behind.

He looked around desperately.

"Where's Brooke?" he shouted at the five gathered there.

And suddenly, Hattie knew not only the identity of the killer, but at last she also knew the motive.

"Howard! Michael!" Alexandra cried. "What's going on? Why are you here?"

Michael was close to panic. "Where's Brooke?" he yelled.

Hattie was on her feet and hurrying toward the kitchen.

"She and Shawn went to the kitchen to clean up the dishes," she called back over her shoulder.

"She's not there!" Michael shouted, following her across the dining room. "I just came through the kitchen. No one's there!"

Alexandra ran after them.

"Michael, answer me! Is Brooke in danger?"

"After what you did to me, Alexandra, I should never speak to you again," Michael roared. "But, yes, Brooke is in terrible danger!" He ran to the kitchen door and looked out at the woods.

Hattie tried to remain calm.

"The dog is missing," she said. "Brooke and Shawn have probably taken him out for a walk." She fought back terror. *Which path did they take?* she wondered. *What horror is out there waiting for them— stalking them?*

"Where? Where did they go?" Alexandra cried. "Which way would they go, Hattie?" Without waiting for an answer, Alexandra took the scarf from her neck, tied it around her head and ran across the porch, heading for the woods.

"Crazy woman!" Michael exclaimed. "Come back, Alexandra!" He, too, bolted from the house, and followed her into the woods.

# 41

Maria DiRienzo awakened late that morning. Slowly she opened her right eye and looked at the time on the clock-radio on her bedside table. It was ten thirty. She had much to do before she and Michael were due at her brother's for dinner at five thirty.

"Michael," she mumbled, "it's time to get up. It's late." She rolled over and wasn't really surprised to see that his side of the bed was empty. She swung her bare feet onto the floor and, without bothering to put a robe over her thin nightgown, padded downstairs looking for him.

The red light on the phone in the den phone was blinking, indicating there was voice mail. As Maria retrieved it, she knew it would be from Michael. She should have checked for messages when she came home.

"Maria," his deep voice enunciated, "I've been held up in town. Lock up the house and turn out the lights, I won't be home until late tomorrow afternoon." She clenched her fists and for one wild moment considered smashing the phone.

Her anger almost consumed her. She'd known that he would be in Philadelphia planning his campaign for a good part of the night, and she had suspected that he might party for a while afterward. But she had also expected that he would come home some time before dawn. *Was he with a woman?* she wondered. Maybe that was why he made it clear to Howard that he didn't want him to go with him. Or maybe he had found out that Howard had sent Shawn to the Eagles game to talk to

Stacey. Maybe he blamed her, too. He had no right to treat her like this! He'll be sorry!

Maria stamped into the kitchen and made a pot of coffee. As soon as it was ready she drank two cups, in quick succession. She ate no breakfast, having no stomach for food under the circumstances. Then she hurried back upstairs to the bathroom off her bedroom where she stood under a hot shower for almost ten minutes.

She felt better when she got out—more decisive. She remembered as she dried herself that Howard had told her last night that he'd be coming over this afternoon. *Howard*, she thought. Howard was the best friend she'd ever had, but she did not want to see him this afternoon, not after what he'd done to spoil her plans. She was almost glad he'd burned his hands...served him right!

She'd always been able to confide in Howard. He had been sincerely sympathetic. She knew he cared. She believed he understood— even when he talked to her last night. Now, in the bright light of day, she began to doubt his loyalty.

It was time to act again. From the back of her closet, where she had stuffed them into a suitcase, she brought out her black wool slacks, heavy black sweater and black wool cap. They bore the strong smell of smoke laced with kerosene.

Fully dressed with her gray hair tucked out of sight under the cap, she returned to the den. She found the key to Michael's gun case in the back of the top drawer in his desk and used it to unlock and open the cabinet. She chose a .22 rifle which Michael had taught her how to use when she was a girl and, armed with the rifle and extra ammunition, left the house.

Maria was almost euphoric as she placed the rifle under a blanket in her trunk. She didn't notice Howard's approaching car. Her plans were uppermost in her mind as she slid into the driver's seat, and she was aware of little else.

It was with great difficulty that Maria kept to the speed limit all the way north on I-95 and then on the narrow roads that eventually led to Hattie's house. How clever she had been when she insisted on picking up Brooke at the Farwell farm last Sunday. How else would she have learned about the hidden lane leading from the housing development? She laughed out loud.

Suddenly she became angry at Howard again. If he hadn't interfered, the house would be in ashes now, and Brooke with it! Never mind, she consoled herself, there will be no mistakes this afternoon, and if that monster dog comes after me, I'll shoot him! This time I'm prepared.

Maria parked around the bend in the lane, far away from the house. She surveyed the area cautiously before removing the .22 from the trunk. No one was in sight. She walked down the lane until she found a path leading into the woods, and then she followed that until she found another that ran parallel to the lane.

At last she saw the house. It looked as if nothing had happened. It should have been burned to the ground. The familiar anger rose in her throat like bile. Her grip on the rifle tightened. She ducked under outstretched branches and moved closer to the house.

For a while Maria stood and stared at the windows. *Wouldn't it be wonderful*, she thought, *if Brooke appeared at one of them?* But that didn't happen. She looked at the kitchen porch where she had ignited the log pile the previous night, but decided against going onto that. That would be too dangerous, and anyway she believed that horrible dog probably stayed in the kitchen.

She turned her gaze to the opposite end of the house and the porch that wrapped around it. She edged her way across the lane toward the gate which opened onto the path leading to the porch. She had her hand on the gate when she saw through the window someone walking past the front door. She ducked out of sight. This would never do. She could be seen too easily. As soon as she felt it was safe, she turned and ran back into the woods.

From her vantage point she saw someone come out onto the kitchen porch. She backed further into the woods and hid in a cedar thicket from which she continued to observe the kitchen porch. No doubt about it, the man standing there could be no one but Shawn. A woman wearing a long dark skirt, a white blouse and a dark cape joined him. Her hair was pulled back into a bun, but Maria didn't waste time staring at her or Shawn, because the woman, who must, she thought, be Hattie Farwell, was holding a leash, and at the other end of the leash was attached that monster of a dog!

Maria watched as Shawn and Brooke with Wolf walked back into the woods at a distance from her. Soon they disappeared around a large rock outcropping, and Maria breathed a sigh of relief. If she hadn't been so concentrated on Wolf she might have wondered why Shawn was so attentive to 'Hattie.'

Dusk was beginning to darken the woods. Maria made her way to a brighter area and found herself on the edge of a clearing. She could barely make out the house through the trees, but she could tell that someone was turning on lights inside.

She remained motionless, wondering what to do next. The soft cracking of a twig made her jump. She turned cautiously and saw not 20 feet from her a buck, placidly chewing some tall late grass. The buck's head suddenly went up, his ears erect. His whole being was alert. *What did he hear?* she wondered.

And then she heard it, too. A car was speeding up the lane. She could see its headlights, and all at once it came to a rapid stop. Then she heard Michael's voice, although she couldn't make out his words. Tense and anxious and more determined than ever to kill Brooke, Maria clutched the .22 closer to her. The movement startled the buck, and with a wave of his white tail he disappeared into the woods.

In moments the outside lights burst to life, and Maria could see frantic activity on the kitchen porch. A slim figure in a cherry-red sweater separated herself from the others and ran toward the woods.

"Brooke!" Maria whispered in glee. "It's Brooke, I'd recognize that sweater anywhere! How lucky can I get? She's coming down the path in my direction!" She wanted to laugh. She placed the rifle stock to her right shoulder and leaned her cheek against it as she attempted to follow the running figure through the sights. She was sorry the light wasn't better as she trained the barrel on Alexandra's scarf-covered head.

# 42

Jim came up behind Hattie. She was standing at the open door, desperately trying to decide what to do. "What's going on?" he demanded.

At that moment Howard pushed Jim aside, darted past Hattie, and before Jim could stop him, ran up the lane. Hattie stopped Jim from running after him. "Wait!" she commanded. "They're all trying to find Brooke before it's too late. Maria DiRienzo is out there somewhere planning to kill her."

"Maria DiRienzo?" Cameron's voice came from the dining room doorway. "Does Maria DiRienzo want to kill Brooke?" Cameron's expression was one of incredulity.

The others piled into the kitchen behind him. "Who wants to kill Brooke?" asked Anna in a voice fraught with fear. "Where is she, Aunt Hattie? What's happening?"

Larry put his arm protectively around Anna. "You've got to sit down, Anna, please."

"Maybe you'd better go upstairs and lie down," Terri suggested.

"No!" Anna exclaimed. "How can I lie down when my sister is out there in terrible danger?"

Terri crossed the room to Jim and Hattie. "Tell us what you know," she said to Hattie. "Did I hear you right? Is Maria DiRienzo trying to kill Brooke?"

"Yes," Hattie said. "And I would be willing to swear that Maria killed Annie, tried to kill Anna and also murdered Stacey Tyburn, the Eagles cheerleader."

At that moment Howard Cole came running back down the lane and over to the kitchen porch. "Has Brooke come back, yet?" he asked breathlessly. "I haven't seen anyone, but Maria's car is parked at the end of the lane near the new development. She left her house an hour and a half ago, and she took Michael's .22 rifle.

"We've got to find her before she finds Brooke!

"Why does Maria want to kill Brooke?" Jim demanded.

"Because she knows who Brooke is," Howard answered. "It was Brooke she wanted all along, but there's no time to go into that now." He turned and ran down the lane, darting into the woods from time to time, searching.

Dusk was beginning to settle over the forest. "We're going to need flashlights pretty soon," Jim said. "Terri, I think you'd better stay here. Keep your eyes open. I'll start looking in the woods, and I think you'd better call for back-up."

Terri was hanging up the phone when a shot rang out in the woods. Jim ran toward the sound while Terri kept the others from following. Jim reappeared in less than four minutes. "Call for an ambulance," he called. "Dr. MacArthur, come with me. Hurry! I'll get my first aid kit from my car."

Terri called for the ambulance while Jim and Cameron rushed back into the woods. Jim led the way down a winding, hilly path to an open area where Alexandra lay face down in the dirt. A crimson patch was saturating the scarf on her head. Michael knelt next to her, talking to her, trying desperately to get a response. When he saw Cameron and Jim he called out. "I think she's dead."

Maria crept quietly away. That was what she wanted to hear. *She's dead,* she thought in elation. *Brooke is finally dead!*

Maria made her way cautiously through the woods until she was out of sight of the house and felt free to run up the lane to her car. She unlocked the door and pressed the button in the glove compartment to release the trunk catch.

She was almost giddy with joy as she placed the rifle under a blanket in the trunk. *I did it! I did it!* she rejoiced. She was even happier than when she'd successfully pushed Stacey Tyburn under the train.

Maria closed the trunk lid and was starting back to the driver's side door when Howard ran from behind a clump of bushes and stood in front of her. "Maria, Maria," he said sadly. "I feel so guilty that I let you get this far. You need help, my dear, we must get you to a hospital."

His bandages made it difficult, but he took hold of her arm and gently helped her from the car. He led her around to the passenger side, where he opened the door and helped her in.

Maria was unexpectedly compliant. She sat quietly in the passenger seat until Howard closed her door and started to walk behind the car to the driver's side. With an evil smile on her face, she pressed the button to lock all of the doors and scooted rapidly over to the driver's seat.

Howard yelled and tried to open the door, but Maria laughed wickedly. She put the car in gear and gunned it rapidly past him. She drove up the lane toward Brookside Farms. Howard ran after her.

To her horror, she never reached the development. A police car blocked her way. A uniformed officer, gun drawn, approached the car. Without warning, Maria let out a little yelp, jumped from the car and charged into the woods.

"Stop!" yelled the officer. "Stop, or I'll shoot!"

He raised his gun, pointed it above the fleeing figure and pulled the trigger just as Shawn and Brooke came from the woods. Maria screamed and continued running.

Before the officer could fire a second time, a great gray dog leapt from a thicket and knocked the terrified woman to the ground. The officer pointed his gun at Wolf.

"Don't shoot!" Shawn shrieked. "It's okay. He's a pet!"

Wolf, snarling viciously, stood over Maria until she was handcuffed and led to the police car. She continued to scream uncontrollably. She didn't see Brooke, but Brooke saw everything that had happened.

"We could use your dog on the force," the officer said to Shawn, after Maria was secured in the back seat of his car. "Calm down, lady!" he told her as he climbed into the driver's seat.

She wasn't listening, but continued screaming and trying to bang her head against the wire screen that separated the front seat from the back.

Howard stood breathlessly, with tears in his eyes, watching Maria.

The officer looked at Howard's bandaged hands.

"What happened to your hands?" he asked.

"I burned them," Howard said. His voice was flat and lifeless. He felt numb.

The officer instructed Howard to sit in the passenger seat of his car while he drove him back to Hattie's house. Shawn and Brooke followed on foot. Maria was still screaming, almost convulsively now.

Terri met them at the gate when they arrived. An ambulance was backed as far as possible into the path upon which Alexandra lay. Its motor was running and its lights were flashing.

The officer turned Howard over to Jim and continued to the hospital with Maria.

Brooke and Shawn ran down the lane to Jim.

"What is it?" Brooke cried. "Who's been hurt? Don't tell me it was Anna again!"

Hattie hurried down the flagstone path to embrace Brooke.

"Oh, darling, you don't know how good it is to see you!" she exclaimed. "Are you all right?"

"I'm fine, Aunt Hattie, but why is an ambulance here?" Brooke responded. Her eyes were still on the emergency vehicle. "Has Anna been hurt again?"

"No, no, Anna is fine. She's in the kitchen, and she's very worried about you. Why don't you go in with me and assure her you're fine?"

Shawn's face was white, and he was obviously extremely upset.

"I heard a gunshot, didn't I?" he asked, after Hattie and Brooke had gone in the house. "Was somebody shot?"

"We don't know anything for sure," Terri answered, "but I can only assume that Mrs. MacArthur was shot. Jim and Dr. MacArthur went out some time ago, and the ambulance paramedics are there now, too."

Wolf cantered down the lane, and after investigating people and vehicles, trotted past the wide open storm door into the house. There, he began noisily lapping water from his dish.

Brooke, who was being hugged by Anna, smiled fondly at him.

"Wolf captured Maria," she said, breathlessly. "She was running away from a police officer when he shot over her head. She screamed, but kept running into the woods to escape. Wolf jumped on her and held her down until the officer was able to handcuff her. Now, will someone please tell me why the police were chasing Maria? And why was she screaming?"

"Because," Michael said from the doorway, "she shot your mother."

Before Brooke could react to this stunning news, a

commotion outside sent them all hurrying onto the porch. Alexandra was on a litter being carried out of the woods. Brooke rushed to her side, but Cameron gently pulled her out of the way as Alexandra was placed in the ambulance.

"Mother!" Anna cried from the porch, but there was no response.

Larry put his arm around her and drew her to him. She burst into tears.

Cameron took hold of Brooke's hand and hurried with her to the porch.

"Girls, your mother will be all right. The bullet grazed her skull and knocked her unconscious for a little while, but her injury is not serious as far as I can tell. She's just a bit dazed right now. I'm going to follow the ambulance to the hospital, and I'll call you as soon as I know anything new."

Anna, still cuddled in Larry's arms, began to cry again, this time with relief.

"Now maybe we can convince you to go back to bed," Larry said, concerned.

"Please, Larry," she begged. "I must find out what's going on."

Hattie, who understood what Anna was going through, looked at her compassionately.

"Why don't we all go into the living room?" she suggested. "Maybe we can unravel this mystery." She turned to the officer standing with Howard. "Please, bring Mr. Cole, too," she said. "I believe he can tell us a great deal."

Michael slipped his arm around Brooke's shoulders as they were walking into the living room. When she sat in an overstuffed chair, he perched on the arm, never taking his eyes off her. She was too distracted by all the activity to notice.

Boss or no boss, Shawn noticed, and his looks shot daggers at Michael. If it had been possible he would have sat on the other arm, but even in his jealousy he knew that would be ridiculous. He did the next best thing and sat on the floor at her feet.

Howard sat on a straight chair near them. Michael had never seen Howard look so completely beaten. Hattie sat in her favorite chair by the fireplace, where the fire had long since died. From her position she could see everyone else in the room. Anna and Larry returned to their original seats on the sofa. Terri and Jim chose comfortable armchairs facing Brooke and her cozy companions.

For a moment nobody spoke. They all looked at one another uneasily. Howard shifted in his seat. Finally he was the first to speak. "The rifle is in the trunk of Maria's car under a blanket. I was just turning the corner on my way to see Michael when I saw Maria run from the house carrying the gun. I was certain that it was Michael's .22.

"She put the gun in her trunk and drove off in a rush. I knew I had to follow her, although I was just about positive where she was headed." He looked at Hattie. "Here to your house, Miss Farwell. I followed her here last night when she tried to burn the house down."

"Mr. Cole told us how he put most of the fire out in the cellar," Terri interjected.

"Yes," Howard continued. "Mike, I'm so sorry. I should have said something to you when I first became suspicious of Maria, but honestly, last night was the first time I realized how truly deranged she is."

"You're in love with her Howard," Michael murmured. "Why didn't I see that before?"

"You've always had too much else on your mind!" Howard spoke bitterly. "You left her alone so much. She was very lonely, Mike. How do you think she felt when she knew about all of your affairs?"

"She knew?" Michael was amazed.

"Of course, she knew, you idiot! Wives always know." Howard was clearly annoyed. "And then there were the years when she tried so hard to give you a baby. Seven miscarriages, Michael! Do you know what that did to her? And you were anything but understanding. Then she was getting older and putting on weight, and there were those beautiful, nubile young women constantly swarming you."

For a minute Michael looked at Howard suspiciously. "Howard, did you and Maria...I mean, was there anything between the two of you?"

"God, no, Mike! What a stupid thing to suggest! You still don't really understand the depth of her love for you, do you? She's crazy with it. I didn't fully understand how crazy until last night. Now it's all beginning to fit together."

Hattie took over.

"It was Maria who killed Annie, wasn't it, Howard? And it was Maria who tried to kill Anna, too. Isn't that true?"

"Yes," Howard said, so softly that everyone leaned forward to hear him.

"Why?" Terri asked.

"I honestly didn't know she was responsible when it happened," Howard said. "It was when she was so mean to Brooke that I began to wonder. Especially the day when she deliberately locked her in the basement at headquarters and unplugged her phone."

"Deliberately?" shouted Michael. "I was the one who got her out of there. The door was just stuck.

"No," Howard shook his head. "I checked it out the next day. True, the door did stick sometimes, but that wasn't what happened. There was a lock in the knob that allowed the knob to be turned from the outside, but not from downstairs."

"I thought Maria was jealous of Brooke," Shawn said in a wise voice. "But is that any reason to kill her? I think Maria kept Brooke away from Michael because she's so beautiful, and she didn't want Michael to make a play for her."

"You're right," Howard agreed. "Maria was insanely jealous of Brooke, but not for the reason you said."

Hattie spoke thoughtfully. "Her jealously, Shawn, was to her a reason to kill. She wasn't thinking like rational people. Her mind was warped, you have to understand that."

"It wasn't just jealously that made her push Stacey Tyburn in front of the subway train. She had to get rid of her, because she was afraid her relationship with Michael would ruin his chances of becoming president. Killing Brooke would have been an entirely different matter, wouldn't it, Michael?"

Michael started to speak, then changed his mind. "Not now, Hattie, please," he finally said.

Brooke looked at Michael, then at Hattie. "If there's something that involves me, I have a right to know what it is."

Howard shifted uncomfortably in his chair.

"Mike, I knew Brooke's secret the first day I saw her. Maria knew it, too. Obviously, Miss Farwell also knows it. Don't you think, in fairness to Brooke, you should be the one to tell her before someone else does?"

Michael looked down at Brooke. She was looking back at him expectantly.

"Eighteen and a half years ago, when I was running for Congress," he began, "your mother was a volunteer in my campaign. She worked very hard in the spring primaries, and we became extremely close—too close." He stopped, embarrassed, and cleared his throat.

"Shortly after that, your father—err...her husband—completed his residency in reconstructive surgery and went into practice with Dr. MacArthur. He was home more often after that, and with the primaries over, I had no reason to see your mother anymore. I bumped into her one day in Center City, and she told me that everything was fine again between she and Doug, and she was very happy. She failed mention the fact that she was pregnant, though I don't know if I would have thought anything about it if she had."

Brooke's eyes widened. She held her breath as she waited for what he would say next.

"Brooke," he started, "Brooke, I never knew until the day you were locked in the basement. Honestly, I never actually knew. That day, when I talked to you and brought you home and had a chance to really look at you, I knew without doubt that I'm your father."

Brooke gasped.

"How can you be so sure?"

"Your coloring was my first clue. I stopped by your grandparents' home several times during the campaign to talk over flyers or photos or something with your mother...anything for an excuse to be with her. Once I met Doug." He looked over at Brooke's sister. "Of course, I knew you, Anna. I often saw your grandparents, and I saw all the photos they had around of the rest of the family. It struck me then that they were all blue-eyed blondes, particularly when I came from a family of brown-eyed, dark-haired Italians.

"You have your mother's features and figure, Brooke, but go look in the mirror. Your eyes and hair are just like mine. Why do you think your mother kept you out of sight so much? Don't you know that it's genetically impossible for two blue-eyed people to produce a child with brown eyes?

"Oh...my God!" Brooke gasped, completely shocked. "But, of course. That's why she put me in boarding school when I was only eight years old. And then there was summer camp every year. I was never home! I thought she just didn't want to be bothered with me once she married Cameron."

Michael took her hand in his.

"I can't tell you how I regret all the years we've missed, but we can make up for them now. I mean, if you want to."

Brooke hesitated for a moment, then her face softened.

"Okay. I just need some time to get used to all this. It's...so much to process." Suddenly, she burst into tears. "All my life, I've lived a lie. I'm not really Brooke Turner. I'm Brooke DiRienzo!"

Michael put his arm around her and handed her his handkerchief.

"I guess I'm in shock," she admitted.

"Me, too!" Shawn piped up. "Imagine me being engaged to the daughter of Michael DiRienzo!" He smiled with delight.

"We'll just see about that engagement bit," Michael told Shawn.

Hattie suppressed a smile. Michael was really taking to being a father.

"There's more to be told," she said. "For example, how did Maria find out about Brooke?"

Howard stood up and began to pace back and forth.

"She knew that Alexandra had had a baby girl. That much was in the paper, in the society column. She told me about it, but not Michael, because she counted backward and figured that the child was his. I told her that the father was probably Alexandra's husband, but she wouldn't buy that. She was convinced that Michael was the father.

"It became an obsession with her. Over the years, she tried to see the child, but she didn't know how to find her. I don't know when she decided to kill her, but one day she was extremely agitated when she showed me a picture in the paper of Alexandra and Cameron MacArthur with Anna.

"She never knew until after she tried to kill Anna that Alexandra had two daughters. She found out last week, when Shawn told her. At that point, I still didn't suspect that Maria was the one who killed Mrs.Turner and ran Anna off the road.

"Maria had once mentioned to me that she'd seen Anna on several occasions at Philadelphia Orchestra concerts, and had listened to her conversations, especially with Larry. That's how she discovered that Anna liked Beethoven, and she also overheard Larry call her 'Annie.'

"She even followed Anna home once and wrote down her address. Finally she wrote the note to 'Annie' and sent the tickets, but I honestly didn't realize that at the time." Howard put his head down and sobbed into his bandaged hands.

Jim and Terri exchanged glances.

"Just when did you find out?" Jim asked.

"Last night, when I followed her and caught her trying to set fire to this house. She got away before I could stop her, but I went to her house after I left the hospital. Michael wasn't home. I confronted her with setting the fire and told her of my other suspicions. Maria poured out the whole story, and I told her she must get help. I didn't believe she would try anything else after our talk, until I saw her today with the rifle. I'm so sorry." He put his bandaged hands over his face again.

Jim walked over to Howard.

"Maria drove two cars, a maroon Chrysler with which she killed Mrs. Turner, and a green van she used to force Anna off the road the night of Mrs. Turner's funeral. Do you know where she got those vehicles?"

Howard glanced at Michael, but Michael simply shrugged his shoulders.

The senator admitted, in stunned tones, "This is all new to me. I'm finding it hard to believe that Maria could be so deranged. I really can't believe it." He looked horrified. "How could I have lived with her all these years and not suspected?"

"Because," Howard said, "you never really paid much attention to her."

"What about those vehicles, Mr. DiRienzo?" Jim asked.

"I don't know anything about them," Michael answered decisively.

"Mr. Cole?" Jim persisted.

Howard didn't answer.

Everyone waited for him to say something. Finally Hattie broke the silence.

"Mr. Cole, isn't it true that the Bertolinos, Maria's brothers, have a chop-shop hidden behind their legitimate business? Isn't that where Maria got those two stolen cars?"

Howard blanched.

Michael's mouth flew open. "Is that true, Howard? I've never heard anything about that!"

Howard struggled with an answer. He looked around the room. His mouth worked but no words came out. At last, he simply said, "Yes," in a small voice. "Maria told me about it."

Jim left the room. His voice could be heard as he talked into his police radio, but his words were indistinct. When he returned, he said that Philadelphia police units were being dispatched to Bertolino Motors. He also said that Maria had been admitted to the hospital's mental health unit.

"Her condition is unchanged," he said. "She's completely out of it. In spite of her mental state, she has been officially charged with two counts of murder and three of attempted murder as well as assault with a deadly weapon and arson."

Howard groaned.

Michael sighed deeply. "I'll call my lawyer." He pulled his cell phone from his pocket and walked out of the room to make his call in privacy.

"I honestly didn't allow myself to believe Maria could be capable of murder," Howard said, after Michael had left the room. "It wasn't until last Sunday, when Stacey Tyburn died under the subway train, that I began to fear that Maria was responsible."

"How was that?" asked Terri.

"Millions of people ride the subway every year," Howard answered. "How many of them fall onto the tracks? I began to wonder how Stacey really died. I mean, think about it: she's a professional cheerleader! Do you know what kind of agility and grace it takes to do some of those moves? That girl didn't fall. So I realized she must have been pushed, and that begged the questions: Why? Who?

"Only one person came to mind. Who had a motive? Maria. Who knew she would be taking that train? Maria, Shawn and I were the only ones. Shawn had called me up when Stacey left him, and Maria listened to our conversation on her extension. She told me so. Then she faked an ulcer attack and left immediately, giving herself plenty of time to reach the subway station before Stacey got there.

"I tried to convince myself that Stacey committed suicide, but it just didn't jibe. Both Shawn and Stacey's roommate, Jane Flynn, said that Stacey was definitely planning to see Michael. It didn't make sense that she would kill herself on her way to meet him."

Shawn stared at the floor, remembering the sweet girl and feeling wretched that he'd made her so unhappy in the last hours of her life.

"I guess," said Brooke, "it was Maria who pushed me down the cellar stairs and Aunt Hattie into the closet in Gram's house. She would have had the opportunity and the key, wouldn't she?"

"Yes," Howard said. "When I confronted her, she told me that she went there to find the note. She said that Miss Farwell and you, Brooke, arrived before she thought you would, and she had to get out of there before she could find it."

"Speaking of that note," said Jim. "It's in police possession now. Could you obtain a sample of Mrs. DiRienzo's handwriting for us, Mr. Cole?"

He looked at Jim and Terri. "Must I be the one to incriminate her?"

"It'll bode well for you when you're charged because you didn't report all this as soon as you knew it," Terri advised.

Howard drew a heavy, resigned sigh. "There are a number of handwritten memos at campaign headquarters," he offered.

"Good. How about if we drive you there right now?" asked Jim, rising to take Howard by the arm.

"Before you leave," Hattie said. "I assume it was Maria who called Cameron the night of Annie's funeral asking for 'Annie' and pretending to be me." Howard nodded his head. "And what about Anna's medicine being exchanged for digitalis in the hospital?"

"I don't know anything about that, but I'm certain Maria didn't do it," Howard stated. "She wouldn't have known anything about digitalis."

"That was probably just what it appeared to be," Terri said. "I looked into the incident, and it really did seem that a clumsy volunteer knocked into the cart, scattering pills all over the floor, and then tried to replace the medicine. It was very bad judgment, and the volunteer is no longer permitted on the floors."

"Good grief!" exclaimed Hattie. "That's horrible! And one more thing, Jim: What about that shotgun blast in the woods? Was that really a poacher?"

"I believe it was, Hattie."

"Well, how about that!"

# 43

Michael returned to the living room to find Brooke still in tears.

"Are you going to be okay?" he asked, putting his arms around her.

"This whole thing is sinking in, I guess," she sobbed. "It suddenly dawned on me that Anna is only my half-sister, and that Gram wasn't really my grandmother at all!"

"Oh, darling," Hattie patted her arm. "I knew your Gram all my life, and she was no fool. I wonder now if maybe she didn't suspect the truth all along, and loved you just as much anyway. Perhaps the timing of your birth and your coloring made her suspicious, but if they did, it would never have mattered to your Gram. She just loved you for yourself."

"Half a sister is better than none," Anna quipped, as she hugged and kissed Brooke. "Dry those tears, baby. I'm every bit as much your sister now as I ever was!"

Cameron walked in as that scene was unfolding.

"Brooke knows, I see," he observed. "It's right that she does, but Alexandra will be very upset."

Brooke stared at him, her eyes still bright with tears. "Cameron, you knew, too? Why didn't you tell me? Why did everyone know about me but me?"

"I wanted you to know, Brooke," Cameron said, "but I didn't have the right to tell you. Furthermore, I didn't have facts, just suspicions. Your mother never told me, and when I once brought up the subject of your coloring, she told me that you looked exactly like her French great-grandfather.

"But I knew that was bunk. You couldn't possibly have been Doug's child. He and your mother were both blue-eyed blonds. It just wasn't physically possible. Who, then, did your mother know who was dark? There was only one answer: Michael DiRienzo. But I never mentioned my thoughts to your mother, nor did I ever again mention your coloring."

"Speaking of Mother, how is she?" asked Anna. "I guess she's doing fine, or you wouldn't be here."

"Actually, she is," Cameron said. "But she's not happy. Of course they had to shave off most of her hair to tend her wound, and she's absolutely beside herself. At this time her head is completely bandaged, but she's having a fit worrying about when the bandages come off. I promised her that I would bring her a selection of wigs to try on as soon as she's better, but that was small comfort!"

"Oh, poor Mother! Of all the people this could happen to, she's the worst!" Anna said sympathetically.

"There's just one mystery we haven't cleared up, yet," said Terri. "Larry, when did you come to see Anna in the hospital?"

"I told you," said Larry, "a teacher friend at the Spruce Street School phoned me with the news. I called my school to get a substitute, and caught the first plane to Philadelphia. I saw Anna that night in intensive care, but she was pretty wifty." He hugged Anna lovingly. "I just figured I'd have to come back when she was more with the program."

"Why did you ever break off your engagement in the first place?" Brooke asked.

"I broke it off," Anna confessed. "My reason was pretty stupid. Larry wanted to go to Seattle and I didn't, at least not then. I didn't want to leave my class, and I didn't want to leave Gram alone in that big house. She would have killed me if she'd known that!

"We fought and said things we never should have, and I guess my pride got in the way, but I gave him back his ring. I regretted it from that moment on, but I was too proud to tell him, and he was too proud to try to get me back. I've never loved any man but Larry." She snuggled against his arm.

Shawn looked miserable. "Michael," he said almost shyly. "I guess you won't be running for president now, will you?"

"I guess not," Michael replied sadly. "I plan to call a press conference first thing tomorrow morning and tell everything in as dignified a manner as possible. You can be sure the police reporters know now that Maria has been arrested. They'll dig up the whole story before morning, so if I want any future in politics at all, I'll have to get the jump on them. And now, I'll have to do it without Howard." He sighed heavily.

"Will you tell them about me?" Brooke asked in concern. "What about Mother? What will this do to her?"

Michael looked at her for a long time. No one had ever come between him and his career. But Brooke, his own flesh and blood whom he realized he cherished, was looking at him so beseechingly. Could he avoid disclosing the existence of a daughter he never knew he had, without hurting his chances of some kind of political career?

What of Alexandra and her life? He felt he owed her nothing, but still he agonized about his decision. Maybe he'd better talk to her before he did anything.

And then, of course, there was Maria. How much of what she had done would become public? All of it, he surmised. Then he would have to confess his affairs with Stacey as well as Alexandra, and who knew how many others would come to light? Of course, he could always say that Maria was crazy and didn't know what she was talking about...

The whole thing was blowing up in his face. A press conference was inevitable, but what could he say? He wished Howard and his lawyer were here. But they were now at police headquarters, where Howard was giving his deposition about Maria.

Everyone in the room seemed to be waiting for his decision. He turned his eyes toward Brooke. *She's so young, so vulnerable,* he thought. *Can I do this to her?* He could wait until his lawyer and Howard were finished and consult with them. That was probably what he should do, but in the end, the decision would be his alone.

He sighed again. His lifetime dream had almost become a reality. It was tantalizingly close: Michael DiRienzo, President of the United States! He had worked so hard!

But look at all the people he'd hurt along the way. What would Maria have been like if he had treated her with love? Annie Turner and Stacey Tyburn would not have been murdered. What about the others? Would Alexandra be able to handle the disclosure of their affair? He couldn't add Brooke to that long list.

He was in mental anguish when he stood and told the group. "I'm going to announce at my press conference tomorrow that I am no longer a candidate for the presidency of the United States, and due to deeply personal issues, I am giving serious consideration to resigning my Senate seat."

*We'll see what happens then,* he thought.

Brooke rushed over to embrace him.

As he held his daughter in his arms, Michael knew that—painful as it was—he had made the right decision.

# Acknowledgments

Thanks to my family and friends for all their encouragement and support, especially during the difficult times when I first started working on this novel.

Thanks, too, to my wonderful sisters in the Red Hat Society, who always serve as an inspiration to me as I work on the Hattie Farwell books.

And thanks to publisher Mary Shafer of Word Forge Books, who believed in Hattie and in me enough to take a chance on us both.

# About the Author

Betty Kerr Orlemann, the daughter of a book editor for a major publishing house, grew up in a home filled with good books. This atmosphere fostered a love of reading and writing, and Betty spent much of her life as a journalist. Until her retirement in 2002, she was a staff writer for the Bucks County Courier Times, where she worked the criminal courts beat at the county seat in Doylestown.

Since then, she has freelanced as a stringer and columnist for several regional newspapers, including a long-running column for the *Delaware Valley News* (Frenchtown, N.J.) and features for *The Morning Call* (Allentown, Pa.) and the *Bucks County Herald* (Lahaska, Pa.). She also hosted her own radio show on WDVR-FM (Sergeantsville, N.J.).

Betty's other activities—teaching ballroom dance in Philadelphia, working as a medical technician, co-owning a gift and antiques shop, and serving as the first woman president of the Greater Glenside Chamber of Commerce—have served as grist for her idea mill...and what grist it is!

Betty is an enthusiastic member of the Delaware Valley chapter of Sisters In Crime, a professional networking group for women mystery writers. Betty is an equally energetic member of the Red Hat Society, an organization of women committed to meeting middle age with humor, verve and *élan*.

Betty is now a full-time freelance writer. Her latest project is a series of murder mystery novels centering around her alter-ego, Hattie Farwell. Like Hattie, Betty is 80 years old. And like Hattie, Betty lives with a dog and two cats in a beautiful cedar woods in Tinicum Township, Bucks County, Pennsylvania.

We hope you have enjoyed this first volume in our Hattie Farwell mystery series. If you'd like to get on the mailing list to be notified about upcoming titles and release dates, there are two ways you can do so.

1. Please send an email to admin@wordforgebooks.com with the subject line "Add me to your Hattie Farwell notification list."

2. Please fill out the form below and mail it in to: Word Forge Books, PO Box 97, Ferndale, PA 18921.

IMPORTANT NOTE: We do not rent, sell or otherwise distribute our mailing lists for postal mail or email, so you can sign up for our notifications with confidence that your privacy will be protected. We don't like spam, either.

- - - - - - - - - - - - - - - - - - - - - - - - -

## PLEASE ADD ME TO YOUR
## HATTIE FARWELL NOTIFICATION LIST

Name

Mailing Address

City                                    State            ZIP

Email

Please also add me to your catalog mailing list.        Yes        No

Word Forge Books and its various imprints are constantly developing new titles that help us achieve our mission of bringing you the world through words, and celebrating what's good about it.

We hope you've enjoyed this book, and encourage you to check out the other titles listed here. You can stay updated about our newest offerings by visiting our website at wordforgebooks.com. **Order online or call toll-free at 888-320-WORD (9673).**

### DEVASTATION ON THE DELAWARE:
### Stories and Images of the Deadly Flood of 1955

The only comprehensive documentary of the record-setting weather disaster that killed nearly 100 people in the Delaware River Valley. This award-winning book reads like a thriller, but the stories are real.
ISBN 978-09771329-0-4                    $19.95

### ALMOST PERFECT:
### Disabled Pets and the People Who Love Them

In a world that reveres perfection and disdains anything less, most of us realize that nothing—and no one—can truly measure up. These stories are about those animals who—through birth or injury—have been rendered less than perfect, and the humans who found love enough to welcome them into their hearts and homes.

Almost Perfect allows you to share the immeasurable rewards those people have found. Give yourself permission to believe once more in happy endings as you're inspired by these and more true, heartwarming stories of animals who have overcome physical handicaps to share happy, full lives with their human companions.
ISBN 978-09771329-2-8                    $12.95